THE BRAGG DYNASTY—
WINNER! REVIEWER'S CHOICE AWARD
BEST WESTERN SERIES 1988-1989

Praise for *FIRESTORM:*

WINNER! *AFFAIRE DE COEUR'S* GOLD
CERTIFICATE FOR EXCELLENCE 1988

"FIRESTORM sizzles, smolders
and erupts with sensuality…
a fabulous read"
Romantic Times

"Brenda Joyce has created characters
that will always be remembered
in a love story that can not be forgotten…
a wonderful read"
Affaire de Coeur

BRENDA JOYCE

Firestorm

AVON BOOKS ◆ NEW YORK

FIRESTORM is an original publication of Avon Books. This work has never before appeared in book form. This work is a novel. Any similarity to actual persons or events is purely coincidental.

AVON BOOKS
A division of
The Hearst Corporation
1350 Avenue of the Americas
New York, New York 10019

Copyright © 1988 by Brenda Joyce Dworman
Inside cover author photo by Volkmann © 1994
Published by arrangement with the author
Library of Congress Catalog Card Number: 88-91572
ISBN: 0-380-75577-7

First Avon Books Printing: November 1988

AVON TRADEMARK REG. U.S. PAT. OFF. AND IN OTHER COUNTRIES, MARCA REGISTRADA, HECHO EN U.S.A.

Printed in U.S.A.

RA 10 9 8 7 6 5 4 3

Prologue

West Texas, 1858

"Go!" Storm shouted. "Go, Nick, go!"

She was very tall, clad in buckskins, a thick braid hanging down her back. She was jumping up and down at the edge of the crowd of youths who had gathered around the two young men wrestling in the dust. A lean, muscular boy was on top, his skin bronzed, coppery, shining with sweat as he strained against his massive opponent. Suddenly Nick's back foot slipped from where it had been digging into the dirt, and in the next instant he was on his back.

Storm groaned and edged closer. "You can do it, Nick, you can do it," she shouted to her brother. Before the words were even out of her mouth, Nick had flipped his opponent and twisted his arm up behind his back, and the intense struggle ceased.

"Nick's won!" Storm yelled, one fist raised in the air. Cheers, laughter, and good-natured boos rang out.

Nick released his opponent and rolled onto his back; both boys lay side by side, panting. He met his sister's excited gaze with his own cool one. "How could I dare lose?" he murmured dryly, rising to his feet, running fingers through thick, straight, blue-black hair.

Lars was a poor loser, just one of his many less-than-endearing traits, and Storm's eyes widened as she saw him rise and leap at Nick from behind. "Nick!" she screamed.

Nick turned just in time to go flying backward in the dust, Lars on top of him. "You cheated, breed," Lars shouted, his face red. His ham-sized fist slammed into Nick's face.

"Stop it," Storm cried, knowing Lars could kill Nick. "Stop it!"

In the next instant Nick managed to twist free through sheer agility, and suddenly there was a long, lethal knife in his hand, the tip touching Lars's throat as Nick jammed his knee menacingly into the blond's groin. "This breed suggests that you calm down and reassess," Nick said softly.

"Rathe!"

Inside the barn it was dim and cool. Storm's thirteen-year-old brother stood so close to the blond girl that his thighs touched hers. His expression was intense and pleading. "Please, Lucilla," he whispered, taking her small hands in his. "Just one kiss."

She stared at the stunningly handsome boy in front of her. "I can't."

"You're so pretty," he whispered, his sapphire eyes riveted on hers. "I haven't been able to stop thinking about you, Lucilla."

She blushed. "Really?"

He grinned. "Really." His hands went to her soft shoulders.

She trembled at his touch, her heart beating madly. He was only a boy, two years younger than she, and a devil at that—she'd known him for years, knew all about his escapades, but this was a side of him she'd never seen. His face was so close. His hands slid to her waist. "Rathe," she managed.

"Just one kiss," he coaxed, his beautiful lips parted only an inch from hers.

"I can't."

"You can," he whispered breathlessly. "Lucilla, sweetheart . . ."

Lucilla closed her eyes in surrender. She waited with bated breath. His lips were soft and gentle, but his body pressed against hers was hot and hard. Lucilla had been raised on a Texas ranch, so she knew very well what that hardness meant. Suddenly it didn't matter that he was only thirteen. She found herself opening her mouth for his probing tongue, found herself whimpering when his hand cupped her small breast. His thumb moved back and forth over her hard, aching nipple.

"Oh, Lucilla," Rathe gasped when they came up for air. "Oh, Lucilla."

The rich smells of the barbecue wafted all around the tiny, sable-haired woman and the large, striking, blond man. They were sitting under a tree, removed from the other guests, his arm draped around her while she snuggled against his side. She regarded him with wide violet eyes; he gazed at her with burning gold ones.

"You are an insatiable old goat," Miranda said, breaking the sexual tension between them.

He threw back his head and laughed. "I can't help it," he said, nuzzling her cheek with his. "We've been at this barbecue all weekend, and I want to go home and bed my wife."

"Derek!" The tone was mocking and teasing.

"Come here, Miranda," he cajoled, his tone a perfect echo of that of his younger son, Rathe.

She nestled closer and lifted her face for his kiss. It was long, intimate, and tender. She clung to him; he was the one who finally broke away. "Let's get the kids and head out of here," he said, clearing his throat.

"Where are they, anyway?" Miranda asked as he helped her to her feet.

"I have no idea, but why don't we start with Storm? If there's a competition going on, she'll be there," Derek said, smiling as he slid an arm around his wife's shoulders.

It didn't take long to find the group of youths watching the wrestling, cheering on their favorites. Miranda froze when she saw the participants, her face draining of color. "Oh, my God!"

Derek bit his lip to stop laughing.

Storm was on the ground wrestling with Buddy Ames, who was seventeen and shirtless. They grappled back and forth with Storm beneath him. In an effort to get him off, she wedged a thigh between his legs; her other leg wrapped around his calf. The kids surrounding them were laughing and shouting encouragement. Derek chuckled.

Miranda turned furiously on him. "Stop the fight this instant! This instant!"

"Yes, ma'am," he said meekly, then leaned down to grab Buddy by the scruff of the neck and lift him off Storm as casually as one might pick up a kitten.

Miranda whirled on her elder son. "Nick! How could you let her fight like this!"

Nick shrugged, unruffled. "I tried to tell her she's too old to wrestle anymore, but she wouldn't listen. You know Storm, Ma."

"Pa!" Storm protested, sitting in the dust in a most unladylike manner, knees spread. "I could have won!"

"I think you had better get up, young lady," Derek said, trying to sound stern.

"You promised," Miranda admonished, sitting on their four-poster bed, brushing her long, thick hair with hard, angry strokes.

Derek stood watching her, agonized. "But, Miranda, she's only a child."

"A child?" Miranda stood. "She's almost seventeen and a woman, Derek, and it's time you faced it."

"But San Francisco!"

"You have to let her go," Miranda said softly, placing a soothing hand on his chest.

"We originally said we'd send her to your cousin Langdon when she turned eighteen," he countered, his gaze worried.

She clasped his hand. "Derek, take a good look at our daughter. She's a beautiful woman, and she deserves a chance at society. She deserves silk gowns and kidskin slippers." She grimaced. "She is certainly too old to be wrestling in the mud with grown men!"

"Damn," Derek said. He paced the confines of their cozy bedroom. "Let me break it to her."

Miranda smiled, looped her arms around his neck, and gave him a long kiss. "I love you."

Derek held her close, reluctant to let her go. "Maybe I could tell her tomorrow?" he asked hopefully. His wife gave him a warning look.

He found Storm downstairs with the boys, whom he sent outside with a stern reminder of chores that needed to be done. "Storm, I've got a great surprise for you."

"What is it?" she asked, smiling.

"Your mother and I were going to wait until you were eighteen, but we decided you're old enough now. You're going to spend the summer with Paul Langdon in San Francisco."

"I won't go."

"Honey, you'll love San Francisco."

Storm was frantic. "Pa, this is all Mother's idea, isn't it? You can talk her out of it, I know you can—if you really want to."

"Honey, as usual, your mother's right. You need to see another side of life. It's only for the summer."

"I don't want to go," Storm said stubbornly. "I'm happy here. I don't want to leave you and Mother and the boys."

"It's only for the summer," Derek repeated quietly. He smiled. "And I know you'll do me and your mother proud."

With the sure knowledge of defeat came the urge to cry. Storm turned and fled up the stairs to her room. They were sending her away, far away to a strange city, away from everything and everyone she loved . . . She didn't answer when there was a knock on her door. She knew who it was.

"Storm?" Miranda entered and sat on the bed beside her daughter. Her hand stroked Storm's thick, gold-streaked hair. "Let's talk."

"I don't want to go."

"I want to tell you a little story," Miranda said calmly, with a slight smile. She regarded her daughter for a moment, the lean, graceful form, broad-shouldered for a woman, with a tiny waist and narrow hips. Her legs were long and strong. She had a striking, unusual face, with high cheekbones and a wide jaw. Miranda suspected that the bone structure came from Derek's Apache mother.

"I know you're frightened, but you're a strong, brave girl with a warm, loving family behind you. You know I was raised in a convent in France. When I was seventeen my father summoned me home to England to tell me that he had betrothed me to a Texas rancher—a complete stranger. I was very sheltered and very innocent and very afraid but I had no choice in the matter. I was sent to Texas."

Storm sat up. "Grandpa sent you to marry Pa?"

"No. My fiancé was actually Derek's best friend and blood brother. John had had an accident, so he sent Derek, who was a captain in the Texas Rangers at the time, to escort me to him. It was very frightening, Storm, to be sent away to marry a complete stranger, knowing I had no control over my life and that I could never go back home." Miranda paused to let Storm think about her words.

"So what happened?" Storm asked. "If you were betrothed to Pa's best friend when you met Pa . . ."

Miranda smiled at the recollection. "That's another story, dear, and a long one. Maybe sometime I'll tell it to you."

Storm studied her knees.

"You're only going to my cousin's for a visit."

Storm bit her lip. "I guess you're right."

Miranda smiled and hugged her. "You have nothing to be afraid of. In fact, I won't be surprised if you have the time of your life."

"I'm not afraid," Storm said.

But she was. .

Chapter 1

San Francisco, 1859

Brett sat at the large, leather-topped mahogany desk with a frown of concentration that deepened to a scowl. He turned the pages of the oversized ledger. Damn. He should have known. This was the first time he'd made an error in judgment about a man, and hopefully it would be the last. Furious now, he snapped the book closed and rose to his full six feet, two inches.

He paced to the window and stared broodingly out at Stockton Street. He was not going to let his bookkeeper's theft ruin this day. A slight smile formed on his ruthlessly sculpted face. Not that he was being sentimental just because it was his birthday. But . . . maybe he was. Today he was twenty-six, and he had everything he wanted. His smile widened.

Not bad for the son of a whore.

Not bad for the bastard of a Californio.

D'Archand did not resemble his mother, who was French, petite, chestnut-haired, and blue-eyed. Instead he was almost an exact replica of his father, Don Felipe Monterro—tall, broad-shouldered, powerfully built, harshly handsome. And dark, very dark, with nearly black eyes that held little softness and short, crisply curling black hair.

The last time Brett had seen his father he had been gray-
ing at the temples, Brett recalled, and instantly grew tense
and angry. A scene flashed through his head, which he
tried, but failed, to ignore.

"I'm leaving, Father," a sixteen-year-old Brett had said,
waiting, begging silently for his father to stop him.

The handsome, lean man remained emotionless.
"Where will you go?"

Brett refused to feel the pain. He was a fool. He had
never been accepted by his father, had never been more
than the bastard in the stable, insurance against the possibility that there would be no other heirs. Now he was no
longer needed. When he had heard Don Felipe's new wife's
infant boy begin to cry, he had wanted to cry, too. Instead,
his face was as cold and stiff as the don's. "I'm going to
Sutter's Fort," he answered.

"Ah, gold," the haciendado said. It was early 1849.

"Yes, sir." He could barely get out the words.

The don gave him a blooded Arabian stallion and a few
hundred pesos. Brett rode out that day and never looked
back.

Unconsciously, Brett's fist smashed against the windowsill, the hard planes of his face rigid. "I won't look back,"
he growled aloud. "For all I care, the old sonuvabitch is
dead. And good riddance! I don't need him. I have what
I want—success, respectability . . . everything."

From outside his office came a loud crash of breaking
glass.

Brett froze, listening, but made no move to leave his
large, elegant office. It was decorated in a classic style,
with mahogany doors, an Oriental rug in coral and blue,
a large sofa in wine-colored leather. There were two
French chairs covered in pin-striped silk, blue velvet
drapes, and wall-to-wall bookcases. His first mistress,
Suzanne, had decorated the room for him under his watch-
ful, critical eye when he had acquired the Golden Lady

and moved out of his other, shabbier offices in the Miner's Girl—his first saloon and first investment.

He had to smile, remembering how he had scraped together enough gold dust to buy into a partnership in that sinkhole. A profitable sinkhole upon which he had founded the wealth he owned today. He almost laughed.

The Golden Lady was one of San Francisco's classiest establishments, every inch as plush and elegant as his office. Even the second floor—where hostesses earned top dollar satisfying their customers—was tastefully decorated. Because of the lack of women in San Francisco—even now, ten years after the gold rush—city government and society tolerated its houses of ill repute. Being owner of the Golden Lady didn't detract from Brett's reputation, because it was the most elegant establishment in the city. Then, too, Brett had diversified over the past five years. He now owned a hotel, two restaurants, a partnership in a shipping line, a freight line, and shares in a ranch across the bay. He had also acquired land just west of San Francisco, which people were starting to buy and build homes on. At the age of twenty-six, Brett was one of the wealthiest men in San Francisco.

He pulled a gold watch on a chain from his silver brocade vest. He had just enough time for a short interlude with Audrey, his current mistress, before meeting his partner in the shipping line, Paul Langdon. He slipped on a black suit jacket and automatically adjusted his black necktie. He had just added his black Stetson when another crash and a woman's scream came from somewhere in the building.

Linda, one of his girls, thrust open the study door. "Brett, you'd better—"

He was already striding past her, his face taut. "What is it?"

"Some loony," she said, hurrying behind him down the

shining waxed floor of the corridor. "He has a gun, and Susie."

Brett paused on the threshold of the saloon, which was embellished with rich mahogany, brass, and green velvet. At this early hour of the afternoon half the chairs were empty. A dozen men dressed in well-cut suits were standing uneasily at various tables. The dealers in their brocade waistcoats looked equally wary. Two of Brett's girls stood white and immobile at the end of the long bar. The bartender, James, stood frozen facing the middle of the room.

There on the floor lay Luke, the two-hundred-pound bouncer, his temple bleeding.

A few yards away stood a dirty man in a flannel shirt and muddy boots. Clenched in a harsh embrace in front of him, the barrel of a gun pressed against her right temple, was Susie, pale and wet with sweat, her kohled eyes huge.

Moving forward to face the man holding Susie, Brett spoke quietly. "Is he dead?"

"No, I don't think so," one of his regular customers answered.

"Linda, go get Doc Winslow." He didn't have to look at her to know she was still frozen in the entryway. "Now, Linda," he commanded softly.

Linda turned and fled.

"I'm going to tend to Luke," Brett told the man holding Susie. He started forward, his eyes never leaving Susie and her captor. The man immediately pressed the gun harder, and Susie cried out. Brett froze. "I just want to check his wound," Brett explained.

"He ain't dead," the man said harshly. "I only hit him with the butt. He's just stunned."

Relieved, Brett wanted to look at Luke, but he didn't dare. He heard James say from behind him, "It's true, boss, I saw it."

The man turned wild eyes on him. "You the boss man here?"

"Yes, I'm Brett D'Archand. And you are?"

"I'm her husband," the man spat. "I'm Bill Hawkins, and this whore is my wife."

Brett momentarily met Susie's gaze and saw her terror. He tried to reassure her with his eyes. Calmly, he asked, "Is that true?"

Susie whimpered what sounded like an affirmative.

"This little whore is my runaway wife, and I'm taking her back. No way you can stop me—but I'd like an excuse, you bastard, so just try."

"Brett," Susie whimpered. "Please."

He had known she was married. Brett did not sleep with his employees, but he carefully screened them all, and when Susie had first come to him he had known he should throw her out instantly. She was just showing her pregnancy, and her face was bruised from a beating. But for just that reason, he couldn't deny her. He'd given her a warm meal and listened to her plea for work. There was no way he could hire a pregnant woman in his establishment, although he knew that other places would take her. So, because she was young, and pregnant, and running away from a husband who had obviously beaten her, he had given her a job as a maid. Because of his support, Susie had asked him to be the baby's godfather, and Brett had agreed, secretly delighted.

After the baby was born, Susie had gone to work as one of the hostesses, wanting the better money. He had objected because of her child, which brought back stinging memories of his own youth. But somehow she managed the child and her job, with help from the entire staff. Even Brett had found himself tending the infant once when suddenly there was no one else available.

Now, as he faced his goddaughter's father, he remembered vividly how Susie had looked when he had first seen her, and he knew he could not let this man take her and the child away.

"There's no need for the gun," Brett said quietly. "Why don't you remove it from Susie's temple."

Bill just stared. Then there was the sound of footsteps behind him, and Brett saw Winslow pushing through the front doors. Bill turned to look. Brett moved.

He leaped at Hawkins, one hand going for his wrist with the gun. Susie screamed, breaking free and running.

Brett's years growing up on the streets of Mazatlán had taught him a few tricks. Though Bill was bigger, they were at a standoff. The gun went off harmlessly at the ceiling, angering Brett, who was thinking of his chandelier and the hole in the plaster. He raised his knee, yanking Bill's gun-bearing arm down hard on his thigh. Brett jammed the arm against his leg again. He knew he was close to breaking the man's bone, but he didn't care. Bill cried out, and the gun fell harmlessly to the floor. Brett released the arm and delivered a shattering blow to Bill's face. The man jerked backward, but Brett caught him and brought him forward as he swung a hard left into his bulging abdomen. A whoosh of air sounded as Bill crumpled forward. One more blow did it. Brett felt the man pass out in his hands and let him thud to the floor.

Brett stood, regaining his breath, then hurried to where Winslow knelt above Luke. "Is he okay?"

"Gash'll need a few stitches. Jimbo, bring me some whiskey."

One of Sheriff Andrews's deputies had arrived and was dragging Bill Hawkins to his feet as the man blinked groggily. "You gonna press charges, Brett?" the deputy asked.

"Absolutely," Brett said. "How long can you lock him up?"

"How long you want him locked up?"

Long enough to help Susie and the baby, he thought. "A few days, to start."

The deputy nodded and started out while Hawkins, stumbling alongside, cursed Brett. Brett watched, then turned to Linda. "Where's Susie?"

"She ran upstairs."

Brett went after her. He found her in her room, rocking her daughter, crying. He sat down on the bed next to her. "It's all right now. He's been arrested."

She looked up at him with frightened, glazed eyes. "Brett, what am I going to do? He'll hurt her, I know he will." She moaned and started sobbing.

Her tears made Brett feel uneasy. "I'm friends with Judge Steiner," he said. "How would you feel about a divorce?"

"Oh! Could you?"

"I'm sure it can be arranged."

She hugged him, almost crushing the baby, and he was embarrassed. "But what about Bill? He'll be so angry."

"I'll take care of him," Brett said.

"How?"

Brett smiled slightly. "I'll pay him off."

And if that didn't work, there were always other means.

"Will you look at that!" exclaimed a man clad in navy woolen trousers.

"I see, I see, I ain't blind," said the second sailor.

The object of their attention was Storm, standing in front of a hitching post and bakery on Stockton Street, holding the reins of two large stallions and waiting for a companion. She was clad from neck to toe in skintight, well-worn buckskins, which molded her superb and striking figure. A worn Stetson on her head shadowed her face, and a brown and gold braid the thickness of a man's forearm hung to her waist.

"I ain't never seen anything like that," said the second man, starting eagerly forward.

Storm heard not only their approach but also their remarks and the undisguised lewdness in their tone, and she was flushed and tensed. This would never happen in San Antone, she thought fiercely. No one there would ever dare to talk about her behind her back, knowing full well that if one of her brothers didn't pursue the matter, her father would. Which made her look at the saloon next door to the bakery where he had told her to wait. Where was he?

"Howdy, li'l lady," said the bulkier sailor, grinning.

Storm ignored him, stiffening her spine as his body odor assaulted her sensibilities. Both her mother and father were sticklers for cleanliness. It was something she had grown up with, and she was acutely aware now of the need she had for a bath—and a bed.

"C'mon, gal, don't turn that pretty back on us," said the other sailor.

She purposely let her thoughts continue, hoping they would walk away. It had been a month since she'd had a decent bed. A month since they'd left Texas—and home. Even now she couldn't believe that they were here. Already. A combination of dread and excitement mingled pleasantly and disturbingly in her veins.

"Hey, gal, you shore are rude, now, ain't ya?"

When Storm felt the large hand closing on her arm, she yanked back, angry for losing herself so completely in her thoughts. "Let go," she warned, meeting the man's gaze for the first time.

He gasped at the sight of her deep blue eyes, at the striking and unusual features he finally glimpsed. This was no heart-shaped, bow-mouthed, doll-like face. Her cheekbones were very high. Her nose was straight and proud and flaring. Her strong jaw was determined. He'd never seen a face quite like this, except maybe on a half-breed squaw.

"Get your hand off me," Storm repeated, her tone not indicating any fear. If she'd outridden a dozen Comanches by herself when she was twelve, why should she be afraid of two decadent sailors? Especially when her father was bound to come out of the saloon at any second.

The sailor reached up to remove her hat. His friend whistled, and Storm furiously jerked back her head, eyes blazing. His hand touched her hair, a glinting riot of browns and golds. Storm sucked in her breath and then, before anyone knew it, she'd drawn a buck knife from its sheath and was flicking it down the length of his arm. He yelped and jumped back, eyeing the scratch she had made from his wrist to his elbow.

Storm eyed them angrily and watched them mutter and back off, finally disappearing down the street. She sheathed the knife, and just in time, too, for her father appeared with his long, deceptively easy stride, his handsome face smiling. "Sorry, sweetheart," he said as she handed him the reins.

Storm grabbed her stallion's mane and vaulted on, Apache-style. "Did you find out where Paul lives?"

"Sure did. Not far from here." His topaz eyes were warm. "It won't be long now."

His words echoed, making her tense, until the new sights of the city captured her attention. As they rode gingerly through the muddy streets of San Francisco, Storm was wide-eyed. Never had she seen a city this big, not even San Antonio, which was completely different—so old and so Spanish.

San Francisco was made up of a conglomeration of ramshackle huts, sturdier wooden Victorian-style buildings, and brick and stone edifices with strange pediments and cornices. There were mansions with elaborate façades enclosed by wrought-iron fences. There were saloons and stores and eating places. Many of the streets had boardwalks and were cobbled, and she saw why—no one could walk through the foot-deep mud on the shoddier side streets. And there was activity everywhere.

Men and women elegantly dressed in the latest fashions mingled with roughly clad men in flannel shirts and denim pants. Short, slim Chinese men with braids mingled with black men and Mexicans in serapes and sombreros. There were sailors and Dutchmen. Wagons drawn by mules vied for the right of way down thoroughfares crowded with elegant carriages carrying chaperoned young ladies. Noticing one such barouche—and inside it, the two parasoled, bonneted young women dressed in frilly white dresses, their blond curls carefully escaping to cling to white necks, and the matron in green beside them—Storm felt a rush of fear. She could never, ever dress or look like that. She would be a complete laughingstock! Both horrified and mesmerized, she continued to stare at the two girls. The barouche had stopped and they were laughing coyly with a gentleman on a palomino who appeared elegant in a brown suit and top hat. Her father followed her glance.

"Pretty, aren't they?"

Storm couldn't speak. Surely no one was going to get her up like that. With her height and funny looks, it would be ridiculous. Besides, she hadn't worn a dress in so long she wondered if she'd trip trying to walk in one.

The urge to flee intensified. "Pa? Please, let's turn around and go home."

He reached out and took her hand as they walked their horses side by side down Market Street. "Honey, it's natural for you to be nervous. But after a few weeks you'll outshine every woman in this town. I know it." His golden eyes were shining.

Storm looked away. He was prejudiced. He had always been prejudiced about her. Her father thought she was beautiful and perfect.

They passed through very different parts of the city as they rode toward Rincon Hill, where her cousin's house was located. The hill was less densely developed, and Paul's house had been described to them, so they spotted it instantly, set almost at the top of the hill. It was a huge brick mansion with white pillars and a white pediment, with balconies on the second and third floors and towers on the roof. The surrounding gardens were just starting to bloom with azaleas and bougainvillea and wisteria. A brick wall topped with a curtain of wrought iron surrounded the grounds. The front gates stood open, and they rode through them.

"Pa," Storm whispered as they walked their mounts up the muddy drive. "It's so big."

"Langdon's done well for himself," Derek agreed. "When he wrote and said he'd made some investments that paid off and built himself a home, I had no idea."

To Storm, the mansion looked like one of the castles in England that her mother had described to her.

They tied their horses at a hitching post shaped like a black jockey, one hand outstretched with a ring to hold the reins. Storm hung back behind her father, her heart thumping, torn between the desire to stay and experience something new and exciting, and the fear of being left alone, away from her family and everything that was familiar to her.

The man who opened the front door looked like an English butler or majordomo. He ushered them inside, not even batting an eye at their appearance, and Storm found herself standing in a black and white marble-floored foyer. A huge curved staircase on their right wound up to the second story, and all around them were doors. The man-servant stepped to a pair of splendid mahogany doors and knocked. Both Storm and Derek could hear from within the hushed sounds of men conversing.

"Sir," the man said. "Derek Bragg and your cousin are here."

"Good God!" Paul exclaimed, jumping up. In several strides he had crossed the room, leaving two men seated within. Derek strode across the foyer to meet him, and they clasped hands warmly in the doorway of the library. "Derek! I didn't expect you and Storm for another few weeks!"

Derek was smiling in pleasure as well. "We left a week early to take advantage of the weather. After all," he added, grinning, "I do have a ranch to get back to."

"Indeed, you do," Paul said, a merry light in his eyes. He turned to Storm and gaped.

Storm had met Paul only once before, ten years ago, when he and her grandfather had appeared unexpectedly at the ranch. Paul, a younger son of an English baron, had been on his way to the California gold fields, and her grandfather, the earl of Dragmore, had visited his daughter's family and the grandchildren he had never seen. She stepped forward, flushing, acutely aware of how she must look in this elegant castle. At least she had had the presence of mind to take off her hat at the front door when her father had done so. "Hello, Cousin Paul."

"My God! You're even more beautiful than your mother!" He hugged her.

The instant she had stepped into view, both men sitting in the background had jumped to their feet, staring. Storm, already flushed, noticed Paul's guests, looking so elegant and urbane, and wanted to die. She wasn't beautiful, and already she was being made to feel a fool. If *only* she were a bit shorter.

Paul released her, his eyes warm and admiring. Then, like the confident host he was, he turned slightly, and the two men came forward. "Brett, Grant, I want you to meet Derek Bragg, my cousin Miranda's husband, and their daughter Storm."

Storm glanced at the two men, apprehension mingling with indifference. Men meant nothing to her except as amusing comrades—with the exception of Lennie Willis, who had tried to kiss her and feel her breasts one day when they were fishing. She'd blackened one of his eyes for that.

But . . . these men were a bit frightening, just like San Francisco. They were dressed like her cousin, one in a brown suit, the other in black, their sophisticated elegance making her feel out of place and ugly and dreadfully inappropriate. She watched as her father shook hands with both men.

"Grant Farlane," said the man in brown, smiling warmly, amusement seeming to dance in his eyes.

Storm grasped the hand he held out and pumped it vigorously. "Nice to meet you," she said, noting the man's surprise, which he gracefully covered.

She turned to the other man and was instantly stunned. He was staring. She wasn't sure what his piercing look meant. It was blazing in its intensity. Did he think she was a freak? She'd had many hot glances in her short lifetime, but none like this. Even the sailors hadn't looked at her like this. She met his gaze and saw that it was almost black. She had never seen such a dark man, as dark as her father was golden. She felt the rushing of her blood, the racing of her heart. Her stomach tightened with a stabbing jolt. He was still staring, but now his gaze swept her slowly, caressingly, and she had the ridiculous idea that he could see right through her clothes. She flushed, holding out her hand.

A small smile curved his mouth, and she found herself staring at his lips, which were surprisingly full in the hard face. "Brett D'Archand," he said, and then, before she knew what was happening, he brought her hand upward and kissed it right above her knuckles. She froze.

His lips were warm, soft, and the skin he kissed tingled. She was suddenly acutely aware that her hands were chapped and callused and dusty.

He released her hand. "A pleasure," he said, his voice deep and rich, his mouth still curved with that slight, predatory smile.

Storm stepped closer to her father, wanting to fall

through the floor. That or slap this stranger. Was he making fun of her? And he was still staring, making her feel both oddly uncomfortable and strangely elated.

Derek was smiling. "We need baths," he told Paul. "And I need a drink or two."

"Of course," Paul said. "You both must be exhausted."

"Paul," Grant said, "Brett and I will leave. Why don't we finish this discussion tomorrow morning over breakfast?"

"Wonderful," Paul said. "Would eight o'clock be convenient?"

The men agreed quickly. "Don't bother seeing us out," Brett said, and found himself looking again at Storm. *"Enchanté,"* he murmured with a negligent tilt of his head. Then he and Grant Farlane were gone.

Derek turned to his daughter, who was gnawing her lower lip. "Looks like you've already got an admirer, Storm."

She was aghast. "What? Who? I don't want any admirers!"

"Brett D'Archand has an eye for the ladies," Paul told Derek. "So did Grant, until he married Marcy." He turned to Storm. "You'll like Marcy. She knows you're coming. I'm hoping the two of you will be friends. She's volunteered to help you with your wardrobe."

"Do I really need a wardrobe?" Storm said in dismay.

Both men stared at her. "I want her to have the best," Derek said firmly. "I want my girl to outshine every lady in town."

"Then we're agreed," Paul said with obvious relief. "You will be the toast of the city, Storm, you'll see."

At that moment Storm wanted nothing more than to wake up and find this was all a dream. She didn't want to be the toast of this city or any other.

Chapter 2

Brett didn't forget the unusual young woman after he left Paul Langdon's. But because the night was young, he went back to his mistress's, took her to Letoile for dinner and champagne, and then back to her lodgings for an intimate birthday celebration. Every now and then during the course of the evening, he had a flashing remembrance of a buckskin-clad woman with huge blue eyes.

The next morning, as he met Grant and they rode together up Rincon Hill, he had a strong visual memory of the young woman called Storm. And he felt an instant, lustful stirring of his body.

Never had he seen such an unusual yet magnificent creature. If he were her father, he would not let her wear those buckskins, which left nothing to a man's imagination. He had never seen such a compelling form on a woman. She was tall, probably five-ten in her boots. Her legs were long and strong, but sensuously curved—legs to wrap around a man as he drove himself into her. Her waist was tiny, a sharp contrast to her surprisingly broad shoulders. And she had full, large breasts that strained against her shirt.

And the way she walked. He had never seen a woman move like that before, as if she could run swiftly, effortlessly, as if she could jump easily from cliff to cliff like a big cat.

He remembered her face in perfect detail. And her

22

eyes—a vivid dark blue, the color of dark sapphires, almost purple. He knew he wanted to bed her. Of course, that was out of the question. He wasn't ready for marriage, not yet, and even if he was, some Texas hick wasn't his idea of a wife. When he married, it would be to a woman of impeccable breeding and birth—perhaps from a blue-blooded eastern family. A woman who could be a hostess for the many social functions they would hold in the house he had recently built. A woman to enhance his respectability and reputation.

"You're pensive this morning," Grant said, shoving a lock of brown hair from his brown eyes. Like Brett, he was self-made, with various interests. Like Brett, too, he had come to California to strike it rich in the gold fields, and had instead made his fortune through hard work, only assisted by Lady Luck.

Brett smiled. "I was thinking about that little hoyden, Storm."

"What a beauty," Grant said admiringly. "And she's not exactly little."

Brett laughed. "No, not quite."

"She's never been out of West Texas before," Grant told him.

"How do you know?"

Grant smiled. "I've known all about Miss Storm Bragg for quite a while now. Paul has recruited Marcy to take her under her wing and help turn her into an elegant lady. Marcy knows more about Storm than anyone except her family, and she's been looking forward to playing big sister for months now."

Brett chuckled. It was just like Marcy to be excited at the awesome prospect of turning a wildcat Texan into a lady of refinement. Marcy's heart was too big—bless her for it. If Marcy weren't married to Grant, she would make Brett a perfect wife, beautiful and warm. If she weren't married to his good friend, Brett would probably be in love with her. She was one of the few women he knew who was a lady but also sensual and responsive, not frigid. A rarity.

"Taming Storm might take some doing," Brett said as they rode through the wrought-iron gates.

"Marcy is a winner," Grant pointed out.

Brett laughed. "She does have the tenacity of a terrier," he agreed. "So, Storm has never been out of West Texas? I wonder what she'll look like in a ballgown." His smile broadened at the thought. Better yet, he had a disturbing image of her naked.

"Do you intend to court her?"

Brett laughed. "Hell, no! I'm not ready for a wife."

"Too bad. Did you see your name in the paper the other day? On the second page, in the article about expanded shipping."

"I saw it," Brett said wryly, dismounting.

Grant laughed and quoted, " 'Brett D'Archand, one of the city's most prominent citizens and most eligible bachelors.' "

"Like I said, I'm not ready."

"Could have fooled all the young ladies," Grant teased. "Building that monstrosity on Folsom Street just for yourself . . ."

Brett glared. "That 'monstrosity' is the height of good taste and refinement."

Grant laughed, and Bart, Paul's valet, butler, and majordomo, ushered them in.

Paul greeted them in the dining room. The long table could seat fifty, but the three men clustered at one end, drinking coffee, eating omelets and potato pancakes, and discussing the prospects of taking on several new contracts with their shipping line as it was, or expanding to do so. Brett was in favor of expansion, and soon they all agreed. The three men hadn't made their individual fortunes by failing to take risks. As it was, Brett knew he was becoming dangerously overextended and cash short. The "monstrosity," as Grant had referred to it, had been an incredibly expensive indulgence that probably should have waited.

Pushing aside his plate and leaning back in his chair, Brett asked casually, "Where are your guests?"

Paul accepted another cup of coffee from the serving maid. "They're out riding," he said. "Storm wanted to see the ocean, and her father decided to take her. He's leaving tomorrow."

"You say he's a rancher?" Brett asked.

"Yes. And before that, a Texas Ranger."

Brett was surprised. Everyone had heard tall stories about that dauntless breed. He was disappointed, though. He had wanted another glimpse of Storm.

"Marcy will be over this afternoon, Paul," Grant interjected. "I meant to tell you."

"Good. Maybe she can take Storm to the seamstress right away. She has nothing to wear. It's such a shame."

Brett raised his cup in silent agreement. At that precise moment, there was the sound of voices, and Storm's rich, clear laughter rang out. Brett looked toward the doorway with a quickening of interest and was rewarded by a view of Derek Bragg. His daughter appeared right behind him.

Brett had forgotten just how striking she was.

"How was your ride?" Paul asked as all three men stood.

"Just wonderful!" said Storm. "We saw the ocean. I've never seen so much water. And the beaches are beautiful. I hate to say it, but they're much nicer than our own coast."

Derek laughed. "What's this? My little Texan is being disloyal?"

She grinned and accepted the chair Grant was holding out next to him. Derek sat down on her other side, and she found herself facing the dark, magnetic gaze of Brett

D'Archand. For a moment his eyes held hers, refusing to let her go. In that instant, which seemed to stretch forever, Storm lost touch with everything and everyone else in the room. She felt compelled to stare back at this strange man, helpless to look away. Her heartbeat quickened.

Grant was saying something.

Storm felt a flush come over her face as she tore her gaze away from Brett. "Excuse me?"

Grant laughed. "I know he's more handsome than I am, but I'm deeply wounded," he teased.

Storm's face burned. Fortunately, the maid intervened to ask her if she wanted any breakfast. "Yes, please," she cried, her heart thumping. God, she was making a fool out of herself! How could she have stared at him like that?

"My wife, Marcy, is coming over this afternoon to call on you," Grant continued.

Storm was startled. "Why?"

"To welcome you to the city," he said.

"You'll love her, Storm," Paul added. "She's only a few years older than you. I'm hoping you two will be great friends."

Storm smiled, somewhat wanly.

"She's going to take you to the dressmaker today, too," Paul added, hoping to please her.

Storm looked stricken. "Today?"

"You do need clothes," Paul pointed out.

Storm stared down at her plate. It was starting already. "Pa's leaving tomorrow," she said firmly, "and I'd rather wait until after he's gone to do that."

"That's okay," Derek said, patting her hand. "As long as your afternoon's cut out for you, I'll take off today."

She was stunned.

"Are you sure you don't want to stay?" Paul asked. "For a few days, anyway?"

"Not only do I have a ranch to run," Derek said, "but I also have the most beautiful, loving woman in the world

waiting for me.'' He grinned. ''I guess I'm a besotted
fool, but I miss her like hell.''

''Pa, please don't go today,'' Storm whispered urgently,
turning stricken blue eyes on him.

''I really have to get back, sweetheart,'' he said easily.
''Chin up, Storm. In a few weeks you'll be having such a
good time you won't ever want to come home.'' As an
afterthought, he added, ''But you will.''

Storm was no longer hungry. Pa was leaving today!
Damn Marcy Farlane for her friendliness, and damn them
all for making him go! She stared at her plate but didn't
see the eggs. She was terrified. She, who had fought ren-
egade Comanches, faced a grizzly alone, and been attacked once by outlaws. She hadn't been afraid then, but
she was afraid now. All her life she had been secure in
the warm, loving bosom of her family. Although Derek
was gone sometimes on trail drives, there was always her
mother and brothers. She had never been apart from her
family.

Across the table, Brett was feeling sorry for her. She
was really only a child. It was so clear she didn't want to
stay in San Francisco and didn't want her father to leave
her. She was a wild, beautiful child. Almost a woman.

Paul spoke. ''Dear, I have some wonderful news for
you.''

Storm managed to look up, trying to hide her dismay.

''The Farlanes are holding a small dinner party Friday
in your honor.''

''What?'' It was a gasp.

''To introduce you to some of the young people of town,
and some bachelors.''

She couldn't believe it. Friday—five days away. Good
God! She was going to have to mix with elegant men and
women—she couldn't do it!

''That's very nice of you and your wife,'' Derek said

easily to Grant, shooting his daughter a hard, uncompromising look.

"It's our pleasure," Grant returned.

"Yes, thank you," Storm managed stiffly, standing. "Excuse me, please," and she turned and hurried from the room.

The four men stared after her, Paul and Grant in surprise, Brett with both surprise and admiration for the rear view of her form, and Derek with grim understanding. He turned to Grant. "Please forgive her," he said softly, "but the truth is, she's never been in a situation like this, and she's nervous. It's my fault. I raised her with her brothers, as if she were a boy. I don't think she really knows she's a woman yet. She's at home in the saddle but not in the parlor."

"It's all right," Grant said, "I understand perfectly."

Storm had brought one good outfit, which Miranda had altered at the last moment because it had been too tight in the chest and shoulders. It was a traveling suit in brown serge, with a short-waisted jacket, trimmed with black lace, and a matching skirt. Beneath it Storm wore a shirt-waist, white, frilled, and high-necked, and her only chemise, pantalets, and two petticoats. Storm felt strangled and ungainly in the outfit, which her father had insisted she wear to meet Marcy.

Storm had tried again, begging her father to take her back home, but Derek's tone had been hard and inflexible, and she had known he would not cater to her this time. Now he was gone. Just like that, abandoning her . . . She stared out the parlor window.

An elegant carriage pulled by a beautiful bay gelding and driven by the single occupant, who must be Marcy Farlane, rolled up the drive. Storm turned away as the vehicle approached the front entrance. Storm was alone in the house except for the servants, since Paul had gone to his office at the bank, which he owned. Some crisis had arisen.

Storm was standing nervously in a corner of the parlor when Bart announced Marcy. Marcy bustled right past him, a beautiful woman with chestnut hair and blue-green eyes, shorter than Storm by several inches, a bit on the voluptuous side. She was wearing a blue gown that seemed to Storm scandalously low-cut. White lace gloves protected her hands, and a matching hat, trimmed with ribbons and lace, sat at a jaunty angle on her head. She moved forward with abundant energy. "You must be Storm. I have been looking forward to meeting you for months, ever since Paul first told me of your coming."

The greeting seemed genuine. Marcy's face was a perfect heart shape, her lips red and full, her skin the color of creamy magnolia blossoms. In contrast Storm felt like a freak. Marcy was beaming and clasping her hands warmly. Storm managed a smile.

"How do you like San Francisco?" Marcy asked.

"Fine," Storm managed.

"Miss, would you like some refreshments?" Bart inquired.

Storm was at a loss. Marcy said swiftly, "No, Bart, thank you. Storm and I have our day cut out for us. I'm going to take her to Madame Lamotte's and give her a tour of our fair city. It's such a beautiful day. Perfect for a carriage ride."

If Marcy noticed that Storm was unusually quiet, she paid no mind. Before Storm knew it, they were ensconced in the carriage and driving through town. Marcy pointed out landmarks and gave a running commentary and history: "See that building? The brick one with the gargoyles. It was burned down fifteen times in the past eight years. See that house? The St. Clairs live there. He's in publishing. *She* is the biggest gossip in town—next to her daughter, Leanne. Don't worry. You'll get to meet them.

That's the Miner's Girl. Brett D'Archand used to own that saloon. That's where he got his start. You met him last night, I believe. Oh! There's my brother-in-law. Randolph! Randolph!''

Storm was staring at the Miner's Girl with interest. It was a typical saloon, and from the sight of two men clad in flannels and Levis, she guessed its clientele consisted of regular laborers. One of the windows was broken. The building needed paint, badly, and the letters in the sign were incomplete. What a squalid place, she thought, curious.

''Storm, this is Randolph Farlane. Randolph, Storm Bragg, Paul's cousin from Texas.''

Storm looked up to see a handsome younger version of Grant, except for the golden color of his hair. He was looking at her with Grant's easy smile. She smiled back. ''Hello.''

''My pleasure,'' Randolph breathed, sitting easily on the chestnut he was riding. ''I hope you've been given a warm welcome, Miss Bragg.''

''Yes.''

''I'm looking forward to Friday evening,'' Randolph said.

Storm nodded, confused. He seemed to be implying that he was looking forward to seeing her again. She said, ''So am I.'' It seemed the safest course to take.

His eyes lit up with pleasure. ''Until then. Unless, of course, you'd care to go riding with me before that?''

Storm was startled, but she loved riding, so she responded with genuine enthusiasm. ''Oh, yes, I'd love to. Demon needs a daily workout or he becomes a bit much.''

''Demon, I take it, is your horse?''

She nodded proudly. ''I raised him from a colt.''

''Well then, I'll ask Paul immediately if I may call on you.'' He grinned, nodded to Marcy, and rode off.

Marcy was smiling. "Randy's a wonderful young man. He's taken with you."

Storm regarded her with confusion. "What?"

Marcy saw the incomprehension on her face. "He thinks you're pretty, which you are."

Storm flushed. "That's ridiculous. He was just being polite."

Marcy studied her. "Didn't you have any beaux back home, Storm?"

She shook her head. "I'm only seventeen, just."

She isn't aware of her beauty, Marcy thought, delighted. Or of men!

"You said Brett owned the Miner's Girl," Storm commented.

Marcy urged the bay forward, careful to avoid the other carriages and pedestrians. She shot a glance at Storm, who was innocently and openly curious. "Yes."

"But—it doesn't seem right."

"Why? Because Brett's such a gentleman?" Marcy laughed. "We all have to start somewhere, dear. Besides, Brett was only twenty-one when he bought a partnership in the saloon, mostly with gold dust although a few poker hands helped."

"He's a gambler?"

"He's a saloon keeper, hotelier, restaurateur, and landowner—among other things." Marcy glanced at Storm again. The girl was showing so much interest in Brett. She began to consider the possibility, but the match seemed an unlikely one. Brett was a rake, for one thing, and so polished. Besides, he liked beautiful, elegant women. No, she couldn't see them together. But . . . stranger things had happened.

"So he still owns the saloon?"

"No, he eventually bought out his partner, then sold out and bought the Golden Lady, which is one of the most elegant saloons in the city. Brett would be upset if he heard me now! *The* most elegant,'' she amended.

''He looks like a gambler,'' Storm muttered. ''Probably never did an honest day's work in his life.''

''That's not fair,'' Marcy said sharply.

Storm looked away, but wouldn't retract what she had said.

Madame Lamotte's was located on the other side of town, just before the buildings of the financial district clustered along Market Street and Embarcadero. Marcy braked the team and climbed down gracefully; Storm lifted her skirts to her knees and leaped to the ground. Marcy stared, shocked.

A man boomed with laughter behind them.

Both women looked up to see Brett on a magnificent gray stallion, clearly a thoroughbred. ''Ladies,'' he said, still chuckling.

Storm flushed, realizing she had just made a mistake, but she hadn't thought about what she was doing. She had been jumping off horses and wagons all her life.

''Good afternoon, Brett,'' Marcy said warmly. ''Where are you off to?''

''The bank.'' He grinned. ''Where else?'' His eyes went to Storm. The suit was awful, but nothing could detract from her startling looks. At the sight of the color in her cheeks, his grin widened. Then he noticed how her hair had turned different shades of dark and pale gold in the sunlight. She was still wearing it in that one thick braid down her back. ''Doing a little shopping?'' he asked.

''We are,'' Marcy said firmly.

''Need any help?'' Brett's gaze never wavered from Storm.

She couldn't look away from his warm, compelling eyes.

Marcy intruded. ''Now, Brett, don't be such a tease.''

Brett touched the edge of his black Stetson with his

forefinger, his gaze again drifting to Storm. Then he turned and trotted away, sitting as if he'd been born in the saddle.

"Storm . . ." Marcy said, not sure how to begin.

"I didn't think," Storm said, knowing instantly what she was talking about.

"Next time watch me. A lady moves gracefully, slowly and deliberately."

Storm was utterly embarrassed that that gambler had seen her leap from the carriage. "Marcy, to tell you the truth—I don't give a damn about being a lady, and I don't want these clothes. I just want to go home to Texas."

Marcy regarded her for a moment, then put a comforting hand on her shoulder, and they strolled toward the shop. "Well, you can either sulk for six months, or take advantage of a wonderful opportunity."

Storm wasn't really listening. Madame Lamotte's was the largest dress shop she had ever seen. There were displays of ready-made dresses for sale. Several women were inspecting the various garments. And accessories—hats, gloves, shawls, slippers, bonnets, pins, lace trim, ribbons . . . Storm had never seen anything like them. A short, plump woman clad in a sky-blue muslin gown hurried over. "Madame Farlane. It's so wonderful to see you!"

"Madame Lamotte, I would like you to meet Paul Langdon's cousin, Storm Bragg. She'll be needing an entire wardrobe as soon as possible. But first we'll purchase a few dresses off the racks. I hope that if they need altering it can be done today?"

"*Certainement!*" The little lady was beaming, scanning Storm's figure with a rapid, practiced eye. "The mademoiselle is so tall. Everything off the racks will be too short."

Marcy hadn't thought of that. Perturbed, she studied Storm, who flushed with annoyance at the hated description "tall." "Don't worry," Marcy said soothingly. "There must be something that can be let down."

"Yes, yes, maybe one or two things. Come. Let's take your measurements."

Storm found herself stripped to her chemise and pantalets, and measured all over. Marcy was babbling away, describing what she wanted for Storm. "With your vivid coloring, my dear," Marcy said, "you must have bold, bright colors. No pastels!"

Storm listened, but she had no idea what they were talking about. She grew tired and sat down to wait as Marcy and Madame Lamotte looked at hundreds of silks, taffetas, muslins, and velvets, choosing fabrics, trims, and styles. Marcy always asked what Storm thought. She always said yes because she felt helpless and overwhelmed.

"We absolutely must have the royal-blue taffeta ball gown for two weeks from Friday," Marcy announced. "And everything that goes with it."

Madame Lamotte nodded. "Ah, *oui*. Mademoiselle will go to the Sinclairs' annual ball, *non?*"

"Yes," Marcy said.

Storm was horrified. In five days she was going to a dinner party. In two weeks she was going to a ball? She did know how to dance, but she'd be damned if she would! She'd break her leg just trying to *walk* in those tiny high-heeled slippers.

"Can we have the cherry-pink silk by Friday morning?"

"For you, madame, of course," Madame Lamotte said. Marcy knew the woman's fee would be close to double for having her girls work around the clock.

Storm was laced into a corset. She had never, ever worn stays. "I can't breathe," she gasped.

"Although mademoiselle is tall, her waist is tiny—nineteen inches," Madame Lamotte said.

"I'll faint in front of everyone," Storm cried. A fine sheen of perspiration appeared on her brow.

"Storm, a lady wears a corset. But you'll get used to it. Loosen the stays, madame."

Storm found herself in an emerald-green silk dress, pin-striped with rose and cream. She looked down at herself and saw her breasts, the same gold as the rest of her, for she had been swimming and bathing naked her entire life. Both Madame Lamotte and Marcy had been stunned at her all-over golden tan, and Marcy had been bold enough to ask about it. Storm had told her the truth innocently enough, noticing their scandalized looks.

"It's too low," she said now, aghast.

"It's not low at all," Marcy countered, glancing at the girl's stricken face. She frowned, considering the evening gowns she had ordered for Storm. The blue taffeta was low, but the girl would be incredibly stunning in it, and the ball was over two weeks away. Wouldn't that be enough time for her to adjust? "Perhaps, madame, to make Storm more comfortable, we can add a bit of cream lace at the bosom," Marcy said.

They added lace there and at the flounced hem, then pronounced the gown a perfect fit. Madame Lamotte left momentarily. "You look beautiful, Storm," Marcy said softly. "Look." She turned her to face the mirror.

Storm stared, hardly recognizing herself as Marcy loosened her thick, gold-streaked hair and tied it away from her face with a pink ribbon. She saw a tall, startlingly unusual girl with golden skin, full breasts, and a breathless expression. She hated the stays and hoops, but she had to admit, somewhat grudgingly, that the gown was beautiful. Now that the lace had been added, and there was no sign of cleavage, she didn't feel so naked.

"Would you like to wear the gown home?" Marcy asked.

She did and she didn't. "I'll ruin it," she said finally.

Marcy laughed but didn't force the issue.

* * *

He lowered his head and nuzzled the ample breasts. She moaned. Smiling, he flicked his tongue around one pointed nipple, again and again, until her hands were clenching his hair. Brett took the hard peak into his mouth and began to suck. She whimpered, trying to push his head down.

Brett trailed kisses down her soft, slightly rounded belly, then over the curling hair protecting her woman's mound. She gasped when his kisses descended, his tongue intimately probing pink, moist flesh. When she moaned, he raised himself up and plunged into her, thrusting smoothly. She moaned again in climax, and he followed.

A moment later he rolled away. He never spent the night with Audrey, his mistress, and was surprised that he had spent the night here, at Patricia Fowley's. But her note had been impossible to resist. Patricia Fowley was married to a wealthy, older real estate investor. On more than one occasion she had flirted outrageously with him, and he had known for a long time that, inevitably, they would become lovers. Her husband was out of town for the week. When she had invited him over for a late supper, he had come eagerly.

He sat up, stretching his lean, muscled body. Patricia was well-versed in the art of lovemaking, a passionate, demanding companion. She smiled at him. She was only twenty-two, with pale blond hair and blue eyes, and now, in the morning sunlight, he could study her fashionably curved body. Her skin was as white as milk, and without stays, she was somewhat heavier than he'd thought. "Good morning," he murmured.

"Um," she purred. "A delicious morning."

Brett stood languidly.

"Don't go, Brett."

"I'm afraid I have to, *chère.*"

"It's the crack of dawn."

He laughed, stepping into his trousers. "Not quite."

When he sat on the bed to pull on his gleaming black boots, she pressed her soft, lush breasts against his back.

"Stay," she whispered. "I dismissed all the servants. No one will know."

"You live too dangerously," he said, momentarily sated and no longer sexually excited by her. "As much as I dislike your husband, I have no desire to be caught cuckolding the poor man."

"Oh, bah! Steve is too old! What am I supposed to do?" She pouted prettily, perfectly.

Brett grinned. "You have a hand—use it."

She gasped, shocked.

Brett laughed and slipped on his shirt. She had let him know last night that she was no stranger to such tactics.

"When will I see you again?"

"In a couple of days," he replied, though he wasn't sure he was really interested. Yes, she had been good, but Audrey was better—less demanding, more giving. Besides, there were all kinds of classy whores in San Francisco, and Brett had never been one to stay long with the same woman. Even Audrey had been his mistress for only a few months.

Brett left shortly after, feeling invigorated despite the lack of sleep. It was early, not even seven o'clock, so he had time for his habitual gallop before going home and changing for the day.

He thought about Susie and her child with satisfaction. Judge Steiner had granted the divorce, and as Brett had guessed, Bill Hawkins had been more than happy to exchange his wife for a few hundred dollars. Yesterday Susie had sworn her eternal gratitude to Brett . . . and now she was happily back at work.

Brett galloped King along the beach and through the surf. The salt air felt good, fresh and clean against his face. He had gotten a loan from Paul's bank yesterday, money he would put up for his share in expanding the shipping line. Paul had approved the loan instantly, saying, "I like your style, Brett." Paul was the only one who knew how overextended he was, but Brett had always been a gambler.

It was a clear, crisp spring day. Squinting ahead, he realized a rider was approaching at a canter. He admired the big black stallion, then with a start realized the rider was Storm. Storm—alone. Instantly he was worried. Their gazes met, and he saw that she had recognized him, too.

"What happened?" he shouted, whirling his stallion around and cutting her off. Both horses pranced restlessly in place.

"What do you mean?"

"Where in hell's your escort?" he heard himself demand with sudden anger.

Her chin jutted up. "I came alone."

He couldn't believe it. "Alone?"

"Excuse me," she flared, her eyes sparking, and urged her stallion past him.

He quickly maneuvered his own mount to cut her off again, reaching for her reins. She gasped and deftly sidestepped away. "How dare you!"

"What's wrong with you?" he shouted. "Foolish child! There's all kind of riffraff running around! Are you an idiot?"

Storm was incensed, as much by his manner as his words. Child? And who was he to tell her what to do? "Let me by!"

He was having trouble comprehending the scenario. She was breathtaking and might as well have been naked, sitting astride that huge, mean stallion, clad in skintight buckskins. Her face was flushed from exertion, and wisps of golden hair blew around her face. "Certainly," he finally said, backing up his gray.

She moved determinedly past, then gasped when he turned to ride alongside her. "What are you doing?"

"Escorting you," he said, regaining some control. "I *know* Paul didn't approve your riding alone."

"I don't want your escort or your company," she flashed. "I can take care of myself!"

He gave her a contemptuous look.

Storm decided she hated him. "I can shoot better and ride faster than any man!"

He noted grimly that she had a six-shooter strapped to her thigh. "That's quite an accomplishment for a young lady," he drawled sarcastically. "Maybe it should be added to the repertoire of all young ladies' training."

She flushed. "I can certainly defend myself better than some dandified city-slicker gambler!"

Brett tensed, and Storm whirled her stallion in the other direction. "Goodbye, Mr. D'Archand. I'm going home, so there's no need for you to further ruin my day."

Brett turned his own mount and continued to ride silently alongside her. He would escort her to her door *and* deliver her into Paul's hands. The girl had no common sense. None at all.

But he found himself staring at her perfect form, so ripe for lovemaking, and her arresting profile. Desire washed over him, and he fought it. He had always been a lusty man, and proud of it, but this time his lust was misplaced.

She glared at him. "It's rude to stare."

"Forgive me."

She looked quickly at him to see if he was mocking her, but his expression told her nothing. She urged the black into a canter.

Brett had to admire her seat. She rode with consummate grace, as if she and the horse were one. He wasn't even shocked that she rode astride, for he had imagined she would when he had first seen her clad in men's buckskins. Now, however, he had an image of her astride something else. Him.

"You ride very well," he said hoarsely.

"So do you."

He grinned then. "Tell me, Storm, do you have a beau back in Texas?" He was sure she didn't. The girl was flustered every time he looked at her. Clearly she didn't know how to flirt.

She glanced warily at him. "No."

He was pleased, although he refused to recognize why that should be. "Why?"

"I'm only seventeen."

He chuckled. "That's old enough."

When he began laughing at her, Storm lashed out. "Lennie Willis tried to kiss me, but I blackened his eye," she said with hard satisfaction.

Brett's smile widened. He could vividly imagine the scene, some young bumpkin trying to steal a kiss from the wild, buckskin-clad girl, her fist flying. He laughed again. Storm glared, flushing.

He decided to change the topic. "How was shopping yesterday? Did you find some pretty things?"

"I have no use for 'pretty things,' Mr. D'Archand. I'm a Texas woman who lives and works on a ranch. As far as I'm concerned, this life is for people like you, not for me."

He frowned. He had only been trying to make pleasant conversation, but it seemed she wanted to fight. "You haven't even given San Francisco a chance."

"That's right," she said as they turned off the beach.

They rode the rest of the way in silence, and when they reached the gates of the Langdon residence, Storm turned a flashing blue glance at him. "Goodbye, Mr. D'Archand."

"Brett," he said easily. "And I intend to escort you to your front door." He had already decided not to confront Paul now, in front of her, for his temper at her foolishness had cooled. He would stop by the bank in town later and have a private word with her guardian. After all, Paul must be informed of his cousin's riding off alone. It was just too dangerous.

They reached the stables to the left of the house. Ever the gentleman, Brett swung down as Storm did. She ignored him, handing her reins to the groom who had hurried over. Brett caught her arm before she could move away. "Until Friday," he said, holding her hand and staring into her eyes.

Then he was gone, swinging effortlessly into the saddle and cantering away without a backward glance.

Despite herself, Storm gazed after him.

Chapter 3

On Friday morning Storm woke up sick with dread. She refused to get out of bed, and soon Paul had sent for the physician. She was flushed with anxiety—tonight was the dinner party in her honor. She intended to stay in bed all day, pretending to have the flu so no one would make her go.

Dr. Winslow arrived just before noon, as did Marcy. "What's wrong?" she cried, genuinely worried, rushing to Storm's bedside before Dr. Winslow could enter.

Storm felt ashamed. Over the past few days she had been squired around town by Marcy, and she had quickly realized that the older woman was unaffectedly warm and friendly, with nothing but kind intentions. Storm liked her, grudgingly. Just as she liked San Francisco, grudgingly. Now she saw Marcy's white, worried face, felt a hand on her forehead, and was at once guilty. Worse, she knew her father would be ashamed of her for acting this way.

"You might have a slight fever," Marcy cried, agitated.

"Please, Marcy, let me decide that," said the man standing in the doorway. He stepped inside carrying a battered doctor's bag.

"I feel much better," Storm said, sitting up. "I'm fine, really." Marcy had gone to so much trouble for this dinner party. Storm couldn't lie to her.

Dr. Winslow pronounced Storm healthy and strong—

stronger than most women, in fact—and he soon left, escorted by Paul. Marcy sat down on the bed next to Storm, who couldn't meet her gaze. Marcy held her hand.

"I think I understand," she said slowly, in a soft voice.

"No," Storm protested. "I did feel ill this morning, but it was probably something I ate last night. I feel fine now."

"Were you trying to avoid coming to dinner tonight?" Marcy's direct question took Storm by surprise, and she flushed guiltily. Marcy's gaze was knowing. "Everyone will love you, dear," she said. "You're a vibrant, beautiful girl."

Storm bit her lip. She couldn't lie. "I'm sorry. I—I couldn't go through with it, not after you've been so kind to me."

"Randolph would be so disappointed."

"What?" Storm was ridiculously pleased. Randolph had taken her riding two days ago, and, because Marcy had made her aware of him, she had noticed that his gaze was openly admiring. In her new riding habit, which, upon her insistence, had a split skirt, Storm had felt very attractive. She knew now that Marcy had been right. Randolph thought she was pretty, and the idea produced a heady sensation. She felt wonderfully feminine, even powerful.

"He's been raving about you ever since he first laid eyes on you," Marcy said with a smile.

Storm smiled, too.

"It will be a wonderful evening, you'll see. I'll send Marie over to help you dress and do your hair." She rose, her gaze warm and compassionate.

Storm watched her leave. Although she was still nervous, she felt relieved to be attending the dinner party after all. Marcy had been kind, and she didn't want to hurt her. Nor could she shame herself or her family—even though they wouldn't know—by pulling such a poor prank.

Marie arrived in midafternoon. Storm bathed in scented

water, then rubbed the lotion Marcy had given her all over her body. It smelled of roses, like the bathwater. She especially massaged the lotion into her chapped hands. Remembering how Brett had kissed her knuckles, a flood of color filled her cheeks. Marcy's hands were lily white and as soft as down. What had Brett thought when he'd touched Storm's callused palm? Even then she had been aware that something was wrong, that she didn't have a lady's hands.

But, dammit, I'm a Texan, and I work a ranch!

She knew Brett was going to be there tonight.

Thinking of him brought all kinds of careening emotions to the surface. For one, she was furious with him. The night after he had come across her riding alone on the beach, she had been lectured by Paul and restricted to riding with Bart, Paul, or another male companion. Ridiculous! She could take care of herself—she'd been doing it for years. She was used to riding free, like an Apache on the desert, not with a chaperone to slow her down. The new restriction was all Brett's fault, and she would have a few choice words to say to him when she saw him. He had no right to go ratting on her behind her back.

Besides, she still hadn't forgiven him for calling her a child.

Marie began helping Storm to dress. First came a sheer, lacy chemise, cut so low that Storm's nipples almost burst free. Never had she seen such a fine garment. Then came silk stockings and pink garters with black rosettes. Lacy, filmy drawers and the hated corset followed.

Storm hadn't worn one since she had been fitted by Madame Lamotte. Now, when Marie held up the frilly, frothy, beribboned contraption, Storm scowled. "No."

"Oh, yes, you must."

"No!"

"Mademoiselle, it is scandal not to wear one. You must. Madame Marcy says so." Despite her small size and soft voice, the French maid was immovable. Storm found herself being cinched up. She groaned. "It's too tight!"

"It is not tight at all," Marie said firmly.

"I can't breathe!" She couldn't. Of course, it might have been due to the dread growing in her.

Marie gave one more tug, making Storm grunt in a very unladylike manner, and began to tie the stays. Storm tried to breathe. She found she could—barely.

"Now hoops," Marie said.

Storm was frowning at herself in the mirror. The corset had pushed her full breasts up and out, making her look more bovine than human. "I can't wear this," she said huskily.

A petticoat was plunked over her head, then tied at her waist. Four more frothy ones followed. The last was black, edged with lace and black diamantes. Finally came the cherry-pink dress.

When Marie had finally finished, right down to dabbing a rose-based scent on Storm's wrists, behind her ears, and in her cleavage, Storm stared at herself in horror and dismay. She didn't recognize the person in the mirror. She seemed . . . elegant . . . different . . . a *woman*.

She didn't like the dress. Half her breasts were exposed. "This is too low," she declared. "I refuse to wear it."

"It is not low at all," Marie responded. "You could show a lot more, and you should. Your body is *magnifique, ma petite*. You should show it off, not hide it."

"I don't want to show it off," Storm said, flushing. At least her hair had been left alone. Marie had merely pulled its thick, wavy length behind her ears and secured it with a black satin headband encrusted with seed pearls. The headband pinched. Her head began to throb. Even the tiny diamond ear studs that had been her mother's hurt her ears.

"Magnifique," Marie declared.

Storm took a few practice steps around the room. Her

feet immediately began to hurt around the toes. The shoes must be too narrow. What she wouldn't give to wear her worn cowboy boots. She smiled at the thought of entering Marcy's salon wearing dirty brown boots. There was a knock on the door, and Paul entered.

"Storm, you look magnificent!" he cried, his eyes bright with pride.

Storm knew he meant what he said, and she took another look at herself in the mirror. "My face isn't heart-shaped," she said doubtfully. "Look how wide my jaw is."

Paul smiled. "You are not conventionally beautiful, no, but you are striking. I can't think of another woman who even touches your beauty, Storm."

She wondered if he was just flattering her, but then she saw that he was serious. "Thank you."

He held out his arm. "Shall we?"

Storm took it, but as they left the thickly carpeted room, she stumbled. She prayed it wasn't a foreshadowing of the evening to come.

"So I begged Papa, and he promised, and isn't that just wonderful?"

Brett smiled at the beautiful brunette chatting merrily. "That's wonderful, Leanne, and I'm thrilled for you."

She clasped his arm. Her flawless oval face, with ivory skin, red lips, and sky-blue eyes, was wreathed in a smile. "Then you'll have to escort me through the park, Brett."

"Indeed, I will," he said, glancing once again at her small breasts, almost completely revealed by the pastel blue silk gown she wore. As she pressed his arm even closer to her side, her bosom swelled, and for the barest moment he thought he could see the faint pink edge of her aureoles.

Although her chatter was inane and aimless, Leanne St. Clair was perfect marriage material. She was beautiful and elegant. Her mother could trace her antecedents back to the English aristocracy, and her father was the grandson of a French duke beheaded during the days of the French Revolution. This was not the first time Brett had escorted Leanne, nor would it be the last. He had yet to kiss her, though. That would be too much of a declaration of matrimonial intentions, which he did not quite have.

Marcy had twenty guests, not including the guest of honor and her cousin, who had yet to arrive—purposely, Brett was sure. Everyone knew everyone, sharing each other's social circles. There were four other well-bred young ladies, two escorted by reputable bachelors, two accompanied by their parents. Marcy had, of course, included several eligible young men, most of them unescorted. The genders were balanced by the addition of two widows. Most, but not all, of the married couples were young, in their thirties.

The grand salon was large and elegantly furnished; huge double doors opened onto a spacious, marble-floored foyer. As Leanne chatted, Brett found himself glancing at the doorway. He was soon rewarded. Paul Langdon appeared with a ravishing woman at his side, and Marcy squealed with delight as she swept forward to greet them.

It took Brett a split instant to recognize the stunning woman as Storm. His body grew tense as he stood in the sudden silence of the salon and stared at the tall, willowy woman in the modestly cut pink gown. She was magnificent. Leanne pressed closer to him, seeking to gain his attention, but he ignored her.

"Storm, darling, you look beautiful!" Marcy cried.

Storm was already flushed. As her anxiety increased, so had her pulse and her temperature, and she was having a bit of trouble breathing. Damn the stays anyway! She was afraid she was going to trip again, and everyone in the room was staring at her as if she were some tall freak. Worst of all, the first person she had seen when she walked in was that nosy bastard D'Archand, and he was looking at her as if he could see right through her clothes. She couldn't speak.

"Come, dear, let me introduce you around," said Marcy.

Storm stole a glance at Brett, and for the first time noticed the exquisite, *short* brunette clinging to him. She felt irritated without knowing why. Her gaze drifted away, then back to Brett, and she froze when their glances met. He smiled slightly, with the faintest hint of amusement, as if he guessed her innermost thoughts, and offered a slight bow. Storm looked away.

"She's so tall," Leanne muttered with a toss of her blue-black head that made the diamonds woven into her hair glint and sparkle. "She's as tall as most men."

Brett ignored her. He had been pierced with desire when their gazes met, the reason for his self-derisive expression. He managed to tear his glance away from Storm when he realized how rude he was being. "Some punch, sweet?" he asked Leanne, wondering, fascinated, why the tops of Storm's breasts were the same golden color as her neck, arms, and face. Just where did her unusual tan end? Would her breasts be white beneath the neck of the gown?

Randolph came forward with open admiration and enthusiasm. "Storm, I've been looking forward to this day forever it seems!" He took her hand and kissed it.

Storm blushed. "Me, too," she said—a polite, harmless lie. Marcy shot her an amused glance.

"Really?" Randolph asked hopefully. "I hope that just a little of your eagerness was due to a desire to see me?"

Storm laughed, a rich, warm sound that carried throughout the room. "You know it was."

Randolph raised her hand and kissed it again. "Maybe later we can take a turn in the garden."

"I would love to," Storm said.

Brett, who had moved closer and was standing behind

her, scowled. She was flirting with Randolph, and he didn't like it—not one bit. Then, before he could get a word in, she was surrounded by the five other bachelors present, all eager to meet her. Marcy began making the introductions, and Storm swept off with them, amid much laughter and gallantry.

Marcy noticed Brett's dark expression and took her husband's arm as he came to stand beside them. "I guess the rest of the introductions will have to wait," she said.

"Your protegée is already a big success, darling," Grant said, kissing her cheek gently.

Marcy glowed.

"Has Randolph called on her?" Brett almost growled. Leanne was still clinging to his arm. He knew he was being rude to her, but with Storm in the room he couldn't seem to give Leanne his full attention.

"He's taken her riding," Grant replied. "He thinks she's the most beautiful woman he's ever seen."

"Brett, let's dance," Leanne said quickly, producing a winning smile. Brett nodded without a word and took her onto the dance floor for a graceful waltz.

"Lord, I hate seeing Brett with that vain twit," Grant said.

"Grant, be generous. It's not Leanne's fault. She can't help being the way she is. I would be that way, too, if I had two parents like hers. Oh, Storm is dancing!"

"You would never be that way," Grant muttered, kissing her again, this time not quite so chastely.

Storm could barely think. She could barely breathe. She had only accepted this dance with the auburn-haired man because she had to get away from such a large group of men. Now she was sorry. Her feet hurt, throbbing painfully. She could keep her balance well enough for walking, but dancing didn't come naturally to her—at least, not this kind of dancing. Give her a rowdy, foot-stomping Texas tune any day! Her headband still pinched, and her stays were constricting and uncomfortable. She couldn't even remember her partner's name.

When she stepped on his foot, she wanted to die. "I'm sorry!"

"It's all right," he said.

"Please," Storm said desperately as she missed another step, "could we stop?"

"Certainly," he said, though not before she trod on his foot again.

Storm walked resolutely away, her face flushed with embarrassment. She would not dance again. She veered away from the group of young men, who had dispersed somewhat with her absence but were now awaiting her arrival like hounds straining at the leash. Instead she headed for Paul, who was talking to an older couple.

"Are you enjoying yourself, Storm?" he asked.

"Yes," she lied, trying to forget how clumsy she had been on the dance floor. She saw Brett strolling toward them—toward her, she knew with sure instinct. Although he seemed relaxed and casual, she could sense the determination in his tall, muscular form. Panic and anger surged up in her.

"Storm," he said, reaching for her hand, covered with short black gloves. "How enchanting you look tonight." He kissed her knuckles, and his touch seemed to sear through the fabric of the gloves. She regarded him venomously and yanked her hand away. He looked taken aback.

"Thank you," she said glacially, her eyes a cold blue fire.

"Are you displeased with me?" he asked coolly.

She raised her brows, not realizing how imperious the gesture was.

"Of course not," Paul said, clapping Brett's shoulder. "How are you, Brett? I see you've brought Leanne tonight."

Immediately Storm strode away, not caring if she was being unforgivably rude, refusing even to be near the man who had caused Paul to forbid her to ride alone. But taking such long strides was a mistake. A delicate heel slipped, and she would have fallen if Grant Farlane didn't reach out and grab her. "Damn!" *Another mistake.*

"It's all right," Grant said kindly.

Her face was red. She glanced around and saw that half the people in the room had seen the mishap, including Brett. "I hate these da—these shoes," she muttered.

Grant grinned. "I myself don't know how you ladies do it," he said, his brown eyes twinkling.

She relaxed. "This is just so different for me."

"You're doing fine," he soothed. "And you've got a bevy of admirers. Leanne St. Claire is green with envy because even she can't compete with your beauty."

Storm didn't understand why everyone kept telling her she was beautiful. Just then a servant announced dinner, and Grant offered her his arm. She took it, thinking that Marcy was very lucky to have him for a husband.

Fortunately, dinner went better than the earlier part of the evening. Sitting down gave Storm's feet a chance to rest, although they didn't stop throbbing. She tried to slip off her shoes under the table, then decided against it—she would never get them back on. As the guest of honor, she was seated on Grant's left, with Randolph on her other side. Unfortunately, Leanne and Brett were directly across from her. Storm ignored Brett, although he kept staring at her—quite rudely, she thought. And not just at her face, but at her overly exposed breasts. She had known the gown was too low.

When Brett spoke to her, she had no choice but to respond, although there was no mistaking her coolness. He finally gave up.

After a seven-course meal, the guests returned to the salon for more dancing. Marcy routinely waived the custom of having the men retire separately from the women, and Grant always supported her decision. Randolph went off to fetch Storm a glass of water, and for the first time that evening she found herself alone. It was a blessed relief.

She was emotionally exhausted, with throbbing feet and the beginning of a grand headache. Having eaten too much, and barely able to stand the corset, she was in great physical discomfort. She had drunk a glass of wine with dinner, and now she began to feel lonely, homesick, and sorry for herself. She moved to the velvet-draped French doors and stared blindly out at the night.

"Somehow I don't get the feeling you've enjoyed yourself this evening," Brett said.

She turned, blinking back the moisture in her eyes. "Go away."

"Why are you angry with me? Because of that little incident on the beach? If so, I apologize." His dark eyes were blazing.

"You bastard! You ran and told Paul about it! How dare you interfere! Now I can't ride alone. You've ruined the only pleasure I have in this damn town."

He was visibly shocked at her rage and bad language, and then a tense, rigid mask slipped over his face. "It was for your own good," he said, exercising great restraint. "Better you ride with others than ride alone and get hurt."

"I can take care of myself. Just go away." Tears welled up in her eyes. She turned her back on him, and moments later, heard him stride away. She felt relief—and disappointment.

"Storm?" It was Randolph.

She wiped her eyes with a knuckle, not turning to him because she didn't want anyone to see she was crying.

But he saw. "What's wrong?" he asked, genuinely concerned.

"Could we take that walk now?"

He set down the glass of water, took her arm, and led her outside through the French doors, ignoring the shocked stares that followed them. Outside, the night was cool, and she immediately shivered.

"You need your cloak," Randolph said. "I'll get it."

"No, it's wonderful," she said, taking in deep breaths of the night air. She started to breathe more easily.

He led her down the steps into the garden, where the wonderful fragrance of honeysuckle assailed them. "Do we have to walk?" Storm said. "I hate to say this but my feet are killing me."

"You should have told me," he said, instantly stopping. They stood and looked up at the crescent moon. Storm shivered again, and Randolph put his arm around her shoulders. She tensed. He was immensely disappointed. He wanted to kiss her, but he knew with certainty that she wouldn't be receptive. Instead, he settled for just having her near him. "Tell me why you're upset," he said softly.

"I'm not upset anymore."

At the sound of soft voices behind them they both turned. From the shadows emerged the dark form of a couple, then, as they moved into the lights cast by the house, Brett and Leanne became distinguishable. Brett stared at them, not smiling but apparently not surprised to see them.

"Fancy meeting you here, Randy," he said, his eyes on Storm.

Storm didn't like the way he was looking at her. She was suddenly aware of how close she was standing to Randolph, and that he had one arm draped casually over her shoulders. She had the insane feeling that Brett had followed them out here. For a long moment Brett and Randolph stared hard at each other, like two stallions ready to do battle.

Storm sighed and moved away from Randolph, limping

to the stone bench and sinking down on it. She moaned and began to unlace her shoes.

"Storm," Randolph said, moving to her, "let me do that."

"I can't stand it another minute," she cried, letting him kneel before her and pull off one shoe. "Oh!"

He rubbed her foot between two large hands. "Better?"

Tears came to her eyes. "I don't think I'll ever walk again." They both suddenly smiled, and as Randolph removed the other shoe, Storm looked up to see Brett and Leanne staring at them. Brett looked furious, Leanne incredulous. Her heart began to pound.

"Brett, I think they want to be alone," Leanne said suggestively, holding on to his arm.

"Probably so, but it wouldn't do to allow Storm to ruin her reputation—not at this early stage," Brett drawled.

Storm gasped. "What?"

Randolph was instantly on his feet. "Brett! You know me better than that. If you weren't such a good friend, I'd knock you down right now!"

"Oh, I'm sorry," Brett said smoothly, sarcastically. "You came out here for the air—not for the lady's kisses?"

"That's right," Randolph said between gritted teeth.

"Let's go, Brett," Leanne said. "It's not your place to interfere."

"Put on your shoes, Storm," Brett ordered harshly. He didn't dare analyze why he was raging with anger. "You're going inside."

She was stunned, then furious, and stood abruptly. "How dare you order me around!"

Leanne gasped.

Brett smiled. "Put on your shoes," he said in a softer tone. "We'll all go in together." Damned if he'd leave her out here alone with Randolph.

"He's right," Randolph said. "We've been out here too long. At any second, Marcy will come running."

But Storm was furious. "No, Randolph. I refuse to be ordered around. He went behind my back and spoke to Paul and ruined my riding, and now he turns up here telling me what to do? No!" She was shouting, the effort making her breathless and dizzy.

Brett reached out and grabbed her arm. "Your shoes can always be put on for you, Storm. I would be most delighted to do so."

"Brett!" Leanne and Randolph protested at once.

"Get your hands off me!" Storm cried.

"Put on your shoes."

She slapped him as hard as she could.

The crack was loud in the silence of the night.

Brett hadn't released her arm. He stared at her, momentarily stunned, then pulled her into a close embrace, with a fierce grip on both her arms, pressing her against his own hard body. He began to throb against her. Her face had become pale as she stared back at him, and he had the insane desire to kiss her, brutally, until she begged for more.

"I can't . . . breathe . . ." she whispered, a strangled sound. And then, suddenly, she went limp in his arms.

"My God!" Randolph cried. "What have you done?"

"She's fainted," Brett said with forced evenness. He swung her into his arms and strode purposefully toward the house, bypassing the doors leading to the salon, heading instead toward Grant's library. Only one light was burning, and the doors were unlocked. Randolph reached ahead to open them, and Brett entered, setting his burden carefully on the sofa. "Damn stays," he said angrily, and with nimble dexterity, he unhooked the back of her gown and loosened her stays.

"Damn you, Brett," Randolph exclaimed.

Brett was kneeling at Storm's side, lightly stroking her pale face. "She doesn't need stays," he said. Then, with an awful premonition, he asked, "Where's Leanne?"

"I don't know. I'll go get Marcy and some smelling salts."

But before he hurried away, the door burst open, and Marcy, Grant, and Paul rushed in. "Good God, what happened?" Marcy cried.

"What the hell happened?" Paul roared, taking in his cousin's disheveled appearance—shoeless feet, unfastened gown.

"She fainted," Brett said calmly.

"Leanne said she was in the garden with her clothes undone, and now she's fainted," Paul said furiously. "Who's the culprit? I'll kill him!"

"Relax," Grant said. "Let Brett explain."

"She took off her shoes, Paul, because her feet were hurting her," he said dryly. "I don't think she realized how inappropriate it was. *I* loosened her stays *after* she fainted."

"She's not used to corsets," Marcy said worriedly, stroking her hair. "Grant, go put a stop to Leanne's vicious gossiping."

Grant nodded and left just as Randolph returned with the salts. Storm moaned. Brett, still kneeling, reached out without thinking to stroke her face. Her skin was incredibly smooth. Marcy was instantly there, shouldering him aside and flashing a warning look. "Fetch me a brandy, Brett," she ordered.

Brett rose reluctantly. He had trouble taking his eyes off the beautiful girl. Paul Langdon shoved past him, and he faded into the background. Shortly thereafter, Storm and Paul left for the evening without once returning to the salon.

Chapter 4

Sunlight poked through the flowery chintz curtains of Storm's bedroom window and woke her. Instantly, she remembered the fiasco of the night before and wanted to die from humiliation. Even lying there in bed, her face began to burn. Oh, God. How could she have fainted?

I will never, ever wear stays again, she promised herself, turning onto her stomach and burying her face in her pillow. What had everyone thought? What had Brett thought?

It was his fault, anyway! She had lost her breath fighting with him. Damn him for interfering once again. What an arrogant dandy, she thought angrily, throwing his weight around when he should be minding his own business.

There was no point lying in bed. Storm was dying to gallop Demon across the beach until she had put San Francisco and everyone in it far, far behind her. But she had overslept, and she not only didn't want Bart's boring, silent company, but also dreaded the thought of running into someone from last night's party. But how long could she hide?

She dressed in her buckskins. To hell with all the fancy clothes. They didn't suit her, it was all too clear. She braided her hair and went downstairs, ignoring the silent disapproval of Bart and the serving girl. At least food was something she could still enjoy. She ate three eggs, a small steak, fresh bread, and fried potatoes, and topped all that off with a piece of melon. Afterward she felt pleasantly full.

"Mrs. Farlane is here to see you, ma'am," Bart said from the doorway.

"Oh, no need for formality," Marcy cried, stepping past him into the dining room. She looked surprised at Storm's garb, but smiled and kissed her cheek warmly. "Good morning, dear. Did you sleep well?"

Looking at her, Storm suddenly wanted to cry. "Not really," she murmured.

Marcy sat down next to her and covered Storm's hand with her own. "How are you feeling?"

"Fine—physically, anyway."

Sapphire-blue eyes met sky-blue ones. "A little faint means absolutely nothing. You're not the first woman to faint, and you won't be the last."

Storm felt moisture welling up in her eyes. "I never want to see any of those people again. Never!"

"Storm . . ."

"No. They all know I'm just some . . . some country bumpkin. I stepped on that man's foot twice when we danced, I practically fell on my face and half the people in the room saw it, and I hate those shoes. And then I had to faint. And it wasn't even my fault! It was that Brett D'Archand's fault!"

Marcy raised a brow. "Storm, last night you were beautiful, and every man there thought so. Randolph is infatuated with you, and so, I think, are half a dozen others. If you aren't good at dancing, then you'll just have to take some lessons. And *I* certainly didn't see you trip. As for fainting . . . well, it's considered very feminine."

Storm grimaced. "But I'm not feminine. I ride and shoot and hunt and track better than most men—Pa says so. I'm tall and gawky, and my feet are too large. My hands are red and chapped and *callused,* and I feel like a freak in all those beautiful gowns. I wish I could go home.'' She swatted angrily at a tear that dared to creep from one eye.

"You're very feminine, Storm, and very beautiful, and I wish you could see yourself the way others do. Your height is striking, and you're one of the most graceful women I've ever seen. You just need to relax, and maybe get used to wearing gowns and shoes.''

"This is all so silly,'' Storm said, sniffing. "In six months I'm going home. Do you know what I do at home, Marcy? I work the range with the boys. I hunt with my brothers and Pa. I can whip up the best meal on the trail you've ever seen. If my buckskins rip, I can sew them up with a piece of sinew.'' Storm put her elbows on the table and her chin in her hands.

"What do you do when you fall off a horse, Storm?'' Marcy asked gently.

Storm looked up. "Get back on, of course.''

Marcy just looked at her.

Storm realized the significance of what she had said. She frowned. "I do want to make my family proud of me, I really do,'' she said passionately. "It's just . . . so hard!''

"I'm going to take you to lunch, Storm. Come on. I'll help you change.''

But the thought of appearing in public made Storm feel sick. "Maybe tomorrow.''

"Storm . . .''

The one thing she wasn't was a coward. She could imagine her pa being there. He would be so disappointed if he knew she was hiding in Paul's big house, afraid to see anyone. "All right,'' she said. "But no stays, Marcy.''

Some time later they were settled in Marcy's beautiful black barouche. Storm was wearing a cream-colored muslin gown striped in pink with a matching hat set at a jaunty angle on her head. Her hair was pinned away from her face and left to wave loosely down her back. Her gloves were crocheted, as was her reticule. The shoes that matched the gown were much more comfortable than the ones she'd worn the night before, with a low heel, and Marcy had thrown out the culprits responsible for her aching feet last night. In truth, as the carriage rolled down California Street and men turned to stare, Storm felt pleased, even elegant.

"What exactly happened last night?" Marcy asked.

Storm didn't mind telling her. "Randolph and I were walking in the garden. Then Brett and Leanne appeared, and Brett insinuated that he was protecting my reputation. He has some nerve! My feet were killing me, and Randolph helped me take off my shoes. Brett became completely unreasonable and insisted I put them back on and go inside. He grabbed me, and that's when I lost my breath and fainted."

"That's so strange," Marcy said. "If you had gone outside with almost anyone else, I could understand Brett's concern, but Randolph is a gentleman and Brett's friend."

"Brett D'Archand needs a lesson in manners," Storm said vehemently.

"Dear, I don't know if you're aware of it, but just be careful when you walk alone with a man. Not all of them have good intentions when they escort a lady into a moonlit garden."

"What do you mean?" Storm asked.

"Well, they'll try and kiss you, of course."

Storm laughed. "Let them try! I'll gladly blacken another eye!"

Marcy smiled. "I guess I don't have to worry about you. Actually, there are other less violent ways of dissuading an amorous gentleman."

"Such as?"

"A firm no."

Storm smiled.

"And, Storm, Brett is a gentleman, and a nice man."

She gave an unladylike snort. "And I'm a dainty lady! Hah!"

Marcy decided not to tell her charge that they were having lunch at Brett's hotel. She couldn't help wondering why Brett had acted so strangely last night. Could it be that he had been jealous when Storm and Randolph had disappeared into the garden? Marcy had seen them go from across the room, and she'd seen Brett and Leanne trailing almost in their wake—as if Brett were deliberately following Storm. But that was silly.

Brett's hotel was an elegant Victorian brick building on the corner of Stockton Street. It was surrounded by shops, eateries, an ice cream parlor—and two blocks down, the Golden Lady. The lobby boasted plush gold Turkish carpets, crystal chandeliers, couches in striped silk, and velvet draperies in white and gold. Huge windows let in lots of sunlight, and the high ceiling was glass-domed. The lobby was an atrium, surrounded on all four sides by the guest rooms, starting on the second floor. The design was original and impressive. Marcy could see that Storm was awed.

The dining room was as elegant as the lobby, also decorated in gold and white, the walls upholstered in a heavy gold fabric showing the Tree of Life in corals, greens, and blues. Starched white linen covered the tables, and crystal glasses gleamed. Marcy smiled at Storm's wide-eyed expression.

Two matrons and another party of three men stood in front of them waiting for the host to seat them. The men were discussing a business venture involving China. Suddenly Marcy heard her last name. One of the matrons, whom Marcy knew slightly, had said, ". . . at the Farlanes' last night." Marcy's ears perked up.

"She was *outside*—with *two gentlemen?*" demanded Mrs. Butterfield.

"Without her shoes on. And then she fainted," said Mrs. Chase knowingly.

"Which one kissed her?"

"I don't know. But to go out alone with two men—I wonder if we've even heard the whole story."

"You don't think . . . What do you think?"

"If she had her shoes off, maybe she had her hose off, too."

Marcy was shocked into momentary speechlessness, and then the host was leading the two gossips to their table. Marcy glanced at Storm, but she was so involved in her rapt perusal of the appointments that she appeared not to have heard a word of what was said. Marcy was furious. She should have known that malicious little Leanne would start spreading rumors as fast as she could. With her mother's help, of course. Marcy intended to pay a visit to Mrs. Chase later that afternoon and tear her apart. *And* set the record straight.

"I've never, ever dreamed a place could look like this," Storm whispered.

Marcy tried to calm down. She didn't want Storm to think anything was wrong. "It's one of San Francisco's most elegant establishments. I thought you'd enjoy it."

Storm smiled. "I just can't believe it."

They were soon seated at a round table for four by a window overlooking the street. Storm spent a good deal of time studying the menu, apparently fascinated. Marcy leaned forward. "Do you need any help with that?" she asked, then looked up to see Brett approaching.

"I just can't decide," Storm said, flashing a smile. "Everything sounds so good."

"Maybe I can help," Brett said.

Storm gasped and looked up to see him standing there, his eyes warm, a soft expression on his face. She was momentarily flustered.

"Good afternoon, ladies," he said, glancing briefly at

Marcy before turning his gaze back to Storm. "You both look ravishing today."

Marcy smiled. She knew the compliment wasn't for her.

"May I?" Brett asked, pulling out a chair between them.

"Please," Marcy said.

Storm stiffened.

"What are you in the mood for, Storm?" Brett asked, his eyes never leaving her face. "Although, as boastful as it may sound, everything on the menu is good."

"I don't know," Storm managed, taken aback by his pleasantness and the way he was looking at her. She wanted to ignore him, or better yet, tell him off, but she knew that would be unbearably rude to Marcy, who was good friends with Brett.

"Try the salmon. Have you ever had salmon? It's a freshwater fish we ship down from up north. It's quite good."

"I'll have the pheasant," Storm said, folding her menu and looking out the window.

"Storm!" Marcy exclaimed, not able to believe the girl could be so rude.

Brett's face closed with a rush of anger. For a moment he didn't speak. "I would like to offer my sincere apologies for anything I might have done to offend you last night," he said.

Storm glanced at him and nodded. She saw his anger deepening. She looked at Marcy and realized that she was stunned and upset with her. She managed a weak smile. "Thank you. Your apology is accepted." She looked out the window again, not wanting Marcy to know she had just lied. She was too angry to accept his apology.

"Thank you," Brett said, his tone cool. "Perhaps, then, we can start over?"

She was forced to look at him. His face was hard and stiff. "Of course."

"Good. How about a ride tomorrow? I'll call for you at two in the afternoon."

Storm gaped. "But . . ."

"That's a fine idea, Brett," Marcy interjected. "You and Storm should get over whatever differences are between you. And two o'clock will be fine. That will give Storm a chance to entertain her morning callers." Marcy flashed him a smile.

"Good. That's settled then," Brett said, standing. "Enjoy your lunch, ladies."

Storm watched his tall, broad-shouldered yet elegant figure as he made his way out of the dining room. She turned to Marcy. "I don't want to go riding with him. And what morning callers?"

"But you love riding. And let him think you already have callers—besides, you probably will." Marcy's tone became reproving. "No matter what, Storm, a lady is never rude. Your behavior just now was uncalled for."

A guilty flush washed over Storm. She liked Marcy. She wanted her friendship and approval. "I'm sorry," she said as contritely as she could.

"And it won't hurt you to go riding with Brett," Marcy declared. "You may even have a good time."

"I doubt it," Storm said before she could stop herself. Seeing Marcy's expression, she added, "But I'll try."

A few minutes later, after they had ordered, their waiter returned to the table with a bottle of French champagne. "We didn't order champagne," Marcy said.

"Compliments of the house, madame." The waiter popped the cork and poured two glasses.

"I don't understand," Storm said.

"The house is the establishment," Marcy told her.

"But why would they send you champagne?"

"I do believe it was for you," Marcy said evenly. "Brett owns the hotel."

Storm gaped.

* * *

For some reason Storm couldn't sleep that night.

The next morning she felt keyed up, restless, with a tingling anticipation. She kept thinking about Brett. Dandified though he was, she had to admit he was handsome. Of course, she was irritated beyond all end that he had taken advantage of the situation yesterday and gotten permission to take her riding. If Marcy hadn't been there, Storm would have told him exactly what she thought of his high and mighty ways.

She did have two callers that morning, Randolph and another gentleman whose name she immediately forgot. Marcy had told her what to do if she had callers—she entertained them in the parlor if it was before noon and had refreshments served. Storm was nervous, having no idea what to talk about, but Randolph saved the day. They wound up talking about horses, then Texas. Storm found herself telling stories about her father when he was a Texas Ranger. Both Randolph and the other man—his name was James she realized when Randolph called him that—seemed very interested. James had even come to California overland, passing through Texas, and he had a few stories of his own to tell. It was close to noon when he left, and shortly thereafter, Randolph did, too.

Storm walked him to the door. "Thank you for coming," she said, smiling, no longer ill at ease.

Randolph's eyes were shining. "I've never had so much fun, Storm. Most ladies talk about silly things—you know, other ladies and balls and such. Your father sounds like quite a man."

"Maybe you'll be able to meet him when he comes to get me in September."

For a moment Randolph's face fell. "I forgot you'll be leaving us." Then he smiled. "But I'd like to meet your father."

Storm ate a light lunch, then changed into a riding habit.

This one had been designed by Marcy and was quite un-usual, but very elegant. It was black. The jacket was bolero-styled, embroidered with gold and silver threads. The split skirt was tight at the hips and flared out to catch the top of her new black riding boots. The shirt she wore beneath it was cream-colored, high-necked, and detailed with fragile lace. She even had a black Stetson to go with it. She admired herself in the mirror and wished her family could see her now. She wondered what Brett would think.

Storm realized she was actually anticipating Brett's ar-rival, a thought that thoroughly annoyed her. He arrived promptly at two. She met him in the foyer. There was no mistaking the admiration in his gaze.

"Brett," she said coolly to hide her strange agitation. She held out her hand.

He gave a lazy smile that made her heart do a flip-flop. He took her hand, holding it for a moment, and Storm was struck by the fact that it disappeared in the largeness of his. For the first time she realized he was a head taller than she was. That thought disturbed her even more.

Slowly, deliberately, he turned over her hand so that the palm was facing up. Storm felt confused. Her blood was pounding in her ears. He raised her palm, holding her gaze, his own eyes dark, then pressed a warm, lingering kiss on her soft flesh. She gasped softly.

He released her. "You look magnificent." He was smil-ing, the corners of his eyes crinkling slightly. "Shall we?"

Before a mutinous expression could settle on her face, he took her arm and tucked it in his, stealing another glance at her. A beautiful blush covered her features. What was it about her that so drew him? She was just another woman, a half child even, but he'd be a damn liar if he pretended he wasn't affected by her. The thought made him uneasy. It had been the same every time he'd seen her since they first met: he was drawn to her, almost against his will. She was the only woman he knew who was immune to his charm, who seemed to dislike him, and that irritated him and fed his determination to win her over.

And . . . something else. He wasn't sure he liked how he felt around her—unsettled, needing. *Needy.*

An image flashed in his mind. A forlorn little boy with a puppy-dog's gaze watching his beautiful mother sweep by without a word, not even noticing his presence. The boy's hopeful expression became closed.

Brett found his heart pounding heavily, hurtfully. His hold on Storm tightened.

I am no longer that boy, he thought grimly, and damned if I care what this woman thinks of me.

He led her outside. The groom had already brought her stallion around and was holding him some distance from Brett's own mount. The two animals wanted to fight.

Brett walked her to the black's side. She took the reins from the groom, thanking him, but before she could slip one foot in the stirrup, Brett grasped her around the waist and set her in the saddle. He couldn't help it. He may not have been born a gentleman, but he was one now.

Her eyes blazed. "I can mount by myself, thank you."

He smiled back. "I couldn't resist."

"Well, try!" she retorted.

He swung gracefully onto his gray, and they set off down the drive, holding the two stallions to a restless, prancing walk. He could see from Storm's expression that she wasn't thrilled to be riding with him and that she was still angry. He shoved his own roiling emotions away.

"How was lunch yesterday?" he asked, hoping to hit upon an innocuous topic.

"I was impressed," she muttered, barely audibly. But Brett's momentary delight at her words was short-lived. "You took complete advantage, Brett. If Marcy wasn't there, you know I would never have agreed to go riding with you." She glared at him. "Why? What kind of game are you playing?"

He raised a brow coolly. "It's quite natural, I assure you, for a single man to want the company of a beautiful, unattached lady." The gallant flattery came unbidden to his lips.

She looked at him for a moment, her blue eyes fierce and doubtful, her mouth stony. Then she sighed. "I suppose after everything the Farlanes have done for me, I should forgive you."

"I thought you had."

"You know I didn't!" she flashed.

He had to smile. What a passionate woman, he thought again, suddenly knowing she would be a wildcat in bed. He wondered if Randolph had kissed her in the Farlanes' garden.

That thought coming out of nowhere made him frown. He focused on what she had said. "Are you still angry because I told Paul you were out riding alone?"

"Yes! That wasn't your business."

"I would do it again," he told her seriously. He held her gaze and wouldn't let go. Then he smiled in admiration at her stubbornness, her spirit, her beauty. "It's just not safe, Storm," he added gently.

She seemed uneasy at his tone and quickly looked away. Had Randolph kissed her? he wondered again, irritated. He wanted to be the first to kiss her. Would she fight him or melt against him? He almost laughed. She'd fight. He'd be lucky not to get a black eye if he tried.

"Still mad?" There was a new, teasing note in his voice.

They were riding down the path to the beach. For a moment, as she let her stallion pick his way, she didn't answer. Then she said, "I guess not." She sighed heavily, as if it required a great effort to give up her anger.

"Thank you, Storm." He grinned. "Next time I will know that a single line of apology will not do."

"Just don't interfere again, Brett," she warned. "You're not my father."

"Absolutely not," he agreed readily.

"Does that gray have any speed?" she asked, tossing her head disdainfully.

Brett's grin widened. "A bit."

"Good. How far shall we race to? That point where the coast curves?"

"Fine with me," Brett said, trying not to laugh. Should he let her win?

"Ready?"

"Ready."

"Go!" Storm shouted, and the two stallions leaped forward as one.

The distance was only a mile and a half or so, and Brett kept his gray nose to flank with the black. Both horses ran hard, with fierce, inbred desire. Brett admired how Storm rode, fearlessly and effortlessly. After a mile, the black stallion began to lengthen his strides, and Brett realized with shock that Storm had been holding him in. He urged the gray on, and the powerful animal pulled even with the black. They were racing neck and neck, nose to nose.

Storm's hat had been flung back, and her head was bare. She shot Brett a wild, excited look, her blue eyes dancing. Then she laughed, a loud, rich sound, and leaned even further over her horse's neck until her face disappeared in his mane. The black surged forward. Brett drove his gray on, but the horse could not get his nose past the black's flank. With a shout of triumph, Storm crossed the point half a length ahead.

She pulled up, her animal shaking his head in protest, still wanting to run. Brett patted his gray, who was also prancing avidly, eager to run farther, but he didn't take his eyes off Storm. Wisps of hair had come loose from her braid and were blowing around her face. She was flushed, exultant, sitting tall and straight and looking impossibly gorgeous. He had never met a woman who could ride the way she did, so fast, so fearlessly. He suddenly understood that she was now in her element. "You won," he conceded, sweeping her a mock bow. "And I'm mightily impressed."

"It wasn't fair," Storm cried, bringing the black closer to him. "Damn, but I'm so much lighter than you! You were so close behind! I know Demon's faster, but we should have had you by more than half a length to make up for how heavy you are."

He laughed.

"No, really. Next time let's go longer, and I'll weight my saddle with something to make it a more even challenge. How does that sound?"

He was still smiling. "How could I possibly resist?

"Good," she said, sliding off her horse. "We'd better walk them a bit."

Brett joined her on foot. The two stallions were getting along better now that some of their restless energy had been spent, and it took only a moment to make sure one wasn't going to kick or bite the other. They moved closer to the water, where the sand was harder, and strolled side by side in silence.

"You can ride," Storm finally admitted grudgingly.

Brett cocked a brow. "Was my riding ability in doubt?"

She gave him a half smile. "I thought the gray was for show, like your clothes."

"I see," he said, irritated. Clearly, she didn't think much of him. Every woman he'd ever met had been irresistibly drawn to him, had admired his looks, his success. Why was she so immune to him?

"Where are you from, Brett? Are you descended from one of the original Californio families?"

He looked at her, trying to tell if she was really interested or just making conversation. "Yes. Although I was born in Mazatlán. My father was a criollo."

"What's a criollo?"

"A Mexican who can trace his lineage back to Spain with no taint."

"Ah, a kind of aristocracy," Storm said.

"Yes."

"I should have known," she muttered. "And now he's an American?"

"He prefers to call himself a Californio."

"Does he have a ranch? Why are you here, not there?"

He hadn't missed her disparaging tone, and his mouth tightened. "I came here in '49 to make my fortune," he said shortly. "My brother will inherit."

There was no need to tell her that it was only after the accidental deaths of his two legitimate half brothers that his father had originally sent for him—the bastard. That his father had only then recognized him as his son and decided to be a father to him. He had remarried the instant his first wife died, in hopes of begetting a legitimate heir— a goal that had been fulfilled promptly in his half brother Manuel, who was now ten years old.

Brett heard the touch of bitterness in his voice but ignored her questioning glance, knowing she had heard it, too.

"Were you raised in Mazatlán?" Storm was asking.

Brett felt a reflexive tightening of his gut. "Until I was eight. After that I was raised in Monterey, on the hacienda." The words had slipped out—he had said too much.

He would never forget the day his mother had summoned him so casually to tell him he was going to live with his father in a faraway land called California. Even now there was a lingering trace of the pain the little boy had felt. But he hadn't let his mother see him cry, and he hadn't begged or pleaded with her to change her mind. Even now he wondered how much Don Felipe, his father, had paid the whore, his mother, to get him.

"Will you ever go back?" Storm asked.

"Never," he said as dispassionately as he could.

"You had a falling out with your father?"

He stared at her in amazement and ill-concealed anger.

"I'm sorry." She had the grace to blush. "I don't know why I'm prying. I am sorry."

She was so earnest he forgot his displeasure. He liked seeing a slightly humble Storm for a change. They walked in silence for a bit. Storm sighed. "I love the water," she said, staring out at the ocean. "Back home I swim every day."

He remembered how golden her skin was at the edge of her bodice, where it should have been white. He became fascinated with the idea that she swam naked. No—it was impossible. Though she might be a little savage, no man would let his daughter do so.

"I miss it," she said.

A wave twice the size of the rest crested and rolled toward shore. Brett saw it as it broke, threw his arm around her waist, and pulled her rapidly up the beach as the tide came rushing in. She laughed, running with him to escape the surf. In that moment they both dropped their reins, but the stallions followed. "I don't mind getting my boots wet," Storm said, smiling.

His arm was still around her, her entire side pressed against him. He could smell the scent of roses, and a silken tendril of her hair caught on his mouth. She stumbled slightly, sinking into the softer sand, and the movement threw one soft, round breast against his ribs. She was firm, but soft, too, and the contradiction thrilled him. She was still laughing, not even looking at him but at the culprit ocean. Her lashes were unbelievably black and long.

In one deft move he drew her completely against him, the arm around her waist locking like an iron band, his other hand going to the back of her head. She gasped, her gaze meeting his in mute surprise just as he lowered his mouth and brushed her lips softly, gently.

She stiffened. With melting tenderness, teasing with unbearable lightness, he moved his mouth again and again on hers. She started to step back, but his arm around her waist and his hand on her neck tightened. His tongue touched her lower lip, traced it. She relaxed, softening. His mouth became more insistent, more searching and demanding. He thought a whimper escaped from deep in her chest. His tongue darted between her lips; she opened them. As he plunged into her, thrusting again and again, telling her with his mouth and tongue how he would make love to her, he grew hard and long against her belly, throbbing wildly.

With incredible strength, she tore herself out of his arms and pulled back her right arm. She was panting. "Bastard!" she shouted, and even though he realized in shock what she was doing, he comprehended too late. A fist hurled into his midsection, making him grunt and double over. Jesus, was she strong!

He reacted instinctively. Before the next fist could take his face in an undercut, he had grabbed her wrist and stopped her. His stomach hurt. It was one thing to take a gut blow prepared, with all the abdominal muscles tensed into a steel wall, but he had never expected her to hit him there. Good Lord, she packed a punch!

"How dare you!" she declared. "If I had my gun I'd shoot you, you arrogant bastard!"

They were only a foot apart. Brett yanked cruelly on her wrist, pulling her so she fell against his chest, but she didn't wince or cry out. Her blue eyes blazed. Her violent anger made him respond in kind, made him want to dominate her with sheer male power. For an instant they stood eye to eye, her face inches from his. She hated him, he could see it, and it fueled in him a wild, uncontrollable desire to possess.

His free hand grabbed her chin so hard that later her skin was pink. He pulled her close and kissed her brutally, savagely, giving no quarter. She fought, but no matter how

strong she was, she was no match for him. Sanity returned
to him. Jesus! He released her and pushed her away from
him.

She landed on all fours in the wet sand. She looked up
at him like a wild, spitting cat. Brett was trying to master
the savagery she had brought out in him, panting as if he'd
run a fast mile, locking gazes with her. When he felt he'd
regained some control, he moved to her and held out his
hand. "Get up, Storm," he said, his husky voice betraying his emotion.

He didn't expect her reaction. With a cry that sounded
like an Indian howl, she grabbed his legs, and he fell onto
his hands and knees in the sand. She shrieked, pouncing
on him. He caught her wrists, going down on his back to
defend himself. Quickly he flipped and pinned her, realizing with irony that for other reasons this was not a safe
position to be in right now.

"I'll kill you," she gasped, fighting futilely.

"God, you're incredible," he said, his breath mingling
with hers. Then, "I apologize. I truly apologize."

"I hate you," she cried. "Let me up! Let me go!
Now!"

"Don't try anything again," he warned.

She made no comment. He got up carefully. He offered
his hand again, but she ignored it, coming fluidly to her
feet in one motion, with a dancer's grace. Still ignoring
him, she strode over to her horse and leaped into the saddle. In the next instant she was cantering down the beach.

He hurriedly mounted and followed her, catching up to
her at a gallop, then slowed to her pace. What could he
possibly say? He had dallied unforgivably with her. He
didn't even know how it had happened. If she hadn't
punched him—*punched* him, by God—he would never have
kissed her again, certainly not so brutally. The whole way
back to Paul's house, he debated the best means of apol-
ogizing.

As they rode up the drive, he knew he had to make his move. "Storm, it was only a kiss. I'm sorry. You're very beautiful, and I lost control." He looked hard at her, meaning every word.

She refused to look at him.

"It was only a kiss," he tried again as she slid off her horse in front of the veranda.

She stared at him. "Your apology is not accepted. Don't ever come near me again."

"Storm!"

"No! You are so vain and conceited. You're nothing but a showy, strutting peacock!" She whirled and slammed into the house.

He stared at the door. A showy, strutting peacock? Is that what she thought?

Other women considered him handsome and virile and powerful. Never had any woman called him vain and conceited . . . a showy, strutting peacock. No.

He turned the gray around. To hell with her, anyway. She was nothing but trouble. He should never have dallied with her in the first place. She obviously detested him, had from the first, and wasn't bothering to hide it.

He ignored his inner turmoil, reaching out for his anger, finding it and clinging vehemently to it. He had lost control and let his lust rule him, and that was a mistake he would not make again under any circumstances. To hell with Storm Bragg. She was nothing but a Texas ruffian, and he liked his women smooth and polished.

Chapter 5

Brett's bad mood lingered for the rest of the afternoon, and it didn't improve when he returned to his house to change into dinner clothes. Sorting through his mail, he found a letter from his uncle.

What in hell did he want?

In all fairness, Brett thought as he slit open the envelope, his heart starting to hammer, his Uncle Emmanuel was the only Monterro who had treated him as if he were not a whore's bastard, as if he were human, with feelings. Brett's own father, Don Felipe, had rarely bothered with him except to observe a particular feat and then to offer either criticism or indifference. In fact, when he had been brought to Hacienda de los Cierros, his Uncle Emmanuel had been the one to insist Brett be educated and reared in the house, not in the stables—much to the dismay of Don Felipe's second wife. Doña Theresa had hated him, of course, for he was a threat to any sons she might bear.

Dear nephew,

It has been too long, and I am so pleased to have finally located you and to have found out that you are prospering and well. My investigator tells me you are well established in San Francisco and a successful businessman. I am happy for you. Somehow, I always knew you would succeed.

It is a great coincidence that, after several years of searching, my man found you just when you are needed most. Brett, your father is gravely ill. I fear that he will not recover. Several years ago he took a bad fall from his horse, paralyzing him from the waist down. Since that time, he has never regained his will to live. Recently, he came down with a cold that turned into pneumonia. I fear that the Lord is going to take him away from us soon.

Brett, I know you are as proud as your father, but I beg you not to let your pride rule your emotions. Don Felipe will never write to you and ask you to come to him, although I have shared with him all my news of you. I know he wants to see you. Please come.

The rest of the family is well. Your brother Manuel is ten, strong, stubborn, and intelligent, just like you and his father. Your two younger sisters, Gabriella and Catherine, both have their mother's Castilian beauty. My own children, Sophia and Diego, are well. Sophia is a new mother. Your Tía Elena is the same.

> *Your loving uncle,*
> *Emmanuel*

Brett put the letter aside, his face a dark mask. He promptly went to the sideboard and poured himself a large brandy. He drank half of it, staring out of the window at the garden and street below. Damn them all.

He was flooded with memories, none of them pleasant. Of himself living and stealing on the streets of Mazatlán, a skinny, dirty boy always one step ahead of the *policía*, failing to appear at home for days and even weeks on end. Not that his mother, the French whore, cared. Whenever he did return, one of her several "protectors" was there. One thing about Mother—she was ageless, beautiful. But heartless. She left his upbringing to the housekeeper, who didn't have time. Only one of the maids seemed to care, a little English girl named Mary. When she caught him running in, usually because he was hungry and had failed to find enough on the streets, she would grab him and make him bathe and change his clothes. He would be gone as soon as his stomach was full, but not before hearing his mother's high-pitched cries and the deep moans of whomever she was ''entertaining.''

He didn't know who he hated more, his mother the whore, or his father the Californio.

He was eight when his life changed—when the don sent for him because his two brothers had been killed. Brett hadn't even known who his father was until that moment when his mother informed him she was sending him away. To this day he had no idea what the relationship between his parents had been, or how they had met.

Don Felipe's first wife, Doña Anna, had not given his father another heir. Old beyond her years, she did not seem capable of producing more children. She died six years after Brett's arrival, having suffered several miscarriages, but by then, Don Felipe was relieved. He promptly married fifteen-year-old Theresa, who came from a long line of male-bearing bluebloods.

At the time of the second marriage, Brett was fourteen. During the years he had lived in his father's household he had been educated but otherwise either ignored or vilified. He learned to read and write in Spanish, French, and English, although he already knew how to speak all three languages. He even learned a smattering of Latin. He became well versed in mathematics, geometry, geography, and history, and excelled at riding, fencing, and handling pistols. He learned to talk and walk and act like a gentleman—which he knew he was not.

Don Felipe seemed not to care about him, except when Brett did not succeed at something, and then his father became angry. Brett was punished, usually with a cane.

He never gave satisfaction when he was hit—he never cried out.

In the six years before her death, Doña Anna refused even to look at him, much less talk to him, although she talked *about* him to others. He knew he was a bastard, but it had never bothered him until he heard his father's wife constantly refer to him as "the bastard." Then he knew a hatred and shame like never before.

The others looked down on him, too. Little Sophia—a cousin near his own age, a startlingly beautiful child with blue-black hair and dark eyes—looked down her aristocratic nose at him, and called him "bastard" in glee, knowing he could not hit her the way he wanted to. She loved taunting him. Just thinking about her now made him turn rigid with anger.

And then, of course, there was Tía Elena.

He had to smile. Exactly what had Tío Emmanuel meant when he said Tía Elena, his wife, had not changed? Certainly he didn't know she was a whore, like Brett's mother?

It had happened when he was almost sixteen. Brett had begun to be interested in girls the year before, to the point where several of the serving wenches had begun to infatuate him. He was starting to dream about them . . . One afternoon he had stumbled cross his aunt and a companion in a hidden spot in one of the gardens.

He was fascinated as he watched his aunt coupling with a stableboy. Neither of them had removed their clothes, which he regretted, but her skirts were pulled up to her waist and her legs were long and white. Brett watched the stableboy pumping into her until he himself lost all control and made the ultimate faux pas by crying out.

In a flash Elena had pushed off the boy, who was actually twenty or so, and pulled her skirts down and her bodice together. "Who's there?" she called.

Mesmerized, unable to speak, Brett stepped into view.

At first she was startled, and then she looked at him, deliberately studied him, and he began to get hard and hot all over again. She smiled. "Pablo, go now. I'll see you another time. Come here, *querida.*"

Brett's heart was pounding wildly as he walked toward her. He didn't know what to expect, but he did know one thing—Tía Elena would be in terrible trouble if anyone found out what she had been doing. She stood, releasing her bodice, and Brett gasped when her full, blue-veined, hard-tipped breasts fell out.

"Such a handsome young man," Elena murmured, taking his hand and placing it on her breast.

Brett was lost. He knew it was wrong because the only person he liked at all was his Tío Emmanuel, but he was sixteen and his blood was raging. His mouth soon followed his hands, and he was wildly suckling her large, hard nipples, making Elena laugh throatily. "You have all the right instincts, Brett."

Soon he was deep inside her, thrusting wildly, mindlessly . . . He had never experienced anything like it before.

In the month before he left, she taught him a lot. Brett was consumed with guilt, but his appetites controlled him. And then Doña Theresa, his father's new wife, bore a son—Manuel—and there was no longer any need for Brett to remain . . .

Brett dismissed his uncle's letter. Don Felipe was still a cold bastard, Sophia still a bitch. Elena was surely still a whore . . . and he didn't give a damn about any of them. He crumpled the letter and tossed it into the fireplace.

"Damn Brett D'Archand!"

Storm paced furiously across her bedroom, still clad in her riding habit. She couldn't stop thinking about him. She couldn't wipe the image of his dark, handsome face from her mind. She couldn't forget how his face lit up when he smiled, or how small lines radiated from his eyes in moments of rare good humor. Damn!

She couldn't forget how his lips felt on hers—how firm and gentle, then savage and brutal. She sank into a chair and covered her face with her hands.

Her body had betrayed her. While her mind had been stunned with surprise as he kissed her, her body had yielded, becoming soft, pliant, warm, eager. She had *liked* his kisses.

Even now, just remembering provoked a similar reaction, one of warmth and racing heat.

She had been kissed only once before, and she had hated it. She had never even liked boys, except as companions with whom to hunt, ride, and wrestle. At the last few social events her family had attended, Storm had felt alienated from all the other girls her age, who had had one topic on their minds—boys. Storm thought they were silly. She was more interested in when the family's prize mare was going to foal, and the bear that was killing everyone's cattle, and the outlaw McRae whom the Rangers were pursuing.

Now Storm was miserable. And angry. And humiliated. She had the awful feeling that Brett knew she had liked his kisses, a thought she found almost impossible to live with. The rutting pig. Vain peacock. Piece of cow dung. She was glad she had had enough sense to realize just how far things were going and had punched him as hard as she could. She'd hurt him, too, she knew it, and the thought pleased her no end.

A maid knocked and came in bearing Storm's dinner tray, making her realize she was ravenous. She attacked her meal immediately and finished every last mouthful of the steak and potatoes, beans and salad, even a piece of cherry cobbler. She had been too ashamed and confused to face Paul at dinner downstairs.

Storm was no fool. She knew about mating. That is,

she'd seen horses and dogs and cows coupling since she was a child. Once, she'd even seen her brother, Nick, with one of their maids in the pantry. Storm had to smile at that memory—Nick had been only sixteen, tall and skinny and lost in the voluptuous Irish girl's charms. So she knew, pretty much, how a man and woman coupled, and she had realized this afternoon exactly what that hardness appearing between them had meant. It had given her the strength to break away, had revived her sanity. She flushed at the thought. Brett wanted to take her the way Nick had taken Rose. Her color increased; her senses tingled with heightened awareness.

She was ashamed. She understood now why her mother and father shared such secret, pleased looks, why they were always touching and kissing. But that was different. They were married. They loved each other. Storm had never even thought about the attraction that exists between a man and a woman, but now that she did, she knew it was right and good when it was between two people who loved each other. She, however, didn't love Brett—she disliked him immensely. Possibly she even hated him. And he certainly didn't like her. So what was wrong with her?

Was she turning into a loose hussy like Beth Ellen?

Beth Ellen was the blond, blue-eyed daughter of one of their neighbors, one of those girls who had been taking walks into the woods with boys since she was thirteen. Storm had never understood why, but there was no mistaking how different Beth Ellen acted when she was alone with her, or around her parents, and when there was a handsome man in the vicinity. When Nick came by, Beth Ellen became flushed and coy, and when she thought no one was looking, she brushed up against him. At other times she was as demure as a mouse. Storm had asked her once what was so great about boys, and Beth Ellen had just laughed.

Storm thought she would never be able to fall asleep

that night because of her distress, but she did, almost instantly. Her sleep was full of dreams, however. At first they were pleasant. She was back home surrounded by her family. Then they were at a barbecue, and Beth Ellen was there, dressed in the kind of gown Storm had been wearing lately, while everyone else wore their usual cotton frocks—except Storm, who was wearing buckskins. She felt ugly next to Beth Ellen's sophisticated beauty.

Suddenly Brett was there, too. He was completely taken with Beth Ellen, and it was mutual. They both ignored Storm. She was hurt—incredibly hurt—to see them together. When they walked in the woods, she followed, only to find them rolling on the ground in each other's arms, getting ready to couple. Brett heard her and looked up. When he saw her, he started laughing. Storm woke up.

It was just a dream, and she had forgotten it by the time she woke again in the morning, for she had other worries on her mind. Tonight she was supposed to go to a small party at the Holdens'. She did not look forward to going. She had the feeling almost everyone from the Farlanes' party would be there, including that arrogant rake, Brett D'Archand.

But go she did, wearing a purple velvet gown cut just as immodestly as everything else she was wearing these days, and without stays—she would not even consider it. She and Paul arrived at seven o'clock and were greeted profusely by the Holdens at the front entrance.

As they moved inside, Storm saw him—looking incredibly handsome and virile in black evening clothes, talking to a pretty, picture-perfect blond and the Farlanes. The blond was standing close, with her arm in his. Storm felt a flash of pure anger. The woman was obviously his companion for the evening. Not that she gave a goddamn. Brett had seen her, too, immediately, but Storm looked right past him and smiled at Marcy and Grant.

"Shall we go say hello?" Paul asked, about to move toward the foursome.

"Oh, no, there's James," Storm cried, flashing him what she hoped was a radiant smile. James came hurrying over.

"Storm!" He bowed over her hand, but his brown eyes never left her face. "I was hoping you would be here tonight."

She smiled. "Thank you, James."

He begged to take her from her cousin, who agreed, pleased with her suitor, and Storm was led away by the eager James to meet some of the other guests. In the opposite direction from *him*.

Soon Randolph and two other young men, Robert and Lee, had gathered around Storm, all laughing as the men tried to outdo one another by telling her amusing anecdotes, each vying for her favor. Storm had never felt so feminine, or so pretty. It was hard to believe she was at this elegant soiree, dressed like a princess, surrounded by four handsome men who were all trying to hold her attention. Just once, she stole a look in Brett's direction, feeling smug because she was sure he was witnessing her grand success. He wasn't. His mouth was close to the blond's ear, and she was blushing gorgeously. Then they gazed into each other's eyes as if they were in love. Storm's heart fell, and she suddenly felt sick.

The evening was ruined. Storm listened and smiled and tried to laugh, but she was not doing a convincing job of it. Randolph asked her what was wrong, but she gave him a wan smile and told him "Nothing." She stole another look at Brett and found him in almost the same position as before. The insipid blond's blue eyes were shining.

Then Storm held court over her group of admirers with determination. As if sensing they had lost her interest, they were beginning to look ill-at-ease, and ready to leave. Storm resolved she would have a good time—or at least

Brett D'Archand would think so! "Did I ever tell you the story of how I outrode ten Comanches when I was only twelve years old?"

"What?" her companions all exclaimed.

"Come on, Storm," Lee said, "you're making that up."

"Most certainly not. I ride better than any Comanche, and if any of you gentlemen don't believe me, you'll just have to take me riding to find out."

That suggestion was greeted with roars of approval, and before Storm knew it, she had three offers to go riding.

"Tell us about the Comanches," Robert said.

"It was a group of renegades that had drifted south, raiding and looting and killing," Storm said.

"How do you know that?" James asked.

"Why, the only time Comanches come that far south, where we live, is when they're renegades. In the past fifteen years they've been almost wiped out by the Texas Rangers."

"So you were twelve and outrode them?"

"I was playing in a lake across the valley from where the ranch house is. I wasn't supposed to be there. I was supposed to be doing my chores." She smiled.

"And?" Lee asked.

"I was wading in the water when my horse snorted and I looked up. There they were—ten Comanches ringing the shore about twenty yards away from me and my mare."

"You're making this up!" Lee said.

"I am not!" Storm's eyes flashed. "I was afraid to run. I was afraid that if I ran they would come after me. So I pretended I didn't have a care in the world and very calmly and slowly walked out of the water to my horse—which, fortunately, was a very fast Arabian mare my pa had bought for breeding. No one moved. I mounted. I didn't even look at them. But the minute I started to trot away, they started after me—at a gallop.

"We raced the entire eight miles back home, across really rough, rocky terrain. All I could think of was that my mare could break a leg and Pa would be furious! At first, they were right behind me, but their ponies were no match for my filly, and I started to lose them. By the time I got home I was way ahead of them, enough so that I couldn't see them."

There was a moment of shocked silence. Then Randolph said, "What happened next?"

"I started screaming. Pa and the boys were out on the range, so me and my mother and our old maid had to hold them off ourselves."

"Wow!" Lee said.

"Don't worry," Storm said disdainfully. "Comanches only hit and run. They gave up after attacking the house for five minutes—took off with some horses and chickens, and set fire to one of the barns, which me and Mother managed to put out." She grinned. "I sure was lucky. If that mare had busted her leg, Pa would have killed me!"

They all laughed.

"But I did get a spanking for neglecting my chores," she added ruefully, then regretted having mentioned this detail since, from the expressions on her admirers' faces, she had an idea they were envisioning that portion of her grown-up anatomy. "Anybody care to race?" she said to change the trend of thought.

"Beware," said a familiar voice behind her. "She does ride like a Comanche, and I can personally attest to it."

Storm whirled to face Brett, who was smiling as if nothing had ever happened between them. The blond, who looked even more gorgeous up close, was still hanging on to his arm. How long had he been standing there? Storm blushed furiously, then gave him a cold shoulder. "Lee, would you escort me to the punch bowl?" she asked in her sweetest voice.

He jumped to comply, and Storm was very aware of

Brett's eyes on her as she walked away, her heart thumping.

He didn't approach again, which was fortunate for him, she thought. Some time later, however, Marcy and Grant joined her group as she was being regaled yet again by tales from the same four admirers. "Hello, dear," Marcy said. "You look exquisite." She was glowing with pride. "Doesn't she?"

"She certainly does," Grant said, kissing her cheek. "I would say life in San Francisco agrees with you."

Storm didn't want to insult anyone. "It has grown on me."

"I heard you went riding yesterday with Brett," Grant said. "Heard you beat his gray, too." He laughed.

Storm grew rigid. "Our first and last ride."

Grant and Marcy looked surprised. "Dear, didn't you enjoy yourself? Brett is good company."

Storm stepped closer to them, her blue eyes blazing. She lowered her voice so her quartet of admirers couldn't hear. "I almost certainly did not! Marcy, I know Brett is your friend, but he isn't mine, and please don't expect me to be civil to him again!"

For a moment silence greeted her, then Marcy asked, "Dear, what happened?"

"He kissed me," she blurted out. "But I don't think he'll try it again!"

They stared at her, Marcy looking scandalized, Grant looking suspiciously on the verge of laughter. "Worse things have happened," he finally said.

"Not to me they haven't." Storm tossed her mane of waving hair. "I bet his belly is still sore from where I punched him." She hesitated, then added, "At least, I hope so!" She stalked away—away from the Farlanes and from her admirers.

Grant started laughing.

"It's not amusing," Marcy said, her brows furrowed.

"Oh-ho! I can see your devious mind at work. It *is* funny! I doubt Brett has ever been punched by a lady before. I wish I could have been there."

"Those two seem to have got off on the wrong foot since they first met," Marcy mused.

"She's the most beautiful woman in San Francisco, next to you, Marcy, so how could Brett not be attracted to her?"

Across the room, Storm was not smiling as she stared out of the windows into the night. She kept thinking about that damn scoundrel and that blond. Who was she? She was dying to know, but was too proud to ask. Then she became aware of the two young ladies standing close to her, talking loud enough for her to hear.

"Yes, yes, that is her!" the brunette exclaimed, momentarily meeting Storm's eyes. There was no doubt she was deliberately speaking loud enough for Storm to hear. She looked away.

"The one who fainted?" her friend asked eagerly.

"In the *garden*," the brunette said significantly. "She was in the garden with Brett D'Archand *and* Randolph Farlane. *And* she had no shoes on."

There was a stunned silence. Storm turned to glare at the two girls, growing more furious by the second.

"Mary, do you think one of them kissed her?"

The brunette was triumphant. "You ninny, I bet they both kissed her! But she was asking for it. Going out there alone with Brett—everyone knows his reputation—and Randolph. Why else would she have fainted?"

"Oh, my Lord," the second girl gasped, staring at Storm again with wide eyes.

Storm's face was red.

"What do you expect—she's from Texas. They do things out in the open there. I wonder if they did more than kiss. I bet she had other garments off, too! I wonder if . . ."

Storm clenched her fists, hard. She wanted to slap the

girl, but this wasn't Texas; it was a ballroom in San Francisco, and she did know better. Besides, she didn't want to live up to their expectations. Nevertheless, it was hard to restrain herself. Storm stepped right between the two girls to face her accuser. "Do you have something to say to me?" she demanded softly.

Mary looked her up and down disapprovingly, then tilted her classic nose in the air. "No, I don't think so."

Storm was so mad she wanted to spit. When the brunette turned back to face her girlfriend and began to walk away, Storm stepped down hard on the hem of her gown. There was a loud tearing sound as her gown ripped beneath Storm's kidskin-clad foot. The brunette whirled, horrified.

"Oh, I am so sorry," Storm said innocently. "Look what happened!"

"You did that on purpose!" Mary cried.

"Of course I didn't," Storm said sweetly. "It's not so bad. Look." As tears of anger gathered in the brunette's eyes, Storm bent and lifted the jaggedly torn hem.

"Just let go," Mary insisted.

"Okay," Storm said, letting go and straightening so abruptly that she jammed her shoulder into Mary's hand—the one holding her glass of champagne. The contents spilled all over her skirt. Mary shrieked.

"Oh, dear, how clumsy of you," Storm said.

"You did it!"

"I saw her," the blond agreed. "She did it on purpose!"

"She tore my gown and spilled my drink all over me," Mary wailed. By now they were gathering more than a little attention.

"Let me get you another drink," Storm offered solicitously.

"Storm," Paul and Marcy cried at once, reaching her.

"She ruined my dress!" the brunette screamed. "That trollop purposely ruined my dress!"

Storm's temper flared. "I'd like to kill her," she muttered savagely before she realized someone had come up to her from behind.

"I think you've done well enough already," Brett said, chuckling.

Storm went red.

"Storm, maybe we'd better go home," Paul said firmly, quietly, taking her arm.

"Not until I set that little wretch straight," Storm said, causing the crowd to gasp. "I fainted because my stays were too tight. And I was not alone in the garden with two men—Leanne St. Clair was there, too. And the only thing off my body was my shoes—nothing else. You're lucky I'm not packing my gun, because so help me, I'd—"

"I think everyone gets the idea," Brett interrupted, his tone heavy with amusement.

Paul tightened his grip on her arm. "I'm sure we can expect Mary to call tomorrow to apologize—in which case Storm will gladly do the same for her rash actions. I am so sorry, Ben," he said to their host.

Ben Holden barely managed to hide his chagrin. "Ah, sure, that's all right, well . . ." He smiled foolishly.

Storm was still furious. "I will not apologize to that foul-minded—"

"Storm, say good night," Paul interrupted.

Feeling duly chastised, she managed to do as she was told. She was very aware of Brett standing near her, of his dancing dark eyes that suggested he thought the incident was the funniest thing he had ever seen. So, just before she turned to follow her cousin into the foyer, she shot Brett the meanest look she could. She wasn't sure, but as she stepped out the front door she thought she heard him laughing.

* * *

"Who was that?"

Brett looked down at Elizabeth's shocked, white face, having forgotten her presence. "Storm Bragg, Paul Langdon's cousin."

"Can you believe what she did? And the language—"

"How about a glass of champagne?" he said, cutting her off. Whatever had possessed him to escort Elizabeth Bedford to the Holdens'? But he knew the answer instantly. Storm!

He smiled as he went to fetch Elizabeth a glass of champagne. He had seen the whole incident—in fact, he had been hard pressed not to watch every move Storm made the entire evening. Surrounded by suitors, *rapt* suitors, ignoring him—was she trying to make him jealous? Not that it would work. Why should he be jealous of that little hoyden? He certainly wasn't. Not in the least.

Did she know Lee was a womanizer? And did she know that Robert, although of impeccable breeding, was penniless? Certainly not an acceptable suitor. Still, he had felt annoyed at their devoted attention. Was she actually flirting with them? Of course not. She didn't even know how to flirt. He had been compelled, finally, to approach and investigate. To find that she was certainly not flirting, just regaling them with an incredible tale.

He didn't doubt for an instant that she had outridden a bunch of Comanche warriors. Most men wouldn't have had that kind of courage, but foolish, brave, impulsive, gorgeous Storm did . . . He wasn't in the least surprised, either, that she had torn Mary Atherton's gown and spilled her champagne. No doubt Mary had deserved it, but Storm had violated an unspoken social rule. A lady did not condescend even to acknowledge such gossip. That thought made him chuckle. Storm was certainly no lady.

Suddenly, he was bored with the evening. She hadn't forgiven him for the kiss yesterday—not that he expected her to. He shouldn't even think about it, he knew that. But as his carriage headed toward the Bedfords' to take Elizabeth home, and as Elizabeth chatted on, he found himself remembering how Storm felt and smelled and tasted, and he was honest enough to admit he was seriously infatuated with her. What a mistress she would make!

He escorted Elizabeth to her door, declining her offer to come inside, bowing over her hand and kissing it lightly. Then he headed promptly to his mistress's home.

Audrey was petite, auburn-haired, and beautiful. She greeted him in a tempting, sheer wrapper, not in the least sleepy-eyed. She dismissed her maid and in a sultry, teasing tone asked, "What can I do for you at this hour, Brett?"

He pulled her roughly into his arms. "I think you know, sweet." His mouth found hers, hard and demanding, and he ran his hands over the soft, warm curves of her body. He closed his eyes. As he fondled her, he imagined that she was Storm. His excitement grew, became almost impossible to control. Even later, when he was driving deep inside her, he kept seeing Storm.

It was quite disconcerting.

Chapter 6

Leaning low over the stallion's neck, Storm let him gallop full out. His black mane whipped her cheeks, and tears blurred her eyes. She urged him faster, faster, but she couldn't ride fast or far enough, she knew, to put everything behind her. God, it couldn't get any worse!

But it probably would, she thought a moment later when she slowed Demon to a trot and then to a walk. Especially if Paul found out she'd been riding alone.

Storm didn't care. She was fed up with what she should and shouldn't do. Everything she did was wrong, anyway. What an insane life it was to be a lady, to be corseted and high-heeled and dressed like a frilly doll and made to attend inane party after inane party, night after night! And the ridiculous rules! Most topics of conversation were unacceptable, a lady must never accept improper advances, she should not walk in the garden alone with a man for more than a minute or two, she did not take off her shoes in public, and she did not—no matter what the provocation—lower herself by acknowledging such insults, much less responding to them.

Storm knew her cousin was appalled by her behavior. He had told her so last night. "This is not Texas, young lady," he had said sternly. "Your behavior only made the matter worse."

"That's not fair," Storm challenged. "A man wouldn't stand for such insults!"

"You are not a man."

That was hard to refute, so Storm tried another tactic. "But, Paul! The things she was saying! She was insinuating that I was kissing both—"

"And your language," Paul said, flushing. "Good God, Storm! You have a mouth like a saloon girl!"

Clearly, he wasn't going to listen to her side of things, and, ridiculously, Storm felt tears rising. "She deserved it," she insisted. "No one can talk that way about me!"

"Go upstairs and think about all this," Paul said abruptly. "It's late. We'll discuss it further tomorrow."

Well, it was now tomorrow, and Storm didn't want to discuss what had happened, didn't want to defend herself. On top of it all, she couldn't understand why a young woman she didn't even know would spread such filthy rumors about her. It wasn't as if they were enemies.

Storm was so involved in her ruminations that she didn't realize, at first, that she had ridden to the point where she and Brett had raced, where he had kissed her. She was even more agitated now as vivid, tactile memories flooded her, of his hands on her waist, on her back; of his mouth on hers, soft and firm, then savage and unyielding . . .

She turned the black around to head back.

And for the first time saw the three riders.

They were still down the beach a ways, but Storm recognized them instantly—she had seen them in town earlier. It seemed too much a coincidence that they were here now, heading toward her. She remembered vaguely that their mounts were all cow ponies, and the men were garbed as cowboys. There was a ranch or two in the vicinity, or so she thought. There was no real reason to be apprehensive, but Storm felt the first prickling of fear. Although she wasn't certain, it seemed that these men had followed her.

As they approached at a trot, she could see that their mounts were wet from running, and she knew for certain now that they had, indeed, been following her. Anger surged through her, and she was glad she had strapped her six-shooter to one buckskin-clad thigh. She pulled the black up momentarily.

"Howdy, li'l lady," said the tall, lanky forerider.

The riders fanned out on the narrow stretch of sand, and Storm's other thought, that she could just ride past them, faded. If they were after her person, they could easily grab her.

"Will you let me pass?" she asked.

"Sure." The leader grinned and gave a mocking sweep of his arm.

Storm knew they weren't going to let her pass. Clamping her mouth tightly shut, she whipped the black around and into a gallop. They would never catch her.

But she'd barely finished the thought when the men started hollering, and she heard the unmistakable whir of a lasso. She sank lower, suddenly afraid, as the heavy rope settled over her shoulders and pinned her arms to her sides. She was yanked out of the saddle, hard, and fell on her back in the sand, choking on the gritty earth.

"We got her," whooped a cowboy.

Storm looked up, spitting sand, and saw she was surrounded, one man holding the rope just right, keeping it taut. She knew she had to get to her gun.

"Jesus, thank you! Ain't she purty!"

"Ree-lax," said the leader, dismounting. "Me first." He grinned down at her.

Storm got painfully to her knees and then to her feet, without using her hands, which were still pinned to her sides. "I won't run," she said evenly, "but this rope is hurting me."

The leader grabbed the black's reins and moved him away, then chuckled. "She won't get far now."

"Please take off the lasso," she said.

"Now, how come you don't look scared?" he said,

stepping close. Storm stood very still, staring defiantly into his eyes. Her heart was pumping madly with a combination of fear and anger. He reached out and touched her cheek, and Storm yanked her face away. He chuckled, touched her face again, then let his hand slide down to her shoulder and over her breast. He squeezed.

Storm tried to step back, but the tight rope painfully restricted her movements, and the cowboy grinned, cupping both breasts now and rubbing her nipples. Storm kneed him as hard as she could in the groin.

He groaned, dropping to his knees and clutching himself. Storm made a mad dash forward, to put slack in the line, and as the rope around her torso started to loosen, she tried to slip it off. But at exactly that moment the man holding the lariat realized what was happening and urged his mount backward, tightening the rope with a laugh. He kept going, and Storm was pulled forward until she was stumbling. She went down face first in the sand and was dragged. A shot rang out.

At first, with her eyes and mouth screwed shut to prevent the gritty sand from hurting her, Storm thought one of the men had fired his gun. Then she heard a voice she would never mistake. ''Make that move and you're dead.''

Brett!

Storm looked up, panting. Brett was astride his horse not far from her, facing two of the three cowboys. The third still lay incapacitated on the sand. Brett looked deadly and furious, and she was more frightened by the expression on his face than by her predicament. He was holding his gun, a small, pearl-handled pistol that didn't look like it could do much harm. As surely as she knew she was still alive, Storm knew the cowboys would challenge Brett. They did.

They drew almost simultaneously. Brett fired coolly, the shots coming so close together that they sounded like one, and both men fell with soft cries. Brett replaced the pistol inside his black jacket and turned to her, his glance hard.

Storm struggled to her knees, yanking off the rope and spitting sand. "Damn," she said hoarsely. She wiped sand off her face and away from her eyes, then watched as Brett checked the two men before striding over to their leader and disarming him. "Are they hurt bad?" she asked.

His face was rigid. "They're dead."

She was stunned.

"Are you hurt?" he asked, his voice cold and clipped.

With the back of her hand, she wiped her mouth and spat out more sand, looking up at him. He was really angry. But surely not at her. "No," she said. "I could have handled it. I was about to draw my Colt."

"Yes, it certainly looked like it," he said with undisguised sarcasm. He took two steps over to her and stood, legs braced, staring down at her. "You need someone to beat some sense into you."

She felt a touch of apprehension. Shakily, she rose to her feet. "I guess I should thank you," she said uneasily.

His eyes hard, he didn't respond.

She took a step back, looking for Demon.

"You disobeyed Paul," he said suddenly, his face taut. "Paul is too soft." He took a step toward her.

She moved away, suddenly afraid. "I needed to think," she cried, searching for Demon.

"I'm sure you would get a lot of thinking done on your back with your legs spread for these three gentlemen."

She gasped, flushing, and lengthened her stride. He grabbed her arm, yanking her around. "Let go!" she cried.

Before she knew it, he was sinking to his knees, taking her with him. For one instant, Storm's fear vanished. She knew he was going to take her in his arms and kiss her, and her blood began to heat and race. Then, stunning her, he wrenched her so she was facedown over his knee, and she realized, in complete horror, that he wasn't going to kiss her at all. ''No!'' she screamed as he hit her across the buttocks, so hard that tears came to her eyes. ''You bastard!''

''Apt,'' he gritted, and hit her again, and again and again.

It hurt. Her buckskins provided no protection, no padding, and he was trying to hurt her, and succeeding. She would not cry. She blinked hard against the tears until he stopped abruptly and threw her away from him. She got to her hands and knees.

''Never,'' he said. ''Never ride alone again. You could have been raped—you were almost raped—and because of your foolishness two men are dead.''

She hated him. With a cry of rage, she threw herself at him, leaping, attacking. She had never used her nails before, considered it girlish and ridiculous, but never had she been so enraged. He caught her wrists, and she kicked him as hard as she could in the shin. He tightened his hold, catching one of her legs between both of his thighs. ''I'll kill you!'' she cried, at that moment meaning it, and sank her teeth into his neck.

He gasped as she drew blood. He pried her off and wrenched her arms behind her back, almost twisting them out of their sockets, causing her to cry out as she struggled to attack him again. He still had her legs clamped between his, and suddenly he grabbed her braid close to her nape, so hard she thought he might pull out her scalp, and he twisted her head back and kissed her.

The kiss hurt. His lips were hard and brutal—he wanted to hurt her, she knew it, the way she had hurt him. But Storm opened her mouth, her body responding eagerly, wanting to give him better access. All the fight went out of her. As his tongue plundered deeply, exciting red-hot currents stabbed through her, and she pressed against him, moaning from deep in her throat. Desire sparked inside her as she rubbed her belly against his hard, hot arousal.

All at once he shoved her away.

She stumbled backward but didn't fall. So many heaving, roiling emotions and sensations were rushing through her body that she couldn't identify or give in to just one. Then, with a cry, she realized the third man was gone. "Brett!"

"I see," he said, his voice husky. But he appeared unperturbed nonetheless. He moved toward their mounts, and leaped onto the gray, then brought Demon to her. "Get up," he said.

She remembered that she hated him, that he had spanked her—then kissed her. Conveniently, she forgot her own reaction to the kiss, and it was lost in her mortification, her humiliation, her fury. She stared at him with all the blazing indignation she could muster.

"You, my dear," he said, "have taken San Francisco by storm."

Brett was hurting her, but Storm would not let him know it, no matter what. He propelled her up the steps, across the veranda, and into the foyer with barely restrained violence. Storm knew he was still furious, but then, so was she.

Bart appeared, his eyes widening at Brett's unorthodox entrance. "Where's Paul?" Brett demanded.

"In the dining room."

"Let me go," Storm said angrily.

"You keep quiet," Brett ordered harshly. "And let me do the talking."

"I can tell my side, thank you," she snapped. If he told the story, it would sound much worse, she knew it. He would spare no details.

"Shut up," he said succinctly, and they stepped into

the dining room, Brett releasing her just before they crossed the threshold.

Paul was reading the paper and drinking a cup of coffee. He looked up in complete surprise. "Brett! What—what's going on?" He frowned when he saw Storm's attire.

Storm started to speak. "Paul, I'm—"

Brett cut her off, grabbing her wrist and squeezing it so hard she thought he would break it. "Paul, I'm afraid there's been a bit of trouble."

"Please, sit," he said, shooting Storm an apprehensive glance.

Brett practically shoved her into a chair next to her cousin but didn't sit himself. Instead, he kept a tight, warning grip on her shoulder. "Storm and I were out riding," he said. "We made plans to do so last night. We were galloping when I felt that King's gait was off. I shouted for Storm to pull up, but she didn't hear me. Anyway, I stopped, and sure enough, I found he'd picked up a stone."

Storm craned her neck around to stare up at him in disbelief. He ignored her. "When I caught up to her, she was surrounded by three characters, and one of them had roped her. Needless to say, it came down to some gunplay. Two of the men are dead, and the third one ran off."

Storm couldn't believe it. Why had he made up such a story? Was he protecting her? But why? It didn't make any sense. She stared at him, but he was looking at Paul as if she didn't exist. "Thank God you're all right!" Paul cried. "Bart! Go fetch Sheriff Andrews or one of the deputies. Brett, thank you."

"It was nothing," Brett said, releasing his hand from Storm's shoulder. "It's fortunate I was with her."

Storm flushed. He meant the irony for her, and she didn't miss it. She felt overwhelmed with guilt. Had Brett told the truth, she would be defending herself like a spitting wildcat. Instead, he had taken the blame for what had happened. She didn't understand. Not at all.

"Did you recognize any of the men?" Paul asked.

"No. Nor did I recognize any of the brands—and there were three different ones. But I did memorize them."

"Storm, dear, are you all right?"

Storm managed to meet Paul's eyes. "Yes."

"I hope you thanked Brett. Dear God! To think if he had come a few moments later . . ."

Storm's color deepened. She knew she could have handled it alone. Or, she thought she could have. She had been on the verge of getting her gun. Well, almost on the verge. Maybe she couldn't have handled it. Then a flash of painful memory reminded her that Brett had gone too far by punishing her himself. No, she certainly wasn't beholden to him. "I already thanked him," she said, her eyes on the linen tablecloth. "May I go upstairs now?"

"Certainly," Paul said, standing. "If the sheriff wants to ask you some questions, which he most certainly will, I'll call for you."

Storm nodded, avoided Brett's dark, intense gaze, which was now riveted on her, and started from the dining room. Just as she left the room, she heard Paul say, "How can we keep this quiet? Storm doesn't need another scandal."

"I'm afraid two dead men assure the whole town will be talking about it," Brett said grimly.

"Thank God you were with her," Paul said. "Imagine if this had happened when she was riding alone."

Storm ran up the stairs, not wanting to hear any more. She didn't want to be the subject of more gossip, but she realized with a sinking heart she had no choice in the matter. She wished she had never come west. She was suddenly miserable, as well as guilty, and she still didn't understand why Brett had protected her. She was astute enough to know that if the real story came out—that she had been riding alone—the scandal would be ten times worse. Was that why he had lied?

Why would he want to protect her?

The scandal broke that afternoon.

Brett had told the sheriff he'd like to keep the incident quiet, and Andrews had nodded. But hoping to catch the remaining assailant, Andrews sent his deputies out asking questions, and before two o'clock Brett found himself being hailed repeatedly on the street as he walked from the Golden Lady to his hotel for a late lunch. Everyone wanted the gory details.

"Hey, Brett! Heard you shot up some riffraff down by the beach!" That from a man he barely knew.

Leanne St. Clair and her mother chose that moment to ride down the street in their carriage. They hailed him, and Brett had no choice but to stop. "Good day, Brett," said Helen St. Clair. Leanne echoed her mother, smiling coyly.

Brett wasn't feeling very friendly. He was still perturbed because he'd had to kill two men, an act that didn't sit well with him. He had killed before, but not often, and not since his wild gold rush days. He hated taking another's life, even in self-defense. In this case it was even worse, because if the wild little chit had had any sense, none of it would have happened. He was still furious with her.

Now he nodded abruptly, rudely, to Leanne, remembering how she had spread rumors about Storm in the Farlanes' garden. She didn't look half as beautiful today in the daylight, just malicious. He felt disgusted.

"So, Brett, the news is all over town! Tell us," Helen said excitedly.

"What news?"

"Oh, Brett!" Leanne pouted. "You know. How you defended Storm from being molested. Was she hurt? Is she . . . ruined?"

"I'm afraid I have no idea what you're talking about," Brett said coldly. "Excuse me, ladies, I am late for an engagement." He nodded and walked by, ignoring Helen St. Clair's gasp at his rudeness.

Unfortunately, two business acquaintances stopped him moments later to ask if it was true—had he gunned down two men in defense of Storm's honor? Brett feigned complete ignorance and did not glance at a soul in the magnificent gold and white foyer of the Hotel Royale. When his own host asked him if the news was true, he almost fired the man on the spot. Instead, seeing heads straining in his direction, Brett changed his mind and turned on his heel, heading grimly, resolutely, back outside. He would skip lunch.

Storm was trouble, spelled with capital letters. As he sought the sanctuary of his own office in the Golden Lady, he wondered if Storm could possibly become a conventional, mild-mannered lady. He doubted it. He still didn't know what had made him lie to her cousin to protect her.

Several hours later there was a knock on his door, and, thinking it was Linda, one of his girls, with a snack he'd asked her to fetch, Brett called out for her to come in. Marcy Farlane closed the door behind her.

Brett immediately stood. "Marcy?" he said, surprised, then worried. "Is everything all right?"

"Oh, yes," she said, flashing him a beautiful smile. "Brett, I'm sorry to bother you, but we must talk."

Brett quickly led her to the sofa, where she gracefully sat, pulling off fine white gloves. "I can't believe you would come here," he began.

She smiled fleetingly. "Why not? I've always wanted an excuse to see what a place like this looks like."

Brett scowled. "The downstairs is merely a bar, you know that."

"But I expected to see naked women running around."

He relaxed when he saw that she was teasing him. "They only run around naked upstairs."

She smiled and put an elegant hand on his. "Brett, please, Storm won't talk—what happened?"

"Et tu, Brute?"

"What?"

He shook his head. "I've been accosted all day by avid townsmen trying to get the 'inside story.' "

"I am sorry. But I'm worried about Storm."

"I know. You've probably already heard the story. We were out riding, my horse pulled up a bit lame, she went on ahead. She was accosted by three men, I shot two of them, one escaped."

Marcy let out her breath. "Poor Storm! Thank God you were there."

Brett frowned.

"Brett, she wasn't hurt, was she?"

"No."

She sighed. Then she looked at him suspiciously. "I find it hard to believe that the two of you were out riding together."

"What?"

"Storm told me she—well, I won't repeat her words, but she let me understand in no uncertain terms that she would not be friends with you, no matter what our own relationship."

Anger began to seep through him. "She did, eh?"

"So I find it hard to believe that the two of you were out riding."

"We were." He would not tell the truth, even to Marcy, but he was angry now, thinking about that ungrateful brat, Storm. "I have no use for her, either," he muttered.

"Oh, damn," Marcy said, startling Brett. "Well, thank God she's all right. Thank you, Brett."

"You're welcome."

Marcy held his gaze. "Are you all right?"

"Of course."

She sighed. "Storm has begged off the next week's engagements, and both Paul and I agree we've pushed her too far too fast. We're going to try to let this scandal die down before the Sinclairs' ball."

"Good idea," Brett agreed.

She stood, and Brett was instantly on his feet, too. "I'm sorry to bother you, Brett." She shot him another musing glance. "Were you two really riding together?"

"Of course," he said easily with his bland poker face.

Suddenly she smiled, taking his hands. "Thank you, Brett." She kissed his cheek.

After she left, he stood gazing at the door for a few moments. Exactly what *had* Storm told Marcy about him?

Chapter 7

She wanted to go.

She was apprehensive, though, too—after all, it was her first appearance back in society after her last fiasco. But boredom drew her out of her self-imposed exile. That and the desire to see Brett.

The past week had crept past. She had ridden for hours every day with Bart, and read Shakespeare and Melville and Dickens until they were coming out of her ears. Then restlessness had set in. She was not used to being confined, with nothing constructive to do. When Paul had to go to Sacramento to inspect some holdings there, she had eagerly accompanied him. She had loved the riverboat ride.

But she kept thinking about Brett.

She wanted to ask him why he had lied for her, but she hadn't seen him all week. She had hoped, while carefully not allowing herself to admit she was hoping, that he would call on her. He hadn't. Randolph had called instead, and James, and Lee, and Robert. They had all politely avoided any mention of what had happened—except for Randolph, who had practically demanded the full details. Not wanting to discuss it, Storm had lost her temper, and like the gentleman he was, Randolph had dropped the subject.

Leanne, too, had come calling with her mother. They had tried to pry the story out of Storm while insinuating that she had been molested, or worse. Storm would have attacked the bitchy girl if Marcy hadn't been there. Marcy had said a few well-chosen words, politely putting Leanne in her place, and the two had left in a huff.

Now Storm stood very still, her heart fluttering, while her maid, Lettie, hooked up the exquisite royal-blue taffeta ballgown. Brett would be there tonight. And she was determined to find out why he had lied for her.

Into her mind there kept flashing an image of how his mouth looked as it was lowering on hers. She shoved it away.

Marcy knocked softly and entered, the picture of elegance in a shimmering gold gown that revealed white shoulders and an expanse of white bosom. The Farlanes would be driving Storm and Paul to the Sinclairs' tonight. "You look wonderful," Marcy cried enthusiastically.

Storm smiled and turned to face the mirror. Her expression faded. The woman staring back at her was radiant, flushed, her bright eyes as blue as the gown. She was a stranger. Storm reached for the bodice to tug it up. It wouldn't move. "This is scandalous," she said.

"It's the height of fashion," Marcy assured her.

"If I bend over, I'll fall out."

"Why would you bend over?"

"Oh, Marcy! I don't think I can wear this."

"Storm, you look wonderful, and the men are waiting. We'll be late."

Storm's color intensified. She couldn't go dressed like this, with her shoulders entirely revealed. The puffed sleeves covered her arms only to her elbows. Almost her entire bosom was exposed. She felt naked.

She found herself settled in the carriage. It was better than standing in front of the mirror. She would pretend she hadn't seen how she looked, or better yet, pretend she had Marcy's elegance and poise and confidence. As if sensing her thoughts, Marcy reached out and squeezed her hand. Storm wondered if everyone had forgotten the incident on the beach.

In the round driveway they waited for five carriages to discharge their passengers at the front steps before they were able to alight, Paul taking a firm grip on Storm's elbow to help her down. By now, she was used to the high-heeled shoes, and quite adept at walking. She was no longer afraid of falling on her face, and since she refused to wear stays, she didn't think she'd faint, either.

Her heart began to pound. They walked inside, and the ladies handed their cloaks to the butler.

There were a hundred couples at the ball, the crème de la crème of San Francisco society, but the instant they entered the vast ballroom, Storm saw Brett. He was standing not far from the entryway, talking to two gentlemen and a lady, looking impossibly virile in a black tailcoat and silver waistcoat and tie. Their eyes met.

She blushed. Even from the distance of forty feet, she felt the heat of his gaze, saw the brightening of his eyes, then felt breathless as his gaze descended, leisurely, pausing on the expanse of her revealed bosom. She was suddenly glad she was wearing the gown. He liked it. Then she realized Brett wasn't the only one staring. Everyone near the entrance of the ballroom was gazing at her. Dismay replaced her heady elation. They were whispering about her.

Instantly her quartet of suitors was upon her, laughing and exclaiming over her beauty, announcing their pleasure in seeing her. As Robert and Lee began quarreling over the first dance, and Randolph took her arm while James volunteered to fetch champagne, Storm forgot that she was the object of so much scrutiny.

She had no more time to think of Brett, but she was always aware of him. Even as she whirled away in Robert's arms, then Lee's, then Randolph's, even as James brought the champagne and she paused to drink it, she sensed Brett staring at her steadily, intensely, standing alone now. She realized he had come without a partner, and was thrilled. A man she didn't know asked for a dance, and she agreed. Then James again. She danced and danced and danced, but on the periphery of her line of vision, as she was waltzed around the floor, she was always aware of Brett.

Her feet were beginning to ache, but she barely noticed. She was having a good time. The men were openly admiring, telling her again and again how lovely she was, and she was starting to feel lovely. The moment a dance ended, there was always someone else to claim her; she couldn't even remember their names. Taking a momentary breather, she sipped another glass of champagne, and carried on a conversation with at least six suitors. This time Randolph whirled her away.

It was getting late, and the waltz had barely started when they were interrupted. "Excuse me, but I'm cutting in," Brett said firmly.

Storm's heart went wild.

He gazed steadily down at her for a moment. She could barely breathe. He took her in his arms, and her body leaped at the exhilarating contact. "Never have I seen a woman so beautiful," he breathed huskily.

She thought she might faint from sheer ecstasy.

He was graceful, smooth, a wonderful leader, and Storm followed easily. She was acutely aware of his hand on her waist, not light like the other men but firmly there, his splayed fingers making her skin tingle through the taffeta and petticoats. His other hand, holding hers, was large and warm and seemed to throb deliciously over hers. She gazed steadily at his face, really seeing it as if for the first time, taking the opportunity to memorize its bold lines and harsh planes. She found herself staring at his mouth— which was just as bold and sensuously full.

"Do you like what you see?" His voice was warm and deep, huskier than usual. It thrilled her.

"Yes," she said simply, truthfully. Their eyes met, his flaring with light.

"Storm," he said, her name a caress.

"Brett?"

He almost smiled. "I think I'm becoming enchanted," he murmured.

Enchanted. He was becoming enchanted. The word echoed dreamily again and again. And she was becoming lost and powerless, lost in the warmth and intensity of his presence.

"Why?" Her own voice sounded different, and she coughed to clear it. "Why did you lie to Paul?"

He gave her a lazy smile. "To save your reputation. You could not have weathered the scandal if people had learned you had been accosted while riding alone."

She looked blankly at him.

"The bitches of this town would say you asked to be raped. Worse, that you were. That I'd arrived too late."

She flushed. Until now she hadn't fully understood the magnitude of what he'd done. "Thank you."

Suddenly she realized he was waltzing her through the French doors and out onto the balcony. "Brett!" But her protest was weak. She was trembling, eager to be alone with him.

They stopped, and his arm went around her. "You must be tired," he murmured, holding her pressed against his side. "You've been dancing all night."

She smiled gratefully. "I'm not tired, but my feet hurt a bit."

He threw back his head and laughed. His eyes sparkled as he studied her. One hand touched her cheek, his fingers trembling slightly, or was it her imagination? "Guileless Storm."

She was too aware of his fingers on her face, of the stillness of the night around them, of the feel of his hip and side and thigh against her. She swallowed.

"Let me get us something to drink," he said quickly. "Champagne or punch?"

"Champagne."

As soon as he left, she let out her breath and realized her heart was pounding wildly, her body throbbing deliciously. She leaned over the rail, closing her eyes, lifting her face to the moonlight. The air was chilly, but she didn't care. She fantasized about how Brett would return and pull her into his arms and kiss her. She was aching for his kiss.

He returned with two glasses, smiling warmly at her. Her heart leaped in response. "What were you thinking about? Or were you wishing on the moon?"

She took the glass he held out and sipped, gazing up at the full white orb. "I was imagining how you'd kiss me," she said, daring to glance at him.

His breath caught. She turned to look fully at him. He took the glass away, setting it aside. "Your wish is my command," he murmured and took her into his arms.

His body was warm and as hard as she remembered. Never had anything felt so right as being pulled against him. He held her so tightly her breasts were crushed against his chest, and she pressed harder, wanting to lose herself in him. Both his hands slid up her back, to her bare shoulders, and captured her head, oblivious of her carefully piled hair. In the bright moonlight she could see his features as clearly as if it were day. His gaze was so intense it sent a shudder through her, and then his mouth swooped down, covering hers.

She threw her arms around his neck and strained against him. The kiss was gentle and brief. He withdrew. She cried out in protest, and then he was kissing her again, this time with savage strength. She opened her lips beneath the onslaught; he began to probe with his tongue. Storm clung to him, moaning from deep in her chest.

She felt his own shuddering response, and more. His maleness rose between them, hot, hard, insistent, and she mindlessly ground her belly against it. His hands, callused and searing, roamed over her bare back, kneading her flesh, stroking. Then abruptly he pulled away, forcibly removing her hands and stepping two paces to one side.

"No," she protested, a whimper of sound.

She saw the strain on his face, the tightly compressed mouth, the pinched nostrils. Then his gaze slipped, and she glanced down to see that her bodice had become askew, revealing one taut, coral-colored nipple. Brett sucked in his breath. Storm just stared dumbly.

She pulled up the bodice with a shaking hand. Then he was there—his hands on hers, taking them away, pulling her against him, and she cried out gladly. His mouth came down again. She kissed him back, frantically, meeting his tongue with her own, and bravely, determinedly, pushing past. She probed deeply and intimately. Brett groaned.

His hands moved from her back to her waist, sliding up to cup her breasts. A searing liquid warmth, bittersweet and demanding, plunged through her. His hands crushed and squeezed, then hard palms slid over her nipples, again and again, making her moan with need and joy. And then his hands were on her back, nimbly unhooking her gown.

He crushed her bare breasts, one in each hand. Beyond all thought, Storm pressed herself more fully against him. His fingers found her nipples and began to caress them until she was shaking with desperate need. He lifted her in his arms.

She knew he was carrying her down steps, into a garden. He laid her down, on her bare back. The ground was wet. "My gown," she managed, her only coherent thought.

"Storm, tell me to stop," he begged, holding her face in both hands.

Their eyes met. With one hand she touched his cheek, amazed at his shudder of response. Barely able to breathe, she moved her hand down to his corded neck, then to his chest, sliding it beneath the layers of clothing until she met his feverishly hot skin and the crisp hair that covered it. He made a choked sound.

His arms went around her waist, lifting her up. His mouth came down, and he began nuzzling and kissing her swollen breasts. When his tongue flicked over one hard peak she gasped and clenched fistfuls of his hair. He teased mercilessly, then took that nipple between his teeth, tugging. She moaned.

"Brett! I'm going to die," she said, sobbing.

"No, love," he rasped. "You won't die." He tugged again, then began to suckle.

Storm thrashed. A hot ache was building, threatening, overwhelming. She felt his hand on her belly, rubbing, and she arched toward it. "Please," she panted. "Please!"

"Yes," he said, and his hand moved lower, one finger extended, rubbing.

Storm shuddered.

And then she felt cool air on her silk-clad legs, knew he had raised her skirts, felt his hand traveling up her thigh. Even over her pantalets, his touch was beyond enduring. She thrashed wildly, frantically, and then his hand was there, covering her womanhood, stroking insistently. He slipped one finger into her underwear to the cleft of wet, swollen flesh. His mouth covered hers.

She cried out. The sound was muted because of his kiss, but the sensations weren't—she thought she was dying. The explosion was intense, a brilliant bursting of fiery lights, of mind-numbing spasms that shook her from head to toe, and then blessed relief. She drifted.

"Storm," he said urgently.

She opened her eyes.

He had both hands on her waist and was kneeling between her spread thighs. His chest was rising and falling as if he had run for miles. "I need you," he said. "Please." His hands went to his trousers, hesitating. She found herself staring at the thick, rigid erection straining against the fabric. He looked at her, waiting for a word, a sign that he should stop.

"Yes," she whispered, as a delicious ache began to build and throb again.

"Sweet Jesus!" a woman screamed.

Brett grabbed Storm and yanked her behind him before she was even cognizant of the fact that someone had intruded upon them.

"Brett D'Archand!" the intruder gasped.

Comprehension began to dawn for Storm, and she grabbed her skirts, but they were already down. Half sitting, she yanked up her bodice as the full import of what was happening started to sink in.

"Helen," Brett said thickly.

Helen St. Clair moved purposefully forward, and Storm looked up to meet her dark, shocked gaze. "I should have known," she cried triumphantly. "I knew it!" She began to hurry away.

With shock, Storm realized what that lady had seen, what they had done. Dear God! What *had* they done? Horror consumed her.

Brett was kneeling, facing her. "Turn around, let me hook you up," he said, his tone urgent.

Numbly, Storm shifted, presenting her back. "Oh, God."

"He won't help us now," Brett said grimly. "Damn!" His hands were shaking. "There." He lifted her to her feet.

"I—I can't go back in," she said fearfully. Her hair had come loose. She was sure there were grass stains all over her gown.

"No, you can't," he said, holding her gaze. "I'm sorry." For a moment they stared at each other. Then they heard people coming, and they both turned, Brett instinctively moving in front of her, shielding her from view.

"Where is she?" Paul Langdon roared.

"Relax, Paul," Brett said evenly. "Nothing happened."

"Helen St. Clair told me exactly what she saw," Paul shouted, and before anyone could move, he had thrown a punch, hitting Brett in the jaw and sending him staggering back against Storm.

"Storm, are you all right?" Marcy cried, rushing forward. But her husband grabbed her arm, dragging her back. "Stay out of it," he warned.

"I'm sorry," Brett said to Paul Langdon, his tone conversational, as if they were alone. "Nothing happened."

"Come here, Storm," Paul said, as if he hadn't heard. His tone was so hard and unyielding that Storm stepped forward immediately, unable to look at anyone. She wanted to die. He grabbed her arm. "We'll go out the back way," he stated. "Grant, I'll send the carriage back for you."

"That's fine," Grant said.

"Maybe I should go with them," Marcy said worriedly.

"No," Grant returned.

"Let's go," Paul said without looking at Brett. Holding Storm's arm, he led her away, while Grant, Marcy, and Brett stood unmoving in the moonlight.

Storm felt numb and detached. She heard Grant say harshly, "Just what the hell is wrong with you?" and she knew he wasn't talking to Marcy, but to Brett. If he responded, she didn't hear.

Paul almost threw her into the carriage, and he didn't say a word during the entire drive home. But once inside the foyer, he spoke, just as she was about to go upstairs. "No, young lady, into my study."

Feeling great trepidation, Storm obediently retraced her steps and followed him across the room and into the study. He shut the doors behind them and stared at her. "Is it true?"

"What?"

"Helen said you were on the ground, on your back. Is it true?"

She hesitated. She flushed. She wanted to lie. She didn't know what to say.

"Your gown was undone."

She knew she had to lie. "He only kissed me."

He didn't look at her. "With your skirts up and your bodice down?"

Storm flushed. That bitch. What else had she said? Who else had she told? Oh, God! She stared at the floor, wishing she could disappear through it.

"Go to your room," he said then, not looking at her. "I need to think."

Only by the greatest effort did Storm restrain herself from running out of the study. Once she was on the stairs, she rushed to her room as if seeking sanctuary. But there was no escaping her thoughts. Her mind a whirlwind, she remained too agitated to sleep, too aghast at her own behavior to calm down. She couldn't believe she had been reduced to a quivering, moaning hussy.

She knew she was going to be sent home in disgrace, a thought that almost reduced her to tears. Her parents would be so disappointed in her. She didn't think she could face them, especially her father. She could picture his disbelieving expression when he first found out, the disbelief changing to a vast, reproachful disappointment.

She was sure Paul would explain in a letter just why she was being sent home. Her only hope was to send her own letter as well in which she tried to explain things from her own point of view. The problem was, she had no defense to offer. She had been a too willing participant.

But at least she would go home. She hadn't wanted to come here in the first place. It had been a terrible mistake, a disaster from day one. The sooner she could leave, the better. She knew her reputation was ruined, that she would never be invited to any social functions again, that she would be shunned. She dreaded the thought of even taking a carriage ride in public. People would point and stare and whisper. Everyone would know what she had done, how shameless she had been.

And then, with horror, she realized it would be close to two months before Derek could arrive to take her home. It would take a month for a letter to reach him, and assuming he left right away to fetch her, almost another month for him to return. Two months! What in God's name would she do for two months in this city where everyone knew about her downfall?

She couldn't face anybody—not all the people she had met, not her cousin, not Marcy, not Brett . . . Brett. Just the thought of him cooled her fear, bringing a surge of warmth, making her blood race in a way she now understood. She remembered the feel of his mouth on hers, warm, demanding, her own wild response—and she flushed in embarrassment. She thought of how he had lied about the incident at the beach to protect her; how when Helen St. Clair had found them he had pushed Storm behind him before she even knew what was happening, as if to physically shield her. And he had done it again, moments later, placing his powerful body between her and Paul and the others . . .

But he couldn't shield her from the consequences of her own actions. No one could.

"I'm sorry," he had said, and she remembered now the fire of his gaze, how it had held her.

She had thought she hated him. Didn't she? Storm placed a hand on her chest as if to still her exuberant heart. She didn't understand what she was feeling.

Her father would be so disappointed.

Brett, her father; Brett, her father . . . She was tortured by thoughts of the two men. And then, out of the blue, just as dawn was breaking, she had the most horror-inspiring thought of all. Pa would kill Brett!

She sat up, knowing beyond a doubt that, despite her own guilt, Derek would go after Brett and shoot him for defiling his daughter. He would kill him. Storm felt sick.

She got up and paced her room, truly frightened now. She had to stop him. But how? Nothing she could say or do would stop her father from exacting vengeance. She must warn Brett! She had two months to convince him to get out of town and stay away when Derek came to pick her up. She'd make him listen. She had to!

She sank back against the pillows, trembling. The situation was getting worse and worse. Once she left San Francisco she would never see Brett again. That thought shouldn't have bothered her, but it did.

I don't even like him, she thought in utter, abject confusion. And even though I didn't try to stop him, he should have known better. He should have stopped. It's really his fault. And now I'm going to be sent home, and I'll never see that rutting bastard again.

She started to cry.

She couldn't help it. She was disgraced, ruined, attracted to an arrogant gambler despite herself, stuck here for another two months, two months before she had to face her father, who would try and kill Brett . . . It just couldn't get worse.

Brett poured himself a double brandy and drank half in two gulps. He sank into a heavily padded chair, setting aside the snifter and burying his hands in his face. What in hell was wrong with him?

Never had he lost control like that. Not ever. He had almost taken a young woman's virginity, had almost ruined her with no thought of the consequences. He still didn't know how it had happened. Vividly, he remembered how he had wanted to stop, and how he couldn't.

How he had been overwhelmed with frantic passion, desperate need. How she had wanted him, too, had urged him on, hadn't tried to stop him. Sweet Jesus!

He closed his eyes, his head pounding. He could still see her, half naked, arching for him, her full, gorgeous breasts spilling free of her gown, her thighs spread, welcoming. She had been so wet and ready for him. A small moan escaped him as he remembered how he had brought her to a quick, stunning climax.

Christ! In the Sinclairs' garden!

He stood and paced and finished the brandy. The thought occurred to him that maybe Storm wasn't innocent—maybe she was one of those young ladies from respectable homes who pretended innocence while consorting with men behind society's back. He became very stiff then, staring blindly into the night, trying to determine if that was true. It didn't seem possible.

Yet he remembered how she had urged him on so frantically. No proper lady would do that.

He remembered how she looked when he had first seen her, clad in buckskins like a savage, so unaware of being a woman. But maybe running free as she did, she had been coupling from an early age with the Lennie Willises of Texas. Damn! He didn't know what to think!

If that weren't the case, then why had she urged him on?

It didn't really matter. Her reputation was ruined. *He* had ruined her.

Brett wasn't surprised when the summons came an hour later. Paul Langdon demanded his presence at eight in the morning. Grimly, Brett crumpled the note and tossed it in the fireplace. He did not want to marry her, but it was the only thing to do.

He spent a restless night tossing and turning, and arrived at Langdon's promptly at eight. Bart led him to the study and announced him. Paul Langdon was standing rigidly amid the plush appointments, and he nodded grimly. "Come in, Brett."

"Thank you." Brett stepped nearer and closely examined his friend's hard façade. "Good morning."

Paul gave him a long, steady look without answering.

"Paul, I'm very sorry," Brett said sincerely. He felt a stabbing guilt for betraying his friend by almost seducing his cousin. However, since he had already come to terms with the retribution he would have to make, he felt slightly better.

"So am I," Paul said. "You're one of my closest friends. I trusted you with her. Tell me—were your rides innocent?"

Brett's face twisted. "Damn! You know they were!"

"You'll marry her," Paul stated without compromise.

Brett's face darkened. Although he had already known it would come to this, Paul hadn't even let him offer to do the honorable thing. The fact irked him, made his spine stiffen.

"She is my responsibility," Paul said heavily. "I could never send her home in disgrace, especially since it was through my neglect and at the hands of my friend that she was compromised."

"I did not take her virginity," Brett said, his black eyes flashing. He was careful how he worded the statement— he still wasn't sure of Storm Bragg's innocence. He would never forget the passion she had shown, and his own uncontrollable response.

"Next Saturday," Paul said. "We'll keep it small and private, with just the Farlanes to witness the ceremony."

Next Saturday was only a week away. Brett found he was furious. "I take it this meets with the bride's approval?"

"Of course."

Brett strode over to the mantel, his back to Paul. Had

it all been a trap from the first moment he'd seen her? Of course Storm would want to marry him, he was the most eligible bachelor in San Francisco. Why should she be any different from all those other simpering young ladies who would love to be caught in an indiscretion with him so he would be forced to wed? He should have known. "Tell me," he said coldly, turning slightly. "Is this Storm's idea or yours?"

"It doesn't matter," Paul said just as coldly. "You'll marry her, Brett."

Brett was furious at himself, at her—and his desire not to wed overcame his brief commitment to doing the honorable thing. "I'm sure there are any number of young men who would be only too willing to marry Miss Bragg."

"I'll ruin you," Paul said softly.

Brett stared. "What?" He had heard, but he didn't believe his ears.

"I'll ruin you," Paul said stridently. "I won't extend your loans. I'll ruin your credit. You have no cash, Brett, and you're overextended. You'll have to liquidate half your holdings."

Brett's mind was working rapidly. He knew instantly that if Paul turned against him he would have to start over. He wouldn't be poor, but it would be a long crawl back to where he was now—and this time he might not make it. "You'd blackball me."

"Absolutely."

"Well," Brett said, "that makes the decision an easy one. Send someone around to tell me what time I should show up for my wedding." With long, barely controlled strides, he reached the door and was gone.

No stupid chit was going to cost him his empire, or his respectability—everything for which he had worked so hard. Not because of one moment's passion. He would marry Storm Bragg.

* * *

Storm ate a late breakfast at noon in her room. She was being a coward—she couldn't face anyone, not yet, not even the servants. She had managed to get a few hours sleep after the sun had risen, but she felt more tired, not less. She could barely eat—an unusual state for her. She was sick with dread, waiting for the summons. It came.

She went downstairs wearing a simple skirt and blouse, her hair in one long braid. Paul was in his study going over papers, but when he saw her he smiled, taking Storm completely by surprise. "Please, come in, and close the door. I have good news."

She couldn't fathom what the news could be, nor could she bear the suspense. She shut the door, leaning warily against it. "Paul—I am so sorry."

"It's not your fault," he said. "Brett is an experienced roué. I don't blame you. You didn't have a chance."

Storm felt hot tears of relief rising.

"He was here this morning," Paul told her.

"What?"

"He agreed that there is only one thing to be done."

Storm was confused. "Have you written to my father?"

"Yes. I didn't think it pertinent to go into the details. I merely stressed that Brett was the best catch in town, that any father would be proud."

"What?" She didn't understand. "Best catch?"

"The wedding will be in exactly one week, next Saturday. We'll keep it small." He beamed. "I know this isn't exactly every girl's dream of a courtship, but Brett is a good man, maybe just a bit too virile. He'll make you a fine husband."

"Husband!" She was stunned. Brett . . . her husband? "And—he wanted to marry me?"

"Of course he did. Brett is an honorable man."

Storm sank into a chair. Finally her mind began to work. "But I can't marry him! Paul, I assumed you would send me home."

"Storm, this is better, truly. You'll have a fine, successful, handsome husband. Why would you prefer to go home in disgrace?

"I don't even like him. I don't want to be his wife!"

"It's too late. Brett has to rectify the damage he's done, he knows that. I couldn't possibly send you home ruined. And you couldn't possibly find a better husband."

"I don't want to get married," Storm said unevenly, "Not now, not ever!"

Paul frowned. "Storm, do you want to be sent home a ruined woman, or would you rather be a successfully married one?"

Storm froze. If she married Brett, maybe her parents would never find out the truth; they would be proud of the match, proud of her . . . Tears came to her eyes. "Paul? Did you tell them any of it?"

"I thought I would leave that up to you."

Storm gulped. It was a choice, and suddenly it was the only one possible. How could she let her family down? Instead, she would pretend she had fallen madly in love, and her parents would be so thrilled, especially because Brett was a good catch.

She would never live with her family again. Never live in Texas again. But she could visit. Brett's wife . . . She wouldn't have to leave and never see him again . . .

"He really wants to marry me?" she said through a sheen of tears.

Paul came over to her. "There, there," he said, patting her shoulder. "I know the past few weeks haven't been easy. Many people have started their marriages with less than the attraction the two of you share. Storm, you've blown into town and taken the bachelor every woman has been after for years. All in two weeks!"

Storm managed to smile. It did sound like an accomplishment. But she still couldn't imagine Brett agreeing to marry her; he was so damn overwhelming, so arrogant, so bossy . . .

"I must admit," Paul said with a sheepish grin, "I did gloat a little in the letter to your parents."

That decided her. They would think she and Brett had fallen madly in love, all in a few weeks, and he the most eligible bachelor in town.

"I'll do it," she said.

Chapter 8

Although Marcy visited every day, helping to prepare Storm's trousseau, Storm didn't see Brett at all during the week preceding the wedding. He didn't even send a note, not a single message, nothing. Storm found it strange—as if the whole thing had been made up, as if there wasn't really going to be a wedding. She had other callers who all wished her well, mournful suitors, including Randolph, who asked her bluntly if she loved Brett. Storm flushed, unable to reply—what could she say? Randolph interpreted that as an affirmative, sadly wished her the best, and left. No young women came to call.

On Thursday, two days before the wedding, Storm felt compelled to bring up the subject of her fiancé. "Marcy?"

"It's perfect!" Marcy exclaimed, surveying Storm in her bridal gown. "The fit is perfect."

"Have you seen Brett?"

Marcy frowned as Madame Lamotte told Storm to raise her arms. "Why, yes, I have."

Storm lowered her arms, and madame told her they could remove the gown. Nimble fingers began to unhook it. "Marcy," Storm said in a quavering voice after madame had left.

"Let's talk," Marcy said, guiding her to a small settee.

Storm took a deep breath. "I just can't believe this is happening! Is it happening? Maybe he's changed his mind.

I haven't heard from him all week. If he jilts me at the altar, I'll die. I can't take another embarrassment, I just can't.''

Marcy put her arm around her. "He's not going to jilt you, Storm. He has every intention of marrying you."

"He does? He said so?"

"Yes." Marcy would not go into detail. She and Grant knew the entire story. Brett was furious at being black-mailed—they had never seen him so angry. She was sure that was why he had stayed away, that and because he had no feelings for Storm other than lustful ones. Or so he said.

Marcy didn't know what to think. She was worried for Storm, but at the same time, she and Brett looked so right together—both so handsome and spirited. Yet they were also both proud and stubborn; the marriage would be one of thunder and lightning. She had told Brett bluntly that she hoped he would be kind to Storm. He had just laughed. Marcy had been almost frightened by his laughter, but she knew that Storm, as vulnerable as she was, could also take care of herself. Maybe Brett was about to be brought to heel. After all, she still couldn't believe he had compro-mised Storm so. Brett knew better. He had mistresses— he was not a man to ruin a good girl. That Storm should make him lose both control and common sense was a good sign. She hoped.

"I don't know, Marcy," Storm said. "For a while I was wondering if Paul made the whole thing up, about Brett wanting to marry me."

Marcy carefully refrained from exposing Paul's deceit. It would not help the jittery girl now to know that Brett didn't want to marry her. She stroked her hair. "Brett's probably been very busy, as busy as you, this past week."

Storm looked down at her hands. "I wish this had never happened. If only I hadn't come to San Francisco."

"That's silly," Marcy said briskly, rising. "You can't

undo what's been done. Come, get dressed. I think we've accomplished enough for today. How about an ice cream?''

Storm smiled slightly. If only she weren't so nervous, so afraid. She still couldn't shake the feeling that Brett was going to jilt her at the altar. It was an awful thought. Last night she'd dreamed it had happened. A horrible nightmare. She shuddered.

She had written to her parents. Most of her letter had been a lie intended to make them happy. She had told them she liked San Francisco, that she was making friends, that the parties were wonderful. She described her new wardrobe as if she loved the elegant gowns. She described her six suitors, boasting. Then she dropped the bombshell, informing them that she was marrying Brett.

The next line had been the hardest of all to write. She told them they were in love. Hah! They could barely stand each other! Then she described Brett, the words flowing easily:

He is as tall as Pa, extremely dark, black-haired and black-eyed. He is probably the most handsome man in California. He is as strong as he is tall, elegant but not foppish. He is actually some kind of Spanish royalty, a criollo. All the young ladies have been after him for years. He is a successful businessman—he owns the most incredible hotel you have ever seen! The whole inside has no roof! All the rooms are on a square around the center, and everything is gold and white! The pillars look like marble. I have never seen such magnificence; it's like a palace. Brett designed it himself. Marcy took me there for lunch my second day in town. I had met Brett the night I arrived. Do you remember him, Pa? He was the one dressed in black who kissed my hand. The day we had lunch he sent a bottle of French champagne to the table. Marcy said it was for me. Of course, I didn't believe her . . .

Storm reread her letter and was stunned to find that it sounded as if she was, indeed, in love with Brett. She had never known she could be such a fluent liar. She was actually raving about him. But she decided not to rewrite it. After all, she'd conveyed the impression she wanted to make. Her letter and Paul's, which also raved about her fiancé, were sent together.

The wedding took place Saturday morning in the grand salon. The only witnesses were Marcy and Grant. There was no music. Paul simply escorted Storm into the room, holding her arm. Brett stood to one side, partially facing the minister. Grant stood next to him as his best man, Marcy on the opposite side. Everyone turned to look as Storm approached, a flush coloring her cheeks. Brett was the last to turn his gaze on her.

He was the only one she saw.

He looked, of course, overwhelmingly handsome and virile in a black suit with a red carnation in the lapel. His face was an unreadable mask. Storm looked into his eyes as she approached and felt a frisson of fear. His eyes were hard and cold, and she thought she saw contempt in them. It shocked her thoroughly, making her falter, but Paul steadied her. Then Brett's look changed, blazed, and relief surged through her. That light that had appeared so briefly, fading even now, she understood—the flaring of hot desire. She felt faint.

Paul handed her to Brett, who took her hand, holding her gaze again, and Storm saw and felt then that he was angry. She didn't understand. She was so confused, weak and light-headed and ill. She didn't even hear the words being said to them. The man holding her hand drowned out all sensations except those of his powerful, intoxicating presence.

Brett's hand was hot and hard and firm. Heat radiated between them, making her heart rate accelerate. She could smell his warm, woodsy, musky scent, very male. His profile was hard and tight-lipped.

And then she was repeating the vows, her voice soft and tentative. Brett's voice was strong, faintly derisive. Grant had handed him a ring, a pale gold band, and he slipped it on her finger. Storm stared blindly at the band through a veil of tears.

He lifted her chin, startling her. Their gazes met, hers tremulous, vulnerable, his cold and aloof, then startled, pitying. The softness was instantly gone. His lips claimed hers, roughly, brutally, in a warring onslaught. If he was trying to hurt her, he was succeeding. Storm couldn't breathe when he pulled away with a savage light in his eyes. She was trembling.

Marcy kissed her cheek first, her expression worried. "Congratulations, dear."

Storm blinked. She couldn't speak.

A maid served everyone glasses of champagne, and Grant proclaimed a toast. "To the newlyweds. A perfect match." He seemed sincere.

"To their happiness," Marcy interjected, her voice brittle.

"To a fruitful union," Paul said, openly pleased.

Before anyone could drink, Brett raised his own glass. "To my beautiful bride," he said, his voice mocking. "And to shotgun weddings." He drank.

Shotgun weddings. Storm turned to look at him, so stunned by the mockery and bitterness of his words that she missed the reactions of their guests, which ranged from surprise to anger. Brett met her gaze, smiling unpleasantly. "I'm afraid we cannot stay," he said, having drained the glass. He took Storm's elbow. "Thank you for coming," he said, his words heavy with sarcasm.

"Brett," Marcy said apprehensively, warningly.

He raised a brow. "Ever the mother lion. Have no fear.

Your cub won't be beaten. I'm not the type. And it's a little late for second thoughts."

Storm found herself being propelled outside and into the waiting carriage. *Shotgun weddings.* He was angry. Very, very angry, and bitter . . . He hadn't wanted to marry her. They had lied. Somehow he had been forced . . . She found herself sitting in the carriage across from Brett, who was staring at her. She started to tremble and looked quickly out the window so he wouldn't see the tears welling in her eyes.

He broke the silence. "Why don't you look happy? You got what you wanted." His words were easy, casual.

"Why?" She blinked at him.

He merely looked questioningly at her.

"Why, Brett? Why did you agree to marry me?"

"That's easy, my dear," he said. "Your cousin would have ruined me."

She sucked in her breath and quickly looked away from his hard, cold countenance. She had been tricked and lied to. Brett hated her. He hadn't wanted to do the honorable thing. He hadn't wanted to marry her. Maybe, deep inside, she had believed he had actually wanted to marry her, that he loved her. "This is a terrible mistake," she managed unsteadily.

He laughed. "It's a little late for that, love."

Suddenly she realized she was afraid of the man she had just married.

They rode the rest of the way in silence. Storm wouldn't look at him. He stared at her steadily. Her heart was beating wildly. This would never do. Somehow she had to get out of it.

He helped her down in front of his house, a Victorian structure of brick and wood with turreted roofs. He led her inside. "This is Peter, my majordomo and valet. Peter will show you to your rooms. Betsy will be your maid—

Peter, send Betsy to Storm to help her undress and see to whatever else she wants. I will return later.''

Storm stared blankly when she realized he was leaving, striding impatiently down the path and jumping back into the carriage, which rolled away. She turned to stare with shock at Peter, who was looking distinctly uncomfortable.

''Madame, will you come upstairs?''

He showed her to her room. It took Storm all of a few seconds to realize she wasn't sharing a room with Brett. Her mind flashed onto her mother and father and their warm, cozy bedroom with the big four-poster bed. She knew they slept in each other's arms. When she was little, she had walked in on that tender scene many times. She glanced around the large, elegant bedroom, tastefully but impersonally decorated in blue and white. Her trunks had been brought in and her clothes had been unpacked. Peter told her he would send Betsy up immediately, and left. Storm saw that even though it was only noon, her bridal nightgown was already draped across the canopied bed.

Good, she thought savagely. I would hate sharing his room anyway!

Brett was feeling something akin to remorse.

And he couldn't concentrate.

He shoved the ledger aside, angry and irritated—a mood that seemed the norm these past few days, especially today, his wedding day. He stood and paced to the window, staring down on Stockton Street. But he didn't see the Saturday strollers, the carriages and horsemen. Instead, a breathtaking vision of his bride floated across his mind.

He wondered if it would always be this way, if every time he saw Storm he would be struck again by her beauty, marveling anew at how much she stirred him. This morning she had looked stunning, young and vulnerable in the white lace and satin gown. He had seen the fear in her eyes when he had looked at her during the ceremony, and the same fear again in the carriage. That look stirred his pity, and maybe some tenderness, even remorse. But he had no reason to feel remorseful. He was the victim, not she.

He poured himself a brandy and sipped it. Was this another trick designed to make him soften? She had trapped him into marriage, but there was one consolation. His bride was waiting for him. Tonight was his wedding night.

It was only five o'clock, but Brett knew he couldn't pretend to work any longer. He wanted his bride. His wife. And tonight he would have her.

It would be an expensive tumble, he thought viciously. It had cost him his freedom. He laughed, grabbed his jacket, and left.

By the time he arrived home he was thoroughly aroused, and disgusted with himself for wanting so badly a woman who had been forced upon him. Of course, no matter how angry he was, he couldn't rape her. He wanted her to want him—as much as he wanted her. He found Peter. "Has she eaten anything yet?"

"No, sir."

"We'll have an early supper. Have the cook send up whatever's ready, along with two bottles of champagne. Immediately." He didn't wait for Peter's reply, but bounded up the stairs, his strides rapid and eager. He even smiled. He felt somewhat like a young boy about to have his first woman. Ridiculous, for a man of his experience. He glanced at her closed door, pausing but not stopping, and entered his own room, shrugging off his jacket.

He washed his face and hands, pulling off his tie and unbuttoning his shirt halfway. He turned to the connecting door and knocked. She told him to come in.

She was sitting in bed, reading. Her hair was loose, a riot of brown and gold cascading over her shoulders. She was clad only in her chemise and petticoats, both of fine white lace and silk. The sight of her, slightly tousled and in bed, made his breath catch and his blood pound. Her eyes widened with surprise at the sight of him.

He smiled slightly and closed the door behind him. "I've ordered us an early supper. We'll eat in here." His gaze swept her admiringly. Maybe it wouldn't be so bad, being married to Storm. He wanted her more than he'd ever wanted any woman. And he wouldn't be the first man to have married from a raging lust.

She swallowed and wet her lips. Her tongue was small, pointed, and pink. "I'm not hungry," she said, her voice cracking.

"You haven't eaten yet," he said, noting her golden coloring. "How did you get tan all over? Are you tan all over?"

Her eyes widened, the blue deepening, a blush coloring her high cheekbones.

"I've never seen a woman whose bosom wasn't white," he murmured. "Unless, of course, she had naturally dark skin. You don't."

Storm shifted on the bed, then looked around—for clothing, he knew. "Don't dress on my account," he said. "You're perfect the way you are."

There was a knock on the door. Brett glanced at her, waiting, one brow arched, while she slid under the covers, pulling them up to her chin. His mouth quirked again, and he opened the door. Peter brought in a tray and began to set the table. Another servant followed with champagne. Brett nodded his thanks and closed the door behind them. Glancing casually at Storm, he uncorked a bottle and poured two glasses, then moved to the bed, where she sat still covered modestly by the spread. He handed her the glass, feeling a flash of annoyance when she didn't move to receive it, merely tightening her grip on the bedding.

"Not thirsty?" he asked.

"Get out."

He stared. Then he smiled, a cold, chilling smile. "Are you talking to me?"

"I'm not talking to the walls," she said, her eyes flashing.

He sipped the champagne. "This is our wedding supper, and our wedding night."

Her nostrils flared. "No."

"Excuse me?" He was incredulous.

Her smile was nasty. "No. Get out. If I had known it was you, I would have bolted the door."

He slowly put down the glass. "I see. You intend to deny me?"

"Yes."

"I did not marry you to have a wife in name only. You are my wife, and you shall sleep in our marriage bed."

"Never," she ground out. "I hate you. Get out."

He yanked down the covers, grabbed her wrist, and pulled her close. "Why do you insist on making this unpleasant?" he snarled into her face.

Tears came to her eyes then, making him curse and abruptly release her. She thumped against the headboard. "Leave me alone!"

He picked up her glass of champagne. "Drink this. It will put a rosier light on everything."

She opened her mouth to refuse, but he gave her such a dark look that she shut it and took the champagne. He knew something was going on in her mind, but he didn't know what. "Drink it," he repeated.

Storm closed her eyes. She wanted to throw the champagne in his face, better yet, claw out his eyes, but she was afraid to. She felt young and alone, naked and vulnerable, and the way he kept looking at her increased her fear.

"Storm," he said, "there's no changing what's been done."

His breath touched her face, and she opened her eyes

to see that he was very close, his eyes blazing. His lips descended, covering hers. She clamped her lips tightly together. His mouth worked on hers, gently but insistently, so unlike the hard, hurtful kiss he had given her in front of their friends after the wedding. But she would not yield—it would not come to that. She hated him. Then she felt his hand on her breast, tenderly fondling, and anger filled her veins. He hated marrying her, hated her, but he wanted to possess her. With a cry of rage, Storm twisted away, at the same time dashing the glass of champagne in his face.

He started, his eyes wide with shock, his face dripping. Storm leaped off the other side of the bed and watched numbly as he visibly tried to control his rage. He walked to the table with stiff strides, picked up a napkin, and wiped his face. Then he turned and left the room without a word.

She was trembling. Without a doubt, she knew, he would be back. Quickly she locked the door connecting their two rooms, then the one leading to the hall. She stood uncertainly in the center of the room, hugging herself, trying to stay calm, telling herself she had nothing to fear. But the fear would not go away.

Time crawled by. The minutes dragged, and she could hear Brett in the other room, no doubt changing his clothes. Then there was silence. What was he doing? What was taking him so long? She moved back to the bed, checked the contents of the drawer of the night table, and waited.

After ordering a bath, Brett stripped completely. He was so angry he didn't trust himself to return to her—he might hurt her. He had never hurt a woman before, but he wanted to beat her. He sipped two brandies to relax, then soaked in the tub, washing his hair, which was sticky with champagne. His anger began to fade, but in its place grew a hard determination. He finished bathing, had another brandy, and slipped on a dark blue silk robe, belted loosely. He moved to the door between their rooms and unlocked it.

She was sitting in bed, still in the sheer, tantalizing lace underclothes, and she gasped and grew pale when he stepped inside. He smiled grimly. He was certainly not foolish enough to give his wife the means to lock him out of her chamber. He moved toward her, resolution in every step. And the sight of her, the smell of her, the knowledge of what was going to happen, of how he would possess her, inflamed and hardened him until passion consumed him. He stopped at the foot of the bed. She met his stare, her eyes wide and frightened, but he refused to entertain pity or compassion. She, not he, had brought them to this moment.

"It's hopeless to fight me," he said hoarsely.

"I will fight you until I die."

"You will enjoy this night."

"You will have to rape me."

"It won't be rape, I assure you." He moved to the side of the bed.

She didn't take her eyes off his face, but her hand went to the drawer of the bedside table. To Brett, his senses overwhelmed with her, his lust painfully filling his loins, it was a confusing gesture. For the first instant when her hand came up, he thought it was to welcome him into her arms, and his heart jumped with excitement. Then, in the dim light, he saw that she was pointing a Colt six-shooter at his heart. He stopped.

"Get out." Although her voice wavered, her hand did not.

"Put the gun down." Disbelief laced his voice.

"No. We are not consummating this marriage. When Pa comes, we'll annul the marriage—if he doesn't kill you for what you've done."

At first Brett didn't hear her, he was so angry that she would pull a gun on him and deny him his rights. He fought for control, fought and lost. He didn't think she'd shoot him, didn't think she was fast enough. He grabbed her wrist with lightning speed, and she moaned and dropped the gun. He kicked it away viciously, sending it slamming into the wall, then he grabbed her by the shoulders, making her whimper, and pulled her very, very close. "Don't you ever threaten me again," he ordered, his teeth clenched, his lips contorted into a snarl. "Do you understand?"

"Damn you," she cried, struggling to be free. She was strong, but no match for him. He tightened his hold until she gasped and went still. "I hate you!" she cried. "I hate you!" She started to cry.

He had been about to throw her beneath him and take her, certain she would soon be moaning in ecstasy. But her sobs were like ice water, reviving his sanity. Rigid with control, he released her. She rolled away from him onto her side.

"So you want an annulment?" he asked, his voice stiff and without inflection.

"Yes," she said, sniffling. "Yes!"

"I thought you wanted to marry me."

"No!" It was a passionate denial. She twisted to face him, her face tear-streaked, her eyes blazing. "They all lied to me. They said you wanted to do the honorable thing. I agreed, but only so I wouldn't shame my family. Now I realize I'd rather go home in disgrace than be married to you."

He stood. He didn't know why anger was rearing its monster head again, threatening to make him violent. After all, he didn't want to be married any more than she did. They had both been duped. He nodded curtly. "Very well," he said.

She was suddenly still, not even breathing.

"We will not consummate the marriage, have no fear. I am in complete agreement with you in this desire." He couldn't smile. In fact, he felt as if he were suffering from lockjaw. "Good night."

He strode out rigidly, forcing himself not to slam the door behind him, although it thudded with some force in any case. Then he stood very still in the center of his bedroom, and ran trembling fingers through his hair. He felt no relief at their solution to this mess, but assumed it was because he was still achingly stiff with desire for her.

She wanted an annulment.

Paul would have no reason to ruin him if her father agreed to it.

Brett shed his robe and pulled on his clothes, cursing angrily because his hands were shaking. Then he left the house. Yet he couldn't seem to get Storm's image out of his mind, in all her fury and tearstained glory.

Chapter 9

The maid looked at him with stunned surprise, her eyes wide. "Mr. D'Archand!"

"Please tell Audrey I am here," he said, stalking past the clearly upset girl to the parlor. He flung off his coat and helped himself to another brandy.

If Audrey saw other men, he didn't care as long as it didn't interfere with his own needs. He paid for her, her clothes and the house. He came first. If she was with someone now, he damn well expected her to get rid of him. With that thought in mind, he walked to the parlor doors and shut them firmly so no one would be embarrassed.

The maid returned to tell him madame would be with him shortly. Brett nodded and stared out the French doors into the small but pleasant garden. A huge oak tree growing very close to the house almost blocked his vision, but it didn't matter. Instead of seeing the azaleas, which were just coming into bloom, and the purple-flowered shrubbery, he saw Storm. Of course. How in hell was he going to get her out of his mind?

It was hard to believe she wanted an annulment. Every other woman in San Francisco would die to be in her place, but *she didn't want him.*

He swung around as the parlor doors opened and Audrey swept in, gorgeous as usual. She was wearing a ruffled silk robe in pink, with black lace edging, and Brett wondered briefly what she had on underneath it. Then, unfortunately, a flashing image of Storm clad in a lacy, virginial chemise and petticoats came to mind. He pushed the thought away.

"Brett!" Audrey's eyes were wide as she gracefully floated forward. "Dear, this is a surprise!"

"So I gathered," he said dryly, accepting her kiss.

She stepped back to survey him. "Darling, this is your wedding night."

He raised a brow. "So it is."

Her face was a perfect ivory oval as she studied him searchingly, then smiled. "I am flattered."

His expression told her the subject was closed, and Audrey knew him too well to pursue it. "Are you hungry, darling?"

"Yes," Brett said, putting down the snifter. "But not for food. We'll eat later."

Audrey smiled without reserve and took his hand. Brett followed her upstairs and into the bedroom. He was already unbuttoning his shirt—there was no need for propriety. Everyone in the small household knew his status, as they damn well better. He let the shirt drop to the floor.

"Let me help," Audrey purred.

As usual, she smelled wonderful, spicy and exotic. Her hands were teasingly light on his flesh. He let her undress him, scowling at the thought that he, Brett D'Archand, was bedding his mistress, not his bride, on his damn wedding night. His anger increased.

He was naked, and Audrey straightened. Brett made no effort to hide his bad mood; there was no need to. Audrey had no right to interfere; she was only his mistress. But she was gazing at him with a combination of speculation and concern. Partly, he knew, because his expression was so dark, and partly because he wasn't ready for her, which was unusual. He remembered how hot he had been for that little Texan and felt a surge of desire just thinking about her. He lifted Audrey into his arms and carried her to the four-poster bed.

As he had suspected, she was wearing nothing beneath the wrapper except black silk stockings and black lace garters with pink rosettes. Her small body was naked, ivory, and curved in all the right places. Her breasts were full, more than a handful, and as he cupped one perfect globe, his desire returned. He lowered his head to suck, thoroughly irritated when a too-vivid image of his bride came to mind. He sucked harder to chase it away, and when Audrey pushed him onto his back and slid down the length of him, murmuring words of endearment, her deft fingers clasping the hot length of his turgid maleness, praising size and prowess, he closed his eyes, her lips banishing all further wayward thoughts.

Something woke Storm. Instantly, she was fully awake, straining to hear. Nothing. She sat up, glancing at the clock—it was just after two in the morning. She grew stiff with remembrance and anger. Was *he* home yet?

She got up slowly, not making a sound, and slipped to the window overlooking the drive and gardens ahead, and to the left, the stable. Then she saw him.

He was strolling from the stables as if he had not a care in the world. She knew it was Brett even though the night was cloudy, only partly illuminated by the moon shining through drifting clouds and by intermittently spaced gas lamps. She looked at him very hard, but he was walking straight and true. He did not look drunk.

She went back to her bed, shaking with something that felt suspiciously like jealousy. Of course it wasn't, but where had he been from six in the evening until now? Her mind refused to answer while something sick and full of dread knotted deep in her belly.

She listened carefully and finally heard his footsteps

coming down the hall. They were firm and even—not staggering. They seemed to pause briefly outside her door, just for a moment, then went past. She heard his own door open and shut softly.

She sat in the middle of the bed and hugged her knees to her chest. I hate him, was her only thought. Yet she still listened as he moved quietly, undressing. She flushed, thinking of him removing his garments, one by one, until he stood naked. Would he put on that thin, blue wisp of a robe, the one he had worn into her room, barely belted, revealing a slice of hard chest, the dark mat of male hair?

Where had he been?

Storm lay back down, her heart pounding loudly. She didn't give a damn. Their marriage was a farce. Thank God he had left her alone. She hoped that wherever he went, he would go there every night! She sighed, and then became very still as her door opened. Immediately she shut her eyes, but not before she saw him standing there, a darker shape in the dim room.

As he moved toward her, Storm feigned sleep, trying to breathe evenly. He paused, she was sure, inches from where she lay. She could feel his gaze on her and was certain he could tell she was faking sleep. She heard him let out his breath, as if he had been holding it, then he bent closer. Even without his touching her, she could feel him, feel his body's warmth. His hand picked up a coil of her hair. Storm fought to keep breathing.

He dropped her hair and moved away, closing her door behind him. What in hell had that meant? Tears came to her eyes, but she furiously blinked them away.

She barely slept, but she stayed in bed pretending sleep until the sun came up. She heard Brett move about and finally leave his room, his footsteps passing her door, then fading into oblivion. Storm bounced out of bed like a shot, whipping on her wrapper, and flung open the door between their rooms. She paused.

His scent was strong in his room. She could still feel his presence. It was a very masculine room, with simple furnishings, not like the elegance of the rest of the house. There was a huge stone hearth. A large, dark blue Oriental rug covered the oak planking of the floor. The bed was four-postered and larger than hers, but the posters were short and thick and carved in a swirling pattern. The coverlet was silk, a simple geometric pattern that looked almost Indian.

His clothes from last night lay on a chair, and Storm started toward them.

At that moment, Peter stepped in, and they both froze, staring at each other in shock. He recovered first. "Good day, madame. Can I help you?" He was polite but clearly puzzled.

"No, I-I think I left a book in here," she managed.

Peter's brows drew together; it was obvious he did not believe her. "If I find it, I will return it to your room," he said in dismissal. Storm didn't move, then was dismayed when he began collecting Brett's clothes from last night. He straightened and looked at her, disapproval in his eyes.

Storm bit her lip, about to retreat. Then, on the floor, almost under the chair, she saw a white sleeve. Peter moved away from the chair, and Storm moved toward it. She pounced on the garment. It was Brett's shirt.

Peter stopped and looked at her.

"You forgot this," Storm said, her heart beating hard as her gaze ran swiftly over the shirt she was twisting in her hands. She didn't see lip rouge. She quickly lifted the garment to her face, inhaling. All she could smell was Brett, but she sniffed again, then thought she could detect something faintly different, a strange spice . . . She couldn't be sure.

"Madame?" Peter's tone was neutral, but he was looking at her as if she were crazy.

She wished she could inspect the damn shirt at her leisure. Instead, she handed it over, smiling the best she could, and hurried back to her room. She sat down, still trying to discern if that spicy scent was tinged with floral. She knew one thing. Brett did not smell of spices. He smelled of leather, male sweat, cigars, brandy, and maybe horses. But not spices. Not slightly sweet spices. But it had been such a faint scent. Maybe she was making it up.

Storm dressed in a simple white blouse and a plain blue serge skirt. She wore only one petticoat, so the skirt hung close to her body. There was no sense wearing a hundred petticoats if she wasn't going anywhere, she thought bitterly. Summoning up courage and defiance, she went downstairs to the dining room, hoping to find Brett had gone. Her stomach started to rumble.

He wasn't gone. He looked up from the paper he was reading, his dark glance flicking over her, seeming to linger on her hips. He sat at the head of the rosewood table, which could easily seat twelve. He had obviously finished eating, but he was still drinking coffee. He set aside the paper. "Good morning," he said politely. "Come in."

Storm came forward then, embarrassed to be caught standing frozen like a frightened schoolgirl in the doorway. As she approached, she saw that a place was set next to Brett, on his right. He was standing. He held out her chair, and as she sat, she became acutely aware of his closeness, his distinctive scent. There was nothing spicy about it. She didn't look at him.

"Madame? Would you like fresh eggs this morning?"

Storm looked up at the butler. "Yes, anything is fine."

He nodded and left. Brett said, "Coffee?"

"Yes, please." She realized he was pouring for her from a silver service. The roles were supposed to be reversed. He handed her the cup and saucer. Storm sipped gratefully. Why did he keep staring at her so?

"Did you sleep well?" he finally asked, his tone impersonal.

Storm looked at him. "Wonderfully."

He cocked a brow, a slight smile tugging the corners of his mouth. "Do you walk in your sleep?"

She froze. "No, of course not."

He tried and failed to suppress a genuine smile. "I could have sworn I saw you standing at your window last night."

She ground her teeth together. "While you were getting home?"

He gazed calmly at her. "Yes."

"You were mistaken," she said as evenly as she could.

"Then I'm glad you slept well."

"And how was your night?"

He was carefully impassive. "No different from any other."

"How good for you," Storm bit out.

"Are you angry?"

"Of course not."

He smiled. "I think I know women well enough to know when they're angry. You are. And you were up last night—I saw you. Were you waiting for me? Did you miss me? Did you change your mind?"

Storm twisted in her chair to face him, glaring. "You conceited boor! I was not waiting for you—I heard something and woke up. I went to the window to investigate, and I saw you. There! Are you satisfied?" She was shaking with fury.

"There is nothing to be satisfied about. But you're still angry." His dark eyes regarded her steadily.

"I'm upset," Storm agreed, her mind fixing on a new, better, safer route.

His eyes brightened. His voice grew softer. "Why?"

She swallowed and looked at him. "I have to send another letter to my parents, one telling them that the first letter was all lies."

They stared at each other. Brett finally spoke, his expression once more closing in, his eyes guarded. "I take it the first letter informed them of our marriage."

She stared down at the tablecloth. "Yes."

"And this letter will ask your father to come for you, for his permission to seek an annulment?"

"Yes."

Brett slapped down his napkin, and stood abruptly. "Write it today," he said harshly. "I will add my own letter as well." He left then, with long, tense strides.

Storm's eyes blurred with tears as she watched his powerful form, broad-shouldered and narrow-hipped, so virile in the tight riding breeches, the loose shirt, the glistening black boots. The dining room doors were open, and once he went through, he was gone from her view. But a moment later she heard the loud slamming of the front door. Why was he angry? She had done nothing, absolutely nothing.

"Madame? Your breakfast."

"Thank you," Storm managed.

Supper was a tense, silent affair. Brett had stayed away all morning, then secluded himself in his study all afternoon. Which was fine with Storm. He did not make one attempt at conversation all through the meal, and Storm, feeling both hostile and miserable, refused to try. After all, their marriage was a farce. Soon it would be over. It could not be soon enough.

"Did you write the letter?" Brett asked, standing. They were the first words he had spoken to her since that morning.

"Yes," she said. Thinking about the letter brought her suspiciously close to tears.

"Bring it to my study," he said, walking out.

Storm stood and fumed. Had he ever asked anybody politely for anything? He had absolutely no manners. And why did he want the letter? Obstinately, she decided she would not jump to his beck and call. She told Thomas, the butler, that she would like a bath and went up to her room.

The bathwater was brought, and her maid, Betsy, helped her out of her clothes. Storm allowed her to do so because she was too distracted thinking how awful life had become to protest. She let the girl pin up her hair, and she slid into the tub. Betsy started to leave. "No, don't!" Storm cried. She was afraid to be alone in her bath in case Brett came looking for her. Hopefully, he had forgotten all about the letter.

Betsy shrugged and started to organize the contents of her dresser. "Shall I help you bathe, ma'am?" she asked later.

Storm came out of her reverie. She had closed her eyes, letting the hot water drain away her tension, thinking about home, about her brothers, whom she missed terribly. Nicky. Silent, strong, he would always protect her, always offer a shoulder to cry on. He would want to kill Brett, she mused, nodding to Betsy. And wild, mischievous Rathe—an impossible tease. Even Rathe, just turned four-teen, would want to go after Brett. He was as good a shot as any of them, perhaps the bravest of them all if reck-lessness could be called bravery. Storm had to smile at the thought of the three Bragg men, Pa and Nick and Rathe, standing side by side facing down and terrorizing a lone, frightened Brett. It was a delicious fantasy.

There was an abrupt knock on the door, and even before she could sink lower, she knew who it was. "I'm bath-ing," she called out, but the door was already open, and Brett stood there glowering. Betsy dropped the soap and sponge and stood, clearly intimidated by him.

"I asked you to bring the letter to my study," Brett said. He was no longer looking at her face. His gaze was scanning the water, trying to scan her, but Storm had sunk every portion of her anatomy up to her chin beneath the bubbles. That chin now tilted upward, her mouth setting into a mutinous line. Brett suddenly smiled.

"Leave," he told Betsy without looking at her.

Storm's eyes went wide. "No," she cried in a panic. "Brett, I'm bathing!"

His smile broadened. "So I see." He motioned to Betsy. "Get out."

Betsy fled. In her terror, she forgot to close the door. Without taking his eyes from Storm, his smile reminding her of a wolf's grin, Brett shut the door. Then he stepped to the side of the tub. Storm sank lower, or tried to. His eyes were very, very bright. She knew he had forgotten the letter.

Brett casually reached down and picked up the sponge and soap, kneeling next to her shoulder. Their gazes locked. She realized he was soaping the sponge, and she became mesmerized by how large and strong his brown hands looked. "What do you think you're doing?" Her voice was a squeak.

His smile broadened. "Helping my wife bathe." The sponge moved over her shoulder. Storm wrenched around and grabbed the wrist holding the sponge. "I'm not really your wife. The annulment, remember?"

The smile disappeared. He tossed the sponge into the tub, straightening. "How could I forget?"

Storm instinctively crossed her arms over her breasts as his eyes sought to pierce the protective layer of bubbles and water. He smiled tightly and casually reached for a towel. "Get out."

She hesitated. "Could you—"

"Get out, and I mean now."

Storm swallowed and stood. The water and bubbles parted, running down her long, lithe, superb body in rivulets. As she stepped from the tub, she was painfully aware of Brett's gaze, which was roaming every part of her—eagerly.

She was so superb, so magnificent, that for a moment, Brett couldn't think. He could only look at her and feel the maddening fullness of his loins. Her body was strong. Never had he seen such a strong, muscled figure on a woman. But it was completely feminine. Completely sensual, willowy despite its strength. Her shoulders were broad, her torso long, her waist narrow. Her breasts were full but high and firm. Her hips were perfectly rounded, her legs long, curved, with the slightest ripple of muscle beneath a layer of softness. And she was golden all over, except for her nipples, which were a darkened coral-rose.

He placed the fluffy towel around her shoulders, trying to control the trembling that beset him.

She jerked away, wrapping the towel tightly around her. Her eyes shone with blue fury. Brett took a deep breath. In one second, he was going to yank that towel away, lift her and throw her on the bed, and to hell with an annulment. "Get dressed and bring me that letter. You don't want me to have to come up here for it again." He walked stiffly away.

He paced his study until he had calmed down enough to deal with the matter at hand. He would not think about her and how she seemed to jolt him beyond control every time he was near her. Instead, he would think about the annulment. He would send their letters tomorrow. It would probably be five or six weeks before Bragg arrived. The other alternative was for him to take her back himself. That would be damn inconvenient—he had all his business affairs to tend to. It would probably be inconvenient for Bragg to drop everything and come for her as well. What if her father couldn't come until the full six months were over, as originally planned?

He grimaced, unable to imagine continuing this farce for that long. He did not think he had the willpower to resist such an enticing morsel when it was under his own roof, day after day, night after night . . . He poured himself a drink, then lit a cigar. He was not going to let his thoughts drift in that direction again.

She appeared in the doorway ten minutes later, clad in a heavy, quilted winter robe. With her hair in one braid, and the robe hiding her figure, she almost resembled a child. Except for that face—it was no child's face. Too extraordinary, too stunning . . .

"Come in."

She did, looking worried. In her hand was an envelope.

Brett moved around his desk and around her to close the door, then he gestured at a chair in front of the desk. Storm sat. "May I?" He reached for the letter.

"It's sealed."

"I intend to read it."

"It's personal," she cried, looking upset.

He studied her. "If you've spoken badly about me, I want to know. If some enraged father is going to come after me, I want to know."

"I haven't," she mumbled.

"Then let me read the letter." Instantly he realized the illogic of his reasoning, but she didn't. She seemed so pathetic and abjectly miserable, he felt a stab of anger toward himself. But curiosity won out, and he took the envelope she handed him, slitting it. He read:

Dear Mother and Father,

I am so sorry to have to be writing this and I'm hoping you won't be angry. I lied to you in the other letter because I didn't want you to know the truth. I wanted you both to be proud of me. I'm so sorry.

From the day I arrived here, nothing has gone right. I hate San Francisco. I'm stuffed into corsets and shoes that hurt unbearably, and I'm painted and dressed like some doll, then shuffled off to boring party after party.

I've made a fool of myself. I can't walk in the shoes, and I fainted because my stays were too tight. I didn't know better, and I walked in a garden with a man, and suddenly the women were saying nasty things about what we were doing in the garden. We weren't doing anything.

I lied about Brett D'Archand, too. We never fell in love. We don't even like each other. But Brett and I were caught kissing. I still don't know how it happened. Paul convinced me it would be better to marry Brett, who is considered a good catch, than to go home in disgrace. On our wedding night we realized how hopeless it would be to stay married, so we never consummated the marriage. We intend to get an annulment. If you approve, Paul won't ruin Brett, which is why Brett married me in the first place. I am so sorry.

And Pa, I think you should know that the kiss was half my fault. Please don't think of hunting Brett down.

> *Please forgive me,*
> *Storm*

Brett looked up, scowling. He wasn't sure why, but the letter disturbed him greatly. He didn't like reading about how sorry she was for failing her parents, and he hated her thinking she had made a fool of herself. She was even trying to protect him, when she could have blamed him completely for what had happened. The innocence of the letter reminded him that she was not yet a woman, merely on the verge of womanhood. Only seventeen. "Do you love them, or are you afraid of them?" he asked softly.

Her face was averted, and when she looked at him he saw how embarrassed she was. "I love them. I miss them—so much." Her face flushed beautifully. "They will never understand why I did what I did. I don't understand, either." She looked away.

Something dangerous and threatening tugged at his

heart, and he found himself kneeling at her side, tilting her chin to face him. "Passion between a man and a woman is normal. I met your father once. It seems to me he would understand passion."

Storm's gaze was so hopeful he felt an overwhelming tenderness. "Do you think so?"

He nodded, smiling slightly. Then he stood and tore up the letter.

"What are you doing?"

"I'll write the letter," he said. "There's no need to humble yourself like this. And you haven't made a fool of yourself," he added with a flare of anger.

"You had no right to do that!"

"As your husband, I had every right," he stated calmly. Now that the offensive letter was destroyed, he felt better. "I'll write something to this effect: 'Dear Mr. Bragg, Your daughter and I have found ourselves to be incompatible. We mutually desire an annulment, providing it meets with your approval. Your daughter is still innocent, if that should be an objection.' Etcetera. There's really no need to go into any further detail."

"Why don't you just sign my name?" Storm flared.

"I doubt they would think you wrote the letter," Brett said easily, sitting on the edge of his desk and picking up his cigar. "Tell me, Storm, why did you protect me?"

Her answer was sullen. "I wouldn't wish anyone dead."

"Dead?"

She turned to him. "Brett, when Pa comes, you have to be ready to hide. If he decides you've wronged me, he'll kill you."

Brett smiled. "Hide?" He said the word as if it were a foreign idea.

"I'm serious!"

He laughed then. "So am I. Why should I hide? You're intact." He frowned. "Aren't you?"

"Pa will probably want to kill you no matter what I say. Can't you understand?"

"Are you intact? Innocent?"

"What?!"

"Are you a virgin?" Brett asked, his tone no longer light, his eyes dark and blazing.

As soon as Storm heard the question, her indignation was lost beneath cold fury. She clamped her teeth together, trembling, so insulted and angry she couldn't speak.

Brett frowned, pierced with disappointment. No answer seemed to be the answer he didn't want. His anger returned full force. He had known it all along, hadn't he? No innocent exploded with passion and climaxed as quickly as she had in a public garden, just from his touch!

"Maybe I *should* let Pa kill you," Storm gritted. *Imbecile!*

"He seems a reasonable man," Brett retorted. *Little tramp!*

"Not only was Pa a Texas Ranger, he's also half Apache. He believes in vengeance, Apache-style."

Brett stared. "What?"

Storm smiled, enjoying what she thought was his fear. "Maybe he'll cut out your tongue, or cut off your fingers. Pa believes in making the punishment fit the crime." She flushed. "You're lucky you didn't . . . that we didn't . . . He'd cut it off!"

Brett barely heard. "You're part Indian?"

"And proud of it. Now maybe you'll listen and hide when he comes to hunt you down."

He couldn't believe it. No wonder she was such a little savage. No damn wonder.

"If you'll excuse me," she said stiffly. He was staring at her as if she were a freak. Now she probably disgusted him.

"You're excused," Brett said, looking away. Part

Apache. It probably explained her striking looks, her unusual form.

Storm paused at the door. "Don't worry," she said as
nastily as possible. "I won't wait up."

His head jerked up. "What does that mean?"

"I feel sorry for the woman or women you keep, to
have to put up with an arrogant bastard like you!"

Anger flooded him. "At least they aren't hypocrites. At
least they don't pretend to be something they're not!" he
shouted.

He was referring to her pretended innocence, but Storm
thought he meant she'd passed herself off as completely
white. "I hope you stay out every night!" she shrieked.
"I can't wait until this nightmare is over!"

"Don't worry," he yelled back as she stormed out. "I
intend to stay out any and every night that I damn well
please. At least some women know how to be women—
not some Texas savage!"

A moment later he heard a door slamming, so loudly
he was sure the walls upstairs shook. He grabbed his
jacket, and being true to his word, stormed out of the
house himself.

Chapter 10

The next morning Storm stared in dismay at her image in the mirror. Her eyes were red. This would never do. Everyone would know she had been crying. Brett would know.

He had been gone only a few hours last night. A few hours, but long enough. Storm told herself she didn't care, that she wasn't crying because of that bastard. She was homesick and alone and lonely. But her excuses sounded hollow even to herself.

There was an ache in her heart, one she wouldn't understand. She kept seeing Brett with some faceless woman, some sleazy, blowzy trollop. She thought bitterly: Good. Anything to keep him out of my bed. What a rutting pig. And a bigot. She was proud of her Apache heritage. It wasn't her fault he hadn't known of it. When she thought how he'd accused her of being a hypocrite, of pretending to be something she was not, a fresh tear welled. Storm furiously blinked it back. He was nothing but some blue-blooded dandy!

She waited until he left for his office, then she went downstairs, ordering her horse saddled and brought around. She couldn't eat, a sure sign that she wasn't herself. Instead she rode Demon for an hour with a groom accompanying her, an Irish lad with a ready grin who viewed her on her horse with awe. Storm didn't mind. She had known Brett wouldn't let her ride alone, and Sian was her own age, although he was a strapping six feet, and armed as well. She was relieved he wasn't an old, brooding fusspot like Bart. Better yet, Sian knew horses, and when she asked questions, he was eager to talk. She liked his brogue.

When it was late enough, Storm and Sian rode to the Farlanes'. Sian moved to help her down, but Storm gave him a cocky grin and leaped down Apache-style in a vaulting motion. His blue eyes went wide. She knew she was showing off, but it felt wonderful. She felt she could enjoy herself with Sian. He was like her brothers.

Marcy didn't have any other callers and hurried into the parlor just moments after Storm arrived, a cry of gladness on her lips. Her expression died the moment she saw Storm's face, pale and red-eyed. She hugged her. "Oh, dear, come, sit down. Lila, bring some refreshments, please."

Storm bit her lip. She thought she was all cried out, but a fresh surge of tears threatened just from being in this kind woman's company. That would never do. She mustn't cry in front of everyone. She smiled wanly instead.

"Do you want to tell me about it?" Marcy asked gently, holding Storm's hand.

"I hate him."

Marcy looked genuinely upset.

"If I had known Paul was forcing him to marry me, I would never have married him. Never."

"Nobody really forces Brett to do anything," Marcy tried.

"They did this time."

"What's done is done," Marcy said softly.

"No. It's not. Brett and I haven't consummated the marriage, and we're getting an annulment." She was shocked at how bitter her words sounded. As if she were hurt and rejected. As if she wanted Brett as her true husband.

Marcy stroked her hair. "Oh, dear. Brett must be in one of his terrible rages. Is he?"

She swallowed. "How did you guess?"

"He's the kind of man who always gets what he wants, and make no mistake, he wants you."

The words were thrilling, but then, with logic, Storm remembered every aspect of their relationship with utter clarity and knew they were false. "No, you're wrong, Marcy."

Lila returned with muffins and croissants, coffee and cream. Storm watched Marcy serve, making the task seem elegant, her hands feminine and sure. Storm couldn't imagine ever being so graceful herself. Her movements were clumsy and rigid. Marcy didn't spill a drop. Storm gratefully sipped the hot, sweet coffee.

"Why are you so upset, dear?"

Storm set down the cup. "I want to go home. I can't stand Brett. On top of everything, he's a damn bigot." Fresh tears rose.

Marcy started. "Now what?"

"I told him Pa's half Apache, that Pa will probably kill him for touching me. Brett told me I was a hypocrite!" She gulped. "Pretending to be something I'm not."

Marcy stared, then comforted her. "Storm, I've never known Brett to be a bigot. That doesn't sound like him at all."

"Those were his exact words. He's angry that I'm not all white; he thinks I was trying to hide my Indian heritage from him on purpose. And he tore up the letter I wrote home. He's so hateful."

Marcy was thinking. "Maybe he was referring to something else. He must have been very angry."

"He's always angry," Storm said, brushing her tears.

Marcy's heart had already gone out to her. Now it went further. The beautiful girl loved Brett, it was as clear as day. Marcy wanted to thrash him, and maybe she would with her tongue. "Why don't you cry, Storm, and let it out."

"No," Storm said, pulling away. "Does Brett have a mistress?"

Marcy froze.

"He does, doesn't he," Storm said, sounding bitter and angry. "He's been out all night both nights."

Marcy gaped. "He went to his mistress on his wedding night?"

Storm tilted her chin. "I refused to let him into my bed, Marcy. Better her than me. I don't care that he sees her, I just can't stand being humiliated in front of the whole damn town."

Marcy was angry. Just because Storm had denied him, he had no right to stomp off in a rage like a little boy. Half the town was probably talking about where Brett had spent his wedding night. His needs weren't that urgent!

"What's she like?" Storm asked.

Marcy was startled. "Dear, if you want to know if Brett has a mistress, you'll have to ask him," she said carefully. She knew that she shouldn't be getting involved in the personal affairs between a husband and wife even if the couple was Brett and Storm, even if they were on the verge on an annulment.

"But you said . . ." Storm stopped. Marcy had indirectly answered her question, but she wasn't satisfied. Of course he had a mistress, she had been sure of it all along. What she really wanted to know was if that was where he had been going these past few nights. How was she going to find that out without asking him directly?

"Well, most men have mistresses," Marcy hedged.

"Does Grant?" Storm realized the impropriety of the question the moment she'd spoken. She flushed. "I'm sorry!"

Marcy smiled. "That's all right. No, he doesn't. The

day Grant takes a mistress is the day he'll lose me forever, and he knows it.''

"He never would," Storm said enviously. "He loves you. You can see it every time he looks at you.''

Marcy knew, then, that she would send Grant to chastise Brett. Not outright. She'd let him pry and wheedle his way first, but if Brett didn't give an inch, she'd make sure Grant told him of the gossip outright. Hopefully, Brett would be ashamed for humiliating his bride, even if they did want an annulment.

"Stay for lunch, Storm. We can go shopping this afternoon.''

Storm was about to say yes, but then she thought of how people would stare at her, people who knew Brett had seen his mistress on his wedding night (assuming he had), and she declined politely. She would spend the day riding with Sian.

Actually, she wanted to ride south to San Diego, then turn east toward Texas. The thought took hold.

"This is a surprise," Brett said.

Grant smiled. "As if it's unusual for us to have lunch?''

Brett toyed with the silverware. His mind drifted to his impossible wife, who wasn't really his wife at all, and the letter he still had to write. He didn't really have time today; maybe he'd write it tonight. What would a few additional days matter?

"Brett?''

He smiled ruefully. "Sorry. Hectic day. You know how Mondays are.''

Grant studied him casually. "I figured with a sweet bride like Storm you'd be on a honeymoon for a few days.''

The change in Brett's attitude was immediate. His face darkened, the muscles going rigid. Even his hands closed like steel traps around the silverware. "Sweet? Yes, as far as taste goes, but that's it. Storm is most definitely not sweet.''

"Trouble in paradise?''

Brett straightened, glaring.

"Just trying to help.''

"Let's order. The roast duck is fantastic.''

"For lunch?''

"I'm starved.''

They ordered, then sat in tense silence, suggesting to Grant that Brett was preoccupied and annoyed. Grant still couldn't believe what Marcy had told him. He decided to go straight for the jugular. "Is it true?''

Brett glanced lazily at him. "Is what true?''

"The rumors I've heard.''

"What rumors?''

"That you spent Saturday night, your wedding night, at Audrey's.''

Brett stared, incredulous, his gaze growing cold. "Jesus Christ! A man can't shit in this town without everyone knowing it!''

"So it is true.''

"It's no one's business but mine,'' Brett said warningly.

"I'm your friend, and when I see you acting like a country jackass, humiliating your bride in front of the entire town, then it's my business to say what I think.''

Brett gritted his teeth and fought for control. His temper was a powder keg these days; it took little to set it off. "Everyone will understand in a few months. We're going to get an annulment,'' he said finally. But he was feeling a twinge of guilt. He shook it aside, remembering the gun, remembering how *she* was the one who had denied him, how *she* was the one who wanted an annulment, *she* was the one who couldn't stand him—the best damn catch in San Francisco!

"Are you sure that's what you want?'' Grant said softly.

Brett stared. "Just because I want to bed her, that's no

reason to marry her," he said crudely. "And, yes, it's what I want. This topic is closed. Here are our meals."

Grant knew he was testing their friendship, but he had to. He saw the way Storm affected Brett—he had seen it that first night she and her father had arrived, dirty and weary from the trail. He had been amused at the sight of the lush girl-woman in buckskins; Brett had been mesmerized. Grant wasn't surprised that Brett had lost all sense of honor and had compromised Storm at the Sinclairs; he remembered how he himself hadn't exactly been an angel when he was chasing Marcy. A man did not ignore social standards like that, did not lose control, did not act the way Brett had been acting ever since the betrothal was announced, unless he was in over his head. Brett just didn't know it yet. And Grant knew his friend. He wasn't a cruel man, maybe a hard one, but God knew, with his unhappy upbringing, it was understandable. Grant was sure Brett was feeling guilty about the gossip, and he wanted him to feel even worse. "Storm called on Marcy this morning."

Brett jerked up his head. His eyes gleamed dangerously. "I see. A conspiracy."

"Storm knows nothing about my coming here, although she did tell Marcy you were getting an annulment."

Brett threw down his fork. "She would air our damn laundry!"

"Brett, relax," Grant said, touching his hand. "I've never seen you like this."

"What else did she say?" Brett demanded, fighting for control.

"Not much. Mostly, she tried not to cry."

Brett sat very still.

"Have you seen her today?"

"No."

"Her eyes are swollen and red from crying."

Brett didn't move, but his eyes flicked to the linen tablecloth. Had she been crying all night? He hadn't heard her. Why had she cried? Because he'd found out the truth, that she wasn't an innocent virgin? Why had she been crying?

"You should be trying to figure out what you've done to make her cry. For God's sake, Brett, she's only seventeen. You treat Leanne St. Clair with kid gloves compared to Storm, and Leanne is a bitch."

"Enough," Brett said, picking up his fork and stabbing his salad. "She's probably crying because she's homesick, or because she hates me."

"It's just not like you to be so unkind," Grant said.

Brett looked up. "It's not every day a man gets blackmailed into marrying against his will, either. Do you blame me for being angry?"

"But who the hell's fault was it to begin with?" Grant persisted.

"Hers!" Brett nearly shouted, slamming his fist on the table and making their glasses jump. "That witch trapped me—believe me, Grant, she's no innocent; she knew what she was doing all along! She trapped me, dammit, and now she realizes she's bitten off more than she can handle and she's changed her mind!" He punctuated that statement with another fist on the table, halting conversation all around them. Brett slapped down his napkin, standing and lowering his voice to a furious whisper. "Well, let me tell you something, my friend. Maybe I've changed *my* mind!" He stalked away.

Grant watched with amazement. Then he smiled, picked up his fork, and continued eating. Marcy would be pleased with him.

Brett went straight home. He was angry that Storm had gone crying to Marcy, blurting out their private business. If she had something further to say, she could say it to him. He left King standing at the hitching post and bounded into the house, bellowing, "Storm!"

There was no answer, so he took the stairs two at a time and barged into her room. She wasn't there. On his way back downstairs, he almost ran down Peter. The man was trying to speak, but Brett cut him off. "Where is my wife?"

"She left this morning on horseback," Peter told him.

"Yes, yes, I know. She went to see Mrs. Farlane." Then he glowered. "You mean she's not back yet?"

"No, sir."

Brett paced the foyer. He pulled out his watch fob; it was almost three in the afternoon. "Peter, what time did she leave here?"

"Around ten, sir."

Brett felt a finger of fear grab his insides. Five hours. She had left five hours ago. He whirled on his majordomo. "She did go with Sian."

"Oh, yes. Sian understands Mrs. D'Archand is never to go riding alone."

Brett experienced a brief but fleeting relief. Sian was good with a pistol, better with a knife, and lethal with his hamlike fists. That was the reason Brett had given the young but capable groom the job of escorting Storm should she ever step out of the house. There would be no repetition of what had happened on the beach a couple of weeks ago. Where in hell were they? "Did she say where she was going after the Farlanes'?"

"No, sir."

She must have stayed at Marcy's, he thought with new relief. It was the only answer. "Send William to the Farlanes' to bring Storm home. He can tell her I'm waiting." With that dictum, Brett removed himself to his study, where he stared out at the blooming azaleas, rhododendrons, and tulips of his garden. Even the dogwoods were in bloom, but he hardly noticed.

William, the coachman, returned twenty minutes later, without Storm. She had left the Farlanes' before noon. Brett was stunned. William didn't move, waiting to be dismissed. Finally Brett found his voice. "Did she say where she was going?"

"No, sir," William said.

Brett stood and waved him away, icy tentacles of fear gripping his bowels, vying with new anger. Now it was almost six hours since she'd gone. Nobody rode for six hours. Where in hell was she?

Something had happened.

Jesus, he thought, rushing through the house and outside, Sian was only twenty, even if he was six feet tall and two hundred pounds. Jesus, there were all kinds of crazy, women-starved scum in the area. "William, saddle King," Brett shouted, then proceeded to do it himself because he was too impatient to wait. He took off at a gallop.

Storm loved the beach. As he thought that, turning in the direction they had once ridden together, the words of her letter came hauntingly back to him: *I hate San Francisco. Nothing has gone right . . . stuffed into corsets and shoes that hurt . . . I lied . . . We never fell in love . . .* Panic rode him as hard as he rode King, panic and guilt and remorse. No matter what, she was his wife, and only seventeen, and he was responsible for her.

Thirty minutes later, when he and King were equally lathered, Brett saw them riding slowly up the beach, toward the path leading over the dunes from where he was surveying the coast. He made out the big black before he could even see Storm, but there was no mistaking the stallion, and that it had a rider. There were two horses, two riders . . . Relief swept him through and through.

He didn't ride down to meet them, for King had been pushed too hard already. But he did go to the trail to wait for them, and when they came into view, he saw that Storm was truly all right, sitting easily, as if she'd been born on that big black stallion. Sian was beside her, oversized on the bay gelding he rode.

Then Brett's relief vanished. Storm's face was flushed and glowing. Her hair was loose, long, golden tendrils falling over her breasts. Her riding jacket was completely unbuttoned, and her shirt was unfastened a good three inches below her collarbone. She and Sian hadn't seen him yet, and they were chatting gaily, merrily, laughing, beaming . . . He couldn't believe it. A huge, hot, hard, impossible rage swept him.

Nobody rode all day.

He would kill Sian. And then he would kill Storm.

They saw him. Storm immediately stopped smiling, an expression that looked like guilt crossing her face. Brett moved King forward, between them. "Where in hell have you been all day?"

Storm looked at him, indignant, then her expression became mutinous. "Where do you think I've been all day, Brett? Where does it *look* like I've been all day?" The last words were gritted furiously.

Her jacket was open, her ripe breasts exposed beneath a thin shirt. Brett noted the faint sheen of perspiration on her chest and face. He looked at her mouth. It didn't look bruised, and the glow from her face could have been from riding for hours on the beach . . . but *nobody* rode all day.

"Go on ahead without us, Sian," Brett said, his voice controlled and deadly. He didn't look at the young man, but sat his horse ramrod straight, staring at his wife. He waited until he knew Sian was gone. Storm's chin thrust up as she waited for the attack.

He rephrased the question. "What have you been doing all day?"

"I went to Marcy's, and then I was riding."

He stared at her mouth again, looking for some swelling, then at her lush breasts. "All day?"

She frowned. "Are you deaf?"

He wanted to hit her. "Your jacket's undone. So is your shirt. Why?"

She stared, her brows wrinkling. "What?"

"Why?"

"Brett, I'm hot."

"Your hair is down."

She stared with dawning comprehension.

"You and Sian get along very well," he said. "I had no idea."

Indignation flared, and her mouth dropped open. A vivid red color—the color of guilt, he thought—flooded her face.

"Did he touch you?" Brett snarled viciously.

"You disgusting lecher!" she shouted, and drove her horse forward.

Thinking she was trying to get past him to escape, Brett moved to block her path. But she drove the stallion right into his, crashing horseflesh against horseflesh, and before he knew it—he just wasn't expecting this kind of reaction— she screamed, a scream that sounded half woman and half Indian, and leaped off her horse—at him.

She leaped viciously, savagely, her face contorted with rage, and they both went flying off their horses and landed on the sand, Brett on his back, Storm on top. He saw she was about to strike, and grabbed both wrists, preventing the small, balled fists from hitting his face. Simultaneously, he jerked up his legs to protect his groin from a lethal knee, and in one deft, practiced movement, he rolled her over and pinned her beneath him so she couldn't move. She was panting and glaring, a wild, spitting animal, her sapphire eyes filled with fury. He was acutely aware of her softness beneath his hardness, of her full breasts crushed beneath his chest, of her open mouth, the soft, fast warm breaths that mingled with his. "Nobody rides all day!" he said.

"All day?" she shrieked. "All day? It wasn't all day— and I do ride all day! Bastard! Pig!"

"Nobody rides all day," he said again, crazed with jealousy. Even he recognized it as jealousy. She wouldn't let him in her bed, but she'd let some groom take her?

"You sicken me," she said, closing her eyes.

There was only one way to find out the truth, he realized. Still holding her wrists, he transferred them to one hand and shoved one knee between her thighs, pushing them open. Her eyes widened as he yanked up her skirts.

"What are you doing?" she cried.

He slid his hand up her wide-legged pantalets, gazing coldly into her eyes. The pants were damp along the insides of her thighs, from knee to groin.

"Brett, no, please," she breathed.

He saw the fear in her eyes, there was no mistaking it, and for a bare moment he hated himself. But no woman was going to cuckold him. With his hand moving so intimately, he felt himself swelling, felt his pulse quickening. He slid his hand into the recesses of her body. He was actually trembling as he moved his fingers over the soft pubic hair in a brief caress. She gasped, eyes widening, and began to struggle. "No!"

"Be still," he rasped, throbbing now, tightening his hold on her. She froze. Brett slid his hand lower, unable to help it, gently caressing her most intimate parts, and felt her shudder. He slid his finger into her. He froze in shock. There was no mistaking her virginity. He had made a mistake, a dreadful mistake. No man's seed was there. She was an innocent. God, what had he done? He removed his hand, feeling the worst sort of heel, and in one efficient movement righted her garments. He stood, pulling her to her feet. "I'm sorry," he said hoarsely.

Her eyes grew bright and shiny, and a tear spilled out, then another and another. "Dammit," he muttered miserably. "I'm sorry, but what in hell was I supposed to think?"

She swiped at the wetness on her face. "You had no right, no right to . . . to . . . do that! I don't lie, Brett!"

He just looked at her. He was feeling terrible for having thought the worst of her, while his body was raging and demanding, straining against his trousers—he wanted his wife. "Your first letter was lies," he said, and he thought about her not being as innocent as she pretended, and felt angry again. He welcomed that emotion.

"I hate you," she said. She turned and mounted Demon. The stallion was sixteen hands, but Storm grabbed the mane and catapulted on as if he were a pony and she a boy. She began trotting away.

For a minute Brett just stood staring after her, trying to assimilate his roiling emotions—desire, remorse, and strangest of all, humility. Then desire won out. He recalled how she had been lying beneath him, soft and warm, how full and magnificent her breasts were . . . and where he'd had his hand. He imagined how it would feel to bury himself deeply in her, as deeply as he could.

He mounted and rode swiftly after her, letting her lead, knowing from the rigidity of her back that she wouldn't talk to him even if he had wanted to converse, which he didn't. He was too embroiled in his own turmoil and hot desire. He looked at Storm's back, at the magnificent cascade of gold and brown hair. Thinking about bedding her naturally made him think about the annulment, which made him recall what he had told Grant. Had he changed his mind about getting the annulment? Why *not* marry for lust? He was certainly never going to fall in love.

She was a magnificent little savage.

Hell, he was crazy. He didn't want to be married. If anything, he should get the annulment and make Storm his mistress. Now *that* was a good, sane idea.

He escorted Storm in brooding silence. For once, he was not a gentleman. Without making a move to dismount himself, he watched as Storm slid from Demon. His eyes never left her until she had disappeared into the house. Then he turned the gray around and headed back into town.

He shut himself up in his office at the Golden Lady with a bottle of his finest brandy. He found himself drinking and staring at the door, but seeing her. He thought about how hot his blood ran for her, and almost changed his mind. Almost went back to the house, to Storm. To his wife.

Then he drained his glass in disgust.

There was a knock on the door. Irritated, Brett got up to answer it. It was Susie. "Brett, Fred Hanks saw you come in and wondered if he could have a word with you over a drink," she said.

"I don't want to be disturbed," he growled, and she hastily retreated while he slammed the door. He leaned against it, brooding. His damn recalcitrant thoughts wouldn't quit. He poured another brandy, then Linda knocked and walked in, uninvited. His jaw tensed.

"Brett, Mary Anne says she's quitting, and that leaves us short a girl tonight. I refuse to work the floor again. Can you talk to her?"

"You're in charge of the girls," Brett said tersely. "You figure out what to do."

"I say we let her go. She's uppity and temperamental—Brett?"

He shoved on his hat and jacket, and strode past her without a word. He slammed out the back entrance and mounted King. The alcohol hadn't eased anything—not his infatuation, not his lust, not his need for the woman who was his wife. And what he didn't need right now was to be bothered by business at the Golden Lady.

He found himself down by the wharves watching the stevedores unloading crates off a merchant ship just arrived from the East. A fat whore with orange hair grabbed his booted foot and offered her wares. Brett smiled slightly.

Two Dutch sailors were arguing across the block; their disagreement soon escalated into a fistfight that became a brawl as another half dozen men joined in. Brett thought it looked like fun.

He paid a gangly boy to watch King and strolled into a crumbling shack with a weathered sign advertising food and ale. The moment he stepped inside, all conversation ceased. Brett looked around. The room was dark, dank, and smoky. Most of the customers were sailors. Two bosomy, haggard women were serving drinks, and the bartender weighed at least two-fifty and was a good half a hand taller than Brett. "Can I help you?" the barkeep asked without expression.

Brett walked forward, removing his hat. "A bottle of your *best* rotgut," he said dryly.

The barkeep met his eyes briefly, then shrugged. Brett took the bottle to a solitary table, shrugged out of his jacket, and downed a few shots. He sighed, leaning back. Conversation resumed. One of the women came over, hanging over him, showing him large, flaccid breasts. "Care fer company, mister?"

"No, thank you," he said easily.

"What a smile," she murmured, then arched her back. "If you change yer mind . . ."

He nodded, watching her saunter off without really seeing her. He drained another shot. Storm. Why did he have to want her so much? What was it about her? He rubbed his face. If he had stayed around tonight, after this afternoon, after having her beneath him like that, after touching her delicate flesh—damn! He was going to fight her every inch of the way. No, fight himself. Fight his attraction for her. Why couldn't she be ugly and meek and boring instead of beautiful and spirited and unique?

Of course, there were benefits to being married. Having a constant companion. A bed partner. A hostess. A mother for his children. He would be the envy of every bachelor in town. She was the most magnificent woman in San Francisco. What were his objections to being married, anyway? How come he couldn't seem to remember them?

Oh, yes. She didn't want him. He wanted her, but she didn't want him.

Just like his mother.

And his father.

But she really didn't have a choice, did she? After all, she was his wife, and she couldn't legally refuse him. If he wanted her, to hell with how she felt—right?

Wrong.

Brett picked up the bottle and was momentarily surprised when his hand closed around air. He tried again, this time successfully. He looked up when a man asked if he could join him.

"Sure," he said. "More the merrier, right?"

The big-bellied seaman sat across from him. "Name's Ben," he said.

"Grab a glass, Ben." Brett grinned. "Hey, doll, bring my frien' here a glass."

They drank in easy silence for a while, Brett thinking about Storm again, reminding himself that his previous thoughts, whatever they were, were wrong. Oh, yes. Something about marriage.

"What you doin' here, mate? You look more like a downtown type."

"Drownin' my sorrows, o' course. Downtown ever'one knows me."

"Women, huh?" Ben was sympathetic.

"Woman," Brett corrected. "The most beautiful, gorgeous, sensuous woman you ever saw. God."

Ben grinned. "She givin' you a good chase?"

"Chase? Hell, yeah, I'd say so, 'specially considerin' she's my wife." Brett grabbed the bottle and refilled their glasses.

"Newlyweds?"

"Very. Damn. Trapped me, she did. Smart gal, huh?"

"An old trick. You're not the first to get it."

Brett started laughing. "That's just it. I haven't got it! Damm it all, I haven't got it yet."

"What?"

"We were caught," Brett said expansively, "in a garden." He leaned forward, a bit too far forward. "My frien' is her cousin and he blackmailed me t' marry her. The thin' is, I was gonna do the hon'rable thin' anyway."

He shook his head sadly and lifted a near-empty bottle, surprised at its lack of contents. He looked up at Ben. "I never bedded her. I married her for her kisses. Now she wants an annulment, an' I agreed, so I have the most beautiful woman in the world in my house, in my bed, an' I can't touch her." He slammed down the bottle, twisted, and waved at the woman for another.

"She's your wife, man," Ben said. "Hell, if I had a beautiful woman like that for a wife, I wouldn't let her go. You want her, you take her. She's yours. She belongs to you."

Brett thought he heard someone say "Wrong," but when he looked around he realized there was no one else with them. "Y'know, I been thinkin' that today myself. She's mine. She belongs to me."

"Damn right. You want her, to hell with what she wants." Ben swigged hard.

Brett followed, slamming down the glass. "Hell, she would like it if'n she jus' tried it."

"Sure she would," Ben agreed.

"Jus' think. Here I am, bein' a gen'man—" He shook his head sadly.

"Hell, man, you're nuts! You gotta teach that gal who's wearing the pants in your family, an' you gotta do it now. You don't do it now, she's gonna be wearin' 'em until the day you die."

"Damn right," Brett said, slapping his palm on the ta-

ble. The barmaid arrived with another bottle. Brett handed
her a few dollars with a grin. "List'n, Ben, this here's for
you. Enjoy." He stood and was shocked to find that it
took a moment to regain his equilibrium.

Awkwardly he picked up his jacket and slipped it on.
He smiled at Ben.

"Don't forget that nice hat," Ben said.

"Oh, yeah." Brett set it on at a jaunty angle. "Take
care, my frien'." He swaggered out unsteadily.

The moment she saw him, all her humiliation returned.

Brett grinned, leaning against her bedroom doorway.
"Hello."

In that first moment she couldn't place what was wrong.
He was slightly askew, when usually his clothes were im-
peccably in place, and he was grinning. It was disarming.
He half pushed himself away from the door, into a standing position, and swayed slightly, then started forward.

Storm sank against the headboard. "Brett, you're
drunk."

He flashed that devastating smile. "Um. And you're
beautiful—have I told you that?"

He reached the side of the bed. Storm found herself
both afraid and strangely exultant. "Brett . . ."

He sank down next to her hip. "So damn beautiful,"
he murmured huskily, his arms going around her.

"Brett, no," she tried, reaching for his arms and re-
sisting without much heart as he pulled her up against the
hard wall of his chest, smiling that drunken, boyish smile.
Something funny was happening to her insides.

"I think I'm bewitched," he slurred, then closed his
eyes and began nuzzling her face with his own.

Storm's heart was thumping. She didn't want him. His
face was coarse and abrasive on hers, but wonderfully so.
His hands moved up and down her arms, feeling surpris-

ingly gentle. He groaned and crushed her, his mouth coming down on hers.

"Please, Brett, don't," she said, pushing him away. To her amazement, he loosened his hold, drawing back and studying her with drunken intentness. She found herself unable to look away.

"I want you," he said finally. "I need you. Give to me, *chère,* please . . ."

She twisted away from his mouth, which landed on her ear. Her relief that he had missed his target soon faded as he began to nibble softly, his breath a faint, feathery touch, sending delicious tremors racing down her body. "Brett." With shock she realized the word sounded like a moan.

"Oh, God," Brett said, pulling her beneath him. "Storm, don't do this to me. Don't send me away. I need you, *chère,* you know that, I need you so much . . ."

There was such a pleading note in his voice, so different from his usual angry command. She froze as he nuzzled her neck, one hand cupping her breast and kneading it gently. She wanted to be angry, and it should be easy after all the horrible things that he had done, but it wasn't. All she could do was feel—heat and hardness, silk and steel— and she was succumbing, unable to resist him.

He was kissing her again and again, tiny, delicious butterfly kisses all over her face, and murmuring at the same time. "Why do you fight me so? Why don't you love me? She didn't want me either—how come it's that way, Storm, how come? It's the ones you don't care about who are eager, when the ones you want, the ones you need, they turn you away, again and again . . ."

She caught his face in her hands, stopping him. "Who, Brett?" she asked, unable to quell her terrible jealousy. "Who turned you away? Who didn't want you?"

He blinked at her, then smiled, closing his eyes and turning his cheek more fully into her hand. He sighed. "Touch me, Storm."

"Who, Brett? Who didn't want you?"

He looked at her. "My mother. My mother sold me to my father. And you know what? It's so funny. For some damn reason, I loved her—even then."

"Oh, Brett," Storm cried compassionately, aghast. "She couldn't have—no mother could sell her own son."

"She did," he said huskily. "The whore did. Come here, darlin'. Um."

Storm wrapped her arms around him and openly returned his kiss. Her hands found his hair, thick and crisp and curling. She spread her thighs gladly as he kneed them apart. Her mind said stop, or at least wait, but her heart and body were in tandem, conspiring . . .

She stroked his back and let him explore her mouth at leisure. Tentatively, shyly, she let her hands drift down to his waist, his hips, lower. They slid over his hard, rounded buttocks. She grew fascinated, freezing, her touch there but motionless. Brett had gone very still, his face buried in the curve of her neck. His breath was warm, arousing. She found that hard curve again and daringly squeezed. A hot jolt seared her and she found herself arching her hips in an unconscious offering.

It took her a moment to realize there was no response.

Storm opened her eyes, her hands still, her heart beating erratically. She peered down at Brett's head. "Brett?"

She tried again. "Brett?"

This time she moved, shaking him with her body. He was a passed-out, dead weight.

Chapter 11

She hadn't seen him all day since she had left him snoring softly in her bed that morning. Storm had no idea when he had gotten up and left, presumably on business. Now, all through supper, he had been quiet and withdrawn. Storm wondered if he even remembered last night—if he remembered how she had encouraged him. Last night he had said he wanted her, tonight he was an indifferent stranger. He had barely looked at her the entire meal. And it didn't just confuse her, it made her angry.

Would she ever understand him?

"Here, sir," Peter said, handing Brett a beer. "This will help."

"What did you put in it?" Brett asked suspiciously, rubbing his temple.

Peter smiled. "You'll feel like your old self in no time." He left.

Brett sipped and met her gaze. This time he didn't look away. Storm didn't either. Finally he put his glass down. "Storm—about last night."

She waited.

He fiddled with his knife. "I . . . ah . . . I was a bit drunk."

"Yes."

He shot a glance at her. "Did . . . ah . . . I hope I didn't disturb you."

176

She gave a slight shrug.

Another quick, shooting glance. "Look, what happened?"

She raised a brow, quelling a smile. "What happened?"

His nostrils flared slightly. "Yes, dammit, what happened?"

"Why, Brett, you said so yourself, you were drunk."

His eyes grew black as he leaned forward. "Dammit, don't play games *now* of all times. Did we— Christ! I woke up in your bed, and I don't remember going there. Did we make love?"

She flushed despite herself. "You were in no shape to do anything except sleep."

He was relieved, disappointed, and still somewhat embarrassed, both for his lack of sobriety and for his lapse of memory. "I apologize for burdening you with myself in such a state."

Storm found herself thinking, I don't mind, then almost gasped at her thoughts. He was doing it again, wheedling her into submission, and she seemed powerless to stop him. She watched him push away his dessert plate. Knowing the meal was over, she felt herself tense with uncertainty. She had to know. "Are you going out tonight?" The instant she said the words, she could have kicked herself for the sarcastic inflection she had put on the word *out*.

He smiled slightly, a warmth that reached his eyes, making Storm uncomfortable, making her fluttery, and she frowned back. The smile broadened, and he put down his coffee cup. When he spoke, his voice was seductive. "Does this mean you care?"

"No," she threw back, "it means I'm curious."

"Only curious?"

"Only curious."

"If you make me a better offer"—his voice grew husky—"I'll gladly stay."

Being naive, it took her a few seconds to understand. She blushed, knowing he would come to her bed if she invited him. "Do you need to . . . to do it every night?"

Brett smiled. "Do what?"

She blushed harder. "Nothing," she mumbled.

Brett fastened his eyes on her. She was wearing a simple skirt and blouse, modestly cut, revealing only the flat part of her upper chest. But her hair was loose, with long curls waving over and around her breasts, and he had the strong urge to lift a strand, wrap it around his hand, pull her close. "Make me an offer," he said huskily.

Her lips parted as she stared back. Her hair was too beautiful to resist. He picked up a heavy, silken strand, coiled it slowly around his wrist, never taking his eyes from her face. She didn't move. The coil grew tight, and he used it as a leash, pulling her head toward him. Her eyes widened. So did her mouth.

His lips were soft covering hers, but there was nothing soft about the jolt that shook him from his head to his toes. The blast of desire had the intensity of dynamite, frightening him with its overwhelming strength. But he deepened the kiss, placing one hand on her shoulder, kneading her flesh, slipping his tongue over and around her lips, teasing their joining, then deftly sliding inside. His tongue touched hers. She yanked away but was pulled up short by her own hair, still coiled and held in his hand.

"Release me," she demanded breathlessly.

"To hell with the annulment," Brett said, his voice deep and uneven.

"Oh, no," Storm said, her eyes flashing defiantly. "Oh, no, I'll never be your wife. Never! One minute you want me, the next you don't. I'm going home as soon as Pa comes."

Her enthusiasm at the prospect of leaving him was a wonderful damper on his lust; he felt the easing of the fullness in his loins as miraculously and quickly as it had appeared. He slipped his hand out of her hair. "Please lower your voice," he said when he trusted his own to sound normal. "Servants gossip."

"To hell with them, to hell with you!" she shouted, jumping up and knocking the chair over. She wiped her mouth with the back of her hand, her face wrinkled in repugnance, revulsion. No woman had ever been repulsed by him, not by his touch, certainly not by his kisses. It was overwhelmingly annoying, irritating, irking, anger-inducing. Brett stood as she fled up the stairs.

Incredibly, he still wanted her. He knew he could seduce her—he could seduce any woman. Within five minutes he would have her trembling and whimpering beneath his hands and mouth. The shrinking fullness in his loins began to reverse itself, and he took a deep breath, seeking rationality.

He hadn't had a moment's peace since he married her. With that thought, he strode grimly through the house. He would never know the meaning of the word *peace* again if he stayed married to her. He knew it beyond a doubt. The woman was too savage, too untamed. The result of her Apache blood, no doubt. Good God! Of all Indians for her to be descended from, no tribe could be worse. He knew all about Apaches—they had been raiding south into Sonora from the mountains for several centuries. Raiding and killing. He remembered how she had attacked him yesterday, and how his dilemma over her had propelled him into a drunken binge. It was starting to come back—how he had, in his temporary insanity, decided to consummate the marriage. God! He didn't need this—not for a woman.

Storm had run upstairs, furious and shaking, ignoring another feeling, one of remorse. This time she was going to make sure. She had almost forgiven him for everything after seeing him so vulnerable last night. Not only had she almost forgiven him, she remembered, she had also nearly given him everything he wanted. Well, no more. He ran hot and cold, and even when he was hot he only wanted to use her, the way he used other women. How could she forget the way he'd treated her yesterday on the beach? They were married, and it was okay for him to visit his mistress, but she couldn't even ride with the groom. She changed in seconds into her split skirt, then waited at the window. The bastard was going out again. She couldn't believe it.

Make me a better offer, he'd said in that rich, low voice. *I'll gladly stay.*

Wearing her moccasins, Storm ran silently downstairs. If she could track a deer across rock flats, she could trail Brett through a bustling city. She was going to catch him in the act and throw it in his face. And use it to force an annulment and tell her pa, and maybe Derek would kill Brett. Right now she was mad enough to help spill his blue blood.

She followed Brett on his big silver stallion at an easy dog trot, the Apache's favorite gait. Her father had told her how Apaches could run for seventy miles like that, day after day, if they had to. He'd done it himself, to rescue her mother, once long ago. In comparison, trotting across town was nothing.

She was breathing a bit hard, but was otherwise unaffected when Brett dismounted in front of a small house with a white picket fence, surrounded by other modest homes with modest yards and fences. The house made Storm frown as she hid in the shadows up the block, because it didn't look like the home of a harlot, but of a family. Brett disappeared inside. Storm ran to the edge of the yard, climbed over the fence, then, keeping low, ran across the small yard and hid behind an oak tree that partially shielded curtained French doors. She peered inside and caught a glimpse of Brett walking past the doorway, apparently upstairs. She leaned against the tree to think—for all of one second. Then she looked up, leaped for a branch, caught it with both hands. She swung her feet up easily until she was clinging upside down like a monkey, then righted herself. She was as good at climbing trees as at riding and shooting. If Brett wasn't visiting his mistress, she would actually be enjoying herself. She started climbing.

Inside, Brett felt both irritated and pensive as he slowly reached the top of the stairs. He didn't really want to be here. He hadn't seen Audrey since his wedding night, so not wanting to see her was out of character—he liked frequent sex. But the past few nights, except for last night, he'd brooded into a whiskey glass in his office at the Golden Lady, not trusting himself to be at home and so near *her*. Her. His damn vixen wife. God, if only she'd invited him up to her room . . . He took a deep breath. That thought brought all kinds of surging desire to the fore.

"Brett, darling." Audrey smiled.

"Hi," he said, kissing her cheek. They were standing on the threshold of her room, he frowning.

"Is everything all right?"

He immediately thought of Storm. "Hah."

"Let me get you a drink," she said, moving to the decanters on the sideboard. "You look like you need it."

I need Storm, he thought, then was shocked at his wayward mind, and furious at himself, too. He walked to the window, unable to get her image out of his head, so that when she actually appeared in the oak tree he was facing, for the briefest moment he thought he was still imagining her. But as they stared through the window into each other's eyes, as shock crossed her face, as he realized she was real, not a figment of his imagination—

They gaped at each other.

And moved simultaneously.

She turned and started to scramble down the tree, but he had already thrust open the window and was lunging out and onto a branch, which groaned under his weight. She was clinging to the trunk like a monkey, and he could hear her harsh breathing, hear the scraping of bark, the rustling of leaves as she frantically descended. He found a new foothold, but when the branch snapped, he jerked his foot back up, seeking another. He started down after her, his feet almost on top of her descending head. Then he heard her cry out. His gaze went from the next foothold he was seeking, to her—except that she wasn't there.

"Storm!" he shouted, freezing as she fell as if in slow motion through the branches, his heart coming into his throat and choking him.

She landed on her back with a loud thump, her eyelids closing, shutting out the blue fire and blue fear.

"Storm!" he shouted. Ignoring his own lack of skill and his heavier weight, he frantically half slid, half climbed down the tree, dropping the last eight feet to land on his hands and knees beside her prone figure.

His heart was beating wildly. He straddled her, took her face in his hands—it was so cold. "Storm? Storm?" She was so lifeless. He didn't want to move her, not if she'd broken anything; he gently touched a forefinger to her throat and found a slow but steady pulse. "Thank God!"

His knees were on each side of her hips, not touching, and he cupped her face with both hands, not lifting or moving her head. "Storm? Storm? Wake up, sweetheart. Wake up, *chère*. Storm?"

Her eyes opened. Even in the dimness of night, he could see how unfocused they were. "Are you all right?" he rasped.

She focused on him. Her eyes closed. "Storm!"

She moaned, her eyes opening again. "I don't think anything's broken," she said finally, shakily.

"Are you sure?"

"Yes."

Relief ebbed; anger flooded in. "What in hell were you doing?" he roared.

"Spying," she said in that same weak voice.

He stared, then had to smile, reluctantly. "I told you," he said, stroking her soft face with a thumb, "you just had to make me a better offer."

Tears welled in her eyes.

"*Chère,*" he said huskily, "don't cry." He used his thumb to brush the tears away. "Next time you want to know where I'm going, please ask."

Their gazes held. Then, after an enigmatic silence, Storm said, "That's the first time I've ever heard you say please."

He smiled, shifting his weight off her. "Can you sit up?"

She nodded. He started to help her rise, but she moaned, and he instantly let her lie back down. "You're not all right," he said accusingly.

"Brett! Brett! What's going on?"

Storm felt Brett stiffen. She stiffened, too, and raised herself to her elbows, straining to see as Brett turned to speak. "Go back inside, Audrey. I need to borrow your carriage. Please send it around."

"Should I get a doctor? Who is it?"

"Audrey—" Brett started, his voice authoritarian.

Storm sat up without realizing it, sat and stared at the incredibly gorgeous, *short* woman holding the lantern, bathed in the glow of lights from the house. "Aren't you going to introduce us, Brett?" she asked as bitingly as she could, nausea rising up in her. She couldn't compete with that woman! Not ever!

"Inside," Brett was saying, his tone harsh. "Now, Audrey. Storm, lie back down," he said, his voice softening as he slipped one arm behind her and pushed her back down.

Storm complied, but it was too late; she and the woman had made eye contact, and Storm had seen the woman's startled understanding when Brett called her by name. More nausea rose. She was dizzy. His mistress was petite and curved and beautiful and feminine and delicate— everything Storm wasn't.

"Yes, Brett," Audrey said softly, dutifully, disappearing.

Storm was going to be sick. She wrenched over, retching. After she had finished, she became aware that Brett had his hands on her, supporting her gently. She wanted to weep. The desire grew stronger when he started stroking her hair. "Don't," she moaned.

His hand stopped. A long moment passed. Storm kept seeing the beautiful woman while fighting waves of dizziness and nausea. Then Brett spoke, his voice soft, low, worried. "The carriage is here." He lifted her easily, and Storm turned her face into his chest. He carried her to the coach, stepped up, sat down, cradling her on his lap. For some reason, being held like that made her lose all control. She started to cry, very softly.

"Are you in pain?" he asked instantly, his body tensing beneath hers, his arms warm and hard around her.

"No," she said through the tears. "My head aches."

"Don't cry, please," he said softly, holding her closer against his chest so she could feel his heartbeat against her breast. She shut her eyes, her face buried in the crook of his neck and shoulder. "Why are you crying, Storm?"

She shook her head. She couldn't talk. The gentleness of his voice merely encouraged her ragged emotions. But she felt his hands, stroking, reassuring, and just before a welcoming blackness took her, she thought that he whispered, "I'm sorry, *chère.*"

She was still unconscious an hour later.

Brett stood next to her, butterflies winging through his heart as he looked at her pale face, so serene right now, as he'd never seen it before, while Doc Winslow examined her. "Well?" Brett said, his voice tense. "Why is she still unconscious? Is she going to be all right?"

"Relax, Brett, your beautiful bride is in one piece."

"What does that mean?" Brett demanded.

"No broken bones, but she does have a concussion. There's a lump back here the size of an orange."

"That can be serious," Brett said, not moving, his voice strangled.

"Not if she has a very quiet week. I want her in bed for the next three days. After that she can have visitors, but only for short periods. No walking, no riding. Separate bedrooms. Lots of rest."

Brett frowned, thinking how he would keep Storm inactive for a full week. "She'll fight me hand and foot," he muttered.

"No fighting," Winslow said. "I want her kept quiet."

"She's got the worst temper I've ever seen."

Winslow smiled. "Don't rile it."

"Easy for you to say," Brett murmured, looking at the unconscious girl on the bed.

"You can give her some laudanum drops for the pain, if it gets too bad," Winslow continued.

"What pain?"

"She'll have a few headaches."

Brett moved to the bed and readjusted the covers, looking down at her, studying her. "Are you sure it's just a concussion? She vomited back there."

"It's just a concussion," Winslow assured him. "No need to come, Brett. I can see myself out."

Winslow left, and Brett sat down on the side of Storm's bed. She didn't stir. He took her hand and held it. It was warm and dry, callused, not silken and soft. He held it, felt it, studied it. It was so strange seeing her like this— she seemed young and vulnerable. He brushed her thick hair away from her temples, then leaned forward without thinking and kissed the spot he had cleared. A tingle of delight and desire swept through him.

I won't do it, he thought. I won't annul this marriage, and that's that.

Having made up his mind, he felt immensely better. He would not analyze it further. Not one iota further. If he thought about it, he'd get furious with himself and start vacillating or change his mind. She moaned.

He stroked her hair. "Storm, *chère*, sleep." His voice was low and melodious. "Shhh, sleep."

Her eyes fluttered open in confusion. "Oh."

"Are you in pain?"

She swallowed. "My head aches."

"Do you want some laudanum?"

She closed her eyes for a moment. "Yes, thank you."

Brett prepared the drops without rising; everything was on the bedside table. "Do you want to put on a nightrail, or do you mind sleeping in your shift tonight?"

Storm frowned, sighed. "I don't care." She watched him. He smiled slightly, slipped one arm behind her, and propped her up. With the other he held the glass, tilting it for her to drink. When she had finished, he set it aside.

"You're not mad?"

Brett looked at her. "We'll talk about everything in a few days," he said. "Storm, if you need anything tonight, more laudanum, I'll be right next door."

Her eyes narrowed. "Why?"

"Because that's where I sleep."

"You could have fooled me," she said, trying to lift her chin, her voice still weak.

To her amazement, Brett did not jump to the bait and get angry. "That's where I sleep," he said firmly.

"You can go back," Storm murmured. "To her . . . fine with me . . ."

Brett felt the beginnings of anger. "Why do you provoke me so?"

"Very beautiful," she murmured, and fell asleep.

He frowned. Did she do it on purpose? Did she enjoy scrapping with him? Was that it? No woman had ever baited him before, much less so incessantly. But she was like no other woman. She was completely, irrevocably, unique.

He moved to his bedroom, keeping the door between

their rooms open. He couldn't sleep. Three times in the night he went to check on her, and every time she was sleeping peacefully.

Storm sighed. The smell of maple syrup permeated her nostrils. Pancakes, she thought, Mother makes the best pancakes . . . She strained for the sound of her brothers, at least Rathe, who was never quiet, always teasing, and Nick's drier tones, her father's amused ones, the clatter of plates, footsteps. The aroma grew stronger, and Storm knew she had overslept; it was time to get up, she had missed her morning chores. She didn't care, not today; she felt wonderful, warm, secure, loved . . . She stretched, sighing, stretched again, and opened her eyes.

For one instant she was utterly confused as she stared into the dark, handsome face of the man standing by her bed, holding a tray.

Then comprehension and a terrible, devastating disappointment fell over her. She wasn't home. She was here, married to this man. This man who disliked her and had a beautiful mistress. Brett.

"Good morning," he said, smiling.

When his gaze roamed her leisurely, Storm realized she had kicked off the covers, and she reached down and pulled them up, sitting. She looked at the tray in his hands.

"Hungry? I brought you some breakfast." He smiled again. Her heart did a flip-flop, and something liquid and warm raced through her body to its very core.

"Starved," she said, regarding him suspiciously.

He set the tray carefully on the bed. "Why are you looking at me like that? Did you sleep well?"

"Like I was dead," she muttered, tearing her glance away. Why was he looking at her as if he were trying to see into her soul? Why was he here, anyway?

Brett chuckled. "Cook makes the best pancakes in town."

"They smell great," she said, and proceeded to eat. She caught him watching, and wished she had had a chance to wash her face and comb her hair, which must be a tangled nest. She looked up again—he was still staring at her, sitting at her knees. "Do I look that strange?"

"What?"

"You're staring."

He smiled slightly, lazily. "It's not unusual for a man to stare at a beautiful woman."

She colored. "Brett." It was a protest.

"Finish eating."

She resumed eating, totally flustered now. Why had he said something so blatantly untrue? What was he up to, disarming her before he started in on her for last night's escapade?

Had he gone back to *her* last night?

"How do you feel today?" he asked when she had finished.

She sipped coffee. "Great." She took a breath. "Okay, let's get it over with."

"Excuse me?"

She raised her head defensively. "I know why you're here."

"Oh?" He raised one brow in that infuriating, superior manner of his.

"To give me hell."

He smiled. "You love fighting, that has to be it!"

"Only when you're my opponent."

He frowned. "I brought you breakfast, that's the sole reason I'm here. Well, that and to see how you feel today."

She met his gaze searchingly. "Betsy could bring me breakfast."

"Most wives would be thrilled to have their husbands bring them breakfast in bed."

"Not this one."

"You are the most uncharitable woman I've ever met," he muttered darkly.

"I don't want charity, not from you or anyone."

"Storm, can we be civil? Why do you always snipe at me?"

"Snipe?" She threw aside the covers and swung her long, half-bare legs over the side of the bed.

Brett caught them, preventing them from reaching the floor. His large hands on her thighs felt very, very warm.

"You're to stay in bed for three days."

"What?"

"Complete bed rest for three days, Storm. And you're confined to the house for a whole week. You have a concussion."

She stared. "You're punishing me for spying on you!"

He stood abruptly, disgusted. "Don't be foolish. Those are Dr. Winslow's orders, and you're obeying them."

"I feel fine."

"You are staying in bed."

"May I use the chamber pot?"

"Of course," he said, not moving.

She sank back against the pillows. "Do you or do you not have something to say to me about last night?"

He smiled slightly, a faint quirking at the corners of his mouth. "Yes, in fact, I do. Next time you want to know where I'm going, please ask."

"You would have told me it's none of my business," Storm said darkly.

"Possibly," Brett said. "Dammit, Storm! You could have broken your neck!"

"I wish I had," she answered, staring past him at the wall.

His jaw clenched. "I'm that bad, am I? Do you know that every single woman in this town would kill to be in your place?"

"I'm not every woman," Storm retorted. "And I would kill *not* to be where I am."

They stared, Brett's frustration darkening his face. "You just won't give a goddamn inch, will you?"

She didn't answer.

Brett turned to the door. "I'll check on you at suppertime." He gave her a hard look. "If I find you've gotten out of bed—" He stopped. "Look, promise me, please, you'll obey the doctor's orders."

She thought about it.

"Storm, I'll beat you black and blue once you're well if you don't take it easy!"

"All right," she said reluctantly.

He slammed the door behind him.

The moment he was gone, Storm felt the sinking weight of depression. He had actually been kind to her for a moment until she had started baiting him. But why? Why the abrupt change? Then the events of last night came flooding back to her in their full horror, and she didn't care that she had been rude and uncivil. The image of the auburn-haired woman, Audrey, hit her full force. So little. So damn beautiful. Storm wanted to cry.

Instead, she had an instant headache, so she lay back down, closing her eyes and trying not to think. It was impossible. Brett's image haunted her, dark and wickedly handsome, intense and unsmiling. Her mind began playing games: she saw Audrey, dainty and delicate, in Brett's arms, his mouth hard on hers, kissing her ravenously. Storm moaned.

Still, her day wasn't as endless as she would have expected. After a morning bath, she fell asleep and slept right through half the afternoon. She ate a little lunch, then read the *Illustrated Varieties*, the city's foremost newspaper.

"Storm?"

She realized it was dark outside, and she had fallen

asleep again. Brett's voice tugged at her, soft, hesitant, as if he wasn't sure whether or not to wake her. She heard him say, "Just put that down here, Betsy. She'll probably be hungry when she wakes up."

"Yes, sir."

"Did she stay in bed all day?"

"She slept most of it away, sir, poor girl."

Silence followed, then Storm heard footsteps and her door opening and closing. She could smell roast beef. She opened her eyes, expecting to be alone. She wasn't.

Brett sat sprawled negligently in a chair, clad in tight riding breeches, gleaming knee-high boots, and a loose linen shirt. His hair was disheveled, and he was staring out the window, giving her a perfect view of his profile.

Storm watched him surreptitiously, beginning with the classic, chiseled profile. Then her gaze drifted, and she found herself studying his legs. She had seen them clad in soft doeskin only once before, for a brief moment. Not like now, when she could stare unnoticed. His thighs were hard and muscled and looked powerful enough to crush her—should she ever get between them. She had a blazing memory of the first time he had kissed her on the beach, of his mouth hard and demanding, of his male hardness pressing eagerly against her belly. Her gaze unthinkingly followed the path of her thoughts. There was no hard, jutting swell now, just a suggestive bulge . . .

She swallowed, feeling her heart race, and glanced back at his face. She gasped and went a hundred shades of red because he was staring at her now, amused and interested. She wanted to die. Better death than to be caught looking at him with such shameless yearning.

"You're awake," he said.

"Yes."

"I didn't mean to wake you."

"That's all right."

"I thought I'd keep you company while you eat."

"That's all right," she said again, not able to look him quite in the eye.

"Eating alone is . . ." He hesitated. "Lonely."

She did look at him then. She couldn't imagine Brett being lonely, but she couldn't imagine him getting staggeringly drunk, either. Or as a little boy, whose mother had sold him . . .

He smiled coaxingly. She found herself smiling back tentatively.

He set the tray on her lap and uncovered the dishes for her. Storm wasn't very hungry, not after being in bed all day. She picked at the meal.

"Are you feeling ill?"

"No, I'm fine."

He scrutinized her. "You always eat like a horse."

She wondered if she should be insulted. "I've slept most of the day."

"I know, Betsy told me."

She knew he knew. She was about to push the tray away, then noticed a small wrapped box on it. "What's this?"

He shrugged.

Storm glanced at him, then tore off the paper. It was a small box of chocolates. She loved chocolates. They were a very rare treat, a once-a-year kind of thing, and she actually squealed in delight.

"It's only candy," he said, but he was smiling.

"I love chocolate, and I never get to eat it. Thank you!" She glowed and popped one in her mouth. "Want one?"

"No, thanks," he said. "Is it good?"

"Very," she said, smiling again.

"Such a simple thing," he murmured, shaking his head in bemusement. "Shall I keep you company for a while?"

She hesitated, wanting to say yes, surprised that she wanted him to stay but too proud to admit it. She shrugged.

He proceeded to inform her of the local news and gossip. Sam Henderson, recently from New York, had invested in a thousand acres north of town for a vineyard. The common consensus was that he was crazy. Potter's Emporium had been sold, but no one knew to whom. There had been a big brawl last night at a disreputable saloon, resulting in two men dead and five seriously injured. Barbara Watkins was expecting, Leanne St. Claire was being courted by James Bradford, there was a party tomorrow night at the Denoffs', but, of course, they couldn't go now. He had stopped by Paul's and told him about the accident, and Paul was going to come calling as soon as he was allowed, in another two days.

"You told him?" Storm gasped, horrified.

"I told him you fell from your horse."

Storm looked at him as if he were crazy.

"I also ran into Grant and told him the same thing— they both looked at me the way you are now. However, I didn't think it was anyone's business that you fell out of a tree."

"You mean that I fell out of your mistress's tree."

"Yes."

The rapport between them was suddenly gone, in its place tension, palpable and sharp. Storm had the feeling that Brett was waiting for her to apologize. She would— when hell froze over.

He finally stood. "I'm keeping you up."

"You can go to the Denoffs' without me."

"I'd rather not." He paused at the door. "I'll see you in the morning."

"Have a good time." She didn't premeditate the comment or the tone, which was very snide.

He had been about to open the door; now he stopped and turned to face her. "What does that mean?" He thought he knew. He had never heard such a sneer from a woman before, but when he looked at her, her expression was angelic. Except for the spitting sapphire blue of her eyes.

"It means have a good time," she said in a normal tone, flushing.

"*Exactly* what the hell does that mean?"

She raised her chin. "It means I know *exactly* where you're going."

"Oh?" His tone was cool.

"Yes."

"Enlighten me as to where you *think* I'm going." It was a harsh command.

"To *her.*"

The muscles in his face ticked.

"But I don't care—I'm glad. As long as you leave me alone."

He counted to ten, then continued to twenty. "For your information," he said slowly, "I'm going to go downstairs to my study to read some papers I didn't get to today— because I lost an hour bringing you breakfast this morning." His eyes were black flames.

She was momentarily speechless, but he pressed on, losing his precarious control. "Why, Storm? Why do you push me over the deep edge every time? Why even bring her up? Why ruin the pleasantness we just shared?"

"Oh? Is not bringing her up going to make her go away?"

"Is that what you want?"

"No!" she shouted, lying and knowing it. "I send you to her! Go! Go and bed her—I don't care!"

Brett stood immobile with clenched fists. "Maybe that's the goddamn problem."

She started to cry. "Just go away—just leave me alone!"

"Gladly," he said, and slammed the door.

Chapter 12

"Marcy!"

Storm had never been so glad to see anyone in her life.

"Oh, Storm, dear." They hugged.

"Hello, Storm," Grant said from behind his wife. "Recovered from your fall?"

Knowing how close Grant and Brett were, Storm flushed but accepted his kiss on the cheek anyway. "Yes," she managed.

"I'll leave you two alone," Grant said. "Where's Brett, in the study?"

"I have no idea," Storm said a touch bitterly.

"Never mind, I'll find him." Grant left the parlor.

"Are you all right?" Marcy asked.

Storm hated being reminded that Brett existed. Where was he anyway? Where had he been these past two days? Three, if you counted today, which was almost over. She had told him to leave her alone, but she had no idea that his doing so would make her angry, miserable, and wretched in general. Not once had he appeared since their last argument, not once!

"Storm, sit down," Marcy said, taking her hands and pulling her onto the sofa. "Well, you look fine."

"I am fine. I've still got three days to go before I'm allowed to leave the house."

"Concussions aren't to be treated lightly."

"I'm so glad you came," Storm burst out. "You're my only friend!"

"Oh, Storm, not true."

"Yes, it is. Paul lied. He betrayed me. He forced Brett to marry me, and now we're both miserable. Marcy, you're my only friend." She was starting to feel sorry for herself.

"What about Brett?"

"Don't even mention that bastard's name to me."

Marcy frowned. "Storm, how on earth did you fall off your horse?"

Storm started laughing. "I didn't fall off my horse. I fell out of a tree!"

"A tree?"

"Yes! And guess whose tree it was?" The laughter had stopped, and tears swam in her eyes.

"Whose?" Marcy asked gently.

"His mistress's tree." It was a flat declaration.

"What?"

"I was spying on him, but, dammit, I had to know for sure if that's where he goes at night—and believe me, it is. Oh, Marcy, I saw them together. And she's so beautiful!"

Marcy was so furious that for a moment she couldn't speak. She realized Storm was trying not to cry, so she pressed her head onto her bosom and stroked her hair. "It's all right, dear. Cry."

"I never cry," Storm said vehemently, lifting her head. "Never. But I've cried so much since I came here . . . I hate him so much."

"You don't mean that," Marcy said.

"I do. Do you know I haven't seen him, not once, in three days? Not once. But I'm glad—we'd just fight anyway. God, I can't wait till Pa comes to take me home."

Half an hour later, Marcy excused herself and marched through the house to the study. The door stood ajar. She rapped briskly and strode in, giving her husband a brief glance. Then her eyes went to Brett, shooting daggers. "I want to talk to you, Brett."

Both men had risen, but Brett's expression grew startled at her tone. "Marcy, hello—"

"How can you be such a brute? Don't you realize Storm's only seventeen, a child, alone in a strange town, with no friends?"

Brett had straightened, the shock disappearing now, a hard expression coming over his face. "You're trespassing, Marcy."

"She's in the salon crying, dammit!"

Brett started—as surprised by her language as by what she'd said. "Is she hurt?" he asked quickly.

"Her feelings are hurt. Can't you think about her feelings for once instead of your own? Can't you leave that damn mistress of yours alone for a few days and woo your wife? Do you even care that she's still alive?"

"You've gone too far!" Brett exploded. "My mistress is none of your business, and my relationship with Storm has nothing to do with you!"

"I think the sooner her father comes for her the better," Marcy shouted back. "You haven't even poked your head in her room to see her in three days. You make me want to wring your wretched neck."

"She told me to stay away," Brett shouted back. "Every time I try and do something nice she throws it back in my face. She's the most ungracious little wretch . . ." He grew calm. "I stayed away for her health, not because I don't care. Every time we're in the same room we start fighting. Why is she crying?"

"Because you've neglected her," Marcy said softly.

He frowned. "That's silly. She told me to leave her alone."

"Oh, Brett, you fool, sometimes when a woman says one thing she means another, especially when she's as proud as Storm is."

Brett stared as if trying to comprehend something completely alien and impossible to understand. "Do you really think she's crying because of me?"

"I know so."

Brett ran a hand through his hair. His heart had done a funny flip at the thought. The past few days had been hell. He had stayed away not because she'd told him to in a fit of anger, but because he wanted her to get well and was afraid she'd suffer a relapse from their fighting. But he'd asked Peter and Betsy half a dozen times a day if she was all right and had everything she needed. At night, when she was asleep, he had peered in on her, the action strangely reassuring, as though, if he didn't, he would wake to find that having Storm in his life was nothing but a dream. He looked at Marcy, no longer angry with her, then hurried from the room.

Storm wasn't in the salon. He knocked lightly on her bedroom door. "Storm? It's me, Brett." There was no answer. He swung open the door. She had been standing very still by the fireplace, but as he entered, her head turned, like a startled doe's. She was wearing a pale blue silk gown, modestly cut, with creamy lace edging the neckline and wrists. Her hair was loose except for a matching ribbon that kept it away from her face. Her eyes found his; they were wary. Brett managed a slight smile, but his heart was hammering against his ribs. He had the intense urge to sweep her into his arms and just hold her. He had never wanted to just hold a woman before. He quietly shut the door behind him. For a moment neither one spoke; they merely regarded each other.

"You're looking well," he said softly, then smiled. "A terrible understatement. You're as stunning as ever."

To his surprise, her mouth trembled, and she glanced away, into the fire, her eyes suspiciously shiny. He moved toward her. She looked at him with that frightened expression again and stepped farther away. Now she stood at the window, he at the hearth. "What is it?" he asked, his tone still soft and alien to his ears.

"What do you want?"

He had the feeling she said it as rudely as she could. The thought produced a glimmer of anger in him. He quenched it. "Marcy said you were crying."

"That traitor," she said, clenching her fists.

"Tell me why."

She faced him, her eyes overly bright. "Let me go home now, Brett. I miss my family terribly, so terribly."

He heard himself say, "I can't."

"I won't let Paul ruin you, I swear!"

He half grimaced. "That's not it."

"Please!"

He came toward her then, and she stumbled back against the windowsill, her breasts rising and falling rapidly—in fear, agitation? He stopped inches from her, close enough to feel her body's heat. He held her gaze and wouldn't relinquish it. "I don't want an annulment," he said.

"What?"

His hand went to her cheek and cupped it. "I don't want an annulment," he said again, huskily. His other hand found her other cheek and he held her face tenderly, his senses singing.

"Brett . . ." It was a whisper, possibly frightened. Her sapphire eyes were huge and tremulous.

They were so close. Her full mouth, the color of berries, was trembling. He was starting to tremble, starting to feel the force of his desire, which was overwhelming. "I'm bewitched," he said, and lowered his lips to hers.

She didn't move. He kissed her very softly, very tenderly, a warm but firm caressing. His tongue stroked her full lower lip, again and again. She shuddered. He slipped his tongue into her mouth, seeking and exploring the texture of her teeth, her inner cheeks, her gums. He thrust deeper, holding her face more tightly, and deeper still.

When her tongue rose timidly to parry with his, a jolt of desire shook him. With tremendous will, he stepped slightly away from her, though he didn't release her face.

Her eyes were closed. Her lashes were almost black, long and spiky, and they fanned against her golden skin. Her lips were slightly bruised, still parted, begging for another kiss. The nostrils of her perfect nose were flared. He had never seen such striking perfection in a woman. She opened her eyes.

He smiled, crinkling the corners of his eyes. "I'm not supposed to excite you, *ma chère.*"

She regarded him intensely, making his desire rage all the more. God, how he wanted her, now, right now. He released her. "Don't say anything," he said. He was afraid she'd spoil the moment. He smiled again, then turned and walked out.

She was stunned. Not by his words, but by her body's reaction to his kiss, the tingling of her lips, the wonderfully searing currents racing through her to her loins. Then understanding penetrated. Still standing at the window, she was struck by what he had said. *I don't want an annulment.*

She became rigid. He didn't want an annulment, but what about her! It was so typical, so damn typical of Brett—he was making a decision by himself that affected the both of them, one that affected the rest of their lives. How dare he!

And why was an inner corner of her mind secretly exhilarated? She shoved that unwanted emotion away, burying it beneath anger at his high-handedness. Had he ever sent the damn letter to her parents? Somehow, she thought not.

Storm paced, working herself up to a fury, waiting for him to come upstairs to bed. She couldn't imagine spending the rest of her life with Brett. What had changed his mind? Some whim of the moment? And then another thought struck her. If he no longer wanted an annulment, then that kiss was just the forerunner of other things to come—consummation of the marriage. At that thought, her breath stuck in her throat and her heart leaped. She could feel his hands, his mouth on her breasts . . . I am so shameless, she thought.

She had heard that her father was quite a scoundrel before he met and married her mother. So was Nick. It seemed to run in the family, she thought, but it was not proper for her, a woman, to be so wanton. She wished fervently that she could be the old Storm, the one who'd blackened Lennie Willis's eye when he'd dared to kiss her. The one whose body belonged totally and wholly to herself. Not this Storm, this strange person in ridiculous gowns, married to a stranger she despised . . . but desired.

So absorbed was she in her own thoughts, it took her a moment to realize Brett was in his room. Sucking in her breath for courage, she opened the door between their rooms and stepped inside.

He was standing by the foot of the bed, bare-chested. His head shot up and he turned, a dark flame leaping to his eyes. Storm instantly forget herself, forgot what she was going to say. She stared.

His shoulders were broad, his chest powerfully muscled and darkly furred. There was not an ounce of fat on him. The dark, curling hair wisped to a vee and disappeared into the waistband of his pants. She had seen men shirtless before, even naked. Well, Rathe and Nick, as boys. The sight had never affected her this way, making her mindless, making the air crack and sizzle.

"Storm, you shouldn't be here," he said thickly.

She looked up, remembering, coming out of her trance. It was a mistake. She saw the hunger in his eyes, saw a pulse beating rapidly in his throat. She knew he wanted to make love to her. The thought thrilled her.

"Brett, you can't make a decision alone that affects me, too."

He started, visibly surprised, then annoyed. "I take it you're referring to the annulment?"

"Yes." She lifted her chin. "I still want one. I don't want to be your wife until the day I die. A few days was no big deal, but not forever. Oh, no."

He inhaled sharply, and she knew he was angry. "That's too bad," he finally said, softly.

She was incredulous. "Too bad? You mean you don't care about my feelings? You don't care that I despise you? You'll keep me your wife against my will?" When he didn't answer, she said, "I'll run away."

He clenched his teeth. Then he relaxed with visible effort. "Oh, I doubt it, Storm. I think I can make you want to stay." He smiled. "I know I can."

There was no mistaking the seductive tone, the sexual innuendo. "You're disgusting," she said. "Why? Why have you changed your mind?"

"Because I want you, and if marriage is the price, I've decided to pay."

She couldn't believe it. For a moment she had nothing to say, then she burst out, "But I don't want you!"

He smiled, clearly amused. "You do, and you will. Trust me." The words were final.

Brett had left town, and it was so different without him. Storm stood in the center of his study, almost able to feel his presence. There was the faint odor of cigars and leather. So very faint, practically nonexistent. Brett would be home today.

He had left early the morning after that strangely tender kiss and his declaration that he no longer wanted an annulment. He had business in Sacramento to take care of, he said, and he would be back in three days. The night of his return he was going to take her to a birthday party.

The hostess was a bit older than she was, and Brett thought they'd like each other.

Storm moved behind the big mahogany desk with its black leather top and sat down. She imagined Brett walking in at this moment; he would probably go into one of his black rages, thinking she was going through his papers or something. She had to admit it, she was curious.

The past three days, the last of her confinement, had been so peaceful. Serene. Placid.

Boring, she thought glumly.

One thing about Brett—when he was around, life was never boring.

Not that she missed him or was looking forward to his return. She was not about to let go of the annulment issue. He wanted her to meet the woman who was having the birthday, as if it mattered—as if she, Storm, was staying. She was not about to spend the rest of her days as Mrs. Brett D'Archand. That thought was too horrible. She even shuddered.

But there was a part of her that was a traitor to herself, a part that was excited at the prospect of his return. How ridiculous! Brett was arrogant, selfish, demanding, peremptory, high-handed, and bigoted. He had the worst temper she had ever seen. The only thing going for him was his incredible looks, which didn't say much.

No, she wasn't looking forward to his return, not at all.

Realizing with horror what a hypocrite she was being, Storm stood up and hastily left his study.

Brett could not deny that he was excited.

Striding down the wharf from where he had just disembarked, he found himself whistling. His good mood had nothing to do with his business trip, which had been mostly an excuse to get out of the house for three days since he didn't trust himself to remain there, not since he had decided he would remain married, with all that that entailed.

Sian was waiting with King, and Brett promptly grilled him. "Has Storm remained in the house? Has she attempted to go out? To go riding? Does she seem fine?" He was satisfied with all the answers and sent Sian home without him, then rode directly to Audrey's white clapboard house.

She entered the parlor a moment after her maid had let him in. He could see from the expression on her face that she was delighted to see him; he hadn't seen her since the night Storm had fallen out of the tree. "Brett!"

She held his shoulders and kissed him. Brett accepted the kiss, but did not let her melt against him, and he ended the kiss before she could deepen it. For a minute, as she stood inches away from him, her hands having slid down to his waist, they gazed into each other's eyes. "I see," Audrey said.

"You always were perceptive," Brett said gratefully. "I intend to give this marriage a go, Audrey. Storm is very proud. Right now is not the time for me to have a mistress."

"You're in love with her," Audrey said. "I saw it the other night."

Brett smiled. "Ah, for once your intuition fails you. No, dear, I am not in love with her, but I do want her. I know this comes suddenly, with no warning. Tomorrow I shall put a generous amount in your account. It will be more than enough until you find another protector."

She touched his cheek. "Brett, I have several would-be protectors lined up and waiting. The gift is not necessary."

"Then buy yourself something you want."

"Thank you," she said simply. She was clad in a satin wrapper with ermine trim, and the silk gown beneath was sheer. She gave him an enticing look. "How about one last time for a special goodbye?"

Brett shook his head. She was a gorgeous woman, and her body was perfectly attuned to his, but he wasn't in the least tempted, not even with her standing there, revealing her wonderful charms. Tonight, he thought, and a wonderful, tingling excitement began racing in his veins. Tonight he would truly make Storm his wife. "I think not, Audrey."

She walked him to the door. "Storm is very lucky. I wonder if she even knows it."

He laughed. "I wish somebody would tell her. She despises me."

Audrey was shocked.

"Forced marriages aren't the best way to start out," he told her.

"Yes, but still. You are—were—the best catch in town. The girl's crazy."

They kissed again, platonically. "Brett," Audrey said, "if you change your mind, I'll always be available. Even if just for a night."

Brett smiled; his eyes danced. "You're good for my self-esteem, Audrey. And who knows? I might take you up on the offer sometime."

"Mrs. and Miss St. Claire to see you, madame," Peter said formally.

With a frown—why were they here?—Storm lifted her skirts and hurried down the stairs. She had been inspecting the gold satin gown she was going to wear tonight. Marcy had told her that with her coloring, gold was a superb color on her. Storm wanted to look her best tonight although she was furious with herself for wanting to look good for Brett.

"Hello, Storm. Why, you don't look ill at all," said Mrs. St. Clair.

"Hello, Helen, Leanne," Storm said. "Peter, please see to some refreshments." Storm didn't realize how regal she sounded. "Please." She gestured for them to sit back down.

Leanne looked stunning in a pale pink walking gown which reminded Storm sourly that Brett had squired Leanne around for at least six months before she herself had even arrived in town. Storm felt gawky, too tall, not pretty. She sat stiffly in a chair.

"We didn't have a chance to call earlier, Storm," Leanne said. "Although we knew about your accident," she added. "I'm *so* glad you're all right."

I'll bet, Storm thought, but she smiled.

"Married life seems to agree with you, dear," Helen said, smiling brightly. "Of course, Brett would agree with just about any woman."

Storm managed another smile. She wasn't sure if that was a compliment or not, and she had a sinking feeling of dread.

"Are you coming to the Wainscotts' party tonight? It's Suzanne's birthday. Have you met Suzanne?" Leanne said cheerfully.

"No, I haven't met her, but Brett said we would go." Storm turned gratefully as Peter set down a tray. "Brett's been out of town for a few days, but he'll be back today." Although she was pouring lemonade, she felt the tense silence that followed. She handed Leanne and her mother their glasses, becoming uneasy. They looked smug.

"Oh, Brett's back," Leanne said happily. "We saw him this afternoon."

Storm's apprehension grew, and she set her glass down carefully, her smile becoming fixed.

"He was going up the steps of a pretty white house with a charming picket fence. Thirteen-thirty Sutter Street," Leanne said merrily.

Storm felt sick. In that instant her whole world collapsed.

"It's so *big* of you, dear, to allow Brett his mistress, and to allow him to be open about it," Helen St. Clair said pleasantly. "Of course, it's the way of the world. All men have mistresses."

"Well, when I get married my husband won't have a mistress," Leanne said. "And Grant Farlane doesn't have a mistress. Isn't it funny that Brett returns after being out of town and goes to see *her* before *you?*"

"Brett can do as he pleases," Storm said, afraid she was going to burst into tears at any moment. "We're getting an annulment," she said with vicious intent, knowing the news would be all over town within minutes after her guests left, then wondering if she should have said it, if she'd gone too far. She could barely breathe.

"An annulment!" Helen gasped. "Why, that *is* news!"

A few minutes later they left, Helen solicitously noting that Storm did not look well and perhaps should lie down. Storm managed to walk them to the front door, then found herself in the parlor again, staring out of the French doors at the beautiful garden, a riot of pink and purple and white and yellow. She saw nothing.

"I will not cry," she said. She already knew about Audrey, so why did she feel this terrible hurt, as if she'd been shot? Had he even gone to Sacramento? Dear God! What if he'd been with her these past three days!

One lone tear crawled slowly down her cheek.

Storm had no idea how long she stood and stared out the window, but when the parlor door opened and closed, she could feel his presence, without even looking. She didn't turn around, not even when he said her name, softly, warmly. "Storm." It was a verbal caress.

Storm continued to stare at the garden, trying to control her terrible hurt. She focused on the pink azaleas, the purple hibiscus. She heard her name again, this time less softly, with some pique. She didn't move. Go away, she prayed silently. Just go away.

She heard him approaching and stiffened, then she was turned around abruptly to face his dark face. "I'm touched at your delight in seeing me," he said grimly.

"Why would you expect delight?" she asked fiercely.

He stared at her. "What's wrong?"

"I must go get dressed for this evening," she said, attempting to pull away.

His hands tightened. "We don't have to leave until seven."

She avoided his eyes. "I have to bathe and wash my hair. Please, let go."

When he didn't, her hands came up to grasp his wrists. "Don't touch me!" she cried, unable to bear it—thinking of his hands on *her* until recently. He let go of her abruptly, and Storm ran out of the room. She could feel him watching her all the way up the stairs.

Chapter 13

Brett was hurt, which was ridiculous. He had been eager to see her, but she hadn't cared less. He hadn't felt hurt since he was a boy living at his father's hacienda, and then only in that first year. He had been vulnerable and wary, not knowing what to expect from the man who had taken him from his mother. That wariness had paid off. After that, he'd learned not to let anyone hurt him with their disdain and rejection. He'd learned how to bury hurt and turn it into anger and resentment.

And he didn't like the way he was feeling now—not at all. It was far too reminiscent of those days, and all because he had faced the fact that he was looking forward to seeing his wife again.

Was she still angry about his decision not to annul the marriage? She would just have to accept it, and he knew she would once he bedded her. She would more than accept it then, he was certain. The passion they would share would change her mind, and he had the feeling that passion wouldn't fade for years. By then Storm would be older, and they might even be friends. They'd have children to solidify the bond between them. Why in hell couldn't she be reasonable?

Brett decided to let her sulk, to ignore her hostility. He had been eager to let her know how generous he had been in giving up his mistress, but now he decided he'd tell her when she deserved to know—and God only knew when that would be. He was annoyed, in general; the bliss of his earlier mood had evaporated.

But when she came downstairs several hours later, he knew it was worth suffering any irritation to have her, and he also knew that he was more than infatuated—he was obsessed. In her low-cut gold gown she looked like a princess out of a fairy tale—no, she looked like a goddess, like Venus, descending to take her place among the mortals. He actually lost his breath. Tonight, he thought, he was finally going to have her. And from the set look on her face it wasn't going to be easy.

But he was a master of seduction.

She stopped at the foot of the stairs without speaking. Her eyes were the bluest he'd ever seen, almost purple. She looked mutinous. He smiled, letting out his breath, and took her hand. "You look ravishing," he said, meaning it. He turned over her palm and kissed it, touching the soft flesh with the tip of his tongue. When he raised his head, he saw she was staring stonily at him. He knew he had his work cut out for him. "Shall we?"

She didn't answer.

In the carriage, Brett continued to get the cold shoulder. "Shall I tell you about my trip?" he asked civilly. Tonight her hair was up, piled in soft curls atop her head, and he wanted to pull out the pins, one by one, and let the tresses fall. He imagined her riding him, the curtain of her hair draping him. His erotic thoughts produced an eager physical reaction.

She regarded him coolly and shrugged.

He felt anger glimmering. "Do you intend to punish me all evening with your silence?"

"Of course not," she said. "It's just that I have nothing to say to you on any subject—unless it's to discuss when we get the annulment."

His irritation was vast. "There will be no annulment, as I have previously stated."

She stared out the window. "Then we have nothing to discuss."

"Fine," he said harshly.

It was a birthday ball. Already the drive was filled with carriages and sleek horses, and inside there were some two hundred people, the women in brilliant gowns and jewels, the men in elegant evening wear. Storm removed her wrap, and Brett led her inside with one hand on her elbow. They paused, glancing around.

Brett escorted her, making introductions, instantly aware of the looks they were getting; there was no mistaking it. When they were face to face with other guests, everyone was pleasant and polite, but Brett could sense keen interest behind the smooth façades. What in hell was going on?

Randolph Farlane came up to them, barely glancing at Brett. "Hello," he said, his eyes devouring Storm. Brett was instantly annoyed.

"Hello, Randolph," he said briskly.

"Hi," Storm said, her face lighting up with pleasure, deepening Brett's annoyance. "Randolph, how come you haven't come to call?"

He smiled then, staring into her eyes, and Brett stood there feeling like an outsider. "I thought it improper considering that you just got married."

"Oh, that's ridiculous. Brett doesn't care, do you?"

Brett stared. "You mean, do I care if Randolph comes to visit? Of course not."

"See? Besides, Brett was out of town for the past three days. I would have loved your company."

Randolph smiled with delight. "I'll come by tomorrow," he said. He looked at Brett. "With your permission, of course."

Thinking about the night of lovemaking ahead, and how it would, undoubtedly, extend through the next day, Brett smiled slightly. "Not tomorrow, Randolph. Another time. Storm will be occupied tomorrow."

"With what?" she demanded tersely.

"With me," he said.

She glared, then took Randolph's arm, muttering something beneath her breath that Brett couldn't make out but knew was derogatory. "Let's dance," she said to Randolph. "Brett doesn't mind."

Randolph looked at Brett, who was, indeed, minding, more and more every minute. "Go ahead," he said, for it would be rude to say otherwise. He watched as they moved onto the dance floor, watched how she smiled up at Randolph and how Randolph smiled down at her, watched to make sure they weren't dancing too close together—and he was irritated, immensely so.

He drank a glass of champagne. The dance was almost over, and he realized he had been staring with unconcealed attention at his wife, so he looked away. A man he knew slightly paused at his side to introduce his cousin, who blushed when Brett smiled at her. A new dance began, and when Brett looked for his wife, he found her dancing again, this time in the arms of Lee Scott. Scowling, he helped himself to another glass of champagne.

"Hello, Brett."

He wasn't in the mood for Leanne, but he gave her a brief smile. "Leanne. How are you?"

"Just fine," she said brightly, taking his arm and holding it against her side. "Do I get a dance, or do you intend to watch your wife all night?"

Ever the gentleman, Brett finished the champagne and set aside the glass. Wondering if Leanne had purposely inflected the word *wife*, he whirled her onto the dance floor, immediately seeking out Storm. Both she and Lee were laughing, obviously enjoying the dance. Storm never laughed with him. Hell, she never even smiled at him!

Leanne chatted away, and Brett responded without pay-ing much attention to her, unable to do so because of his preoccupation with his wife—and anticipation of the night to come. He was determined to claim Storm as soon as this dance was over, but Leanne clung to him and insisted on introducing him to her cousin, a newly arrived gentleman from Philadelphia. Now Storm was dancing with Robert, another ex-suitor, and Brett was more than irritated, he was incensed.

He debated the possibility that she was trying to make him jealous. If so, it most certainly wasn't working, because he most certainly was not jealous. He grabbed her for the next dance, rudely leaving the cousin from Philadelphia in midsentence. "My turn, sweet wife," he said.

"I'm afraid my feet hurt," Storm replied, lifting her big blue eyes and looking straight at him. "And I am so thirsty."

Brett controlled himself, barely. "Let me fetch you some champagne," he said stiffly.

"Thank you," she murmured.

The evening was not going according to plan.

When he returned with two glasses of champagne, she was surrounded by Randolph and Lee and Robert, making the same calf's eyes back at them that they were making at her. Brett was about to shove his way to her side when he realized how foolish it would look. He didn't have to compete. She was his wife. "Here," he said, handing her the glass, and stalked off to do some flirting of his own.

But it was hard to flirt when he was married and obsessed with his own wife. After standing out the one dance he had asked her for, Storm proceeded to dance the next hour away. Brett was so furious at her behavior—for lying about her feet, for snubbing him in public—that he stood and glowered and drank champagne, occasionally waltzing some lady or other around the floor. He was having a horrible time, while Storm had never seemed happier.

"Is it true?"

Brett turned to see Paul Langdon, noting that the man looked grim and angry. "Hello, Paul."

Paul glanced briefly at Storm. "Is it true, Brett?"

"Is what true?"

"Jesus! The damn rumors are flying around this room so thick—that the two of you are getting an annulment!"

Brett stared in complete shock, then a red rage started creeping over him. No wonder the strange glances. He had told no one. Only Marcy and Grant had been privy to that information, and they both knew he had changed his mind. Which meant . . . He looked at Storm, truly wanting to strangle her.

"No, Paul, it is not true."

Paul sighed in relief. "Who in hell started the rumor?"

"I have no idea," Brett said grimly. He drained the champagne. He was getting drunk. Which was good because if he didn't do something he would drag her home. Drag her home and seduce her and make her his forever. Then he realized that leaving so abruptly would feed the appetite of the gossipmongers. So he stood there drinking champagne, pretending to be having a good time and looking unconcerned over his wife's behavior. Finally he decided he'd had enough, that it was his turn to dance with her.

As casually as possible he cut in on Randolph, who was dancing with her for the third time. Storm immediately stopped smiling, going rigid in his arms.

"Smile, *ma chère,*" he said, smiling himself, "or I will break your neck." So much for seduction.

He wanted to kick himself.

Storm gasped. The warning in his voice disturbed her, as did the barely leashed tension pulsating through his body. She tried to smile. He pulled her completely against his frame, his hand on her waist sliding down her hip, much lower than was seemly. "Brett, stop," she said, acutely aware of the physical contact. Was he trying to embarrass her in front of everyone?

"If you won't smile . . ." he said. He left the sentence unfinished. He lowered his mouth to hers and kissed her, right there, in front of everyone. This kiss was hard, not brutal yet totally uncompromising. He forced her mouth open to plunder inside with his tongue. Storm felt the rush of blood through her veins and stiffened against it, against him. This was not right. He was angry; she could feel it in the hard tautness of his body, in the barely restrained way he was kissing her. The deliberate control and expertise he was exercising alerted all her instincts for self-preservation. But she didn't dare push him away, not in public.

He lifted his face, smiled in satisfaction, and whirled her back into the dance. "That should give them something else to talk about," he said.

"Are you drunk?" she demanded, not sure if the breathless quality of his voice was due to nerves or to his effect on her.

"Not quite," he said, his tone pleasant with effort—too pleasant.

When the dance was over, he took her hand. "Thank you, sweetheart," he said. He lifted her hand and kissed it.

The pressure on her elbow was possessive, but when she protested and tried to dislodge him, he squeezed even harder. Storm settled back stiffly in the carriage, not looking at him, her heart pounding. He wasn't looking at her or talking to her, which was fine. She had nothing to say to him. She decided to ignore him and his bad mood. She wished the space of the carriage was not so confined, that Brett wasn't sitting so close, his knee brushing hers.

Her feet ached unbearably from hours spent dancing. She had wanted to get back at him for going to his mistress, and it seemed she had succeeded. Even though Brett didn't care about her, she had known he would hate to see his wife flirting in front of all the world. Her arms were crossed tightly in front of her.

Once home, Brett helped her carefully from the carriage and up the front walk. He slowed his pace when he realized she was struggling to keep up. Both Betsy and Peter were there to greet them, and Brett sent them away. He turned slowly to Storm.

She instantly knew she was in trouble. "I'm tired," she began, placing one hand on the banister.

His hand came down on her wrist. "Tell me, *chère,* just whom did you tell about the annulment?"

She swallowed and knew she had to lie. "No one."

"Then how is it possible, Storm, that our upcoming annulment was the focus of gossip tonight?"

She felt a burning, betraying blush. "I don't know," she quavered.

"No matter," he said lightly. "We'll just have to set the record straight." He turned away, walking with long strides into his study.

She fled up the stairs, extremely apprehensive. She had known the minute she told the St. Clair women that it was a mistake. Was that why he was angry? Because it made him look foolish? Well, good! How did she look when he was at his mistress's, with them married only a week? And why was he hiding his anger behind that guise of politeness when he should be ranting and raving?

"We'll see about setting the record straight," Storm muttered to herself.

After she had gotten into her nightrail—a high-necked blue silk gown, flimsy and clinging but not nearly as revealing as some of her nightclothes—she dismissed Betsy and crawled into bed. She was exhausted, both emotionally and physically.

She had barely closed her eyes when Brett walked into

their room through the adjoining door. Storm bolted upright when he lit the lamp by her bedside. He looked at her. She knew, then, why he was there, and she shrank against the headboard. His navy silk robe was so carelessly belted she could see his navel and the curling hair descending from it. "Brett, I don't want to talk right now," she managed.

"Good," he said. "Neither do I."

In his eyes she saw a glittering heat. "Get out."

He put one knee on the bed. Storm lifted the bedclothes higher. The bed sank; he moved on top of her, his strong, large hands taking her shoulders and pulling her beneath him. "No," she said, a mere gasp.

His eyes were getting brighter, like black flames. He shifted and slipped the covers from between them. "Storm," he said huskily, and then he was holding her face and kissing her.

The kiss was incredibly soft and gentle. As he brushed her mouth with his, he pushed his knee between her thighs, forcing them open. He settled himself between her legs, and Storm felt with panic the heat of his rising maleness. She started to twist away.

"Relax, *chère*," he whispered, his breath warm and arousing. His hand stroked down her arm, and the sensation on her silk-clad flesh was exquisite. Storm saw that he was smiling slightly. She turned her head away from his kiss. Brett laughed, a sexually excited sound, and began nibbling the side of her throat. Her blood pounded thickly, searingly. Beneath his groin her own was swelling in response. When his tongue touched her earlobe with infinite care, she gasped.

His hands found her breasts, touching lightly over the silk, barely brushing her nipples into straining erections. His mouth and breath on her ear were devastating. Storm heard a labored moan, and realized it came from herself.

"That's it, *chère,*" he murmured. "Oh, yes, let yourself go—for me, Storm, for me."

His words registered. He registered. His touch was perfection. He was deliberately using his superior skill to seduce her, and she was falling for it. His mouth moved back to hers, his tongue lightly probing the joining of her lips. One of his hands had roamed down to clasp her buttock. With his other hand he was teasing a nipple. Storm was on fire, yet she refused to open her mouth.

She was infuriated.

"Open your lips, Storm, open for me," Brett breathed, clutching both her buttocks now, lifting her against the grinding hardness of his erection.

"No," Storm said—a mistake.

His tongue darted inside her mouth, thrusting intimately, powerfully, suggestively. Her mind ordered her to tell him no again, but her body was spinning out of control, and her hands came up to clutch his shoulders, then entwine in the short hair of his nape. Brett groaned.

The distinctly male sound and his simultaneous shudder increased the insistent throbbing of Storm's body. Of their own accord, her hands found his powerful buttocks. Brett gasped, lifting his hands. "God, Storm, I want you . . ."

"Yes," she panted, pulling his hips against her and wrapping her legs around his. "Yes, Brett, yes."

He groaned in response, and suddenly she felt the heat of the swollen tip of his shaft probing past her inner thigh, sliding intimately against her. A shudder shook her from head to toe as she arched wildly against him, moaning again, kissing him back, nipping his lip. Her tongue darted out, traced his mouth. Brett ran his hands up her body, groaning, catching her breasts, holding them, squeezing them. Their teeth grated and cut and caught as they kissed.

She thrust her wet womanhood against his hips. His hands slid down her back, holding her up as his mouth traveled down her throat, her collarbone. He nuzzled her lush breasts, again and again, groaning her name, raining kisses upon first one, then the other. He took a peak in his mouth, sucking, tugging with his teeth, lapping with his tongue. She cried out.

His organ, hot and hard and slick, moved steadily against her, rubbing over her moist cleft again and again. Storm thought she was going to die. She *was* going to die. She lay open and wet and waiting. "Please," she moaned. "Please, please, oh, Brett."

His hands found her buttocks, lifted them.

Brett plunged in, tearing instantly through the wall of her virgin's membrane. Storm gasped at the unexpected pain, and Brett instantly stilled, deep inside her.

Gradually the pain subsided. Storm contracted around the huge member inside her, and Brett gasped. He began to move, slowly at first, gently, small easy strokes. Storm moaned again and again, moving with him, easily, naturally, clutching at his buttocks to take in even more of him. He moved faster, harder. She whimpered, gasping. His strokes became intent, determined, faster and faster. Storm couldn't bear it. The pleasure was nearly agony. And then she shattered in a violent, wrenching release, crying out again and again.

As his heart rate slowed, sanity returned. Brett became thoroughly aware of the woman with whom he was coupled so tightly. Good God, he thought, stunned by the intensity of their passion. Warm, jubilant feelings rushed over him. For just a moment his hold tightened, and he breathed in her fragrance. And then he was flooded with the triumph and elation of possession. He grinned.

He eased himself off her, to her side, already anticipating making love to her again. He smiled anew at that thought and looked at her, his hand sliding down her arm, relishing the silken skin. Her gown was tousled around her waist, and he enjoyed the sight. But she gave him a look to freeze his soul, then turned away from him so abruptly that the mattress bounced. Brett tensed, wondering what this new nonsense was. He slid his hand up her back, and desire started to fill his loins again.

"No," she cried, and her shoulders started shaking.

For a moment, Brett couldn't believe it—she was crying. "Storm?"

"Get away," she gritted in a pathetic voice. "Get away from me."

He tensed, staring at her back. Why was she upset? She had wanted him as much as he had wanted her. She had shared his passion, he knew it. He frowned, touching her waist. "Storm?"

Her body went rigid, as if repulsed at his touch. He removed his hand, his heartbeat accelerating. "Why are you crying?"

There was no answer, just muffled sobs.

His mind was racing, working frantically. Jesus! Had he been too rough? He hadn't meant to be. He felt a surge of fear. "Did I hurt you? Storm? Damn."

"Get out," she said in a voice broken with tears. "Please, please, get out."

I hurt her, he thought, a strangled feeling wrapping around his guts. "I'm sorry," he heard himself say in a strangely humble voice.

She whimpered.

He wanted to comfort her, to hold her, to rock her, but now he was afraid to touch her. He found himself reaching out, touching her hair. Her body stiffened.

"Storm," Brett began, hesitantly. "I . . . it's all right." He stroked her glorious hair. "I'm sorry. It only hurts the first time. There won't be any pain the next time."

She sat upright, and he saw that she was furious. "Next time? Next time! There won't be a next time!"

He stared.

"You tricked me," she cried. "You seduced me. You

bastard, you know I don't want to be in this marriage. You know I don't want you. I despise you, you bastard . . ." She started crying again, tears of frustration as much as anger.

His hand had frozen—his entire being had frozen. He stood stiffly. She didn't want him. Those words were an echo, more than an echo, a cruel reminder of another time. Something sick and unsure filled him. He had just given her more passion than he knew he had, and she didn't want him. She despised him. He had known it all along. How could he have forgotten?

As he moved across the room, he caught a glimpse of himself in the mirror, saw the stark, bleak look on his face. She hadn't wanted him to begin with, and she didn't want him now. He could make her body respond, but the victory felt empty, hollow, like defeat.

His eyes didn't move away from her reflection. He was glad she had turned away so he couldn't see her face. "It won't ever happen again," he said, his voice sounding raw and bitter even to his own ears. "I swear it."

Brett woke up early the next morning, a bit hung over from lack of sleep and an excess of champagne. His first waking thought was of Storm, and instantly a self-pitying hurt flooded him. He rose and prepared to dress. There was no sense in brooding over what had happened, he thought with determination. He had done what he had done; it would never happen again. She would have to come to him. He would certainly not make a fool of himself by begging for his wife's favors.

He washed and dressed, then paused to knock on Storm's door with some trepidation. He refused to analyze why he wanted to see her, check on her. There was no answer. She was probably sleeping; he should let her be. He went downstairs and ate.

It was eight o'clock and he was in the midst of his

breakfast when Sian appeared, cap in hand, looking uncomfortable. Brett gestured him inside. "What is it, Sian?"

"Sir, I don't know what happened, but Demon's gone."

Brett put down his cup. "What?"

"Yes, sir. I was just feeding the horses, and when I got to his stall, I realized he was gone. Him and all his tack, sir."

Brett jumped to his feet, a terrible foreboding bolting through him. "Saddle up King, Sian," he ordered.

He bounded up the stairs and barged into Storm's room without knocking. She wasn't there. The bed was unmade, a crimson splotch marring the whiteness of the sheets, another reminder . . . He noted instantly that the armoire was open and clothes were on the floor, as if she had been searching in haste for something in particular. "Betsy!" he bellowed.

She appeared instantly. "Sir?"

"Where's Storm?"

"I—I thought she was sleeping," Betsy said, taking in the room and the bed with wide eyes.

"What's missing?" he snapped.

She started looking through the wardrobe. "Those foul buckskins of hers, and those dirty boots and old hat. She wouldn't let me throw them away."

Brett's heart was catapulting wildly. She had run away—sometime since he had last seen her. He had left her room around one or one-thirty, but he had been up until three, unable to sleep. If she'd left then, that gave her a five-hour head start . . . damnation!

Maybe she had just gone to the Farlanes', or Paul's. When he found her, he would . . . God! Riding at night, alone . . . He felt panic rising up in him, flooding him.

Brett's first stop was the Farlanes' at eight-twenty in the morning. He was tense with anxiety as he dismounted and ran up the front steps. Both Marcy and Grant were in the dining room.

"Good morning," Grant said, standing. "Brett, is—"

"Is Storm here?" Brett cried.

Marcy stood also. "No, Brett, she's not. What happened?"

"Damn," Brett said. "She's run away."

"Oh, my God," Marcy said. "Are you sure?"

"Demon's gone, and she's in her buckskins. Grant?"

"I'll be glad to help."

Marcy stopped Brett. "Maybe she just went riding, Brett."

He regarded her with miserable eyes. "No, Marcy, not after last night. God, if only . . ."

Marcy squeezed his arm.

The two men left. "Where do you want to go?" Grant said, after asking for his horse.

"I want us to split up, Grant, just in case she's in town somewhere." Brett met his glance. "But I know she's heading home, to Texas. That means she's gone south to San Diego. I *know* it. I'm going home to get another horse, and if I have to ride them both into the ground to catch up with her, I will. You comb the town. If by any chance I'm wrong and you find her, get word to me."

Grant clasped his arm. "I will. Brett, she'll be all right."

Brett was sick with worry. "She's out there alone. She's only seventeen."

Grant regarded him with sympathy.

"I've got to find her," Brett said hoarsely. "It's all my fault."

Chapter 14

She had to stop. Demon was exhausted. The sun was just setting, hanging crimson over the ocean. She had been pushing on for close to fourteen hours, she figured, since she had left in the dark hour before dawn.

Wearily, Storm dismounted and unsaddled the stallion, who nickered gratefully. She rubbed him down with brown grass, then gave him a few handfuls of grain, with which she had filled her saddlebags. She hadn't thought to grab any food for herself. She'd eaten some jerky that had been left in her packs from when she and her father had come to San Francisco. She was starved.

She left the black grazing by a stand of scrub oak and headed deeper into the bush, rifle in hand. Luck was with her, for there was still some light, and she scanned the ground, noticing deer droppings in the grass. She stepped farther into the trees, ignoring a squirrel fleeing up a trunk. She didn't want squirrel for dinner. Moving without making a sound, she parted several branches, stepped past, then froze.

The hare sat motionless, listening. Storm raised the rifle slowly, sighting. She cocked it, and the hare leaped away, but too late. A single blast caught him right between the ears. Storm went to fetch her prize.

She skinned the hare on the spot, decapitating it first, then making one neat incision and pulling off the entire pelt. She returned to the spot where she would make camp, setting aside the hare to start a small fire. In no time at all, meat was roasting on a spit, and by nightfall she was eating hot, tasty roasted rabbit.

It satisfied her hunger pangs, but not the other pain that had been tormenting her all day.

She had never felt so debased in her entire life.

Storm had been raised on steadfast love. Her mother had always been there, usually with a firm hand but never giving any reason to question her devotion. Storm's father had openly adored her, and she was secure in the knowledge that should anyone ever dare to insult her, if she couldn't rectify the error herself, her two brothers would—with their fists. From time to time she had been punished—for small crimes, for mischievous pranks or neglecting her chores. Usually her privileges had been denied. She had never been hit, not by her parents, although as a child she and a neighbor kid had gotten into more fistfights than she could count.

Storm was used to being loved and respected.

But Brett didn't love her. He was a ladies' man, and she was just another conquest. He desired her, that she understood, but that was as far as his feelings went. Storm felt sick when she thought how he had been blackmailed into marrying her. And now he had so expertly and easily seduced her, completely indifferent to her own wishes. And she had responded to his skilled touch—how she had responded! That he could touch her and turn her into a wanton beast, make her do his bidding, that she desired him, too, filled her with shame and fury.

For the first time she knew what helplessness was.

She was helpless to protect herself from Brett, helpless in the face of his passion. And that made her terribly afraid. She couldn't handle sex—her body being used—without love.

But she kept hearing Brett, his voice hoarse and filled with remorse, saying, *Storm, God, I'm sorry.*

I'm sorry . . . I'm sorry . . .

"Go away," she said to the night. "Can't you leave me alone, even now?" Tears welled. She could feel his hand in her hair, soothing and comforting. Her father had stroked her hair like that when she was a little girl crying over some incident.

She would make it home or die trying. Make it home, into her father's and mother's arms . . . If only she was there now.

Storm rolled out her bedroll and curled up in it. She gazed at the stars, wishing she could get the sound of Brett's voice out of her head, wishing she hadn't heard the remorse there. She also wished she could wipe out her memory of the lust that had flared between them, of the feel of his body in hers, driving deeper and deeper, his hands on her buttocks, lifting her to him . . . She didn't know what was wrong with her. Even now, the memory of his touch was making her ache. She closed her eyes and sought sleep. It finally came.

Something woke her. Demon, snorting, stomping. Storm, fully awake now, kept her eyes closed, straining to hear . . . There was another horse. She wished Brett hadn't confiscated her Colt. Her hand closed around the butt of the rifle that was beneath her blanket, her finger curling around the trigger. She lay absolutely still.

Then she felt pressure on the rifle as it was being pulled away, and she grabbed it harder, her eyes flying open as Brett said, "I don't know whether to shout in relief or scream bloody hell!"

She sat up, struggled briefly over the gun, briefly and uselessly because her strength was no match for Brett's. He wrenched the gun away and tossed it aside, out of reach, then he grabbed her.

She couldn't believe it. She couldn't believe he had found her! How had he even caught up with her? And

then, in the next instant, as her partly frightened, partly
dismayed gaze swept past him, she saw that he had two
horses, the gray unsaddled and tied to a bay. Her head
snapped back to his. She thought she saw intense relief in
his dark eyes, but she wasn't sure. "Are you all right?"
he demanded, shaking her.

"Yes," she snapped, twisting free, but only because he
let her.

He stood then, his hands clenched on his hips, looking
down at her. Storm met his gaze with a barely summoned
bravado. She hadn't seen relief in his gaze, she couldn't
have. This man was grim, so grim. "Listen to me carefully, Storm," he said.

His tone made her sit very still, at full attention.

"If I had to ride all the way to Texas to find you, I
would. Do you understand?"

She didn't—why would he bother? "Once I made it
home, you'd never get your hands on me again, you blue-
blooded pig!"

A wave of anger swept his face. His fists tightened,
released. He squatted, his face inches from hers. "I should
whip you for running away. It's my right."

"Go ahead," she said, thrusting out her chin, horrified
because she was going to start bawling at any second.

"Damn you," he said softly. His hand, so large and
strong, cupped the side of her face. "Don't cry, I didn't
mean it," he said very softly.

She slapped his hand away. "I wouldn't put it past you,
not after that night."

He was proud of himself for his control, his calm. "And
just what does that mean?"

"It means you have no morals, none at all. You don't
give a damn for anyone other than yourself. Even though
you knew I wanted an annulment, my feelings didn't count
with you. Not as long as you got what you wanted."

He held back his anger. "Ah, 'that' night. How could

I think we'd get past that? Let me remind you of something, Storm. You wanted me as much as I wanted you, and you have from the moment we met.''

''No!'' she denied hotly, and in despair she knew she was lying. Even now her pulse was pumping vigorously in response to his presence.

He studied her blackly. ''I should beat you. You could have been killed, you damn fool! Or raped many, many times—and believe me, it wouldn't have been anything like what happened between us. If you ever try and run away again—''

''I will!'' she cut him off. ''Don't worry about that!''

''Don't push,'' he warned, then abruptly with one hand he pushed her back onto the blanket. ''It's almost midnight. We'll head out at first light.'' He stood, picked up her rifle, and carried it with him to his horses. He untacked the bay.

Storm's hand slid of its own volition to her knife. Dare she? Could she get the drop on him? She had seen the derringer in the band of his breeches. He had laid down her rifle, and his own rifle was still in the scabbard on his saddle. She bit her lip. Now or never, her mind whispered. Home, she thought.

She was sure he would never beat her.

That decided her. Storm rose and started toward Brett. About to slip the bridle off the bay's head, he glanced at her from over his shoulder. He paused. His look was suspicious, then it slid over her buckskin-clad body, making her feel naked, yet warm, too. Her nerves stretched tighter and tighter. His glance moved to the rifle at his feet. ''What are you doing?'' he asked.

She stopped a foot away from him. She hesitated, then placed her left hand on his chest. She heard the sound of his breath, felt his hard body go rigid. ''Brett? I'm sorry.''

He stared at her.

Her mind raced frantically. Without taking her gaze from

his chin and mouth, she knew exactly where his gun was. Her body was trembling. She swayed closer. Her hand slid up, covering the slab of his pectoral muscle. "Brett? I . . ." She lifted her eyes to meet his and was shocked to see the hunger there. But it gave her the inspiration she needed, for she couldn't think of a damn thing to say. She stretched up, lips parted, and touched his mouth with hers.

He stood very still. His mouth didn't move, so hers did. She slid her left hand up to his neck. Her right hand went to his waist, resting lightly inches from the gun. She would grab the gun instead of her knife. It was so close. He began to move his lips against hers, opening his mouth, responding. She ignored the pleasurable sensations sweeping her. He still hadn't touched her.

With her right hand she kneaded his flesh. She slipped her fingers lower, closer . . . She closed her hand over the butt.

And his hand closed over her wrist.

"Let go," he said.

With a cry of outrage, she did. He was still holding her wrist, and her own furious gaze met his. With the speed of a snake, she reached down for the handle of her knife sheathed on her right side. She drew it up, jabbing the point into the skin of his throat. "No," she said softly. "You let go."

His expression was incredulous. Then it grew hard. "Maybe now is the time to find out just how much you hate me," he murmured, tightening his grip on her wrist. "You'll have to cut me, Storm. Can you do it? Will you slit my throat? Gloat while I bleed to death?"

"Yes," she declared. "Yes, gladly. Let go!"

He laughed.

She increased the pressure on his throat, causing a speck of blood to appear, to start to trickle down. He stopped laughing. But her heart was pounding wildly. She couldn't kill him. Good God! She had killed a Comanche in self-defense, but she couldn't murder Brett, not her husband. He let go of her hand.

She felt a wave of hot triumph.

But that same hand went to the wrist holding the knife at his throat. Storm's eyes widened. His were now amused. She wanted to press the blade forward, but she couldn't, and he knew it. His strong, hard hand closed around her wrist and pulled it away. "Put that thing down," he said, turning his back to her.

She stared at him, completely vulnerable, and sheathed the knife. He threw the bridle on top of the saddle, turned and took her arm. "We both need sleep," he said softly, guiding her to the bedroll. She couldn't see. Her eyes were blinded with tears.

He pushed her down, gently, and she crawled between the blankets. When he slid in beside her, she went rigid. "What are you doing?"

"Sleeping," he said, turning onto his side, giving her his back.

She lay very still. "You have your own bedroll," she accused.

"I won't touch you," he said wearily. "It's cold. We'll keep each other warm. Now go to sleep."

She couldn't. But he did, instantly. She was still awake when he rolled over to face her, throwing his arm over her waist. She immediately shoved it aside. It returned to hold her close.

She looked at him.

His face was relaxed in sleep, looking younger, softer, even vulnerable. Her heart seemed to skip a beat. He was so handsome. His breath was warm on her neck, his body hot against hers from her shoulder to her toes. And his arm actually felt comfortable across her waist, once she was used to it.

Experimentally, she rolled onto her side, nestling her back against his chest, her backside into his groin. She closed her eyes as a wonderful comforting warmth enveloped her, and fell into an exhausted slumber.

They arrived back in San Francisco close to midnight, having left at dawn. Storm was exhausted, hungry, and apprehensive. Brett hadn't said more than a dozen words to her all day. He was furious over what she had done, she knew it. She tried not to care. She would have to try to escape again and again. She could not spend the rest of her life as his wife.

Storm managed to get her boots off before collapsing in bed, where she instantly fell asleep. When she awoke the next morning, she dozed in a partly aware state for a long time, not wanting to move, enjoying the soft bed and a delicious sense of lassitude. Finally she opened one eye to realize it was late, close to noon. She yawned.

Sitting up, she realized she was stark naked. Immediately, she wondered who had undressed her—and the thought of her husband doing so, leering at her, studying her while she was unaware, made her grit her teeth. She swung out of bed and opened her wardrobe. She gasped.

It was empty.

Everything was gone.

Storm ran to the chest at the foot of her bed where her spare buckskins were kept, but they, too, were gone. What in God's name was going on?

Then she saw a pale blue silk nightgown and robe. She slipped them both on. The nightgown was sheer, sleeveless, with a low vee neck ruffled in lace. The matching wrapper was of the same material with a frilly collar and cuffs. She had admired the set before, but she had never worn it—it revealed instead of concealing. She certainly could not go downstairs like this.

She reached for the door handle, intending to call for Betsy and demand an explanation. To her shock, the door was locked from the outside. For a moment she refused to believe it. She tried again, yanking on the handle. Quick as a whip, she ran to the other door and pulled on that with the same result. The bastard had locked her in!

It was then that she saw a tray on the table with a silver coffeepot, a pitcher of juice, and several covered plates. She ignored them and stomped over to the window. She already knew there was no way out of the room, not unless she had some rope. It was two stories to the lawn. And she certainly couldn't appear outside dressed like this. Even now, the gardener was trimming hedges. Damn Brett D'Archand!

What did he mean by doing this?

She strode to the door and began pounding on it. She pounded and pounded, yelling for Betsy, Peter, or Brett, until she was hoarse. She knew someone must have heard her, but clearly they had been ordered to ignore her. I'll kill him! she thought.

She paced the room. There wasn't much she could do, not unless she was to tie the sheets together and prance around the lawn naked. Because she might as well be naked for all the negligee hid—or revealed.

So she was to be punished.

Kept a prisoner.

Just who in hell did he think he was?

For lack of anything else to do, she tasted her breakfast, but she had no appetite. She was too angry. She threw aside her fork and began to pace the room. He could not keep her like this for long; it was so ridiculous it had to be a joke. She could not take it seriously. Or should she? She felt panic. What if Brett intended to lock her away indefinitely, without even coming to see her?

She calmed down. Someone would have to come to empty the chamber pot and bring her bathwater, her meals. Surely Peter and Betsy would defy their master in this!

The day seemed endless. No one came. She refused to eat, furious one moment, desperate the next. He was a monster, truly a monster, and she was married to him.

Her spirits sank lower and lower, and then she thought of the injustice of her confinement, and she grew furious again. Anger was a relief. Unlike despair, it was an emotion she understood.

She was pacing once again when she thought she heard footsteps. She froze, straining to hear. She hadn't been mistaken—someone was coming. Storm stared at the door, heard the key in the lock, almost held her breath as the door swung open. Betsy stepped inside, followed by Peter, both carrying buckets of hot water.

"Betsy!" Storm exclaimed, at the same time yanking a sheet off the bed and holding it in front of her. "Where are my clothes? You have to help me. That bastard's locked me in!"

Betsy gasped, Peter bit his lip, and Brett laughed from the doorway. She whirled on him. "How dare you!"

"What? You don't want a bath?" He wrinkled his nose.

"You know what I mean!"

Having filled the tub, Betsy and Peter picked up her tray and left. Brett shut the door behind them, leaning against it, crossing his arms negligently. He was no longer smiling, no longer amused, not in the slightest.

"Brett, I'm warning you . . ." Storm began.

"No," he interrupted coldly, "I'm warning you. You'll stay locked up like some untamable wild animal until I can trust you, Storm."

"What!" She was aghast.

"You heard me," he said.

"You can't do this!" she cried. "You can't! How can you be so cruel?"

"Easily," he said steadily. "You ran away. Not only did you run away, you also managed to make close to fifty miles, putting yourself at the risk of being raped or murdered. You are lucky I found you, which, I might add, I only did after riding hard for eleven hours, almost destroying two of my best horses in the process."

Storm fell silent.

He continued. "Then you started to seduce me to get my gun. When that failed, you pulled a knife on me." He raised a brow. "And you wonder why I'm doing this? Do you think I want to come after you again?"

"I can take care of myself," she said defiantly. "I had my rifle and knife. You should have let me go."

"Probably," he muttered. "Your bath is hot. Peter is bringing us a meal. I thought I'd join you. You must be dying for company, any company, even mine."

"Damn you, Brett D'Archand," she sputtered.

He shrugged and slipped into a chair, sprawling casually, at once elegant and totally male. He was wearing black trousers and a fine lawn shirt with the slightest detailing of ruffling. Storm sat down hard on the bed, trying to assimilate that she was, indeed, the prisoner of this intractable man.

"If you promise me," Brett said, "that you will accept being my wife and will not run away, I will release you."

She stared, then bit her lip. Promise? Could she give him her word, then break it? Of course she could. This was no time for scruples. "I promise," she said unevenly.

He growled. "You little liar. I saw every thought running through that deceivingly gorgeous head of yours. You have no intention of honoring your word."

She held back tears of frustration. She couldn't refute him. It was true. "I wish I had slit your throat," she said, standing and dropping the sheet.

She was expecting anger, not the sharp inhalation, not the flaring light in his eyes, not the way he devoured her body with his gaze. She crossed her arms over her breasts to shield herself from his prying eyes. He smiled but continued to stare. She reached for the sheet at her feet.

He sucked in his breath, and too late Storm realized her breasts had nearly swung free of the gown, revealing their hard nipples. She was pressing the sheet to her, flushing, too aware of her body's pulsating response to his interest, when he yanked the linen easily out of her hands. She gasped.

He was standing in front of her. His face was masked, but nothing could hide the burning hunger of his eyes. "Damn," he growled. A wonderful and terrible wanting assailed her.

He clenched his fists at his sides. With shock, Storm realized he was trying to control himself, that he didn't want to touch her. Her eyes widened, watching the play of ragged emotions on his face. Finally he let out a breath and stepped away from her. "Your bath is getting cold."

Storm fought a feeling of vast disappointment. "I don't want a bath," she lied, unable to keep from looking down—he did want her! Physically, at least, if not mentally. She didn't understand. Worse, she recognized the hurt she was feeling.

He had turned away, pulling out her chair. The table was laid out with their meal, the plates covered to keep the food warm. He seemed to be studying the table, his knuckles white on the back of her chair. Storm couldn't move.

"Then let's eat," he finally said without looking at her.

She hadn't eaten all day, and nothing last night, and the wonderful aromas assailing her made her stomach turn over in anticipation. Brett uncovered their plates and Storm sat down, eager for the diversion as well as the food. She didn't look at him. She wouldn't. She began to eat.

She didn't look up once until she had finished everything on her plate and was more than comfortably full. Brett was watching her intently, the trace of a smile on his mouth. "What a little savage you are," he said softly.

She heard the tender, teasing note but dismissed it. "I may be a savage, but at least I'm not a cold, greedy city-slicker fop! A gambler! A dandy!"

Brett looked startled, then chuckled.

"Blue blood," she accused, shoving aside her plate.

Brett went completely still. She said the word as though

it were tainted. She couldn't know the significance it had for him, yet she was using it as an insult, and he felt fire flaming between his ears. He leaned across the table, closing his hand over her wrist. "What did you call me?"

"Citified fop dandy!"

"After that."

She met his gaze with her own stormy one. "Blue blood! I should have said blue-blooded pig!"

"I believe you called me that once before," he said, almost lightly. His grip tightened; she winced in protest. "Don't you ever call me that again."

Her eyes widened. "Blue blood?"

He made a sound like a growl. He was a moment from turning her over his knee and walloping her. She obviously had found out he was a bastard. He stared.

"I'm sorry," she said nervously.

He stood and pulled her to her feet, jerking her close. She didn't even look sorry, maybe a bit apprehensive, still as mutinous as ever. His grip lightened, and he slid his hand up her silk-clad arm, cupped her shoulder, moved to her neck. She went tense. His fingers splayed around the column of her neck, his thumb on the soft underside of her throat, moving caressingly. She was frozen, not breathing, like a bird trapped in the jaws of a cat. He felt the tension between them, stiff and unyielding. He could so easily break her neck. He could so easily move his hand down, stroking, urging her to passion. He found her gaze, wide and tremulous. With a barely human noise, he dropped his hand and spun for the door and wrenched it open. He slammed it behind him.

Brett was furious with himself. What was wrong with him? Around her he acted like a stallion around a mare in heat. He had been instants from losing control and forcing her. There must be no repetition of what had happened the other night, by God! He had hurt her so badly that she had run away, risking her own life to do so. If anything had happened to her . . . The mere thought made him sick. If Storm had been hurt, or worse, it would have been his fault for making her life with him so unbearable that she had to run away.

Tomorrow morning he would return her clothes to her. He had no intention of keeping her locked up until he could trust her because he wasn't sure how long that would be. He merely wanted to teach her a lesson—and the punishment seemed appropriate, more so than anything else he could devise. After all, if the shoe fits . . . Let her think the imprisonment was indefinite. Let her panic and be filled with contrition and remorse. Hah! If only that were possible! Just what in hell was he going to do with this Texas hoyden of a wife who had come into his life and overturned it completely? How in hell was he going to tame her?

Of course, he would have her watched during the day. He would have the stables locked at night. He was certain she would try to escape again. He almost laughed. Was life with him so unbearable? Was he so despicable? Was it so awful being his wife? He had told her that a repetition of the other night would not happen. He meant it. What more did she want? Did she think him a liar?

He strode into his study, pouring himself a brandy and taking a long swig. The alcohol worked, its warmth stealing across him, soothing him. He reached for the pile of mail. A sense of foreboding took him when he saw a letter from Monterey. Another one. Was his uncle going to beg again for him to come home? Had his father died? Or had he finally swallowed his pride and written to his son? But why should he? Don Felipe had never given a damn about him, not when he was a boy, so why would he care whether he came to visit now? Or had being on his deathbed raised some familial affections? If that was the case, Brett wasn't interested. To hell with the old man.

He tossed the letter aside.

After he'd gone through all the rest of his mail, it was late, almost midnight. Brett poured himself his second brandy, lit another cigar, and found himself staring at the letter from Emmanuel.

Unable to resist, he tore it open, angry with himself for his curiosity. This time the letter was short, a mere paragraph:

Dear Brett,

I wish I were writing under happier circumstances. A great tragedy has struck the hacienda. Your little brother, Manuel, and your sister, Catherine, died of the chicken pox. Your father is worse. One of my own grandchildren was also taken, God rest his soul. Please, Brett, think about coming. If you don't, when your father is gone, you may regret it for the rest of your life.

Your loving uncle,
Emmanuel

Brett stared at the fireplace. Manuel, only ten, whom he had never known, newborn when he'd left the hacienda for the gold fields, dead. His sister, dead. A cousin, dead. His father worse. Why was he struck by the tragedy? He didn't care for any of them except his Uncle Emmanuel.

He abruptly decided they would leave on the afternoon stage tomorrow.

As soon as Brett awoke the next morning he went to tell Storm of their trip. He knocked. "Storm, it's me." He unlocked the door between their adjoining rooms and stepped inside.

Instinct and fine-honed reflexes made him duck. The missile, which he realized was a silver-backed hairbrush, sailed inches from his head and bounced against the wall. He straightened, about to protest, then quickly ducked again as another object came flying. This one hit the wall and shattered. "Storm!"

"You can't do this to me," she shouted, now hurling everything she could get her hands on from the bureau where she had been brushing her hair. A hand mirror, bottles of perfume, a jar of cream, a delicate porcelain dish, a thick hardcover book. All her missiles found their mark. She was clad in her blue negligee, making an incredibly enticing picture. Brett growled and strode forward.

Finally she ran out of ammunition and glanced wildly around, then started to back away. Brett grabbed her. "Jesus! What's wrong with you?"

"What do you think?" she cried, then started to laugh— Brett smelled like roses, strongly, vividly. She couldn't imagine him going about his day smelling so sweet.

His gaze dropped from her face to her full, lush breasts, the hard peaks straining against the silk. Desire rose up in him, hot and fierce. His hold loosened. He pulled her closer until she was almost touching him. "That is not the way," he said thickly, looking into her stormy blue eyes.

She stared indignantly at him. "I want my clothes, Brett. You can't keep me locked up."

"Betsy will help you pack," he told her, releasing her before he did something he might regret.

"Pack?"

"We're going to Monterey," he told her. "To my father's hacienda."

Storm stared, puzzled. "You want me to meet them?"

He glanced up from regarding her long legs, set defiantly, the soft silk molding them perfectly. "I have to go, and I don't want to leave you here," he said. "There was a disease—my brother and sister and a cousin died. They were only children. And my father is not well."

At first he didn't see her expression because he was tantalized by her seductive shape, imagining what he might do to seduce her—forgetting his intention to leave her alone until she came to him.

"Oh, Brett," she breathed, and he felt her hand on his arm.

He looked into her eyes, warm and compassionate, and was completely startled. But . . . he liked her looking at him this way, without anger, mutiny, or hostility. He opened his mouth to say something, but nothing came out.

"Are you all right?" she said softly, tightening her hold on his arm, her voice filling with tenderness. "I'm so sorry."

Brett realized what was going on. She had no idea he didn't know his relatives. She did not know his family history. She was close to her family and assumed it was the same for him. Her touch on his arm, warm even through his shirt, was meant to comfort him. He looked down so she couldn't see his eyes. "I . . . Storm." His voice was broken and husky because he was aching so badly for her.

She moved closer, her hand going to his neck. Her palm was warm and soft, barely callused now. He closed his eyes, and somehow her fingers moved to gently touch the side of his face. His body felt as finely tuned as a bowstring. A shudder took him.

"What can I do?" she whispered.

He reluctantly opened his eyes, having never been offered such comfort from a woman before, and forced himself to raise his head. God, her hands . . . He could imagine them drifting over his chest, his shoulders, lower, stroking his hard shaft, which was already alive and pulsating. "Thank you for your understanding," he whispered, ignoring a tad of guilt.

An idea was forming in his head, a wonderful idea.

Chapter 15

With two carriages and three servants it took four days to make the trip to the Hacienda de los Cierros. The trip was pain free, achieved effortlessly in the smooth barouche, but Storm found it disturbing nevertheless. For those four days Brett was always at her side. He rode in the carriage with her. When she rode astride, to break up the monotony of the trip, Brett chose to do so, too. He placed his bedroll next to hers at night, and when she awoke in the darkness, she was curled up against the hard length of his body with his arm possessively around her.

She couldn't help it—she felt sympathy for him. A great tragedy had struck his family. Storm knew she would grieve endlessly if anything had happened to her own brothers or her parents, and Brett was so stoic, trying to act as if nothing had happened. Now and then, when he wasn't aware she was studying him, she could see the pain cross his face. She wanted to hold and comfort him and help him forget his tragedy. Once or twice Brett goaded her into losing her temper, but she was instantly contrite. She would as soon kick a crippled animal as fight with Brett when he was suffering from his personal loss.

The Hacienda de los Cierros had once claimed the entire valley, but the gold rush had brought hordes to the territory, Brett told her. After the frenzy had died down, many had become squatters, turning to ranching and farming, settling on sections of the vast land grants owned by the Californio families. The Monterros did have an original land grant that dated back to the first expedition sent by Spain, led by Portola in 1767. But California's admission to the Union in 1850 marked a death knell for the Californios, because the squatters, mostly Americans, now had legal rights to the land they had claimed. Many old Californio families were losing land that had been theirs for centuries. Because of the high cost of ranching, most of the families could not afford the cost of years of litigation. Even those who had come only since independence from Spain were losing their land in the courts to the new settlers. Brett told her all this dispassionately, as if he were a detached observer, not the son of the haciendado.

Storm looked down at the magnificent valley, lushly green after all the winter rains, speckled pink and yellow with wildflowers, dotted here and there with cattle and horses, and rimmed by majestic hills. On a high rise sat the hacienda, of white adobe and red-tiled roofs. There were many buildings—stables and smaller villas—but the majestic villa of the Monterros, covered with bougainvillea, dwarfed everything, as large as a castle, Storm thought. She felt a moment's apprehension. Was she ready to meet Brett's family?

Some time later, their small cavalcade moved into the courtyard, where servants came running to help them alight. Brett assisted Storm down, his face tense and dark, and Storm felt his unease and knew she must be mistaken; grief must be responsible for his reticence. His bearing became even more rigid when she heard a woman calling his name, and they turned to look toward the villa. Storm took Brett's hand in hers and blushed when he glanced at her, lifting one brow sardonically. Embarrassed, she made to release her hand, but he held on to it tightly.

"Caro mío! Dear, dear Breton! *Como esta usted?* How was your trip?"

Storm looked at the beautiful woman, her hair jet black, her brown eyes huge, her face the color of ivory. She was clad in black for mourning, and Storm wondered if this was Brett's mother. She had never asked about his family, and Brett had volunteered little information. He released her hand to take the one the beautiful woman had offered and bowed over it. "Indeed, Tía Elena, this is a . . . pleasure." He lifted her fingers to his lips without touching her delicate white skin.

"So gallant! And who, dear Breton, is this?"

Storm flushed when she realized Brett's aunt did not know she was his wife. He gave her an apologetic look, and Storm realized with shock that he hadn't even told his family about their marriage. How could he! Deeply embarrassed, she felt her face flame even more when the woman studied her assessingly.

"My wife, Storm. This is my aunt, Tía Elena."

Storm managed a smile.

"You must be tired," Elena purred, expertly hiding her surprise. "Ah, here come the rest of the family."

Storm was so humiliated, she wished she didn't have to stand there and greet them.

"Brett!"

"Tío Emmanuel," Brett said, and a genuine smile flashed upon his face.

The two men stood facing each other. Storm stared at Brett's uncle, then tried not to look stricken as the kindly, gray-haired gentleman turned to her. "And who is this, nephew?"

"Uncle Emmanuel, this is my dear wife, Storm."

"Ah, you have married. And such a beautiful woman, with such an unusual name, *niña.*" He gave her a warm smile.

"Brett!"

Storm looked at the young woman who had spoken and felt instant dismay. She must be Tía Elena's daughter, for she was an exact but younger version of Brett's beautiful aunt. She was perfectly gorgeous, black-eyed and black-haired, of average height but voluptuously curved, with the smallest waist Storm had ever seen. Her lips were ruby red, and were now smiling seductively at Storm's husband. His voice a caress, Brett said, "Well, well. If my cousin Sophia hasn't grown up."

"And you also, Brett," she flirted, holding out a delicate white hand.

Storm glanced at Brett, saw the smile, and failed to catch the mocking light in his eyes. Her heart turned over. She had the insane notion that he and this woman had been childhood sweethearts. She was so beautiful, any man would love her. And Brett was staring at her, looking at her—she knew that look.

Then he did a surprising thing. He stepped closer to Storm, taking her hand in his. "Sophia, my wife Storm."

Sophia looked her up and down with disdain, almost tossing her glossy black head. "How nice," she murmured, as if she were repulsed. "You are so . . . tall."

"And you are so . . . plump," Storm heard herself say, wanting to scratch her eyes out.

Sophia stared, stunned, then smiled, thrusting her chest forward. "Perfectly so," she said, removing her gaze from Storm. She looked at Brett, into his eyes, her lips pouting invitingly, then at his chest. Her gaze traveled lower and stroked his thighs, shocking Storm. She had never seen a woman stare so lustfully at a man, at his groin. She had the urge to smack Sophia's pout right off her perfect face.

Brett chuckled, his arm going around Storm's waist, pulling her against him. "We are extremely tired," he said.

"Of course," Elena said. "It already grows late. I shall

have bathwater sent to your rooms. Perhaps you would like a dinner tray brought up?''

"That would be fine," Brett said. "Tío Emmanuel, I hope everything can wait until morning.''

"Certainly, Brett. Your father is asleep right now. He takes laudanum for his ease. He will sleep until the morrow.''

"I am sorry about your grandson, Tío . . . Tía," Brett said. "I am sorry, Sophia.''

"Thank you," Sophia said, looking suddenly stricken. "He was only a baby . . .''

Elena put her arm around her daughter. "And Sophia just widowed, too. Come, daughter, help me see to the comfort of your cousin and his wife.''

Storm was shocked to realize Sophia was a widow and a mother, and older than she thought. Compassion for her cousin-in-law replaced her earlier hostility.

Sophia paused at the threshold of the villa, glancing over her shoulder. She flashed Brett a marvelous smile, fluttered inky black lashes over her eyes, and swept away, her rounded hips swinging. One glance at her husband confirmed for Storm the fact that he was watching Sophia walk away with intense concentration, and Storm felt as if someone had stabbed her in the heart. She was suddenly so tired, she felt the urge to cry, and she leaned against him.

"You are exhausted," he murmured, his grip on her tightening. Storm saw warmth his eyes and was flustered. She didn't understand this man who was her husband, not at all.

They were shown into a suite of rooms. Brett retired to the sitting room so Storm could bathe first, with Betsy to aid her. Storm was exhausted, hungry, and still mortified that Brett hadn't bothered to tell his family of their marriage. She did not linger in the tub but washed quickly, dried herself, and slipped on an emerald silk gown and negligee adorned with delicate cream lace. She began to brush her hair, listening to Betsy inform Brett he could take his bath now. Brett told her she was dismissed, and when Storm looked up, he was standing in the doorway, watching her comb out her wet tresses. She met his glance in the mirror and was touched deep inside when he smiled. He moved forward, pulling off his shirt.

For a moment, Storm stared at his chest, then she pulled herself together. "Excuse me," she murmured.

He was unbuckling his belt, unbuttoning the fly to his breeches. Storm's eyes widened; she colored and fled. She thought she heard him laughing softly, but she wasn't sure.

A tray of food was waiting, but it would be rude to eat without him, so Storm sank into a plush chair and poured herself a glass of wine. The sitting room was huge and plush and elegant. There were three sofas, a settee, many chairs, and a desk. The floors, which were made of pine, were covered with Oriental rugs. All the furniture was upholstered in thick brocades or fine silks. The curtains were velvet. The room reminded her of her own home in Texas—very European.

The downstairs, however, had been Spanish, from the red-tiled floors to the heavy walnut furniture and beamed stucco ceilings. It suddenly occurred to Storm that Brett was French, his family Spanish. She frowned at this—even his last name was French. Then she understood. His father must have been French, and he had married the Spanish daughter of the hacienda, who had been the sole heir. For there was no mistaking the resemblance between Brett and his cousin, although the short, merry-cheeked Emmanuel did not seem related at all, as far as looks went.

"So pensive," Brett said, his voice warm and melodious.

Storm glanced up, coming out of her reverie. He was wearing a black silk robe with red lapels. His body was damp. The robe clung to his powerful chest and thighs. Storm shifted uneasily.

"Hungry?" he asked, coming to sit next to her and refilling her glass, then pouring one for himself.

"Yes, starved." She met his eyes. They were so soft when not filled with anger, a dark, rich brown with gold flecks instead of near black. His mouth curved slightly upward, and Storm felt something tugging at her heart. He handed her the glass. She reached for it, and her wrapper opened, revealing the low neckline of her gown, edged in cream lace. Brett's gaze dipped to encompass the view, brightening considerably. Storm flushed and pulled the wrapper together.

"Shall we adjourn to the table?" he asked, standing, revealing a glimpse of hard, black-haired thigh. He held out his hand. Storm took it, rising, and he seated her as if they were at dinner party, holding her chair for her, then seated himself.

"Allow me," he said, smiling, and he served her first.

They ate in silence. Storm was starved until she realized he was barely eating. She looked up and recognized the hungry, rapt expression on his face, felt the heat of his eyes. Her body went hot, something liquid started to build deep inside. She lowered her eyes and continued to eat.

"Tired?" Brett asked once she had finished. His tone was soft, kindly, yet too suggestive.

Storm thought about the single oversized four-poster bed in the other room, and her heart began to race. She thought about the night he had seduced her. Instead of becoming angry, she felt her body start to throb, remembering the incredible sensations he had made her feel, the ecstatic responses she had given.

"Let's go to bed," Brett said, standing. His tone was hard to define, but Storm didn't dare look at him. He had said he wouldn't touch her again. For some reason, she knew he had meant it, and she trusted him.

She preceded him nervously into the bedroom. Brett could feel her anxiety, but he no longer smiled. It was so hard to be this way with her, barely dressed, alone, and not grab her and hold her and stroke her all over. He could think of nothing else now but his lust for her, which was threatening to make him insane. She was so ripe, so lush, her breasts so full, her nipples hard against the green silk, mesmerizing him, demanding his attention. He watched as she slipped off the wrapper, not looking at him, and he managed not to suck in his breath too loudly. The silk clung to every inch of her superb form, molding the thrust of her ample bosom, the flat curve of her belly, the upward tilt of her saucy behind, the shapely line of her legs. And then she was sliding under the covers, closing her eyes as if she were asleep already. He should have smiled. He couldn't.

He turned down the gas lamps before moving to his side of the bed, not wanting her to see his arousal and guard against it. He slipped in beside her, not touching her, stretching out on his back. He was achingly aware of her just six inches away from him. He could smell her. He could feel the heat of her body.

Brett sighed raggedly.

After a moment he did so again, more loudly although he was sure she must have heard the first time.

"Brett?"

Not answering, he rolled onto his side, his back to her. He sighed again, like a hurt, wounded animal.

"Brett? Are you okay?" Her voice was soft, a whisper. He knew she was leaning close to his back; he felt a tendril of her silken hair.

"I'm . . . fine," he said hoarsely.

She greeted that statement, with its heavy innuendos, in silence. Then the bed shifted as she lay back down, and Brett cursed without thinking, audibly. She was instantly poised on her elbow again. "Do you . . . want to talk?"

He waited a few heartbeats, as if he had trouble talking. "Storm . . ."

He tensed when he felt her hand on his bare shoulder, light, then firmer. "Can I get you something to help you sleep?" she asked, kneading the taut muscles of his shoulder.

"Storm . . . the memories," he said. Her hand stopped, then moved again, kneading deliberately. "I know," she whispered.

He sighed and rolled over so that his knee slid against her silk-clad thighs, his face poised inches from her soft breasts. Her hand on his shoulder froze.

Taking a deep breath, Brett snuggled his face into the bounty of her lush breasts. Heaven, he thought, restraining a shudder of pure desire. "Hold me," he whispered raggedly, hoping he sounded like a man grieving, not like one with a rigid arousal.

She didn't hesitate then, but cradled his head deeper into her bosom, her hands moving in his wavy hair. Brett sighed, nuzzling against the silk of her gown, his closed eyes pressing against bare flesh. His knee slid casually against her lower thigh, slipping between her legs, forcing the silk to hike up and retreat. She continued to stroke his hair.

He shifted his face, moving the silk of her gown down, working it down further with another nuzzling movement until one soft, rich globe was bare against his cheek and lips. It was so hard not to kiss that swollen flesh. He moved his hand from between them onto her waist, then down to the ripe curve of her hip. His splayed fingers almost enclosed one buttock.

Storm had been carnally aware of Brett for days, although she was trying to ignore that and be compassionate. Now her heart was racing wildly, her breasts tingling, her groin swelling demandingly. She shifted without thinking, and the result was that her nipple, achingly hard and somehow bared, moved closer to Brett's mouth, catching his nose. Her buttock moved, too, and his hand shifted over the silk until his fingertips were resting inches from her womanhood.

Brett nuzzled the offered breast with a groan. Storm's hands on his head suddenly tightened, pushing him closer to the hard bud. His hand tightened on her buttock, squeezing, releasing, and then he kissed the soft underswell of her breast. "Beautiful. Beautiful . . ." he murmured.

His brushing lips were torture. Storm shifted again, seeking his mouth with her nipple, and her knee brushed the hard, naked tip of his swollen phallus. She gasped, then was silenced as he pulled the hard peak into his mouth, nipping it again and again, making her moan, and then he was suckling like a baby.

She cried out as his teeth caught and teased, as his tongue soothed and lapped, darting, only to give way to sharp, tugging teeth again. His other hand kneaded her buttock, dipping low, sliding between her thighs, rubbing insistently. He caressed her swollen mound from behind, teasing it with a bare finger, tracing the outlines of the lush folds, then sliding upward to tease a throbbing apex. Storm threw her thigh over his torso to accommodate his search.

"Storm," he groaned. "I need you, *chère,* badly . . ."

"Yes," she panted. "Yes, Brett."

His hand bared her other breast, and his mouth found her other nipple, his tongue emerging to flicker repeatedly over it, to lick, tingle, tempt. A hard, seeking mouth closed over it, teeth catching, tugging insistently. Storm cried out.

Brett had already pulled the offending gown up to her waist. With her thigh thrown over his hips, her knee bent, she was open and waiting for him. He fondled her buttock leisurely now, intent on devastation, caressing and stroking, threatening to dip into that inviting, wet sanctuary, yet not doing so. Storm's behind began to move frantically against his hand. She moaned. "Please . . ."

"Yes, darling, soon," he told her, still suckling her taut nipples. He moved his hand to her belly and explored the soft flatness there. She whimpered demandingly. His hand strayed lower; his fingers slid through soft, tangled curls; one finger delved even further. He slid into that wet delta. Storm gasped. He retreated, barely able to breathe, releasing her nipple, pausing to concentrate on the exquisite torture he was intent on inflicting.

His finger explored, teased, slid slickly into deep recesses, moved up and began to rub rhythmically. Storm writhed against him. She pumped against his hand. She panted wildly. Brett shuddered, pressing a kiss to her ribs when she cried out, loudly keening, and he shoved three fingers into her, hard, pumping, amazed at the strength of her contractions, his thumb still on the apex he had been manipulating so deftly. He could feel the entire mound quivering again and again under his hand.

"Oh, Storm," he moaned when she lay still and breathless on her back.

He closed his eyes to regain control, and when he had found it, he knelt over her, studying her.

The green gown was twisted around her waist. Her eyes were closed, her hair in disarray, streaming over the pillows and between and around her full, ripe breasts. He noted that the nipples were still hard, and, unable to resist, he mouthed one briefly. Her eyes flew open. Brett smiled at her dazed look.

Her long legs were spread invitingly. Her curls were damp and dark. Her woman's flesh glistened invitingly. Brett grabbed her hips and lowered his head. When his mouth kissed the tender pink folds, she gasped. He tightened his hold on her, kissing the soft perimeters, then moving closer and closer. His tongue flicked out to trace the depths of the long cleft. She clenched his head, whimpering.

When her hips were thrusting uncontrollably against his seeking tongue, Brett raised himself up and moved the tip of his member over her slickness. She gasped, her wide eyes meeting his. He rubbed himself leisurely against her, smiling.

"I love you," he rasped, moving languidly over her.

She gasped again.

He bent his head over her. "Tell me," he demanded, moving suggestively, the engorged head of his shaft dipping and rubbing and stroking. "Tell me how much you want me." For the first time he kissed her, claiming her lips savagely. When he raised his head, she gasped his name in a plea.

"Do you love me, Storm?" he panted, sliding slickly over her. "Do you love it when I do this? And this?"

She moaned.

"Do you love it when I'm deep inside you?" He poised at the threshold of her entrance without penetrating. He tested that small entry gingerly, prodding it. "Tell me!"

"Yes! Yes! Yes!"

"Oh, God, I want you," he said, and he thrust into her.

They came together wildly, fiercely, straining against each other, slick and wet. Brett thrust harder and harder, having lost all control. *My Storm,* was all he could think. And then she cried out, contracting against him, around him, while he throbbed inside her, and he cried out, too, pumping his seed into her, draining himself, moaning her name.

Storm awoke to find herself entwined intimately with her husband.

Memories of the night before came rushing upon her. Wonderful memories, of his touch, his mouth, his hands playing her. Burning memories of how he felt, so warm and hard against her, on her, in her . . . He had said he loved her. Had he meant it? Storm remembered vividly exactly what he was doing when he said those three words, and she flushed. A more complete recollection flooded her. The things he had said to her! The things he had made her say back! How he had made her beg for him, and how she had meant it. Dear God! Certainly a husband didn't treat a wife like that. Like a whore.

She wrenched away and sat up, her heart starting to pound. Every fiber of her being went stiff when she felt him move next to her. She would not look at him. She could not let him treat her like that. She felt his hand drifting down her thigh. Storm threw both legs over the side of the bed, lunging to her feet in one hard, abrupt movement.

In a second she was flat on her back, Brett on top of her, pinning her, his eyes black and alert, as if he hadn't been sleeping at all. "Storm?"

"Let me up," she gritted, struggling.

He loosened his grip but didn't move. "Is this the way you greet me?" His gaze was piercing. "Are you angry?"

"Of course not," she said with dripping sarcasm.

A look of genuine confusion crossed his face. "After last night," he murmured, "I would expect you to be purring with pleasure, not leaping out of my bed."

"You arrogant boor," she snapped.

Suddenly all confusion and indignation were gone. He smiled, his dark eyes brightening. "If you're trying to get my attention," he murmured seductively, "you needn't have gone so far." He shifted, grinning, and the throbbing tip of him caught her inner thigh. Storm gasped. Brett covered her mouth with his, hungrily, as if he hadn't made love to her four times that night, his tongue darting within, thrusting eagerly.

Storm's whole body began to burn. She ignored it. He

wasn't going to get away with this. She twisted her face away.

"Oh, *chère,*" he breathed, lifting his head, "how I want you." He rubbed himself against her thigh. "That's how much I want you, love." Their eyes caught. His widened when he realized she was glaring.

He found himself shoved rudely off. "Now what?" he asked, trying to sound annoyed, but how could he be annoyed? He had just spent the most incredible night of his life with the most incredible woman he had ever known—and that woman happened to belong to him. His wife. His alone. No one else could have her. It was a heady thought. A million strange, warm, uplifting feelings were shooting through his body, wrestling in his heart. He put an arm around her hips and smiled up at her stormy gaze. Nothing could dampen his mood. "Now what?" he repeated.

"Last night . . ." she began, stopping and giving him a look as sharp as daggers.

His grin widened, and he nuzzled her long neck.

"Stop it, dammit, Brett! I'm serious!"

"So am I, sweetheart," he said, and in one deft, unexpected movement he had pulled her down and on top of him. "This is our honeymoon," he purred.

Storm's eyes filled with tears.

A pang of fear seized him. "Storm, what is it?" He was horrified—horrified that the thought of their honeymoon would make her cry. But how could he have thought she would change after one night spent intimately with him? He had almost forgotten, she despised him. One night was not going to change his stubborn wife's mind.

"I don't like being treated like a whore, Brett," she said furiously. But she was sniffing, and he saw that she was hurt.

Brett sat up, pulling her up with him, cradling her. "What are you talking about, *chère?*" His voice was soft and tender. His forefinger removed a crawling tear from her cheek.

"The things you said to me," she whispered, as if afraid to be overhead.

"What?"

"No man talks to his wife the way you talked to me." She blushed.

He suddenly understood, and bit off his laughter. "How would you know?"

"I just know."

He stroked her cheek. "Sweet, you seemed to enjoy it last night." He grinned. He couldn't help it.

She looked away.

"No, Storm, look at me. Anything you and I do together is all right as long as we are both willing and it pleasures us."

She regarded him doubtfully.

His hand slid to her shoulder. "I want to give you pleasure. I want you to be as excited as I am." He cupped one full breast. He palmed her nipple. "We're married. You are not a whore. You are my wife. It's all right to tease in bed to increase our pleasure. Trust me." His voice had dropped to a whisper.

She wanted to trust him, wanted to believe him. It was getting hard to think, hard to remember why she had been so angry. She was very aware of the movements of his fingers on her nipple. "Brett."

He cupped her face, staring into her eyes, one thumb brushing the corner of her mouth. "You're my wife, Storm," he said. "Never forget that."

Chapter 16

It was noon when they finally left their apartments and came downstairs. Storm kept stealing admiring looks at her husband when she thought he wasn't looking. She couldn't seem to keep her eyes off him. She couldn't stop remembering the passion they had shared, both the frenzied, savage times and the strangely tender ones, too. He was so handsome! And she liked the way he was dressed now—in skintight riding breeches and high black boots, and a simple linen shirt. He was so broad-shouldered, so powerful, so male and virile. As they passed through the empty salon on the first floor, Storm saw the second looks the two maids gave her husband and felt a momentary thrill of pride and possession. This man is my husband, she thought, amazed. Mine!

They were eating breakfast in the high-ceilinged dining room, alone in companionable silence. Feeling Brett's gaze, Storm looked up from her piece of melon and was rewarded with a warm smile. Her heart turned over, and she stared, unable to look away. He leaned close to her and tenderly brushed her lips with his. For another moment their gazes met. Storm's heart was bursting with the love his eyes contained.

"How quaint," Elena said from the doorway. "How picturesque."

Brett stood. "Good morning, Tía."

She swept to him and poised her cheek for his perfunctory kiss. Then she gave one of her own to Storm. "Did you two sleep well?"

Storm blushed while Brett laughed. "As well as could be expected," he said, flashing Storm a warm glance and sitting down.

"Don Felipe is up," Elena said casually, sitting opposite them. "He knows you're here." Her glance held Brett's, and Storm had the feeling a silent communication was exchanged.

Brett shrugged. "I will pay my respects after I eat. How is he?"

"Dying," Elena said.

Storm gasped.

"My dear," Elena told Storm, "if you knew him as we all do, you, too, would know his days left with us are limited. That is why Sophia is here." She looked at Brett. "After losing her son to that dreadful disease, and her husband barely six months in the grave, I did not want her to be alone with a houseful of servants."

"Of course not," Brett said without inflection. "No cousin Diego? Has he not joined us to await Father's grand departure?"

"Brett!" Storm gasped.

Elena remained unperturbed. "Diego comes by almost daily."

"And where is Doña Theresa?" Brett asked.

"She is either in seclusion in her rooms grieving for the loss of her children, or she is with Don Felipe. He can't stand her, you know. He usually orders her away after only a few minutes. Her tears and moaning lamentations drive him crazy."

Storm looked at Brett's aunt. The woman was undeniably beautiful, even in her black mourning dress, which was cut as low as a ballgown, revealing voluptuous breasts. Her skin was white and satiny smooth, and her waist was narrow, her hips round but not ample. She was very beautiful, and very cruel. Storm felt it in the marrow of her being. She also did not like the way she looked at Brett, as if he amused her, as if she knew some wonderful secret joke, as if she knew him—in the biblical sense.

"There you are," Emmanuel said, striding into the dining room, smiling with genuine affection. "Good morning, you two. Brett, she is a ray of golden sunshine." Emmanuel's admiration was frank.

"Isn't she," Brett said, looking at Storm with rapt and warm attention. She had never felt more lovely.

"Finish up, my boy," Emmanuel said. "Don Felipe is eager to see you."

Brett stood and laughed. "Has he said that?"

Emmanuel grinned sheepishly. "Not quite."

"Hah! I'll bet the old badger has pretended he doesn't even know I'm here!"

"He knows," Emmanuel said. "Ease up on him, Brett. He still has the Monterro pride."

Brett shrugged. "It doesn't matter to me," he said casually. He leaned down, tilting Storm's chin up and kissing her fully on the mouth, deeply, despite his aunt and uncle's presence. "They have a quaint custom here, *chère*," he said in a low voice. "It's called a siesta." He grinned.

Storm knew what a siesta was, of course, and she blushed, managing not to look at either of Brett's relatives.

"Ah, to be young and in love." Emmanuel sighed with good-natured exaggeration.

Storm's color deepened as they walked away, her gaze on her husband's beautiful masculine form. Am I in love? she wondered, and knew the answer instantly. Yes! Her whole being was filled with Brett. She didn't know how it had happened, it just had.

"How long have you been married, dear?" Elena asked, watching her closely.

Storm stopped her daydreaming. "About two weeks," she said.

"I see." There was a moment of silence, and Storm continued eating. "How do you like the hacienda?"

"It's beautiful," Storm said honestly. "Now I understand why Brett is so—so—polished."

Elena looked at her. "Whatever do you mean?"

"Why, his being raised here," Storm said.

Elena laughed. Storm didn't like her laughter, especially since she did not understand the joke. At that precise moment, Sophia swept in, a younger version of her mother, breathtakingly gorgeous. "What's so funny, Mama?"

"Sweet Storm," Elena said, her laughter subsiding, "understands how Brett has come to be so polished."

Sophia frowned, sitting and pouring herself a cup of coffee. "I don't understand." She gave Storm a short glance. Storm did not miss the rudeness. Sophia hadn't even said hello.

"Brett's being raised here," Elena said significantly.

Sophia chuckled. "Just how well do you know your husband?" she asked pointedly.

Storm felt her hackles rising. "Very well in some ways," she said with her own innuendo, remembering how Sophia had looked at Brett yesterday. Sophia was attracted to Brett, Storm knew it, and she felt a moment of triumph. Brett was hers. Sophia might want him, but she couldn't have him.

"Any woman can know any man well in those ways, dear," Elena droned tolerantly.

Storm was instantly deflated. The lovemaking they had shared—what he had done to her, how he had made her feel—Brett had shared those moments with other women. The reminder was enough to shatter her mood of euphoria. In fact, she had forgotten how he had been with Audrey before he had come home to her after his trip, then taken her against her will. Damn! Damn, damn, damn!

"Brett is certainly looking fine," Sophia said, breaking into Storm's thoughts. "Emmanuel says he's quite the success in San Francisco."

"Yes," Storm said, pride slipping through the moment of despondency. "He was the most sought-after bachelor in the city. He has a saloon, a hotel, several restaurants, and he owns quite a bit of land. The saloon and hotel are the most elegant and refined in the city. He is also partners with my uncle in a shipping line."

Sophia and her mother exchanged glances. "Who would ever have thought," Sophia finally said, "that my bastard cousin would grow up to be such a man." She stressed the last word.

Anger rushed through Storm. "Excuse me?" She couldn't believe what she had heard.

Sophia raised a brow.

"How dare you," Storm said, standing. "How dare you call my husband names."

"Relax, dear," Elena said, touching her wrist. "We're all family here. Sophia didn't mean to insult Brett. She was speaking matter-of-factly. After all, it is unusual for a penniless bastard to become so successful and so cultured."

Storm was stunned. She couldn't grasp what they were saying. "Brett is a bastard?"

The two women looked surprised. "Surely you knew that much?" Elena said.

Sophia laughed. "Not only is Brett a bastard, Storm, but his mother was a common whore in Mazatlán. French, but a whore."

Poor Brett, Storm thought, remembering how she had called him a blue-blooded pig, and how furious he had been.

Then she remembered all the times she had called him

a bastard, and she was horrified with herself. Why hadn't anyone told her? Poor Brett!

"I do believe we've shocked her, Mama," Sophia said, smiling slightly.

"Please sit, Storm, and finish your breakfast," Elena said.

Storm sat, still assimilating all she had learned. She remember how Elena and Sophia had laughed over her comment about Brett's refinement coming from having been raised here. She remembered how Brett had been grim and cold when she had asked him if he'd had a falling out with his father. The night Brett had come home drunk, he had said his mother had sold him to his father. Had it been true? Oh, God! Suddenly Storm thought she understood. But she wanted, desperately, to understand better.

"Good morning," boomed a male voice from the doorway. "And who is this?"

Storm looked up to see a man clad in the traditional garb of the Californios: tight belled black pants riveted with silver studs, a short bolero jacket, a crisp white shirt. He was dark and extremely handsome, every inch the son of Elena and the brother of Sophia.

"Diego, come greet Brett's wife," Elena said.

Diego strode forward, his black eyes bright with interest. "*Cara*, I am overwhelmed," he said, taking her hand before she even knew what was happening. "Never have I seen such beauty, never!"

Storm blushed. She didn't know what to say to such an outrageous comment. Then he kissed her hand, his mustache tickling her skin, his lips lingering, and she was sure she felt the tip of his tongue. She gasped, trying to pull away and failing. "I hope you will honor me by letting me escort you around Don Felipe's beautiful hacienda."

"I—I don't know," she managed.

"Ah, cousin Brett will not mind. He and Don Felipe have much catching up to do, believe me."

"Perhaps tomorrow," Storm said. She needed to talk to Brett. She wanted to hold him and tell him he didn't need to keep any secrets from her. Not anymore.

"Tomorrow, then," Diego said, smiling. His teeth flashed white against his dark skin. "Now, where is my cousin?"

Brett stared at his father, momentarily shocked. Then Don Felipe turned his head, his black eyes brilliant and gleaming and unchanged, and their gazes locked. Brett shoved away his pity. The once leonine man might be shrunken and white-haired, but his spirit remained undiminished. Brett almost felt sixteen again beneath the impact of that baleful stare. It was judging and condemning and condescending. He felt like "the bastard" again.

"Come here," Don Felipe ordered.

He was sitting in a chaise, a blanket pulled to his waist. He was no longer a giant of a man, but thin and scrawny, shrunken even in height, Brett could see. His voice, too, was weaker; it quavered.

Brett moved forward. "Father," he said evenly. Etiquette called for more of a greeting, but the old bastard had never treated him like anything but a curse, so why should Brett bother?

Don Felipe's eyes scorched him from head to toe. Then, looking into Brett's face, he laughed. "Still the rebel, eh, boy?"

There was nothing to say to that. Brett just stood, hating himself for feeling ill-at-ease.

"Why did you come?" Don Felipe said shortly.

"Emmanuel begged me."

"Ah." The black eyes were assessing. "Perhaps you came like the others, to wait for my death. I'm not ready yet, boy."

"Why should I care whether you live or die, old man?"

Don Felipe chuckled. "At least you're honest, Breton,

that's one thing about you—you're honest. It's more than I can say for the rest of the schemers who surround me, with few exceptions. Have you met your sister Gabriella yet?''

The change in topic took Brett by surprise. ''No.''

''If you think I'm going to leave all this''—a thin arm swept out—''to you, you're wrong.''

It was Brett's turn to laugh. ''Good. I don't want it, not one damn acre!''

They glared at each other.

''Why the hell not?'' Don Felipe shouted. ''You're my son.''

''I'm your son now? Ten years ago I wasn't your son— just your bastard.''

''You were—and are—both my son and my bastard,'' Don Felipe said. ''Even God can't change that fact of life.''

''No, He can't.''

''Emmanuel says you're a rich and successful business-man.''

''Quite.''

''With a new wife.''

''Yes.''

''You should have married a californio.''

''Never,'' Brett said, appalled at the idea. ''I am sorry you are lacking heirs, Father, but there is Diego.''

''Never.'' Don Felipe snorted. ''That weakling nephew! All he does is gamble and wench. Did he save Emmanuel's hacienda? Did he fight for what was his against the greedy Americanos? If I left him this, it would be gone, destroyed, ruined, within a few years.'' Don Felipe was red with rage and breathing harshly, but Brett only clenched his fists rigidly until the don caught his breath. He coughed. ''Those two female vipers and that spineless rakehell have been awaiting your arrival like Christians waiting to be tossed to the lions.'' He laughed, pleased.

"They want all this. They're afraid we'll reconcile and I'll give it all to you."

"If you do, I'll sell it," Brett warned, meaning it.

"As if I'd leave you anything," Don Felipe rasped, his black eyes locking with Brett's.

Brett hated him. "I told you, old man," he said softly, "I don't want it, and I never have."

They glared. "You made that clear," Don Felipe said, "when you walked out of here ten years ago."

"You didn't even try to stop me." It was a standoff, and they both knew it, but Brett wondered what he had expected: a confession, an apology?

"Let them simmer, greedy bastards," Don Felipe said finally. "To protect Gabriella. I don't trust Elena and Sophia."

"What are you saying?" Brett demanded.

"Gabriella is betrothed. I intend to live until she is married in three years, to Salvador Talaveras, a fine Californio. They will inherit everything."

"Fine with me," Brett said grimly. But an ugly thought came unbidden. *He chose my little sister, a woman, over his own son.*

"Go back to the city, boy. We'll let them think you will inherit it all. When the day comes that they read my will, they will be surprised." He chortled at the thought.

"Sophia is a widow," Brett said. "Where is her rancho?"

"Far south, near Los Angeles. They have lost three-quarters to squatters since annexation by the United States, and they could lose it all in litigation over the title. Once, it was a fine place. Now it is neglected and run down." Don Felipe glared at him. "The damn Americanos have taken everything away from us, Brett. Our lands, our way of life. The Californios are a dead breed." He began to cough.

When he didn't stop, Brett grew alarmed despite himself, and pounded him on the back, surprised at the strength of his father's body, which was not as frail as it looked. Brett handed him some water and the old man drank, the fit passing. "Are you all right?" Brett asked.

"Do you care?" he shot back.

"If I'm riding down the road," Brett said, "and I find a starving, maimed mutt, I care enough to put it out of its misery."

"I'm not starving, maimed, or a damn mongrel," Felipe shouted. "I'm your flesh and blood."

"Barely," Brett shouted back. "And through no choice of mine. Why, old man? Why did you want me to come?"

"I didn't, you ungrateful bastard," Don Felipe yelled. "Do you think I care? Go back to the city, back where you belong!"

"Gladly," Brett gritted. "You don't have one drop of compassion in your entire body, do you? Do you have one damn drop?"

"What is all this shouting?" Emmanuel asked with concern, running in.

"Ask him," Brett managed, striding out of the room.

"Felipe, are you all right?"

"He is every inch a Monterro," Don Felipe said with satisfaction when Brett was out of hearing. "And every inch my son."

"Why don't you tell him you are proud of him?" Emmanuel asked gently.

"Bah!" Felipe spat. "Praise is for women and dogs, not men."

Brett slammed into his and his wife's rooms. He was profoundly agitated. God, he hated that old bastard! But what did he expect? A kind word? If the old tyrant hadn't shown him a single kindness when he was a boy, why would he now? Had he really expected it, wanted it, come all this way for it?

"Brett?"

He whirled, not having expected Storm to be there. Immediately, he started to soften. "What are you doing?"

"I was waiting for you," she said gently. Her blue eyes were filled with tenderness and compassion, as if she knew what was raging in his heart and soul.

"Come here," he said gruffly. The urge to wrap himself around her, bury himself in her, and escape all this was overwhelming.

Surprising him, she did, and he lifted her abruptly and carried her to the bed, where he slid down next to her. He cupped her face in his hands and began kissing her. Sure enough, as soon as her lips were soft and open beneath his, her tongue coyly enticing, he forgot the interview with his father and could think of only one thing. He began stroking her superb body, finding her breasts and crushing them in his large hands. "I need you," he murmured, pulling down the bodice of her dress, tearing it in the process.

"Brett," she protested, but she was clinging to him.

"God, I need you," he heard himself groan as he unbuttoned the fly of his breeches. He did. He needed her desperately, like a starving man needs food.

"I find myself insatiable around you," he murmured, wrapping her in his arms.

Later, she met his glance, and he saw the pleasure their lovemaking had brought. She touched his cheek gently. Brett didn't move, drowning in her gaze, more aware of her than he had ever been aware of a woman before. She raised her head and kissed him, gently, lovingly. Then she smiled and laid her cheek against his shoulder.

"You're so beautiful, Storm," Brett said, stroking her hair.

"So are you," she said softly, exploring his waist.

"Isn't this better than fighting, *chère?*"

"Oh, I don't know." She grinned. "Brett? How is your father?"

He stiffened. "Don't even bring that old bastard up, Storm."

"If you don't want to be called names, you shouldn't call others by them," she said gently.

He rolled onto his side, dead serious now, regarding her steadily. She flushed. "Who told you? Tía Elena?"

She nodded.

"The bitch."

"Brett! She's your aunt."

"And a complete bitch, Storm, as I well know. Her daughter's no different."

"They're your family," Storm said with consternation, sitting up.

"By no choice of my own, and barely," Brett said, frowning and sliding up against the pillows.

"What does that mean?"

He shot her a look. "My mother was a two-bit whore. If I didn't look like a Monterro, there would be no proof of my paternity."

"But you do look like a Monterro. The resemblance is strong."

Brett shrugged. "We shouldn't have come. Hell! I don't know why we did come."

"Brett, please. Your father is old and sick and possibly dying—"

"Hah! That despot will live another three years at least, I guarantee it." Seeing her confusion, he added, "To see his daughter married. I know him. He's not as ill as you think."

"You hate him," she whispered, aghast.

"What is it to you, Storm? Are you suddenly taking more than a carnal interest in your husband? Well, don't bother! Just keep out of my personal affairs!" He lunged to his feet.

Storm was shocked, and hurt to the quick. Brett strode out of the room, adjusting his trousers. She brushed away a tear. So much for caring, she thought.

Brett walked back in and instantly froze. "Damn," he muttered.

"Go away," Storm warned, quickly wiping her eyes. "I mean it!"

"I didn't mean to make you cry," he said, sitting next to her and pulling her into his arms. Storm struggled, but Brett wouldn't let her go. She quieted and he held her close, kissing her hair. "Storm, the old man is a sonuva-bitch, believe me. I grew up here being treated worse than the servants. Sophia and Elena never let me forget I was a bastard. The old man never had a kind word, not ever. Uncle Emmanuel made life bearable, but barely. You don't know how it was."

Storm gazed at him, putting her arms around his neck. "And you were just a little boy," she murmured, trying to imagine how it would feel to be seven or eight, and motherless, suddenly thrust into a household of Monter-ros. "A little boy needing love."

"I survived," Brett said gruffly, the look in her eyes unsettling him.

She played with the hair at his temple.

"Brett, your father loves you, I know he does."

Brett laughed. "You're wrong. If he loved me, he would have made an appearance in my life before I was eight, before my two older brothers were killed. He was only interested in me then because he had no male heir, just as he's only interested in me now because Manuel died."

Storm refused to believe it. "That can't be true, Brett, it can't."

"He knew about me, Storm, all along, because my mother was his mistress, and when she got pregnant he supported her until she could work again. But he never came to see me, not once. I never even knew who my father was until the day my mother so casually told me she was sending me away to live with him.''

Storm's heart was breaking. ''Oh, Brett, how could she send you away? She must have done it out of love, knowing you would have a better life with your father than with her.''

Brett laughed. ''I told you, my father paid her for me.''

''Is she still alive?'' Storm heard herself ask.

Brett shrugged. ''I have no idea, nor could I care less.''

She gasped. ''Brett, you must love her a little!''

''Love that whore? Storm, my family was not like yours. You were lucky. My mother birthed me and that was the end of it. I'm surprised she didn't abandon me on the streets for all the attention she gave me those first eight years of my life. Sometimes I got a pat on the head when she walked by. Usually I was told to get out of the house. She didn't like her customers seeing she had a son my age. Whenever I did happen to run into one of them, she would tell them I was the cook's boy.'' Brett stiffened when he saw that tears were slipping down Storm's face. ''Don't cry for me,'' he said brusquely.

She cupped his face. ''I guess I never knew how lucky I was. Brett, I want you to meet my family. You'll love them.''

Brett was feeling all kinds of self-pity, emotions with which he was totally unfamiliar. She was making him feel them. And her hands on his face, so warm and reassuring . . . The urge to wallow in self-pity, hide his face on her chest and let her comfort him as if he were a boy, welled up in him. Instead, he rose abruptly to his feet, giving her a smile. ''I'd love to meet your family,'' he said, changing the topic. ''Is your mother like you?''

Storm smiled. ''Not at all. She's a tiny woman, short and petite and dark-haired. But she's very strong. Pa bends over backward to do her bidding.''

Brett laughed. Storm became so enthusiastic and animated when she was discussing her family, the love she felt for them clear in her eyes. He couldn't help making the comparison with his own family, and he struggled to quell it.

But he couldn't quell one thought. Don Felipe preferred a child-woman as an heir to his bastard son.

Chapter 17

She is beautiful, Brett thought, staring. Then he smiled. "Hello, Gabriella."

The twelve-year-old had been regarding him with shy, blushing curiosity, looking as if she were about to take flight. Now, at his words, she stepped bravely past Elena's skirts. "Hello."

"I'm Brett D'Archand, your brother," he said, studying her with something like awe. She had jet-black hair and skin the color of gardenia blossoms. Her eyes were huge, black-lashed, and amber. This child was his sister. Still young and innocent and vulnerable. It was a heady thought that was provoking some strange and warm feelings in him.

"I know," she said seriously. "Tío told me."

"I am sorry we haven't met sooner," Brett said softly, taking her hand and kissing it. "What a beautiful girl you are."

She blushed.

Brett was feeling sad as she scooted away to the safety of Elena and Emmanuel. She was his sister. He hadn't known Manuel and Catherine—and for the first time, he felt touched by their loss. Had they all been so beautiful, real flesh-and-blood creatures?

Brett sighed and looked across the room at his wife. Diego was chatting with her, and Storm was smiling. That

271

sight irritated him, although from the look on her face he suspected she was merely being polite. Still, he remembered very clearly that Diego had been an insatiable rake when they were growing up, though he was only three years Brett's senior. By the time Brett had left for the gold fields, two of Diego's bastards had been very much in evidence on the Monterro lands. He started toward them, purposefully.

"Wait, Brett."

Brett was stopped by a soft, cool palm on his hand. Sophia smiled into his eyes with promise and intended seduction. He already knew she was the whore her mother was—he had surmised that the instant they met. "Hello, Sophia." His words were cool. Although she was a ravishing creature, her voluptuous endowments generously displayed in the low-cut gown, her mere presence brought back so many hateful memories that he felt a surge of anger. He would never forget the sound of her childish voice taunting him, *Bastard! Bastard! Bastard!* Then she would laugh, because he couldn't hit her . . .

"How does it feel, Brett," she purred, "to be home?"

He laughed. "Home? This isn't my home, cousin, and it never was."

"Tsk. You lived here for close to ten years. How ungrateful. Surely the streets of Mazatlán are not your home."

"Most assuredly not." His gaze was fixed and mocking and cold. "And believe me, I am most grateful for the kind and tender care I received here."

She touched the sleeve of his black jacket. "When you left here you were just a boy," she murmured. "I can't get over the change in you."

He had no response to make to that, but a quick glance across the room showed Diego still monopolizing his wife. He felt a flash of jealousy, and was stunned by it.

"Brett, surely you don't hold the mischievous teasing

of a little girl against me?'' Sophia's eyes were momentarily wide.

''You were a mean child, Sophia, and I suspect you are a cruel woman.''

She gasped, then laughed. ''You haven't changed! You are still right to the point!'' Her amusement disappeared, her hand tightening on his forearm. ''Brett, it wasn't out of meanness, I assure you.''

He raised a brow.

''It was out of jealousy.''

Now it was his turn to be amused, and he smiled. ''Ah, of course, how foolish of me.''

''No, I was jealous,'' she insisted.

''Of the bastard.''

''Of you and Mama.''

Brett stared, no longer smiling. ''Excuse me?''

''I saw you together,'' she whispered, her eyes brightening, her voice trembling. He watched the excitement flare in her face. ''Even though you were only fifteen, Brett, what a man you were, how big you were . . . the way you took her, like a bull . . .''

Brett recovered from the shock and an unexpected sensual onslaught. He shrugged carelessly. ''Your mother was most accommodating.''

''I enjoyed watching,'' she whispered, leaning closer.

Looking at her, he saw her arousal. Her lips were slightly parted, quivering. Her eyes were intensely bright. He imagined a skinny thirteen-year-old watching an inexperienced boy humping clumsily in the arbor. He was sorry she had seen them. Even unknowingly, he did not want to think that he had contributed in any way to her warped sensibilities. ''I'm glad you were amused, Sophia,'' Brett said dryly and walked away. He knew he had not mistaken her reaction, or what she wanted—him.

''I'm so pleased that you and Sophia are getting along,''

Elena said, causing him to halt politely beside her and Emmanuel.

"Of course. Why should we not?"

Elena smiled. "I seem to remember the two of you fighting like cats and dogs when you were children."

"That was long ago, Elena," Emmanuel said. "Brett, tomorrow I'd like to take you riding and show you the land."

"I'd enjoy your company," he said carefully. He didn't want anyone thinking he gave a damn about the hacienda. "Would you mind if Storm came?"

Emmanuel hesitated for the barest moment. "Of course not."

Brett realized his uncle wanted some time alone with him. "We'll go alone," he amended, feeling tenderness for his uncle. He tried to shake off the feeling, since it brought him discomfort, but it lingered. For an isolated, self-sufficient man, he was suddenly in a strange position—with a wife who made him warm deep inside, a sister who raised protective instincts, a dead brother and sister whose loss he inexplicably regretted, and an uncle whose kindness was irresistible.

Emmanuel smiled his pleasure.

Brett joined Diego and Storm, possessively taking her arm and leaning down to kiss her cheek—a tender, sensual brushing of his mouth across her skin. She looked at him from wide blue eyes, and when he smiled with promise, she blushed.

"You are a very lucky man, cousin," Diego said easily, watching Brett.

"Yes, I think so," Brett replied. "Has my cousin been regaling you with tales of our growing up together?" he asked Storm.

"Some," she said. "Has Sophia been reminding you of your times spent growing up together?"

Brett smiled. "Jealous, *chère?*"

"Of course not," she answered, lying.

"Don't be," he murmured.

She flashed a bright smile at Diego. "Diego is taking me riding tomorrow, Brett. He is going to show me the hacienda."

"It will be my utmost pleasure," Diego said, his eyes bright on her face.

Brett heard himself say, "No."

"What?" Storm thought she hadn't heard correctly.

"No."

"Surely, cousin, you can't object. Your wife is safe with me," Diego said.

"I can and I do," Brett replied, feeling ridiculous but not able to help himself. He hated the lecherous looks Diego had for his wife. "Storm, I will gladly show you around."

She pulled her arm free, glaring. "You will not allow me to ride with Diego?"

"Really, Brett, you have her forever. I only want to spend the afternoon with her," Diego cajoled.

"I will take you riding," Brett insisted. "I'm a possessive bastard, Diego."

"You have a nerve," Storm said angrily, trying to keep her voice low. "You drool all over your cousin, but won't allow me to ride with Diego?"

"What?"

Diego smiled, then quickly quelled it. "Brett, I have no ill intentions—"

"Damn right." Brett looked at Storm. "We'll finish this discussion later."

"Damn right," Storm shot back. She gave Diego a sweet, utterly provocative smile. "I will see you tomorrow, Diego."

He took her hand and pressed it to his lips. "Until mañana."

Storm brushed away without giving Brett a glance, and

he watched her approach his uncle and aunt and Gabriella. Diego was speaking, but he only half heard him. "Really, cousin, such a display. If I had dishonorable intentions, I would not seek her out so openly."

Brett was about to reply when everyone hushed and stared as a manservant entered pushing a wheeled chair before him in which sat Don Felipe. The don was smiling, his lower body covered by a blanket.

"Felipe," Emmanuel cried, rushing forward. "What are you doing?"

"I decided to join you for dinner," Felipe said calmly. "I want to eat with the bride and groom."

There was a moment of shocked silence.

Elena broke it, moving gracefully forward to the don's chair. "This *is* a wonderful surprise," she purred, placing her hand on the old man's shoulder and smiling at the assembled family.

Don Felipe met Brett's gaze directly, and for an unbroken moment they stared at each other. Then he said, "I want to meet the bride."

Brett recovered, taking Storm's arm and leading her forward. "Father, this is my wife, Storm."

He studied her. "How old are you, girl?"

Storm's chin came up. "Seventeen."

"How did you ever wind up with my scoundrel son?"

Storm's jaw tightened. "I fell madly in love with him," she said, and Brett relaxed, almost smiling, at her side.

Don Felipe looked from Storm to Brett. Emmanuel came forward. "Why don't we eat," he said, nodding the manservant away and taking the chair. The assembly moved slowly into the dining room, surrounding the don in his chair. He was rolled to the head of the table. Brett held back with Storm, waiting for the others to sit first. Elena moved to sit on the don's right, but he waved her away. "I want my son and his wife on my right and left," he said brusquely.

"Oh, of course, how silly of me," Elena said, smiling magnanimously.

Brett escorted Storm forward and seated her, his hand squeezing her shoulder reassuringly. He seated his aunt on his own right, and finally himself. Wine was poured, and the servants entered bearing platters of food.

"Where are you from, girl?" the don asked. "And who are your parents?"

Brett was grim, but Storm smiled. "West Texas," she said. "I was raised on a cattle ranch there, the D&M. My father and mother settled it in '45, after the Comanche threat had settled down."

"Who's your father?"

"Derek Bragg," she said proudly.

"Who were his people?"

Storm's gaze did not waver from the don's face. "His father was a trapper. His mother was an Apache."

A hushed silence greeted this news. Storm's head tilted proudly. "Before he was a rancher, he was a captain in the Texas Rangers. One of the best."

"So you're part Indian," the don said.

"Part Apache," Storm corrected. "And proud of it."

"And I'm proud, too," Brett intervened smoothly, smiling into Storm's startled gaze. Their eyes held, then Brett reached across the table and squeezed her hand.

"What about your mother?" Don Felipe asked.

"She's English," Storm replied. "Her father is the earl of Dragmore, Lord Shelton. One day my older brother Nick will take over his estate."

Sophia gasped again.

"What an absolutely fascinating family history," Elena said brightly. "Why, Brett, it quite makes yours pale in comparison."

"Thank you, Tía Elena," Brett said. "Father, your questions are rude."

"Why are they rude?" the don shot back. "She's proud

of who she is. She's not trying to hide anything. Reminds me of you.''

Brett wondered if he had just gotten some kind of oblique compliment. He wasn't sure.

''How do you like this hacienda?''

''I love it,'' Storm enthused. ''It's absolutely beautiful. Don't forget, I was raised on a ranch. I learned to ride even before I learned to walk.'' She smiled sheepishly. ''City life's all right, but I miss the ranch sometimes.''

Don Felipe smiled for the first time. Then he looked pointedly at Brett, picked up his knife and fork, and began eating. So did everyone else.

Emmanuel spoke. ''I'm going to show Brett the land tomorrow, Felipe.''

''Good. He should become reacquainted with it.''

Acutely conscious of Elena and Sophia's silent, tense dismay, Brett continued eating.

''Brett's a big success in San Francisco,'' Don Felipe said to the family at large.

''Yes, he is,'' Emmanuel added proudly.

Don Felipe looked at Brett. ''A man with a good business head—why, I bet he could do well with a place like this.''

Elena choked. Diego drained his wine and reached for the bottle to refill it.

''Especially with a wife who's used to ranching.''

Storm raised puzzled eyes to Brett, who met them in a silent communication.

''Tell me, Gabriella, what did you do today?'' the don asked.

She smiled. ''My lessons, Grandpapa, of course.''

''And did you do well?''

''Yes.''

''Good girl.''

''Tomorrow Brett is taking me riding,'' she ventured shyly.

The don looked at Brett, then raised his glass in a gesture of approval. He drank half, then set it down, his sharp eyes landing on Diego. "And how much did you win—or lose—last night?"

Diego coughed. "Excuse me?"

"You heard me, boy. You think I don't know what you spend—to the peso—on those damn games of yours?"

Diego went red.

"Diego was keeping me and Sophia company last night," Elena said. "Perhaps you heard his guitar? He plays so beautifully."

She and Diego exchanged glances, his grateful, hers wary.

Don Felipe grimaced. He turned to Storm, ignoring the others. "Tell me about what it was like on your ranch."

Storm smiled, her eyes brightening, and for the rest of the meal they talked about ranching and cattle and horses, excluding everyone else, Brett listening and watching—with pride.

Brett left the dining room and wandered out onto the patio. It was a beautiful morning, the sun glittering and golden, the air warm and promising summer. Not a cloud broke the clear expanse of sky, and he paused to admire the backdrop of crested mountains, mauve against blue. He sighed, trying not to think about Storm.

He had finally given in. They had fought about Diego again last night, after dinner, Storm becoming increasingly stubborn as the argument progressed. He had finally made wild, passionate love to her, effectively ending that fight—for the moment. She had fallen asleep in his arms, while he had brooded over the energy they had wasted arguing over something so inane—and all because he was being unreasonably jealous. He had never been jealous before. Not ever.

He had looked down at her while she slept, and an incredible tenderness had stolen across him, wrapping warm, vibrant tendrils around him, seeping through him like the warmth of brandy. My magnificent Storm, he had thought, and then wondered if he was falling in love with her.

That thought had struck him with a panic that was close to terror.

He had shoved it away, buried it. He enjoyed his wife tremendously, but that was that. Love was for romantic fools, not for him. What he felt for her was carnal, nothing more. Well, maybe admiration, too.

She wouldn't quit. They had argued again before breakfast until Brett had heard himself give in. He still couldn't believe it. But as much as he hated to admit it, he was wrong. She was right. When in hell had that ever happened to him before?

He was used to whores and mistresses, women he paid for, who accepted his authority without question. Even now, thinking how he had conceded to her will, denied his own wishes, made him uneasy. And if Diego touched her . . . His fists clenched.

He walked farther into the gardens. The old man had been his usual irascible, proud self last night, but Brett had noted one thing—he liked Storm. He had interrogated her during most of the meal, and Storm hadn't been intimidated by him.

Brett understood Don Felipe's ploy. Everyone was afraid he, Brett, was the heir, because of the don's interest in him and Storm. Brett didn't really blame him for such a deception. Elena and Sophia were vipers. Emmanuel was too kind and too blind to thwart them should they attempt to gain control of Gabriella and her fortune. Brett resolved right then and there to make his sister's welfare his concern, whether Don Felipe lived to see her married or not.

What a sweet, beautiful child she was. He was stunned to realize he was feeling something like pride, like brotherly affection, for her. He had promised to take her riding before he and Emmanuel went out. He was looking forward to it.

But Storm was still angry with him.

Their kisses and lovemaking had not dimmed her wrath. She had told him that Apaches hold grudges. Brett had told her that this Apache had better not. Then he had stormed down to breakfast alone, the wonder of their morning lovemaking dissipated. He hated fighting with her.

"Brett?"

He turned, stiffening, at the sight of Sophia hurrying toward him. Now what? he thought. He wasn't in the mood for another confrontation, especially since Storm had ignored him when she had come in to breakfast, making their argument known to everyone.

Sophia walked as if she were on air, swaying toward him, the sunlight glinting off her blue-black head and her ivory breasts, swelling above the black bodice of her gown. Few women looked good in black, but Sophia was one of them. She paused in front of him, smiling. "I was hoping to find you out here," she murmured.

"Don't bother, Sophia," he said curtly. "Whatever you want with me, don't bother."

"My, we are cross today!" Her tone lowered, her fingers came to rest on his chest. He was wearing only a linen shirt and could feel the warmth of her palm through the material. Her voice dropped. "But I understand why," she said throatily.

He covered her hand with his, then deliberately removed it. "You do?"

"A virile man like yourself, fighting with your wife," she said, smiling. "How hungry you must be!" The same hand moved back to his body, this time stroking the flat of his abdomen.

"No," Brett said, both amused and repulsed, "how hungry *you* must be."

"I'm always hungry," she said, her hand moving down the front of his breeches.

"I'm afraid I can't oblige you," Brett said, grasping her wrist and removing the offending hand. "If you need to get laid, I'm sure someone else will be more than happy to oblige you."

"I want you, Brett," she whispered, her voice thick. "Brett, I want you to make love to me the way you did with my mother."

He was still holding her left hand tightly. Her right hand came up and cupped the soft bulge that was his manhood. Angry now, he cursed and grabbed that wrist, too, yanking her forward, the jerking motion bringing her against him. Her full, soft breasts were crushed against his chest. He was not aroused. He was annoyed.

"Oh, Brett," she said with a groan, rubbing her pelvis against his groin, her breasts against his chest.

"Brett!"

His head whipped toward the sound of Storm's voice, and he froze, instantly comprehending the compromising position in which she'd found him. Her face went stark white, her eyes wide as she stood frozen in her tracks, staring at them. Brett pushed away Sophia, who laughed huskily. "Storm, wait!" he cried.

She was running, back the way she had come. Brett took off after her, cursing Sophia, cursing himself, cursing fate. Storm disappeared through the hedges. He followed, turning a corner. Dogwoods and magnolia trees in full bloom greeted him, but there was no sign of his wife. "Storm! Storm! Damn!" he cursed.

"Brett?" Sophia said from behind him.

"Don't come near me," he snarled, wanting to strike her. He plunged farther into the gardens. This time he didn't call out for Storm, because he was sure she wouldn't answer.

* * *

"I had no idea you were so eager to go riding with me."
Diego flashed Storm a white grin.

She managed a stiff smile. Did he know something was
wrong? Could he tell that her heart was breaking? That at
any moment she was going to lose the precarious control
she had been exercising and become hysterical? Oh, Brett,
how could you!

She had evaded him and somehow had run right into
Diego and convinced him that she wanted to go riding
now—not a moment later. She had been so stunned and
frantic, her blood pumping so wildly, that she hadn't even
judged Diego's reaction. She couldn't remember anything.
Not going to the stables, not waiting for their horses to be
saddled, not mounting, nothing. Now they had put the
hacienda behind them and out of sight. All she could think
of was Brett with that beautiful woman in his arms. How
could you, Brett? It was a silent wail.

"Tell me what is wrong," Diego said quietly.

Storm tried to smile but failed. "Let's gallop," she said,
and then Demon was running, Storm crouched low over
his neck.

Clinging like a monkey, she let him run full out. She
rode blindly; she couldn't see because of the tears streaming down her face. The stallion's mane whipped her
cheeks. How could Brett? After this morning and last night
and yesterday and the night before, after his hands and
mouth had worshipped her with such emotion, as if he
needed her, wanted her, loved her. As if she were the only
woman in the world for him. As if . . . as if . . . A sob
tore from her chest.

She wasn't aware of stopping, or that the black had
eventually slowed on his own accord, that Diego had
caught up with her and grabbed the reins, and halting both
mounts. She was aware of nothing. Then she felt his hands
as he pulled her down and into his arms. "Tell me, *cara*,"
he said, holding her. "Tell me why you cry."

She sobbed hysterically. Her face was buried in his neck, for he was only an inch taller than she, and she clung to his jacket while he stroked her hair and back, the Stetson hanging down her shoulders from the chin strap. Finally awareness sank in, and she realized she was crying with abandon in a stranger's arms. Still, Brett's betrayal made her own seem irrelevant.

Diego cupped her face and lifted it until she was forced to look at him. "You can only be crying like this for a man," he said softly. "For Brett?"

She nodded.

"And only if there is another woman."

She nodded again, miserably.

"It is the way of the world, *cara*. Men have wives and mistresses. It is the way."

"I hate it," she cried, not able to look at him, not wanting him to witness her pain and humiliation. "I hate him!"

"I think you love him," he murmured. "I think he is very, very lucky."

"I hate him," she cried again.

He held and rocked her, his body warm and comforting. Eventually she had no more tears left to cry. Sniffing, she pulled away, and he released her, watching her steadily. "Perhaps it is better you find out now, *cara*, and not later, when you love him more."

"I already knew," she said, accepting his handkerchief and wiping her face. "He has a mistress in San Francisco. A beautiful woman, as beautiful as Sophia."

"So it was my sister," Diego said, his gaze narrowed but unreadable. "It doesn't change anything, *cara*, not for you. You are still his wife. When you go back home, Sophia will stay here. She will be forgotten."

"Not by me," Storm said savagely. "I'm going to divorce that sonuvabitch." Her eyes glittered dangerously.

"You are frightening and magnificent," Diego breathed.

"I'm sorry, Diego," Storm said suddenly. "What must you think?"

"That you are beautiful beyond belief," he murmured.

Storm suddenly saw the hot light in his eyes. Not knowing how to respond, she said nothing.

"Let me comfort you, *cara,*" Diego said softly, reaching out to touch her face. "Let me take away all thoughts of him. I can do that."

She was frozen. Her desire for vengeance was strong and overwhelming. Yes, her mind shouted. Let Diego kiss you, touch you, even love you—then throw it in that bastard's face! Her desire to avenge herself and hurt Brett was suddenly vicious. Diego stepped closer and took her in his arms, accepting her silence for acquiescence. Storm gazed steadily up at him, her heart starting to race.

He groaned softly and lowered his face to hers.

The moment his lips brushed hers, the moment his mustache touched her skin, tickling her, she felt a surge of revulsion. "No," she cried, and wrenched away. "No, please, just be my friend."

He stared at her as if debating. She touched his shoulder timidly, tentatively. "Please, Diego, I need a friend."

He relaxed. "For now I will be your friend, but I want to be your lover, *cara*. He need never know."

She shook her head. "I can't."

"Because you love him?" He was intent.

"Yes." She turned to Demon, mounting. Because her back was to Diego, she didn't see the anger cross his features, and when she smiled down at him, he was smiling back. As if nothing had happened.

"Where have you been?" Brett demanded.

She ignored him, calmly removing her Stetson and placing it on a chair, then began unbuttoning her bolero-style jacket.

"Storm, dammit, why did you run off like that?" Brett moved to her, his face taut with worry.

"Don't," she said, a hot, angry gaze searing him warningly.

"It wasn't what you think," he said, clenching his hands at his sides. "How could you think Sophia and I—"

"I know what I saw," she cried, her voice breaking. "Stay away from me—just stay the hell away from me."

"You didn't see anything," Brett insisted, grasping her upper arms. "No, don't struggle, I want you to listen!"

"I hate you," she said tremulously, tears glittering in her eyes. "I truly do."

"You don't mean that, I know you don't." He was afraid. "Storm, listen to me."

"How could you?"

"I didn't! I didn't do anything! She grabbed me, and I grabbed her to get her off. She was pushing against me— we weren't embracing, for God's sake."

Storm laughed bitterly. "Do you think I'm that stupid?"

"Why won't you trust me?" he demanded. "After the past few days, how could you even think I'd look at another woman?"

"I was deluding myself," she said honestly. "I really thought it was special."

"It is, dammit!"

She turned her back on him, pulling off the jacket, her shoulders shaking. She was hurting—over him—but nothing had happened! Her pain tore at him. He pulled her into his arms from behind. "Please believe me," he whispered. "Storm, darling, it was not an embrace or anything more. Not that Sophia wouldn't like more—although God only knows why when she knows I can't stand her. Please, Storm, trust me."

She twisted in his embrace until she was facing him, and Brett was agonized to see that her face was tearstained. He didn't want to hurt her. "Trust you?" she said. "The man who went to his mistress and humiliated me on our wedding night?"

"That's unfair," he said stiffly, "and you know it."

"Then what about when you came back from being in Sacramento? You went straight to her! Leanne St. Clair couldn't wait to tell me how my husband had visited his mistress before me. Then you had the gall . . . the nerve . . . You pig!" She struck him on the chest.

"You listen," he roared, capturing her wrists and holding her against him. "Dammit, why do you always think the worst? I did go to Audrey's that day—for all of fifteen minutes. To terminate our relationship. It's over. I wanted to start our marriage off on the right foot, dammit."

"Really?" It was a hopeful squeak.

He relaxed, gazing down at her. "Yes, really. How could I want her, or any other woman, when I have you?"

Storm bit her lip. "I want to believe you."

"Then believe me," he commanded, wrapping his arms around her. "Please, believe me. I'm not a liar, Storm. If I wanted another woman and you found out, I wouldn't deny it. I wouldn't be the first man to have a wife and mistress. But I don't want another woman."

Her face crumpled, and she buried it against his chest. She wanted so desperately to believe him, and she did. Not being a liar herself, it was hard for her to understand that another human being could be purposely deceitful. She clung to him. "Oh, Brett!"

He buried his face in her hair. "Oh, *chère*," he sighed. He had been so terribly afraid, and now the relief was overwhelming.

Chapter 18

She stood bent over at the waist, her hands gripping the footboard of the huge bed. "Ah," she moaned. "Harder . . . yes!"

The man pounded into her, standing behind her, her hips clenched in his hands. "You are still a damn bitch in heat, Sophia," he rasped. "God!"

Sophia cried out softly while the man thrust one final time and shuddered with a gasp. For a moment he sagged against her, and then she dislodged herself and climbed nimbly on the bed, a fine gleam of sweat covering her. "You haven't lost your touch, Diego," she purred, stretching sensually. An image of Brett flashed through her mind, stirring her desire all over again.

"Damn," Diego said in a low voice. "We shouldn't have done that."

Sophia laughed. "That comment is ten years too late, brother."

He was looking for his pants, flashing her an angry glance. "You know what I mean. Not here. Jesu! If someone found us . . ."

"That's half the fun," she said. Then she reached out and grabbed the waistband of his pants as he was about to button up the fly. "Don't leave. That was just a taste."

"You get crazier and hungrier every day, Sophia," he growled. "Someone—"

"Everyone's asleep," she said, her tone sharp now. "And we need to talk."

"Talk?" He chuckled. "Okay, *hermana mía,* talk. But 'm putting on my clothes, to be safe."

"Coward," Sophia murmured. "Remember the first ime? Remember how I came to your bed at Papa's?"

"I'll never forget," he said, smiling. "Damn, you were ¡ot! And all of fourteen, the tightest little virgin . . ."

Sophia laughed. "Come, sit here," she said, patting the ›ed beside her, "and afterward we can play again."

He sighed. She was one of the most beautiful and ex-:iting women he had ever known, the kind of woman who :ould never get enough. And she was his sister. The com-›ination was so titillating he could not resist. He sat. 'What's on your mind?"

"Brett D'Archand," she said promptly.

"Another conquest."

"Not yet."

"No?" He was surprised. "That's not what Storm told ne. She saw the two of you today."

"I couldn't have planned it better, Diego." She laughed, t rich sound.

"So? If you want him, seduce him. That should be easy :nough."

"I want him for myself. I want *her* out of the way." She regarded him steadily.

"What do you mean?"

"I know you want her," Sophia said coyly. "I think we should work together on this."

Diego felt excitement gripping his insides. He smiled. 'What?"

"I will get Brett in my bed, and she will find out. You will take her away. Brett will think the two of you have run off. He will be so furious he'll wash his hands of her."

"What if she won't come?"

"Force her." She looked at him. "Why don't you take

her to my place? There's no one on that decrepit ranch
except for the peons. You'll have plenty of privacy to do
as you like.''

He grew hard. He thought about having her there, even
against her will. She might scream, but no one would
come. She would fight. His pulse began to throb. ''What
if Brett comes after her?'' It never occurred to him to
consider that his sister might fail to seduce Brett.

''He won't. Tomorrow Papa has to go to San Diego, so
he will be out of the way. Mama will probably use the
opportunity to disappear with that vaquero she's been bedding. Felipe is no problem. I intend to drug Brett after
supper tomorrow—a little laudanum. I'll keep him drugged
through the following day. By the time he starts after you—
if he does—he'll never catch up.''

''Why don't you keep him drugged for a few days?''

''Diego, be sensible. Brett is no idiot. I will convince
him he got drunk, spent the night making love to me, then
overslept.''

''You are going to a lot of trouble to bed a man.''

She laughed. ''Bed him? I want more than that, Diego,
much more. Yes, Brett is beautiful, but he is rich—*rich*.
He can take me away. Do you really think I intend to
marry another Californio just because our damn uncle orders it? Spend the rest of my life trapped on some godforsaken hacienda bearing some stupid clod's sons? Oh,
no.'' She stared passionately at Diego. ''But I have to get
rid of *her*. Brett has to take me away from this godforsaken
life we lead. San Francisco!'' Her eyes lit up. ''Silk gowns,
jewels, fine restaurants, theater, balls . . . I want it all!''

''When Papa finds out what you've done—''

''He won't be able to stop me. I'll be gone. If I had a
peso, Diego, I'd go by myself, right now. But we are all
so damn poor, except for damn Don Felipe. And who
knows? Maybe Brett will marry me one day. I will spin a

web around him that he can't resist!'' Her eyes glittered, making her outrageously beautiful.

Diego felt a stab of jealousy. ''I can't decide what motivates you more, Sophia, wanting Brett in bed and under your power, or wanting to leave all this.''

''I want him,'' she said simply. ''I wanted him when I first saw him and Mother together, but he refused. I still want him, and I always get what I want.'' She leaned back against the pillows, smug and confident. ''And, Diego, when you finish with *her,* get rid of her.''

His eyes widened in shock. ''Kill her? That's going too far!''

''Then sell her south of the border. Just make sure she'll never come back and can't be found.''

Diego felt a twinge of guilt before desire fueled his resolution. He need not ever get rid of her, he decided; he could keep her indefinitely and visit her as the whim took him. He smiled.

He felt Sophia's hand and looked down to see her fondling his erection. ''Which excites you most, *caro?*'' she whispered. ''How you are going to stick that huge cock in me now—or rape her, later?''

He groaned, rolling on top of her.

''This is beautiful land, Brett,'' Storm said, gazing down the rocky cliffs at the blue, blue bay.

''Yes, beautiful,'' he murmured, gazing raptly at her.

She looked at him and blushed.

Brett grinned, his body quickening. Never had a woman fed his desire like she did. It grew each time they made love, every time he looked at her. I must be falling in love, he thought, dazed by the enormity of that thought.

''Come on,'' he said, flashing another smile.

Storm followed, her own blood racing, for she knew that look in his eyes well. That hungry look, as if he were moments from losing control and ravishing her. She shud-

dered with anticipation. Never had she dreamed a ma
could do what he did to her. Never had she thought a ma
could hold her every waking thought, and her dreams
too—that she would become weak-kneed from a glance
that her heart would soar at the mere sight of him.

They trotted their horses through a green meadow sprin
kled with pink and yellow wildflowers. Brett dismounted
and Storm followed. They tethered the horses, then Bret
pulled down the blanket and picnic basket.

Storm found herself watching his large, strong brow
hands. They were powerful, she knew, but also gentle an
sensuous. He laid out the blanket, his movements gracefu
and natural, then knelt, sorting through the contents of th
basket.

Her heart was fluttering at the memory of how he ha
touched her last night, bringing her to an incredibly swee
yet desperate yearning. And how he had filled that need
Her cries had been so loud he had had to clamp his han
over her mouth. Where had this passionate side of he
nature come from?

She studied Brett's hawklike profile. He was a ruthless
looking man, his features harsh, almost cruel, but he wa
immensely handsome, and if she were honest with herself
she had to admit she had been attracted to him like meta
to a magnet from the first time they had met, on th
threshold of her cousin's library. As Brett bent now, cla
in high boots, breeches, and a lawn shirt, his thigh
bulged, and the muscles in his back rippled beneath th
damp, clinging material. He looked up.

She didn't blush. There was a terrible ache between he
thighs, and she wanted him, now. Her eyes were dark an
bright, and she met his gaze steadily.

"I wonder if you know how you're looking at me," h
said.

His response gave her a heady feeling of power, on
she was testing with sensual relish. "It's so hot," sh

murmured, and took off her Stetson, her movements slow
and unrushed. Her hair was braided in one long plait, but
wisps had escaped to curl damply around her face. Feeling
like a female animal, and a provocative one at that, she
began brushing the wisps off her face, then she reached,
slowly, for the top buttons of her jacket. She unfastened
them.

She saw that he was watching with interest. His eyes
were on her hands, now moving over the buttons on her
bosom. He lifted them, briefly, his gaze so hot and hungry
that Storm froze. "Don't stop," he whispered thickly.

She pulled off the jacket. The lace-edged shirt clung
perfectly to her, molding her superb contours, and Storm
wished he would rip it off. She unfastened the top button
at her throat and the two on her neck. She looked at him.
"Brett?" It was a plea.

He took a step toward her, then stopped, clenching his
fists at his sides, restraining himself. "Take off your
clothes, Storm. Take them off for me," he said hoarsely.

She unbuttoned and removed her blouse, then her split
skirt, standing only in pantalets, boots, and a thin, sheer
chemise. She was amazed she didn't feel shy. Instead, she
felt like a seductress, every movement she made seeming
sensuous and exciting. She looked up slowly and saw that
he hadn't moved. The hard, long, thick line of his arousal
caught her attention. His nostrils flared.

She bent over, giving him a clear view of her lush
breasts, partially baring the erect nipples, and pulled off
one boot, then the other. She straightened, reaching for
the hem of her chemise.

"You're teasing me," he muttered.

She gave him a wanton look and pulled the chemise
over her head. He groaned almost inaudibly. She stepped
proudly out of her pantalets and stood naked before him.

She smiled, reached for her braid, and with slow, deliberate movements, separated the strands spreading them out, shaking out the long tresses. She looked up at him.

For one instant, his hot gaze roamed her, lingering on her full, firm breasts, then on the triangle of hair between her thighs. "You are so beautiful," he said thickly, moving to her.

In that next instant his mouth was on hers, his hands everywhere, stroking and caressing, sliding over her arms and shoulders, cupping and squeezing her breasts, tugging at her nipples. He ran his hard hands gently over her hips and thighs, coming back up to fondle and knead her buttocks. He pulled her against him, rubbing suggestively. Storm was whimpering.

"Mine," Brett whispered in her ear, nibbling and then licking hotly. She shuddered.

His hand found one lush breast and began to stroke and play. "You are mine," he said again, and his mouth swooped down on hers, hard and insistent.

Supporting her with one arm, he slipped his other hand between her thighs, searching and seeking until she was trembling and moaning with need. With a triumphant laugh he lifted and carried her to the blanket, laying her down. Still fully clothed, he knelt between her spread thighs and gazed at every inch of what she offered.

"Oh, Storm," he said. "I want you, and I'm going to take you, now, and again, and again, until you beg for mercy."

"Brett," she moaned, gripping his shoulders. "Please."

"Tell me how much you want me," he demanded ruthlessly.

"Yes," she said, shuddering. "I want you . . . Brett . . . please."

With a languorous hand, he caressed her inner thigh until she was quivering and panting and arching against him. "Tell me," he demanded.

"Brett, I shall die if you don't take me now!"

"Maybe I will take you like this," he said thickly, and lowered his head, parting the folds of her glistening flesh, kissing and searching with his tongue. Immediately, her hands settled in his hair and she cried out his name, raggedly, again and again.

He laughed with pleasure, desire, and power. That she was so desperate and ready for him filled him with a sense of triumph. He began inflicting the sensual torture of his mouth and tongue again, with ruthless determination. He could never get enough of her. "Sweet," he murmured against her dampness. "So sweet."

"Brett," she gasped. "I want you inside me. Please, Brett!"

He rose above her, in one motion feeling his hard, huge manhood, and pressed the gleaming tip against her. She cried out in protest; he smiled savagely and lowered his head to take a hard nipple between his teeth, tugging and sucking, probing with the head of his shaft, teasing mercilessly.

She thrashed wildly. Finally he couldn't control himself any longer, and slid, slowly and tantalizingly, into her. She sobbed. He withdrew almost completely, and her nails dug into his back while she moaned and gasped in raging protest. He thrust in wildly then, pumping into her, battering her, and she rose to meet him as savagely as he was taking her. She wrapped her legs around his waist, screamed and clung, and he cried out her name, shuddering convulsively into her.

After he drifted back to awareness, he cradled her tenderly in his arms, stroking her waist absently. He looked down to see her gazing up at him, and to his amusement, she blushed. He chuckled. "Wild little wanton, aren't you?"

"You like it," she replied boldly, her color deepening.

"Indeed I do, *chère.*" He grinned, then hesitated. He

was filled with intense feelings right now, and he could no longer ignore them. He had been with too many women not to know that the joy and tenderness he was feeling toward Storm was unique. In a low voice, he found himself saying, still lazily touching her, "Do I make you happy, *chère?*"

She rolled onto her side, onto him, her face on his chest. Silence followed his question, making his heart flutter, and he knew a vast and angry disappointment. But then she spoke, so softly he almost didn't hear. It was a single word. "Yes."

He moved onto his side to face her, cupping her chin so he could look into her huge sapphire eyes. The warmth shining there momentarily left him breathless. He wanted to ask her how she was feeling now about their marriage, but instead he grunted and said, "This marriage is made, and it won't be unmade." He looked at her for her reaction.

She didn't refute him. She lay very still, her gaze steady upon his, her lips slightly parted. He saw no rebellion in her eyes, only a kind of worshipful hoping. Again he felt breathless. "Do you care about me, *chère?*"

She didn't flinch. "Yes."

He trembled and rolled her beneath him. "Oh, Storm," he began, unable to express the rest, the feelings too new and too huge. His lips found hers tenderly, instead.

"What is it you want, Diego?" Brett asked, sprawled negligently in a chair.

"We have barely exchanged a dozen words," Diego said, smiling. "Is it so strange for me to want to talk with my cousin?"

"Slightly," Brett said, then shrugged. He thought of Storm waiting for him in their bed and felt irritated.

"Brandy?" Diego asked, already pouring a second snifter.

"Thank you," Brett said. He also accepted the cigar and began to puff with relish. Diego sat in an adjoining chair, watching with a thoughtful smile. "Well?" Brett asked.

Diego grinned. "So tell me about your life in San Francisco."

"There's not much to tell," Brett said, sipping the brandy.

"I hear you are very rich."

"Ah," Brett said, flashing a cold, mirthless smile. "Need a loan?"

"Very funny," Diego said stiffly.

"Defending your family's title was very expensive," Brett said. "Litigation has broken most Californios. Your family's not the first."

"Damn Americanos," Diego flashed. "Stealing what is ours!"

Brett had to agree, for it was the truth. "It's too bad."

"Just a few years ago we were rich," Diego said. "Cattle was selling for fifty, sixty dollars a head. Now—this." He made a gesture. "Squatters and litigation. All the great ranchos broken up. Poverty where once there was riches. Still"—his eyes flashed—"your illustrious father will not live forever."

"No, he won't."

"You don't care, do you?" Diego snapped. "Don Felipe won and is still rich. You will have all this one day, and you don't even care."

"No," Brett said, leaning forward to pour himself another brandy. "No taste for liquor tonight, Diego?" he asked, noticing that his cousin hadn't sipped at all. He yawned as a sudden and overwhelming sleepiness assailed him.

Diego didn't answer, just watched him.

Abruptly Brett felt dizzy and lethargic. A heavy languor was creeping stealthily over him. He looked at his cousin, who had become a blur. He tried to move and couldn't. And in that instant before black oblivion took him, he realized he had been drugged.

Upstairs, Storm moved from the bed to the balcony and stepped outside. She was clad in a whisper of blue silk, the sheerest chiffon gown and wrapper. The railing was cool to her touch; a gentle breeze fanned her face. The night glittered with stars, ebony and silver, onyx and diamonds. She sighed, closing her eyes, and inhaled the sweet scent of magnolias and honeysuckle.

Brett, she thought. "Brett," she murmured. She smiled, remembering how he had loved her—so thoroughly, so savagely. With him, lovemaking was rarely tender, never halfhearted. The gentlest of caresses exploded into an unrestrained passion, and her own ability to meet the depth of that passion with her own savagery continued to shock her. He unleashed something dark and wanton and primitive from deep within her. How she reveled in it! How she reveled in him!

After their lovemaking the way he held her was so gentle compared to the previous ravishment, so tender. Did he know his soft, sensual hands spoke for him? And this afternoon he had said he loved her again. A thrill swept her as she recalled his words. Had he meant them? She was no fool. The words had come in the heat of passion, just like that first time, moments before they had both attained a rapturous release. Would he ever say them in a sane moment? Did he really love her?

She wanted a declaration from him so desperately!

She moved restlessly back inside, wondering where he was. She had come up to bed an hour ago, and Brett had gone into the library with Diego for a brandy. She sighed, thinking she was being silly, for they had spent the whole afternoon together. Yet she still hungered for him, for his presence as much as his touch.

She slipped into bed, waiting. Minutes ticked by, and she grew sleepy. She didn't know when she fell asleep, but when she awoke, she wondered how long she had been sleeping, and why Brett wasn't there beside her. At that realization, she was instantly awake. She lit the lamp at her bedside. "Brett?"

She got up and saw he wasn't in their sitting room or in the adjoining dressing room. She found his watch fob—it was two in the morning. She felt a sudden chill. Where was he? Was he still downstairs with Diego? By now they would be drunk. Storm hesitated, debating whether or not to go after him. Then she realized he would not appreciate that. She shivered. She felt a touch of disappointment that he would prefer staying with his cousin to curling up with her, then told herself sternly that she was being unfair. Brett and Diego hadn't seen each other in ten years. Although she knew there was no love between them, maybe now that they were both older and more mature they were becoming friends. That thought pleased her, and she crawled back into bed, though she did not sleep.

Two hours later, she began to wonder if Brett had drunk too much with his cousin and passed out in the library. Surely Diego would help him upstairs. But what if Diego, too, had passed out?

She slipped on a heavier wrapper and silently made her way downstairs, holding a candle to light the way. There was no one in the library. Where was he?

Storm paced the room, doubt and confusion assailing her. Where could he be?

Diego might know. She didn't care that it was unthinkable for her to go to his apartment. Diego and Sophia and their parents all had rooms in the south wing, adjoining the wing where she and Brett were staying. Purposefully, Storm left the library and moved along the corridor with a stealth her father had taught her. She moved up the stairs,

then paused in the long corridor. Wall lanterns lit both
ends, but the hallway in between was bathed in darkness.
Which was Diego's room? She didn't even know. This was
crazy!

Obviously, Brett and Diego were no longer drinking.
What if they both had gone out wenching? There were
numerous young women on the hacienda, and some of
them were quite comely. Storm felt a tremendous rush of
fear. She knew she was being paranoid. She was being
ridiculous. She moved to the first door on the right, and
her hand went to the knob. Very, very quietly she turned
it and pushed the door ajar.

The gray light of dawn was just coming through the
windows, enough for Storm to make out Emmanuel's
slumbering frame. That meant the next door down would
be Elena's. Storm backed out and closed the door sound-
lessly.

She crossed the hall. The first door on that side was
slightly ajar, making her task much easier. Her hand
gripped the knob, and she pushed open the door. The
hinges squeaked and she froze, waiting, but there was no
sound. She pushed the door wide enough to slip in, and
then, unable to prevent it, she cried out.

In the four-poster bed facing her, Sophia lay sprawled in
voluptuous nakedness. Equally naked, Brett lay on his
stomach, his arm thrown around her, pressing her breast
upward. His head was turned into her shoulder, and one
of her white legs was thrown over and between his.

Storm shut her eyes, stunned, praying that when she
opened them a different scene would greet her. Then she
looked again, and this time clasped a hand to her mouth,
both to prevent herself from crying out again, and because
she was suddenly, terribly, sick. She backed out, right into
someone's hard body.

With a sob Storm turned to flee. Strong hands caught

her. She struggled, kicking. "Let me go!" she cried wildly.

"Cara," Diego said.

Storm broke free and ran, stumbling and tripping on the steps, then falling in a rolling headlong rush from top to bottom. She lay on the floor below, unable to move. She moaned, the sound inhuman, like an animal dying.

"Cara!" Diego cried, rushing down and kneeling beside her. "Storm! Are you all right?"

She looked up at him and moaned again, and then she clutched herself, rocking.

She was barely aware of being pulled into his arms and held, of his mouth pressing against her temple and hair, of his stroking, soothing hands, of soft whispers in Spanish, tender endearments. She clung to him, whimpering broken sobs.

Brett had betrayed her.

He had never loved her. He had been with Sophia that day in the garden, and talked Storm out of believing what she had seen. But there was no mistaking what she had seen tonight, and there was no explanation, no excuse. She was filled with grief. She felt as if someone she loved had died.

"I'm so sorry, *cara,* so sorry you had to find out this way," Diego was saying.

Storm realized where she was, and with whom. "I hate him," she whispered, gazing up at Diego's face with its genuine concern, her eyes glazing over again.

"He does not deserve you, *cara.*"

"Help me," Storm cried, clutching the lapels of his robe. "Help me to run away, Diego. Help me to get to Texas."

He looked at her.

"Please," she begged, "please, help me, please!"

Chapter 19

Sleep left Brett in gradual stages, lingering then fading like a mist. Slowly, a hazy, heavy consciousness pervaded. He was aware that he was thirsty, and that he had a slight headache. He was tired, as if he hadn't slept at all, and Storm was so warm and lush next to him that he had not the slightest desire to open his eyes and get out of bed. He tightened his hold on her, nuzzling the silken skin next to his face. She rolled toward him, he felt the movement, and then her lush breasts were enveloping his face, her hand sliding sensually across his flanks.

He sighed, nuzzling the two full globes, running his hand over her buttocks. A nipple hardened against his cheek, and he rubbed his face against it. She sighed, sliding her hand down his buttock, stroking deftly, almost but not quite touching the soft pouch between his legs. He grew harder and caught the teasing peak between his lips, beginning to suckle.

He sucked voraciously, thinking that this was certainly a most delicious way to awaken, still heavy with sleep. He gasped when he felt her stroking his phallus, skillfully and erotically, and then they were rolling together, she beneath and he over her. His eyes still closed, still in a strangely torpid state of languor, he closed his arms around her and began rubbing himself against her.

She was so slick and warm and inviting.

An instant later, a funny feeling in the back of his mind surged to the fore. The hair tickling his face seemed different, coarser, not as silken. The lips beneath his seemed softer, not as firm, and her waist did not fit into the span of his hands . . .

He lifted his head from hers, opening his eyes.

For a scant second, as Sophia's white face met his gaze, he thought he was dreaming. And then it registered—it was Sophia he was gazing at, and he froze, his shaft throbbing against her swollen flesh. He stared, shocked.

She grabbed his hips and arched against him.

Brett leaped out of her arms.

What had he done?

She moaned. "No, don't leave me," she whimpered. "More."

What in hell was he doing in bed with Sophia when he had gone to bed with his wife? Brett sat heavily, staring at her with revulsion and contempt. A tide of self-loathing swept him. Then the thought—good God, where was Storm?

He looked out the windows and saw that it was already afternoon.

Sophia's hand closed around his manhood, her lips nibbling at his hips.

Brett stood, pushing her off. "What the hell is going on?" he shouted, furious, his head filled with pain.

She smiled. "*Cara*, you do not need to be told." She stretched seductively, her white, shapely body glinting in the sunlight, her breasts so pale he could see the blue veins. "You were magnificent last night, *querido*, but this morning leaves something to be desired."

"Last night?" he said, shocked to the depths of his being. He thought rapidly. He had had a drink with Diego . . . and then he knew. He had had one drink, but it had been drugged. And now he was finally coming to, only here, not in his own bed, *here*, with *her*, not with his beloved wife . . . "You little bitch," he snarled, and pounced on her.

She cried out when his hands closed around her throat, squeezing with a primitive savagery. Her face paled; her mouth opened like a fish. Brett instantly released her, stunned by the viciousness of his hatred, by his desire to murder her. "My brandy was drugged last night," he said grimly. "Why, Sophia?"

"What are you talking about?" she cried, rubbing her throat. Her eyes were bright with renewed desire, and the fact that his violence had aroused her sickened him.

"I can't believe you would go to such lengths to get me into your bed! Was it worth it?" His voice was heavy with sarcasm.

"Soon it will be, *querido,*" she purred. "Let me make you hard again." And she reached for him.

Furious, he knocked her hand away. "Why, damn you, Sophia, why?"

"I always get what I want," she said. "Why fight what you want, too?"

"I only want my wife," he said in disgust, and then he was pulling on his pants.

Sophia was out of bed in a flash, rubbing her breasts against his back, her hands sliding down to stroke the soft bulge of his groin. She was unprepared for the violence that greeted this move. One instant she was there, trembling with excitement, her nipples hard against his back, her womanhood wet and warm against his buttocks. Then she was on her back on the floor, the wood cold and hard on her bare body.

She looked up, throbbing wildly now, lying there spread like a whore at his feet.

He pulled on his shirt, regarding her with contempt. "Just like your mother," he said softly, and a moment later he was gone.

Sophia lay there, gasping. With a moan, she reached

down and caressed herself intimately, writhing in ecstasy as she imagined Brett thrusting into her.

As he hurried upstairs to their room, Brett was thinking desperately, trying to come up with an excuse for why he had not come to their bed last night. God, he would kill Diego and Sophia! And he still didn't understand why they had done it. Why would Sophia go to so much trouble to get him into her bed?

What was Storm thinking?

What was he going to say?

He was not a liar, he had never been a liar, so he would tell her the truth. With one omission—he would not tell her he had nearly bedded Sophia. She was not going to believe his story anyway, he was sure. He wanted to lie and tell her he had passed out downstairs, but she might have gone looking for him, and he did not want to be caught in the lie. Damn it!

"Storm," he cried, bursting into their bedroom.

She wasn't there. He searched the adjoining rooms. Where was she? He needed a bath, needed to get the stink of Sophia off of him. He ordered hot water from a servant, who had not seen his wife. Then he went downstairs. No one had seen her.

In the stables Demon was missing.

Of course, he thought, she must have gone riding. He wanted to go after her now, but he felt so damn unclean, so damn violated—

"Did she go alone?" he asked a vaquero.

"I don't know."

No one had seen her leave, so she must have gone very early. Another inquiry revealed that Diego's horse was also missing, and had been all day. Brett was both relieved and furious. Relieved because he didn't want Storm riding alone, and furious because she had spent an entire day with his lecherous cousin.

Not that he didn't trust Storm, he did. But if Diego touched her, he would kill them both—Diego and Sophia. They would pay.

He went back to the house and bathed, unable to think of anything but Storm. He needed to explain what had happened last night. What was she thinking? It all depended on whether or not she had gone looking for him. It was possible, he supposed, that she would be indulgent, thinking he had passed out in the library—that all his worry was for nothing.

But there was still the guilt, and the dirtiness that seemed to stick to his skin no matter how hard he washed. Just the thought of touching that whore, of practically being inside her, made his stomach turn, made him physically ill. If only he had opened his damn eyes! And how in hell could he not have noticed the woman he was holding was not his wife? Especially if he loved her?

And he knew, without a doubt, that he did love Storm.

By the time Brett had finished bathing and dressed, he was becoming worried to the point of panic. Storm and Diego were still gone. The grooms rose at sunup, but did not feed the horses until an hour later. It was then that Demon and Diego's stallion had been noticed missing— and that was ten hours ago.

A terrible suspicion crossed Brett's mind, and was gone as soon as it appeared. He paced their apartments, spending most of the time staring out the French doors to the balcony. What if she was hurt?

"Brett?"

He whirled, furious to see Sophia standing in his room. "Get out," he shouted, his eyes flashing dangerously.

"Brett," she said, not moving. "I think it's very suspicious that your wife and my brother have been gone the whole day together. No one has told Don Felipe, of course, but everyone is talking about it. Diego was so besotted with Storm."

"What are you saying?" he demanded.

She held up a piece of paper. "Diego left me a note saying he had business to attend to and would not be back."

"Let me see that," he said, tearing it from her. The note said exactly that, with no details. But he knew that they were together, he suddenly knew it, and they that had been together since sunrise. She had gone with him. Wherever his business was, Storm had left him and gone with Diego. Because she had found out where he had been last night. Brett was suddenly sure of it.

"I think she went with him," Sophia said. "Diego was very persistent, and he told me he wanted her. He's like me—he always gets what he wants."

"I'll kill him," Brett said, crumpling up the note and flinging it across the room. He had only a few hours till dark, but it would be enough to pick up the trail. Why in hell hadn't he gone after them earlier?

Because he hadn't wanted to think the unthinkable—that Storm had discovered his supposed infidelity, had not waited for him to explain, had not trusted him, had not believed in him—had left him.

"If he touches her . . ." Brett growled.

"What do you think they are going to be doing tonight? Playing poker?" Sophia looked triumphant. "You may as well know, Brett." She smiled.

"Know what?"

"Last night when you were sleeping she walked in on us. I was still awake."

For an instant his heart stopped; he couldn't breathe. And then, when his functions started again, they raced. "What did you say to her?" he demanded hoarsely.

"I didn't have to say anything." She smiled again. "A picture tells a thousand words."

With great effort he stopped himself from striking her.

"After she left, I heard a noise and went out to investigate. I saw Storm and Diego at the bottom of the stairs."

He stared.

"Embracing," Sophia said. "He was comforting her. She left you, Brett. She's run away with another man."

Brett felt as if he was suffocating, but in a moment the sensation had passed. "She's heading for Texas," Brett said with certainty. "And if he touches her, I'll kill him."

It took Storm several moments to realize that they had stopped. She sat on Demon unmoving, numbed with hurt and disinterested in her surroundings. Diego had dismounted and was holding up his hand to her. She focused on him. Dusk was settling. "Why have we stopped?" Her voice was unrecognizable, cracked, old, reed-thin.

"*Cara*, we must make camp for the night." He smiled gently. "Come."

It was so easy to obey and not think. Storm slid off her stallion into his arms, where he held her for a moment longer than necessary. She was only vaguely aware of the feel of the length of his body, of his hands in her hair, of his breath on her cheek. She hurt so badly inside, in her heart, a terrible stabbing. Brett's image, his face harsh and mocking, kept looming in her mind. Then the image of them together.

Diego led her over to his bedroll, and Storm sank down upon it, curling up in a tight ball. She shut her eyes, awaiting sleep's mindless comfort.

Diego watched her for a moment, then went to their horses, untacking them, rubbing them down with dried grass, giving them each several handfuls of grain. After hobbling them, he paused to look at her. He would not make a fire. He wouldn't take the chance. He knew Brett's resolution, his determination. He had no intention of being murdered in his sleep in the dark hours of the night.

As Diego studied Storm, lying with her back to him, he

felt a surge of lust. Tonight he would take her—whether she wanted it or not. And she undoubtedly would not be receptive. Then, imagining a numbed, passive recipient of his passion, he frowned. He wanted her fighting or eager, but not like this—not stricken with hurt, lifeless, dulled. He moved to her. *"Cara?"*

It was a moment before she turned so she could see him. He was shocked at how pale she was, how swollen her eyes, how red her nose. Where was the magnificent creature he had known, fiery and unsurpassable? This woman looked like a child, hurt, vulnerable, disheveled, dirty. His jaw clenched in anger. He held up the canteen. "Here, drink. We dare not make a fire. Here's some jerky. Take it."

Curling up and giving him her back, she shook her head, a sound like a low sob escaping from her mouth. "No," she said.

"You must eat," he insisted, irritated.

She didn't answer.

"Storm, how do you expect to ride all day tomorrow—you must eat."

"Please, Diego, just leave me alone."

He stood, unsure. What was he doing here, in the middle of nowhere, with a woman who was more dead than alive? God, was he crazy? Sophia, of course, had once again manipulated him into doing her bidding. It had been that way all their lives, and it angered him tremendously. He stalked away, needing to think.

The first thing Storm felt when she awoke the next morning was pain, accompanied by remembrance. She sat up, quickly glancing around in the blush of first light, noting Diego stretched out on a bedroll a few feet from her. Then something happened. She felt a surge of anger, and she clung to it.

She closed her eyes, seeing in her mind's eye images of Brett since she had known him. The first time she had met him, standing in Paul's library, both virile and elegant in a black suit. She would never forget that moment, or his eyes, so black and intense. She hadn't understood the look, then. She remembered the first time he had kissed her, on the beach, his shock when she had punched him, the incredible passion that had helplessly swept them away at the ball. Then other images, awful images, flooded her—Audrey's perfect form and face, Sophia lying naked and entwined with him, their wedding, and the time at the beach when he had accused her of being with Sian and had mercilessly and crudely examined her. She got to her feet. Leaving him is the best thing that I could do, she thought unsteadily, fighting to believe it. She smoothed her hair away from her face, determination molding her features. "Home," she said. She clenched her jaw. "Home and a divorce. That man is a bastard, a terrible bastard, and I never loved him." Resolutely, anger in every stride, she moved to her horse and began to saddle him.

That was how Diego found her, fiercely clinging to anger, resolved to head out and ride all day. She glared at him. "We have to put as much distance between Los Cierros and us as possible, Diego. I'm almost certain that bastard will come after us, not because he loves me but because I am his possession, I belong to him—or so he thinks." She gave a short laugh.

Diego was elated. He grabbed her shoulders, spinning her around before she could mount, refusing to release her. *"Cara,* thank God! I was afraid you would waste away from self-pity."

She raised her chin, her face hard, almost ugly. "One day I will make him pay," she said softly, causing a chill to run up and down Diego's spine. "But for now I just have to get away from him. He is stronger than me—I need the protection of my family." She leaped astride Demon. "Let him *dare* to try anything around my father and my brothers! They'll be only too glad to carve him into bits and pieces, Apache-style!''

Diego's pulse began to pound. He imagined her with a knife, straddling Brett, her husband begging for mercy. The fantasy changed irrepressibly until she was straddling him, the knife at his throat, while he was naked and aroused, being forced to do her will. He sucked in his breath and hurried to his horse.

Storm rode hard all day, and Diego found himself pressed to keep up with her, and irritated because of it. There was no way Brett could be closer than several hours behind them, maybe a lot more. Already they were half-way to San Diego. Tonight they would arrive at Sophia's abandoned hacienda. There was no need to push so hard. He wanted to conserve his strength for when they arrived at the rancho.

"I don't want to stay there," Storm told him firmly when they had pulled up at the turnoff.

He was stunned, but recovered. *"Cara,* a bath, a bed. Don't be foolish."

She looked at him. "You go, Diego. The ranch is eight miles west of here. Eight miles. We're going south. I'm not stepping one foot in another direction." She urged her horse forward.

Angry, Diego caught up with her and grabbed her elbow. "Don't be an idiot," he shouted. "We need rest, food. It's still several days to San Diego. Brett is far behind us, have no fear."

"How do you know that?" she asked sharply. "I know Brett. He might be ten miles behind us."

Diego smiled. "Sophia would not be so quick to let him out of her bed, *cara.*"

Storm inhaled sharply, then twisted away so he couldn't see her face. "I'm not turning off. You don't have to come with me."

Diego had no intention of letting her go without him,

but he certainly had no intention of riding with her to Texas. He spurred his horse forward, thinking. He would probably have to hurt her, beat her into submission, tie her up. He grew hard as various images flooded his mind.

They stopped a short time later as the sun set. "We won't make a fire," Storm told him, slapping Demon's rump as she laid down his saddle. She kicked her bedroll so it rolled out, then stretched, leisurely, arching her back. When she saw Diego's hungry gaze, she instantly stopped, suddenly concerned. Her mind flew back to the attraction he had shown for her when they had first met, during those first days at the hacienda, and she grew uneasy. She looked at him again.

He smiled. His eyes were hot. He stepped toward her, and instinctively, Storm stepped back. Nervously alert, she said, "Why have you come, Diego? I was so stunned when we left, I can't remember any of it."

"How could I not come to your aid?" he said, his voice rasping. "How could any man not come to your aid?" Then, as if sensing her wariness, he turned from her, going to his horse. "I will see you as far as the stage in San Diego," he said, his tone neutral, his back to her.

Everyone knew about the new stage which traveled from St. Louis to San Diego, the Butterfield Overland Mail, scheduled to start operating that summer. "Is it running?" she asked eagerly. She hadn't thought far ahead, but she knew she didn't relish the idea of riding alone through hundreds of miles of Apache-infested territory. If she made it, her father would certainly kill her for trying.

"I believe it started operating several weeks ago."

They ate jerky in silence. Diego was still sitting up, not looking at her, when Storm crawled beneath her bedroll. She did not undress, but she did take off her six-shooter, which she placed carefully near at hand. She wasn't thinking of Diego as she did this but of her husband.

She had trouble falling asleep. Brett. Anger softened,

hurt reared. It was impossible, but if she had a choice, what she wouldn't give to be held in his arms right now. She forced her tears away. She didn't love him. She was terribly attracted to him, but that was all. He was a bastard, truly—and then she almost laughed. He was a bastard in every sense of the word.

But she kept remembering how hurt he had looked when she wouldn't tell him she was happy. How his warm expression had become cold and guarded. She started to think about the little boy growing up with a prostitute for a mother who had no time or love to give him, a poor, ragged dirty boy who lived on the streets stealing and begging to survive. Then she found herself imagining what it would be like to be sent abruptly to the hacienda, to be suddenly surrounded by all those selfish, grasping people, to grow up with the don, knowing you were only a bastard son. She felt a flood of sorrow for Brett, all of which she resolutely denied.

She dreamed of Brett. She dreamed they were together, and although she knew him for what he was, although her mind said no, her body throbbed beneath his touch. It was so real—hands on her breasts, teasing her nipples into tautness. Even his kisses were real. And then there was something funny, something that shouldn't be there—it tickled. She smiled, then dreamed Brett had found her, was making love to her, and she moaned. "No."

Storm woke and for an instant thought her dream had come true, that Brett had crawled into the bedroll with her. A hard male body covered hers, throbbing with urgency; warm lips and hands teased her flesh. Then the hair of a mustache tickled her neck, and understanding flashed. She arched in protest, her hands going to Diego's shoulders to force him off. "No!"

One hand grasped her braid, holding her head still, and his mouth came down hard on hers. She thought she would vomit. She twisted, tearing herself away only by nearly pulling her own hair from her scalp, screaming in fury. "Get off!"

"Dios, por Dios!" His hands found her breasts, squeezing. Storm felt him jabbing between her thighs with his member, and was shocked to realize he had pulled her pants down. Instantly she relaxed. His hold tightened, then he shoved up her shirt. While she feigned submission, her right hand moved over the ground searching for the butt of her Colt. It wasn't there.

Horror, then fury, seized her. He had moved one groping hand to toy with her privates, and Storm's knee came up, along with both hands, simultaneously. Her knee caught his rib cage, forcing out a whoosh of air, while her closed fists pounded glancing blows at his cheekbones. For a second he was immobile.

She used that instant, her nails coming up to claw viciously at his face even as he moved again, reaching for her wrists. He caught one, missed the other. Five nails brutally raked open his flesh from temple to jaw. He roared, twisting her arm behind her back so hard that she thought he would break it.

He grabbed her other wrist, imprisoning it, but almost immediately Storm's head was up, her teeth bared viciously, and she was biting into his neck, drawing blood. She refused to let go. He screamed, rolling off. Storm jumped up, stumbling over the buckskins entwined around her ankles. Pulling up her pants, she looked around frantically. Where was her gun?

She heard him, threw a glance over her shoulder, saw him coming after her, bleeding and frenzied with rage. Storm saw the rifle. She bent, grabbed it, heard and felt him coming as she whirled and cocked it in the same motion. He was lunging; she fired. At such close range death was instantaneous. Eyes wide, he reeled and fell over on his back.

She stepped backward, her own eyes huge. She couldn't

stop staring at what had been Diego. She began trembling violently. "Dear God!"

Storm stumbled backward, feeling bile rising, unable to take her eyes off the man she had just killed. What have I done? she thought frantically. I've shot an unarmed man—oh, God!

The rifle dropped from her shaking hands, and she turned and vomited, falling to her knees. The heaves finally stopped. What to do? She couldn't think. Not just any man, Brett's cousin—she had killed Brett's cousin. But he'd been trying to rape her. Maybe he would have stopped. That didn't matter! She should have wounded him—she hadn't meant to do this!

I'm a murderer, she thought.

The sound of the horses snorting and moving restlessly brought her back to her senses. She didn't want to hang. She wanted to go home. At that word, a sob tore through her. She had to get home! She would have to hide the body, no—bury it.

It wasn't easy touching him, much less getting him on Demon. She pulled and tugged and managed to lift him, sweat pouring from her face, her hands covered with sticky blood. She didn't bother tying him to her stallion. She sent the other horse running, then led Demon farther off the road, into the hills, until they were swallowed by darkness.

After what seemed like hours she found a partial crevice that would serve. She meant to slide Diego's body into it; she wound up dumping him in. She tried to move the rocks that formed the wall of the crevice to cover him, but they wouldn't budge. She pushed and strained—they had looked so loose—and tears streamed down her face. She finally gave up, cursing, dumped several handfuls of stones over his body, then pulled brush to cover him.

She knew it wouldn't work. By sunrise the buzzards

would find him, and then a sheriff would come. She had to find enough stones to hide the evidence.

Wiping away the tears, she spent the next few hours gathering rocks by torchlight until the body was thoroughly covered. She didn't realize she had been at it all night until the sky paled to gray. And then a thought struck her.

She had no money.

She needed money for the stage.

She looked at the stones that covered Diego's body.

On her hands and knees, tearing her skin and nails, she uncovered Diego and rifled his pockets. She found a hundred dollars and change. By the time he was re-covered, the sun's position told her it was close to seven.

She sat on her haunches, exhausted, forcing herself to survey the grave. If people rode past here, she doubted they would bother to inspect the site unless they were specifically looking for a buried man.

She stood, sighing, and took her canteen from Demon to drink. By chance, she looked down at herself and almost screamed in frustration. Her shirt was stiff and stained with blood—lots of blood. It seemed that this morning was going to be endless, and every second she delayed, Brett could be getting closer. She held back a hysterical sob. She had to pull herself together.

She found a stream and bathed without taking off her clothes. Most of the blood came out, but the stain was still evident. To her eye, there was no mistaking what it was. As she wearily mounted Demon, she tried to think of what she would say if anyone commented on it. She couldn't come up with anything; all she kept seeing in her mind's eye was Diego after the first moment of impact, before he slammed backward onto the ground. God, would she ever forget?

But gradually the horrible image receded to the back of her mind. Weariness came to the fore, and Storm fought to stay astride, to keep going, willing herself onward, not daring to stop and rest. Now that she was alone, she kept off the main road, paralleling it, riding along the mountain ridge as the Apaches did, making it easier to see her enemy. Her enemy. Brett.

That night she slept, too tired to eat, barely managing to untack and feed Demon. The next day she was fully refreshed, ravenous, and as she ate the last of her jerky she debated the wisdom of making a fire and taking the time to hunt. She decided against both and pushed on.

It was hard. She passed a homestead and was desperate to ride in and buy a loaf of bread, anything—but she didn't dare. She wasn't going to leave a trail for Brett. That night she took the chance and made a small fire and roasted a squirrel. But even though her hunger was assuaged, she didn't sleep dreamlessly. Images of Brett haunted her. She was in his arms, then she was suddenly standing aside and watching him take a naked Sophia into his arms. Just when she thought her heart would break all over again, Diego would appear, urging her to run, but Storm screamed and shot him . . .

She rode into San Diego the next day at noon. The stage east had just left. She bought a ticket, took a hotel room, and settled down to wait.

Chapter 20

Home!

Storm pulled up a lathered Demon. She had made it: she was finally here, finally home. Below her from where she sat Demon on a rise, the many timbered barns and buildings of the D&M sprawled before her in the valley, brownish now under summer's insistent onslaught. Oak and juniper rustled in a dry breeze, horses and prized bulls filled the corrals, smoke rose lazily from the half-dozen chimneys of the two bunkhouses, the kitchens, and main house. And beyond all that, dotting the valley and the hills, longhorns grazed, speckling the panorama black and brown and beige.

Storm urged Demon into a gallop. It was about three weeks since she had run away, but it had been an endless three weeks, fraught with anxiety. She had been so certain Brett would catch her. Maybe he hadn't even tried. She ignored the slight tug of dismay that thought brought, because she would never forgive him for taking Sophia to his bed. No, it didn't matter anymore; she was safe now. The worst part of the trip had been killing Diego; after that there had been no problems, not even with Indians—it was a miracle.

She had already pushed Demon hard, but not to his limit, especially since the pace of the stage he had been tied to had been an easy one. It was early evening, and with growing excitement Storm knew everyone would be home soon. She urged the stallion into a gallop and raced down the hill, past the barns and corrals, her heart beating wildly. She was off the horse before he had come to a full stop, her long legs eating up the distance, propelled by momentum as she ran into the house, shouting for her parents. "Ma! Pa! Ma!"

She headed straight for the stairs, not sure whether they were in their bedroom, changing, or already in the drawing room, awaiting dinner. She was halfway up when her father called her from below.

She stopped, turning, and tears sprang to her eyes. He looked stunned, then his face lit with pleasure, and she flew into his arms, clinging to him. She started crying, like a child.

"Storm, are you all right? What's happened? Sweetheart, what?"

She lifted her face to meet his worried golden eyes, and then she saw her mother, and she wrenched away, throwing herself at Miranda, hunching over so she could bury her face in her mother's neck. She started sobbing, quite hysterically. Her mother held her and stroked her hair.

"Storm's crying," Rathe said in complete bewilderment, coming in to stand next to his brother in the foyer.

"Shut up," Nick said tersely, grabbing his arm.

"What is she doing here?" Rathe asked.

"Darling, it's all right now," Miranda soothed, using a mother's particularly maternal tone, rocking her daughter, who was a head taller than she. "Come on, we'll go upstairs, and you'll tell me all about it."

Storm realized how she must look, how she was behaving, and pulled away, wiping her eyes. When she looked around and saw how stricken her father was, and that both her brothers looked exactly the same, she realized she was frightening them terribly. "I'm all right . . ." she started, sniffing.

"Where's your husband?" Derek asked quietly. His tone was firm, authoritative, a tone that willed an answer.

The words poured out of their own accord. "I've run away, Pa. Brett's a whoring bastard and I hate him. And— oh, God, I killed a man!"

Absolute silence greeted this statement, and Storm wished she could take it all back, not because she wanted to hide anything, but because she needed to explain rationally. Her father had that look, grim and awful, like he might kill someone—and so did her brothers. She ran to her father.

"It was self-defense," she babbled. "He tried to rape me. But he was Brett's cousin! I thought he was helping me run away from Brett. Pa, you have to help me get a divorce!"

Her father blinked in dismay, then took her arm, guiding her to her mother. He managed a smile that didn't reach his golden eyes. "Go on upstairs, honey, with your mother. After you've bathed and eaten, we'll talk." He looked at the boys. "Aren't you two busy with something?"

Nick's strong jaw was clenched, his hard, worried gaze on his sister, but he turned away first. Rathe ran to Storm, throwing one arm around her. "What did he do to make you run away?" he asked grimly, his blue eyes flashing.

His concern made her eyes misty again, and she couldn't speak.

"Rathe," her father said curtly, and he strode away, giving Storm one last, measuring look.

With her mother's arm around her, Storm went upstairs. The moment of elation at being home was gone. She didn't know why she didn't feel full with happiness—instead depression was wrenching her heart like a clamp. She kept thinking of Brett.

Finally, Brett thought.

His blood was pounding wildly. How long had it bee

ince he'd begun chasing her? Six weeks? If he found her
own there—and he was sure he would—she would be
with her parents. He would kill her. If Diego was with
er, he would kill him, too. If Diego had touched her, he
would kill them both. God, he couldn't wait to get his
ands on that little savage!

Pray to God she was there, unharmed.

He moved his horse carefully down the rocky slope toward the cluster of ranch buildings below. It was late,
usk. He could have stayed in town after bathing and shav-
ng, maybe even eased himself with a whore. The problem
was, he thought angrily, Storm had bewitched him, as the
ast six weeks had shown; he had refused, without the
lightest interest, the few sluts who had offered their
harms to him at the various towns through which he
assed. All he could think of was Storm, with a kind of
read-filled panic. She had to be here. She had to be all
ght.

Then he would strangle her.

He knew she had taken the stage, just a day before he
ad arrived in San Diego. At the stage station the clerk
ad grinned lewdly when he'd described her, adding,
Who could miss that? Big ones straining that shirt, out
here . . .'' Before the man had raised his hands to
dicate the size, Brett had grabbed him by the throat
d slammed him repeatedly against the wall, until he
alized he was taking out all his frustration on this in-
cent bystander. He had dropped him, then, demanding
s ticket and asking if Storm was traveling alone. As far
the clerk had known she was, indeed, traveling by
erself.

That was when all his troubles had begun. The stage
d been in operation only a few weeks, and it was three
ays late returning to San Diego. Then, just out of Fort
uma, they had been attacked by Pawnees. At the Mari-
osa Springs way station they had lost a wheel. On the far

side of Apache Pass, they had been attacked by Apaches and in El Paso the driver had been killed in a gunfight All in all, there had been thirteen days of delays. Bret hadn't seen Storm in almost six weeks, six long, agoniz ing, celibate weeks, and he felt like a starving man.

His heart was pounding hard, unbearably. How could he talk sense into her when all he wanted to do was hold her and reassure himself that she was real, not some won derful fantasy he had dreamed up? He would never let her out of his sight again. He wanted to feel the full, warm alive length of her against him. He wanted to stroke her hold her, feel her, tell her he'd been sick without her, that he loved her.

He'd fully accepted his love for her the day she had lef him. It had been an awful, heart-stopping realization. On that came a day too late. He hadn't wanted to love her He hadn't wanted to need her, not like this, so desperatel' that the thought of losing her made him feel like a fright ened boy. He didn't want to want Storm's love.

He kept remembering how she had held and comforted him when she'd thought he was grieving over the death of his little half brother and sister. Then he kept remem bering how he'd once been a hungry boy waiting desper ately for a sign from his mother that *she* cared—a sign tha' never came. And the awful hurt, if he let it rise. The sam scenario repeated with his father . . . No, he didn't wan' to want Storm's love, but God help him, it was too late.

He raised his hand to pound on the door, but voice drifting from an open window halted him. Rich mal voices, and then a feminine one, not Storm's. He strained to hear as a man made a comment, and a jumble of warr male laughter reached his ears, laced with Storm's rich trill. His blood surged, his heart leaped. His fist smashed down on the door, once, twice, three times.

Kill her? Hah! He couldn't wait to get his hands on her The door opened, and Brett blinked. The boy standing ere was Storm's height but a few years younger than she as, his face the image of Derek Bragg's without the ughness of maturity. A beautiful boy, with Storm's col-ing. He smiled, and Brett's heart turned over because it as her smile.

"Howdy." Rathe grinned. "What can I do for you?"

Brett was looking past him, but all he saw was a narrow, ne-floored foyer and a large, carefully wrought oak stair-se. He met the boy's bright blue gaze. "I've come for y wife," he said levelly. "Storm."

Rathe stiffened, all amiability vanishing. Brett saw it d tensed, too. Hadn't he expected this? Hadn't he known e would malign him to her family? "Where is she?" he ard himself ask coolly.

"You can leave now," Rathe said tersely, moving to ock Brett's path with his body. "Before I carve you up— ith pleasure."

"Don't make this difficult, boy," Brett said grimly. It as obvious the boy was itching for a fight. Beating up r brother was all he needed to further ingratiate himself ith Storm. Brett pushed past him into the foyer.

"Hey, Rathe, who is it?" came a male voice.

Brett's gaze met a tall, dark-haired youth entering the yer from a hallway. Rathe said, "It's *him,* Storm's hus-nd. You want the honors, or shall I?"

Shit, Brett thought.

Nick advanced with a predatory stride. Brett fleetingly ought that the tall youth looked half Indian, but that was far as he got because a knife appeared in the boy's nd, then at Brett's throat. Nick's eyes were dark and ld. Brett almost laughed, the situation was so ludicrous. t, hell, he had never seen a knife appear so quickly in s life. Now he knew where *she* had learned to wield one.

"I want the honors," Nick said softly, his breath warm-g Brett's cheek.

"Drop it," Derek commanded. Nobody had heard him

enter, but all three pairs of eyes went to the tall, golden haired man standing by the stairs. He didn't have to repeat the order. Only a second slipped by—albeit a long second—and then Nick's knife disappeared. Brett stepped past the boys, his gaze on Derek.

He saw the blow coming, but too late. He himself was slightly taller than Derek, but Derek was built like a lumberjack, thick with muscle. Brett managed to turn his face just in the nick of time, and the blow glanced off his jaw, not breaking it but possibly dislocating it. Brett slammed backward, into the wall.

"For my little girl, you sonuvabitch," Derek gritted, pouncing on him again.

Brett's head was reeling. A wave of pain shook him, but instinctively he was already straightening, with Derek half pulling him up. He realized the man wanted to beat him up, if not kill him. What had Storm told him? he thought, and then another massive blow took him in the stomach, making him gasp and double over.

"Fight," Derek said, waiting, tensed.

Brett came upright. His eyes blazed furiously, and he wanted to hit back, badly. "No," he said. "I can't fight you, dammit."

"Coward," Derek taunted.

Brett clenched his fists.

"Coward," Derek said again, this time softly. He swung, but Brett was already moving sideways, one arm coming up to block the blow, and with all his strength, he jammed his fist in an undercut to the man's jaw. There was a cracking sound, but Derek's head moved back only slightly. Their eyes met. Derek smiled grimly. "Good," he muttered, just before landing a blow on Brett's cheek, barely missing his eye.

Brett grabbed him, throwing him backward against the stairs. They grappled, too close to exchange blows now.

"No!" Storm screamed. "No! Pa! Stop! You'll kill him!"

Brett's heart careened at the sound of her voice, but when he realized she was pleading for him, he felt anger and disgust. His lack of attention caused Derek to get a knee up and into his stomach. Brett grunted but wouldn't release his hold, and they rolled off the two steps and onto the floor with a thud.

"Derek Bragg, stop it this instant!" Miranda's voice cut through everything.

Miraculously, Brett thought, the man who was now on top of him relaxed, and an instant later was on his feet, helping Brett to his own feet. Derek was panting, his gaze on his wife. "Miranda . . ."

"What is wrong with you?" she said fiercely.

Brett barely saw the tiny, angry, sable-haired woman. He was looking at Storm, his beautiful Storm. She was standing very still, her blue eyes huge, her lips parted, quivering. Brett forgot everyone and everything else. He moved to her. She didn't back away. Her gaze locked with his.

"Storm." It was a husky whisper. Her mouth parted as if she would speak, but no sound came out. She swallowed. His hands found her shoulders, closing over flesh and muscle and bone, and he pulled her against him. She came. For an instant she remained stiff, her face barely touching his chest. He tightened his hold, crushing her to him, and she relaxed, a sound like a moan coming from deep in her throat.

"I should kill you," he said huskily. "God, you could have been killed, dammit, Storm. Why couldn't you trust me?"

She shuddered and he felt wetness seeping through his shirt and knew it was her tears. "I didn't think you were coming," she whispered. "I thought you were letting me go."

"Never," he said fiercely, pressing her closer, stroking her hair, his mouth finding the flesh of her temple. "Never! God . . . I . . ." He suddenly wrenched her away, his eyes blazing. "Where is Diego? Is he here? If he's here, I'm going to kill him." He grasped her chin as her eyes widened. "Has he touched you? Dammit! Answer me!"

She wrenched away. "It would serve you right," she yelled suddenly. "How dare you—how dare you—" Sputtering, she broke off.

"Just tell me," he said harshly. "Where is that sonuvabitch?"

"Dead," she spat.

He stared, then became aware of the tense, curious silence around them, and scanning the rapt faces of her family, he grabbed her arm. Ignoring her struggles, he opened the first door he found, shoved her inside, and slammed the door closed behind him. From outside, he heard the small woman say warningly, "Derek."

They were in a withdrawing room. There was a fire in the hearth. Storm had stepped away and was standing staring into it, trembling. Brett's gaze seared her back. "Tell me."

She whirled. "He tried to rape me. I shot him."

"God," he said, the blood draining from his face. He moved swiftly to her. She backed away, then stopped as the heat of the fire flared behind her. Brett stopped a foot from her, his gaze searching her face. How to win her back? How?

"Storm," he said, trying to control his voice and failing, "never, never, do this again. You could have been killed, raped. Sweet Jesus! Have you no sense? Have—"

"What made you decide to come?" Her heart was pounding painfully. She wanted to launch herself back into his arms and forgive him, love him, make him hers. She could do it; she knew she could. He cared enough to come for her, and that was a start. She could make him love her.

He paused. Then he looked partly rueful, partly derisive. "Don't you know?"

"You got bored with Sophia," Storm said, flushing at the thought. "Two weeks in her bed . . ." She stopped. He hadn't even spent two weeks in her own bed! The thought hurt, so badly that she turned blindly away.

"You fool," he said, and before she knew it, he was holding her from behind, pressing his cheek to her temple. "Listen carefully, Storm. Sophia is a sick bitch. She's been toying with men since she was a child. She's like her mother, who took my virginity before I was sixteen. That last night Sophia slipped laudanum into my brandy. When I woke up, I was in her bed, but I hadn't put myself there. I detest Sophia. No woman holds any interest for me except you—believe me." He said it firmly, a command.

She trembled. "I . . . I can't believe she would do that."

"Would you prefer to believe I chose to go to her when I could have had you? Good God! What's between us is unique, rare. Storm, I—" He broke off, cursing.

She was tense in his arms. "It took you long enough to come after me."

He almost laughed, but what was happening between them was too important to make light of in any way. His life hung in the balance. *"Chère,* I reached San Diego exactly one day after your stage left. You don't know what my trip has been like."

She twisted around, still encircled in his arms, so she could look in his eyes. "You came after me immediately?"

"The night after you left, I departed before dark." He met her gaze levelly. "At first I didn't believe you'd run away. I was praying you didn't know, but Sophia laughed and told me you had walked in on us."

She saw a look of loathing cross his eyes. "Did she really drug you?"

"Yes."

She believed him. Not only was the truth in his eyes, but she knew Brett. If he wanted her for a wife and Sophia as a mistress, he would consider it his right. She had to know the rest. "When you woke up in her bed, did you—what happened?"

He winced, then met her gaze levelly. "I was very groggy from the drug. I thought I was in our bed. I had no reason to think otherwise. But I realized the truth in time."

Storm swallowed. His hands went instantly to her face, cupping it tenderly. "I'm telling you all this because I want it out in the open and finished. I wouldn't tell you if I didn't . . . if I didn't care."

She stared, tears blurring her gaze. She believed him, but it still hurt. Thinking of him with Audrey still hurt, too.

"I was a victim," he said in complete humility. His eyes begged her for understanding, for trust.

"I believe you," she said, meeting his gaze. Then she quickly lowered her eyes. She was thinking about what he'd said—*I wouldn't tell you if I didn't care*. What did that mean? She didn't want him to care. She wanted him to *love* her. She suffered her disappointment in silence—was she a fool to dream of more?

"Storm, come back with me to San Francisco. We'll start over. Please." His tone was ragged, humble.

She was shocked. He was asking, not demanding, not strong-arming her, and if he got down on his knees, it couldn't be more eloquent.

He met her stunned gaze again. "Will you come back with me?"

That decided her. If he had threatened her, claimed her as his possession, she would have refused, no matter how hard that would have been. Because even if he didn't love her, she still loved him—she wanted to be his wife. "Yes, Brett," she said solemnly.

Immediately he was there, wrapping his arms around her, his mouth on her cheek insistent. Something else insistent was rising, demanding, against her belly. Storm closed her eyes, leaning into him while he held her for an endless moment, his cheek against hers. "We had better face your parents," Brett finally said, clearing his throat and stepping away from her.

"My parents," Storm mumbled. She looked at Brett, and she felt the heat of his need as if he were still pressing against her. There was bold promise in his gaze—and something else too, something warm and tender and unfamiliar. She wanted to fly back into his arms.

"And I think you should introduce me properly to your parents and brothers." He quickly kissed her mouth. "What did you tell them?"

Storm bit her lip. "That there was another woman. And I told them about Diego."

Brett tensed. "Why? Why did you have to air what's private and between us?"

"I love my parents. They wanted to know what would make me run away from a man I loved enough to marry." Her words weren't sarcastic, but they reminded him of the letter she had sent, the one full of lies.

"Let's not fight." He touched his jaw gingerly. "Do you think he'll come after me again?"

"No, Mother won't let him."

They left the drawing room. The foyer was empty, of course. "We were eating," Storm said. "They're probably in the parlor."

They were, all four of them, Brett saw ruefully. And waiting for him. Storm's mother, a breathtakingly beautiful woman, was embroidering. Derek was leaning against the mantel, his muscular frame stiff with tension. The tall, dark boy, Nick, was staring out a window. Rathe was pacing in the center of the room. Everyone looked up and stared at their entrance.

"This is Brett," Storm said. "My husband."

Brett put his arm possessively around Storm and locked stares with Derek. The man was still hostile, barely restraining himself.

"Are you hungry, Brett?"

He focused on Miranda, who had risen. He smiled, unconsciously working his charm. "No, thank you, ma'am. The only thing I need is my wife."

"I would like a few words alone with Mr. D'Archand," Derek said in a steely tone.

"Pa, everything's all right," Storm said. "And I'm going back to San Francisco with Brett."

Derek turned his hot golden gaze on her. "Is that so?"

"Yes, that's so," Brett said coolly before Storm could open her mouth. "Storm, *chère,* I'd like to speak alone with your father." He smiled at her. "Don't worry." He tilted her chin and gave her a hard, short kiss.

Miranda shooed out her brood and closed the doors behind them. Brett watched the older man turn away, restlessly, rigidly. He waited. Then he said softly, "I understand how you feel. But you have to let her go. She's not a little girl anymore."

Derek whirled. "Give her to the likes of you? You hurt her!"

"Not purposely," Brett said. "Never purposely."

Derek seemed to take in his words and the emotion laden in them. "When she came home, she wasn't the same. She wasn't the happy child who left." It was an accusation.

"I didn't mean to hurt her. She knows that. She's forgiven me. That's all that matters." Brett's eyes were dark. "Haven't you ever made a mistake?"

"Not where my wife was concerned," Derek said hotly.

"Not like you. I know there was another woman." He clenched his fists.

Brett had no intention of going into detail with this man. "I'm taking her back with me. And I intend to make her happy. You won't stop me. And it has nothing to do with the fact that the law's on my side. Even if it weren't," he said, "you wouldn't stop me."

Derek stared. Then he squinted. "You sound like a man in love."

Brett smiled mockingly. "Even the mighty fall."

"Then how could you do it?"

Brett faced him squarely. "I didn't. Storm didn't trust me, and she jumped to the wrong conclusions. To be honest, I haven't wanted another woman since I first met your daughter. You'll just have to trust me and accept the fact that I intend to take good care of her."

"Shit," Derek said, running a hand through his hair.

Brett suddenly had a disturbing thought. "You're not going to repeat this conversation to her, are you?"

Derek's gaze shot up. "Why not?"

Brett clenched his jaw. Jesus! He could always deny it . . .

"You haven't told her," Derek said incredulously. Understanding crept into his voice. "You haven't goddamn told her how you feel!" He started laughing. "I can just see it, two mules . . ." He laughed harder.

"More like two battering rams," Brett grumbled.

Derek laughed harder still.

Brett relaxed.

Chapter 21

"Brett," Sophia cried in delight, touching him warmly.

We shouldn't have come, Storm thought, rigid, seeing once again in her mind's eye Sophia sprawled wantonly and nakedly in bed with Brett. But it was she who had wanted to come, to resolve things for Brett with his family, she who had insisted, who had made Brett promise that they would stop on the way back to San Francisco. But the way Sophia was looking at Brett now was not the look of a guilty woman, or a woman who had given up. Rather, it was the look of someone ecstatically happy to see her lover again. Storm couldn't even swallow. She was furious. If Sophia again laid a hand on Brett . . .

Sophia looked up at Brett. He was thunderously angry, and not even trying to hide it. "Don't even come near me," he said clearly.

Sophia's eyes widened, but she didn't retreat. She glanced over her shoulder to see who was approaching. It was Emmanuel. Then she looked directly at Storm. "Where is my brother?"

They had already decided to lie, for neither Brett nor Storm wanted to hurt Emmanuel. His tone constricted with anger, Brett replied, "Diego is dead."

"What?!" Sophia actually paled.

"He tried to defend me from a mountain lion," Storm managed, hating the lie. She didn't know how to tell falsehoods, even to protect someone.

"He can't be dead," Sophia said, gasping. Then, at their unwavering gazes, she wheeled and fled.

"I didn't know she cared about anyone other than herself," Brett said grimly in a low voice that only Storm could hear. "Hello, Tío."

"Brett, Storm, I'm so glad you're back. You both left so—well, we won't talk about that." He was beaming, and he hugged them both.

Storm felt so sorry for this man who was so kind but had been cursed with vipers for a wife and children. Then she took back her thoughts. It was bad to think ill of the dead, especially when she herself was a murderess.

"Tío, please, sit." Brett took his uncle's arm.

"What is it, Brett, what's wrong?"

"I'm bringing bad news, unfortunately. Come, sit, please."

Storm collapsed upon the bed. The trip back had not been exhausting; in fact, it had been nothing at all like her flight from California. They had stayed a week with her parents, a week during which Brett had spent most of his time trying to get her away from the house and into the fields, where he would fall on her like a starving man. Storm knew Brett had been trying to be polite and not obvious about what he was up to, but because her father no longer seemed angry—rather, amused—Storm doubted Brett had succeeded. Her brothers' hostility had also faded. Storm had no idea what Derek had said to them, or what Brett had said to Derek. That one night they had stayed closeted together for an hour. Brett refused to tell her how he had won her father over.

Her mother adored him, of course, for what woman could resist his charm when he applied it? And both her mother and her father knew how she felt. Derek had taken her aside after Brett's arrival. "Honey, just tell me whether or not you love him," he had said, and Storm had blushed wildly and confessed the truth. Her father had seemed satisfied. He must have told her mother, for she had given Storm a lecture on men's characters in general: how they were all like little boys behind the brawn and bravado, and one would never be intimidated by a little boy; how they needed love and approval just like anyone else; and sometimes, the ones who acted the most self-sufficient were, indeed, the most desperately needy. Storm had thought about that a lot.

Brett had barely let her out of his sight that week at the D&M, and on the stagecoach he never did. Not that Storm minded. He was charming in the extreme and anticipated her every need and request, amused her with stories, laughed warmly with her, held her hand, and on several nights, despite the lack of privacy, despite the fact that everyone slept in a common room, he had very discreetly and quietly made love to her under their blanket in the corner. Storm blushed just thinking about how shameless they had been.

Now her head was pounding mercilessly. The headache had started that morning. Just knowing they would arrive later had set it off. She hadn't been sure how she would act when faced with Sophia. Brett had known without her saying anything. He had cupped her chin in his large hand. "It's not too late to change your mind, *chère*," he had said quietly.

She loved him for his sensitivity, a side of him she was seeing more and more often since they had been reunited. But she had refused to back down. They must come, at the very least to tell Emmanuel and Elena of Diego's death.

The guilt was lessening slowly. Sometimes it seemed that Brett could read her mind, for he always seemed to sense when she was brooding over what had happened. Then he would take her hand, if they were in public, and smile reassuringly into her eyes. If they were alone, he used other ways to chase away Diego's ghost . . . intimate, soul-soothing ways.

"You're so quiet," Brett said now, reaching for her in the privacy of their room.

Storm relished the feel of disappearing into his warm, hard embrace. "I wish we didn't have to lie."

"So do I," he said softly, his hand in her hair. "But I don't want to hurt Tío Emmanuel with the truth."

Their eyes met in an intimate understanding, but just then the door to their room flew open. Storm's gaze widened at the sight of a pale, red-eyed, and volatile Sophia. "What—"

Sophia leaned against the door. "Tell me what happened, you bitch. Diego would never have defended you— or anyone—at the risk of his life. Tell me!"

Storm couldn't speak. She wanted to tell this witch, who was still breathtakingly beautiful despite her grief, to get out. She opened her mouth, but no words came.

Brett grabbed Sophia's elbow and began to shove her from the room. "No one talks to my wife that way, Sophia. Now get out."

"No! No! Bastard, no! What happened to my brother?" She twisted wildly in his grasp.

"He was killed by a mountain lion," Brett said firmly.

"Trying to save that *puta?*" Sophia spat. "Never. Diego was selfish, completely—"

Brett grabbed her face cruelly. "Don't speak of my wife that way, Sophia," he warned.

She laughed. "Oh, Brett," she mocked, "don't tell me you have forgiven her for lying with Diego? I didn't think you would."

Brett yanked her. "They didn't sleep together."

Sophia laughed. "Diego was so hot for her. He told me that the minute he got her alone, even though she'd fight, he intended to take her and hurt her." She laughed again. "I know Diego. He had her, all right! And she probably loved it, loved every moment. Diego was almost as big as you, Brett, and what he lacked in size he made up for in other ways.''

Brett stared, momentarily shocked.

She laughed again. Her voice became a purr. ''Does it excite you to think about me and Diego, sister and brother, together?''

''God,'' Brett said, ''I should have known.'' He pushed her away. ''Get out. And don't come near my wife again.''

''What happened to my brother?'' Sophia demanded.

Brett shoved her out the door. He turned back to Storm, who was deathly white. He went to her and took her in his arms. ''It's all right.''

''Brett, I killed him, and Sophia knows!''

''She doesn't know, love. Shhh. You did what you had to. You did what was right. A man who rapes deserves to die.''

''Sophia loved him,'' Storm said in confusion.

He kissed her temple. ''I guess she did—in her own sick way. Diego was scum, Storm. Even if you hadn't killed him, someone else would have sooner or later.''

She studied him searchingly. ''Do you really think so?''

''I'm sure of it,'' Brett said. ''Did you know Diego has three or four bastards? Do you know how he got them?''

She shook her head.

''He raped the women. They were Monterro peons, and to him that made them less than human. One of the girls was just thirteen. She died birthing her baby before she was even fourteen. I think tomorrow I'm going to take you to this girl's family. I want you to listen to what they have to say about Diego. Your guilt is understandable, but completely unnecessary in this case. The women on the Monterro lands used to run when he came. And he enjoyed it.''

There was a knock on the door.

Brett looked at Storm. ''Feeling better?''

''Yes,'' she said honestly.

Brett smiled. ''Come in,'' he called.

A servant entered. "Don Felipe wishes to see you, Se-
ior Brett."

"Sit down, boy."

Brett grimaced. Only his father could make him feel
welve again with three words or a mere glance. This time
ie refused to take the bait, noting that Don Felipe looked
etter than when he had left. His color was healthier. He
vas sitting in his wheelchair, a blanket covering his legs
nd hips. "Hello, Father."

"Surprised you came back," Don Felipe said bluntly.

Brett eased himself into a straight chair, wondering at
is lack of tension.

"What happened?"

"Excuse me?"

"Don't play the fool with me, boy. I may have lost the use
f my legs, but I can hear, among other things. Your wife
an off with Diego. Now Diego's dead. Did you kill him?"

Brett fought for control. He opened his mouth to speak,
o tell Don Felipe about the mountain lion.

"And don't give me a pile of shit about Diego throwing
imself in front of some lion to save your beautiful wife.
Ve both know Diego was a coward, not a hero."

Brett clenched his jaw. "In this case," he said very
uietly, pleased with the tone of his voice, "Diego was,
ideed, heroic." The lie almost choked him.

"Bah! What'd she run off with him for anyway? Can't
ou keep your wife content enough so that she doesn't go
unning away?" Don Felipe smiled snidely.

Brett stood.

"Don't you dare leave." It was an order.

Brett slowly faced him.

"I already know," Don Felipe continued. "At least, I
uess. That coward nephew of mine tried to force himself
n her, didn't he? It's the only way he enjoys a woman. Yes,
know. You think I don't know everything that goes on

around here? But your wife isn't just any woman. She defended herself. Well?''

Brett couldn't speak. It was uncanny. It had always been this way. The old man had incredible powers of deduction. He always knew.

"Or did you kill him? Did he rape her? If so, what you did was right.''

"No, he didn't succeed,'' Brett said.

"She killed him?''

"Trying to defend herself.''

Don Felipe nodded. "A fitting end for a coward, don't you think?''

"I don't want Emmanuel to know the truth,'' Brett said.

"Neither do I.'' Then he laughed. "Odds are Diego isn't his spawn anyway, but because he's always refused to see what's in front of his face, no sense in shocking him now.''

"How kind of you,'' Brett said dryly.

"Is she pregnant?''

"What?''

"When do I get a grandson?''

Brett couldn't even answer.

"So why did you come back? To bear the 'sad' tidings?''

"Yes. But mostly because of Storm. She wanted to come back.'' Brett regarded his father steadily. "She had some insane notion that I needed to spend more time in the bosom of my family, that things needed to be *resolved.*''

Don Felipe chuckled. "Helluva woman.''

Brett lifted a brow. "But, Father, she's not a Californio.''

"Neither was your mother.''

"I had no choice in the parents I got.''

"True. But, surprisingly, you turned out the best of the lot.''

Brett couldn't believe his ears. "Am I hallucinating?''

"Don't go getting ahead of yourself. Considering the

ot only consisted of you and those two perverted cousins
f yours.''

Brett suddenly laughed. ''Thank you. Forgive me, I almost thought I was being praised.''

''Praised? Praise is for the weak or the dead.''

''Ah, of course, how foolish of me.'' Brett didn't look
way from the old man. For the first time in his life he
idn't hate his father. He felt something else, something
lien and indescribable. ''You're wrong,'' he said finally.

The don lifted a brow.

''Praise is for those who deserve it, and those who need
.''

Don Felipe laughed. ''What, still mad because I didn't
oddle you as a boy? At least you're no weakling.''

''Jesus,'' Brett said, realizing he had just gotten a com-
liment from the old man, probably the only one he would
ver receive. He was surprised to find he didn't care.

''When are you leaving?''

''As soon as possible,'' Brett said, staring at the shrunken
an in the chair, a surge of pity welling up in him. For this
an. This old, withered man who believed canes and hard-
ess were the way to foster strength of character.

''You should go,'' Don Felipe said. ''You've been away
om your business too long. What kind of businessman
gone for months at a time? You get back, you'll find
meone has stolen you blind.''

Brett chuckled. Don Felipe was never going to change.
e was opinionated, domineering, rude beyond belief. But
this instance he was right.

''You think that's funny?'' the old man demanded.

''No. Not at all.''

''I want to see her before you leave, boy, and I want a
randson I can be proud of.''

''How can I possibly sire a son you could be proud of?''
rett asked mockingly.

Don Felipe stared at him. "You expect me to fill your ears with pretty compliments?"

"Absolutely not," Brett said, smiling. "I just don't understand how the inferior bastard son of a whore could sire a grandson that a blue-blood Californio like yourself could possibly be proud of, much less acknowledge as kin."

"Don't you smart-mouth me," Don Felipe said, but he was grinning. "Just give me that grandson."

And Brett realized that that was the biggest compliment he could possibly receive from his father.

As he closed the door behind him, he found himself chuckling. The old man had lost his touch. He had actually, indirectly and inadvertently, said two nice things to him that day. In all his previous confrontations with his father, Brett had never laughed after seeing him, but this time he did, all the way back to his room.

Where was Brett?

It felt like déjà vu, and Storm didn't like that.

He had been so different all day, his face relaxed, the tension drained away, actually smiling and chuckling from time to time. He had made love to her playfully that afternoon after seeing his father, with much laughter and teasing, as if it were a celebration of sorts. She had never seen him like this before, not in bed, not out of it. She loved this side of him.

They had dined in their room since everyone else was in mourning, and now Brett had disappeared. Storm wanted him again. She wanted him to curl his big body around her, hold her tightly, laugh and tease, and then make wonderful love to her.

What was he doing?

Storm got up, securing her wrapper, and padded out into the hall. She found Brett standing a distance away on the patio, his head lifted to the cool, sweet night air, his perfect profile illuminated by a full moon. Storm felt her heart contract with love. She started forward, then suddenly stopped.

"Brett."

Storm would know *that* voice anywhere. Sophia. At the sound both she and Brett turned toward it. Sophia appeared at the other end of the patio in a thin, clinging nightgown, gracefully drifting toward Brett. She reached him and put her arms around him.

"*Caro,*" she said huskily, "your wife and Diego have been unfaithful to us both. Forget them. Forget Storm. Leave her, Brett. Take me back to San Francisco with you."

Her anger rising, Storm watched silently in the shadows as Sophia pressed herself against Brett. This was one time too many. Sophia needed a lesson, Apache-style. She turned and ran back upstairs.

In their bedroom she found her hunting knife, which she hid in the folds of her wrapper, and rushed out of the room, slamming the door behind her.

She raced down to the patio, her blood pounding. A vivid fantasy was etching itself on her mind—Sophia in terror as Storm held the knife to her cheek just before she scarred her in vengeance for her crimes. But Sophia was no longer on the patio. Nor was Brett anywhere in sight. Storm raced through the house to Sophia's room—and found her alone, standing before her mirror.

"What do you want?" Sophia asked coldly without turning. Their gazes met in the glass.

Storm smiled.

A flicker of irritation crossed Sophia's face. She turned. "What do you want?"

Storm was still smiling coldly. "You need a lesson."

Sophia was startled, then incredulous. "And what, child, could *you* teach *me?*"

Storm stepped forward until she was directly in front of Sophia. The older woman drew back instinctively against the dresser. Something flashed. The long blade appeared in Storm's hand, its tip against Sophia's nose.

Sophia's eyes were huge.

"He belongs to me," Storm said softly, increasing the pressure on the blade without breaking Sophia's fine, white skin.

Sophia gasped. "You're crazy!"

"Do you know what Apache men do to unfaithful wives?" Storm asked conversationally. She did not expect an answer—she did not receive one. "They cut off their noses."

Sophia made a strangled sound.

"Do you know why they choose that as punishment?" Storm asked coolly, looking into Sophia's terrified eyes. "Do you?"

"No . . . *please!*"

Storm smiled again. "Because no man wants to be with a mutilated woman." She let that thought sink in and pressed the blade hard enough to draw a speck of blood.

Sophia whimpered. "Please, don't. *No! I'll never . . .*"

"If you come near him again," Storm stated, "if you ever even look at him again, I'm Apache enough to do it. Nothing—*nothing*—would give me more pleasure."

She drew away, watching with hard satisfaction as Sophia crumpled onto a stool. Somehow she didn't think Sophia would be so eager to flirt with Brett anymore.

Storm found him pacing their room impatiently, clad in his navy silk robe, which was barely belted. At the sight of him Storm felt a surge of love.

"Where have you been?" he demanded.

"Teaching Sophia a lesson," she said honestly, moving into his arms.

He was puzzled. "Storm, what—?"

She cut him off, looking directly into his eyes. "I love you, Brett."

He was momentarily startled. Then his gaze grew warm,

and he cupped her face. "Yes, *chère,* oh, yes." His mouth found hers.

Storm opened her lips, drinking him in, her heart expanding and filling with joy. "I love you," she murmured against his slanting mouth. "I love you," she breathed again, running her hands up and down his broad back.

He crushed her against him, burying his face in her hair. She could feel his heart racing wildly. "Oh, Storm," he groaned. He held her face in his hands, his dark eyes searching hers. "Tell me," he said hoarsely. "Oh, please, tell me again and again."

"I love you," she said simply, her voice breaking.

He crushed her in his arms again, desperately. His body was hot and throbbing with need, shaking. He pulled her to the floor. He began stroking her with trembling hands, straddling her.

"I'm obsessed," he said thickly. "No other woman will do. Do you know that?"

She gazed up at him. His hands had stopped on her shoulders, holding her almost painfully. She could see he was fighting with himself. "No," she said softly. "I don't know that."

He half groaned and half laughed. "Since the day I first saw you, you turned my life upside down. I couldn't stop thinking about you. I tried to tell myself it was just lust. That I didn't need you." He looked at her, taking a deep breath, and slid down the length of her until she could feel the fullness of his arousal against her groin. He reached for his fly. "I can't wait."

"No," she said, firmly stopping his hand. Their breath mingled. "Finish."

"Finish?" he asked stupidly, then laughed shakily. "Yes, *chère,* that's what I'm trying to do if you'd let me open my pants. Finish what we've started."

"You know that's not what I mean, Brett."

"What more do you want?" he cried, his grip on her shoulders tightening.

She cradled his face, the skin already rough with stubble.

"Damn," he said brokenly. He pulled her hard against him, crushing her. "Don't you know. I've fallen in love with you . . ."

"You love me," she said on a sigh. "Truly?"

"Yes." His voice became strained. "Tell me again . . . that you love me."

"I love you," she said, suddenly comprehending how much he needed her.

A look of elation crossed his face. "Prove it to me," he demanded. "Prove it to me, now."

She was about to kiss him and show him, with her mouth and her hands and her body, just how much she loved him. But something stopped her, some timeless womanly intuition. "No," she said softly, a slight smile on her mouth. Her eyes shone with invitation. "You prove it to me."

His nostrils flared. "Gladly," he said hoarsely. His black gaze held hers, and what she saw there, freed at last from the burdens of his past, was more of an aphrodisiac than any words could be.

His mouth descended slowly, and she opened to him. After a while he said huskily, his mouth against hers, "I will spend the rest of my life proving just how much I love you, Storm."

"Yes," she said. "Yes."

America Loves Lindsey!

The Timeless Romances
of #1 Bestselling Author

GENTLE ROGUE	75302-2/$5.99 US/$6.99 Can
DEFY NOT THE HEART	75299-9/$5.99 US/$6.99 Can
SILVER ANGEL	75294-8/$5.99 US/$6.99 Can
TENDER REBEL	75086-4/$5.99 US/$6.99 Can
SECRET FIRE	75087-2/$5.99 US/$6.99 Can
HEARTS AFLAME	89982-5/$5.99 US/$6.99 Can
A HEART SO WILD	75084-8/$5.99 US/$6.99 Can
WHEN LOVE AWAITS	89739-3/$5.99 US/$6.99 Can
LOVE ONLY ONCE	89953-1/$5.99 US/$6.99 Can
BRAVE THE WILD WIND	89284-7/$5.99 US/$6.99 Can
A GENTLE FEUDING	87155-6/$5.99 US/$6.99 Can
HEART OF THUNDER	85118-0/$5.99 US/$6.99 Can
SO SPEAKS THE HEART	81471-4/$5.99 US/$6.99 Can
GLORIOUS ANGEL	84947-X/$5.99 US/$6.99 Can
PARADISE WILD	77651-0/$5.99 US/$6.99 Can
FIRES OF WINTER	75747-8/$5.99 US/$6.99 Can
A PIRATE'S LOVE	40048-0/$5.99 US/$6.99 Can
CAPTIVE BRIDE	01697-4/$5.99 US/$6.99 Can
TENDER IS THE STORM	89693-1/$5.99 US/$6.99 Can
SAVAGE THUNDER	75300-6/$5.99 US/$6.99 Can